STR
UNIVERSE

STRIDER'S UNIVERSE

Book Two of The Strider Chronicles

Paul Barnett

ORBIT

An *Orbit* Book

First published in Great Britain by Orbit 1998

Copyright © Paul Barnett 1998

The moral right of the author has been asserted.

A CIP catalogue record for this book is
available from the British Library.

ISBN 1 85723 601 7

Typeset in Times by M Rules
Printed and bound in Great Britain by
Mackays of Chatham PLC, Chatham, Kent

Orbit
A Division of
Little, Brown and Company (UK)
Brettenham House
Lancaster Place
London WC2E 7EN

For Jo, with love, because she likes
space battles the bestest.

Acknowledgements

As ever, Catherine, Jane and Fionna must be mentioned: they are much loved and have been good to me. Dave Langford took a great deal of the weight off my shoulders when I was starting this book by helping me out a lot with *The Encyclopedia of Fantasy*. Robert Kirby and Simon Trewin, with their usual friendliness, helped out on the business side. Monique Peterson cheered me up greatly with happily timed e-mails that made me laugh. Ron Tiner and Rikki Horn were a joy as well, and also, without knowing they were doing so, extracted me from a rare episode of writer's block by buying me a meal at the Ramada. I am particularly grateful to my copy-editor, Nancy Webber: embarrassments might have abounded. Sincere thanks to all.

Contents

1

It's Not a Cat, But I Guess It's Kinda Cute

'Come here, dammit,' said Strider, her head stuck into one of the storage units on the command deck of the *Midnight Ranger*. She'd called the ship the Bredai had given them *Midnight Ranger* on whim, and now wished she hadn't: something like *Autarch-Buster* or *Shaft of Vengeance* might have seemed – she searched for the word – more *macho*. The other thing she was searching for was Loki.

The damned cat . . .

Loki – whose sex had yet to be determined, if in fact gender-identification was possible or meaningful – had been picked up during the *Midnight Ranger*'s last planetfall. No one had been able to work out how the creature had been able to get aboard the spaceship: she, he or it had certainly not passed through the airlock. Hence the naming of the beast: it was a trickster, and had the habit of melting into or even through walls when it wanted to. It had clearly decided to stay for a while in this storage unit, whose door Nelson had inadvertently left open.

'Here, pretty one,' said Strider, futilely. There was not the slightest stir inside the storage unit. This was in a way good news: there were items in there that could be severely damaged if one of Loki's scales slashed through them. Normally the little creature could be relied upon to keep its scales flat to its sides but sometimes, for no perceptible reason, it could become a ball of cutting edges, like a morningstar without the handle or the chain.

Strider's major fear was that the cat would have a crap in there, so that the command deck would be stunk out for days on end. It had happened before. Cute and affectionate Loki might be, but there was a limit to what one's nostrils could take. The first time this had happened, before Strider had to her profound irritation become fond of the little animal, she and particularly Maloron Leander had proposed to stick it out of the nearest airlock. The boy Hilary had promptly offered to take full responsibility for the pet, and some of the time he actually did so.

Loki most certainly wasn't a cat, but the crew of the *Midnight Ranger* couldn't think of any better term. They'd all seen ancient holos where starships had cats aboard, presumably to hunt down and exterminate all those infestations of alien mice. As starships had decontamination systems that eliminated vermin right down to the viral level, the holos always evoked chuckles.

On the other hand, Loki had somehow got aboard . . .

The real difficulty with Loki was that it was fascinated by Segrill. He was of the Trok species, and stood no higher than Strider's raised thumb. One of these days either Loki was going to remember that every time it ventured to investigate the Trok it got hit on the jaw or Segrill was going to lose patience and strike back with one of his small but lethal weapons.

'Kitty, kitty,' said Strider, too aware that, as she groped here on her knees, her bottom was sticking up in the air. There was nothing wrong with the bottom *per se* – or so she had been told by several lovers when neurosis had struck her in the darkness – but sooner or later someone on the command deck was going to crack a joke.

To hell with the friendly approach.

Strider settled back on her haunches, drew her lazgun from

its holster, and pointed the weapon in the general direction of the storage unit's interior.

'Look, kitty, I'll give you the count of ten to be out of there. Otherwise you're dead meat.'

By the count of three the creature slunk out, looking guiltily with its single eye up at Strider before scuttling off to the far corner of the command deck.

Strider was astonished. The little animal must be more intelligent than she had realized. Was it telepathic?

Then she took a deep breath, and coughed.

'Hilary!' she bellowed at Lan Yi and Maria Strauss-Giolitto. 'Get the goddam kid up here on the deck at once. This is *his* pet.'

The *Midnight Ranger* was tiny by comparison with the *Santa Maria*, the craft which had brought Strider's mission here to The Wondervale: it was barely more than a hundred metres long and less than half that wide. The Bredai had rescued the Humans after the latter had succeeded, with the help of the Images and the Trok, in destroying the stronghold of the Autarch Nalla on Qitanefermeartha – not to mention the Autarch himself. The trouble was that Bredai and Humans were built on incompatible scales. Bredai were as big compared to Humans as Humans were to Trok, but were very much more careless. Also, they breathed a methane atmosphere, so that outside the sealed areas that had been demarcated for Humans and Trok one had to wear a spacesuit the whole time: everyone joked about the smells inside spacesuits except when they were wearing one. The Trok had learnt over generations to live with their clumsy allies – in their odd, hopping way, the Trok were nimble – but the Humans hadn't, and so, after too many fatalities, there had been a mutual agreement to part ways. The Bredai had adapted one of their ship's escape pods to create the independent craft which Strider had dubbed the *Midnight Ranger*.

3

The *Santa Maria* had been over three kilometres long and mightily outfitted with drive units. On Strider's original expedition from the Solar System, heading for Tau Ceti II there had been forty-six people aboard, if you counted the bot Pinocchio. Two years from home the plodding craft had fallen into one of the countless wormholes that linked distant parts of the Universe, and the dazed Humans had found themselves in The Wondervale, an elliptical galaxy in orbit about a giant spiral galaxy, Heaven's Ancestor. Almost immediately the Images had discovered them, and had taken over their lives. Strider had remained captain of her mission, but the Images had taken most of the decisions from her hands.

Just as well, because otherwise the *Santa Maria* would have been destroyed within hours. The Wondervale had not yet erupted into full-scale rebellion against the Autarchy, but it was about to do so. There was no way home, and circumstances had forced the Humans – aboard a *Santa Maria* reconfigured almost entirely by the Images, and equipped by them with the tachyon drive – to ally themselves with their new galaxy's insurgents. Even stranger circumstances had conspired to let Strider and a few of her personnel – not to mention Segrill's army of Trok – be in at the death of the Autarch himself.

The remainder of the Humans, assisted by data acquired from the Spindrifters, one of The Wondervale's ancient species, had departed in the *Santa Maria*, with luck to rediscover the wormhole that would take them back to the Milky Way. Since then there had been casualties.

I started off with forty-six, thought Strider glumly, *and now there are only eight of us, two of whom are aliens. Let's magnify the figure flatteringly by counting in the cat: nine. And it's some mission you've been conducting when you can't even stop the cat crapping.* She settled herself in her seat and looked through the view-window at the planet they were approaching. The reddish disc seemed to be expanding visibly, and it was

4

difficult for her to relax even though she knew that the ship's two Images – Pinocchio and Ten Per Cent Extra Free – would have everything under control..

A claw touched her shoulder.

'Hi, Polyaggle,' she said without turning round. From a distance the Spindrifter looked beautiful, but close up Strider found Polyaggle's appearance disconcerting. At first glance the face looked as if it were a Human's, but almost immediately you saw the proboscis where there should have been a nose: it coiled and uncoiled whenever Polyaggle spoke. Her mouth was diamond-shaped, with four lips. Her face was covered in short black bristles, and a high crest of the same material – it looked like hair – ran from the top of her forehead towards the rear. None of this would have concerned Strider much – she'd encountered some fairly peculiar-looking specimens of *Homo sapiens* in her time – but the alien's slanting eyes were something else. They were utterly black, so that when you looked into them you had the unsettling feeling that you were staring into eternity, into a time before the Universe had formed.

There was also Polyaggle's inexplicable sexuality. It was difficult for Humans to concentrate on what they were saying when they spoke to her face-on. Probably 'sexuality' was the wrong word, because the allure went far beyond sex.

'We will soon be at The Pridehouse,' said the Spindrifter. 'It is something I anticipate with great pleasure.'

Polyaggle's chirruping made no sense to Strider, who heard it simultaneously with the translation into Argot which one or other of the Images supplied.

'Yeah,' said Strider, 'I can understand.'

She could. Polyaggle was almost certainly the last of her species, although she was nurturing a brood somewhere inside her and, when the time was right, would give birth. Strider's mind boggled at the biological complexities that must be involved in the gestation, for Polyaggle was a colonial organism:

if need be she could dissolve into myriad tiny butterfly-like creatures, and they in turn could dissolve into . . . something else entirely, things that were as elusive as quarks. Strider had seen it happen once – Polyaggle had performed the feat in order to start the regeneration of the *Santa Maria*'s Main Computer – and, although the display had possessed a bizarre beauty, she rather hoped she would never see it again.

The Spindrifters were – had been – one of The Wondervale's ancient species. The Pridehouse were another. The ancient species were the ones who had first evolved in The Wondervale, and who had explored both this galaxy and Heaven's Ancestor. A few million years ago, when younger and more aggressive species – the Comelatelies – had emerged and the Autarchy had been bloodily installed, the various ancient species had retreated to their home planets and tried to make their cultures seem as uninteresting and unexploitable as possible, biding their time until the Autarchy dissolved. Within the past year or so, however – Strider still found herself thinking in terms of years – this had changed. Kaantalech had destroyed Spindrift and annihilated the Spindrifters; it had been by sheer chance that Polyaggle had been with the Humans when this act of barbarity was performed. What could happen to one ancient species could happen to another. The Pridehouse, the Lingk-kreatzai, the Wreeps, the Semblances of the Eternal, the Fionnoids, the Janae, the We Are and countless further cultures had quietly declared that their patience was exhausted. If the Autarchy would not of its own accord disintegrate over the aeons of history, they would encourage it to do so. They had waited long enough.

But they were not warriors. Millions of years of stubborn neutrality had deprived them of the ability to make war – although their defences, as Strider had seen during the destruction of Spindrift, could be impressive. The Onurg of the Pridehouse had told Polyaggle – and, through her mediation, Strider – that the ancient species should be led by the commander of the extragalactic ship that had somehow fallen into The Wondervale and had already done so much damage to the Autarchy.

No wonder Polyaggle yearned to reach The Pridehouse. The people of that world might not be of her own species, but at least they were not Comelatelies. She had more in common with them than with most of the other species of The Wondervale – and certainly more than with the Human on whose shoulder her claw was resting.

In a way, Polyaggle was going home.

'We'll be there soon,' said Strider, feeling that the remark was hopelessly inadequate. She found there were tears in her eyes, and wondered if there were tears in Polyaggle's. She didn't dare to turn round and look.

Ten Per Cent Extra Free spoke to her.

WE SHALL BE IN ORBIT AROUND THE PRIDEHOUSE IN JUST OVER TWO HOURS, the Image said. His voice was like a song.

'I want to communicate with them,' said Strider. 'Can it be arranged?'

IT CAN.

'How soon?'

AS SOON AS YOU WISH.

She leaned forward and put her head into the Pocket in front of her. The Images had installed Pockets in the *Santa Maria* and now they had done the same for the *Midnight Ranger* although, the command deck being so much smaller, there was room for only three. At first all she saw was the standard projection – a depiction, in startling detail, of the exterior of the *Midnight Ranger* with, behind and beneath it, a graphic portrayal of their position in relation to The Pridehouse – but within a few seconds there was a flicker and she was looking directly at the face of one of the ancient species.

It could have been a wolf's face were it not for the third eye, near the tip of the snout.

'Are you the Onurg?' said Strider. It was difficult as yet for her to tell the individuals of the Pridehouse apart. But this wolf's coat seemed greyer than the Onurg's startling silver.

'I am not,' said the face. 'My name is Hein. Are you Umbel Nelson?' The Images translated between the species, but the effect was always that of a badly dubbed holo.

'No. I'm Leonie Strider.'

'My apologies.'

'And mine.'

The wolf's third eye momentarily disappeared into the fur of its nose, then re-emerged blue rather than grey.

HEIN IS SMILING AT YOU, warbled Ten Per Cent Extra Free inside Strider's mind. IT WOULD BE POLITE TO SMILE BACK. I SHALL CONVEY TO HEIN THE MEANING OF THE FACIAL CONTORTION.

Strider dutifully smiled, and again the Pridehouse's third eye disappeared. When it resurfaced it was an astonishing green – the green a child uses when painting a tree – which reminded her that . . .

'Please wait a moment,' she said, and withdrew her head from the Pocket. 'Has that damned boy cleared up the mess yet?' she yelled at no one in particular.

'I'm doing it,' said Hilary sullenly. She glanced over her shoulder towards the storage unit. Seeing the expression on his face, she hastily jabbed her head back into the Pocket again.

'You have taken a long time getting here,' said Hein at once.

'Less than a year. We're not equipped with the tachyon drive.'

'You're not?' Ten Per Cent Extra Free made the wolfish face produce a semblance of astonishment.

'The Onurg knows.'

The decision had been Strider's. The tachyon drive allowed instantaneous transport from one side of The Wondervale to the other – or to anywhere else in the Universe, for that matter, so long as you knew where you were going – but it was not

8

unobtrusive, and if there was one thing that Strider wanted to be at the moment it was unobtrusive. After the death of the Autarch, Kaantalech had moved swiftly to take power. There were other potential claimants to the throne, and Kaantalech was dealing with them as ruthlessly as she had the Spindrifters. Kaantalech was going to win the contest for the autarchy – there could be little doubt of it – but still a few warlords held out against her, as did various rebels against the institution of the Autarchy itself. Strider knew it was only a matter of time before the tyrant's thoughts turned again to the Human intruders: the longer the moment could be put off the better. Kaantalech could find the *Midnight Ranger* any time she chose, because she had sensors capable of detecting the Humans' protoplasm, which was quite unakin to anything else in The Wondervale, but she must have other things on her mind as she tried to stamp out the last pockets of resistance to her usurpation – or so Strider had reasoned. A few Humans in a small craft represented no threat: they could be dealt with later, after the might of the rebel Helgiolath fleet had been countered. That said, there was no reason at all for the Humans to advertise themselves as they gathered their forces among the ancient species.

'Ask him,' said Strider, feeling suddenly weary. She wasn't in the mood to explain. Back in the Solar System – so long ago – humanity had felt reasonably proud of itself that it could construct a spaceship capable of achieving a reasonable percentage of lightspeed. Now Strider was not going to apologize because the *Midnight Ranger* could drift along at only a few hundred times the velocity of light.

She yawned.

I DID NOT TRANSMIT THAT FACIAL EXPRESSION, said Ten Per Cent Extra Free helpfully. THE PRIDEHOUSE MIGHT HAVE THOUGHT IT DISCOURTEOUS.

'Thanks,' Strider subvocalized.

Hein's face had turned away. The wolf was clearly talking

9

to someone else, but had switched off the audio channel of the Pocket. From the way that the Pridehouse nodded from time to time – again Ten Per Cent Extra Free was adjusting the body language – Strider realized that someone was explaining her reasoning. Hein must be a junior officer. Strider felt vaguely insulted.

The audio channel crackled back into existence.

'Our decontamination procedures are very simple,' said Hein, 'and will cause you no pain at all.'

'Oh, great,' said Strider without enthusiasm. The various species within The Wondervale were terrified of the microbes that could be passed on to them by other species. Only a tiny proportion of those microbes could in fact transmit from one species to another, but there was good reason for the fear: a single transmitted bug could destroy an entire culture. Strider had been through a full decontamination several times. The experience was not pleasant: you felt stripped so naked that your soul was showing. She was pretty certain the Pridehouse's system would be no better, whatever Hein said.

'How many of us will be allowed to come down?'

'Yourself,' said the Pridehouse. 'The Spindrifter. The Trok. None others.'

Strider raised an eyebrow. She gestured behind her to Polyaggle, and a few moments later the alien's face was sharing the Pocket with her own. A rapid argument started between the members of the two ancient species. After a few moments Ten Per Cent Extra Free gave up trying to translate for her. She stood back, leaving Polyaggle sole occupancy of the Pocket.

'Glad I'm not on the receiving end of what she's giving out,' said Strider to the Image. The Spindrifter's wings were moving agitatedly in and out of their pods. They were coloured in rather more hues than the Human eye had been built to encompass.

SHE IS EXPLAINING TO HEIN THAT YOU HUMANS ARE SOCIAL BEINGS, AND ARE BEST NOT SEPARATED, said Ten Per Cent Extra

Free in Strider's mind. SHE IS TELLING HIM THAT YOU FUNCTION AS A GROUP, NOT AS INDIVIDUALS. SHE IS MAKING THE ARGUMENT FORCEFULLY.

'I guessed that last bit,' said Strider. How odd that Polyaggle, a colonial organism, should see the Humans aboard the *Midnight Ranger* as forming a composite creature like herself. Or perhaps it wasn't so odd. Strider hadn't been looking forward to leaving Leander, Nelson, Strauss-Giolitto, Lan Yi, Hilary – who had grumpily finished his task – and even the cat out in orbit while she was ferried down to The Pridehouse with Segrill and Polyaggle. Maybe the nine of them did indeed form some sort of *Gestalt*, however much they bitched at each other whenever there wasn't enough else to do.

Polyaggle reared back out of the Pocket. 'It has been arranged,' she said. 'They are constructing a suitably sized spacestrip so that we may land the *Midnight Ranger*.'

Strider was incredulous. 'But we'll be there in a couple of hours! They're not expecting us to hang around in orbit for the next six months, are they?'

Polyaggle clacked her claws together in what Strider had learnt to recognize as the Spindrifter's equivalent of a laugh. Just to make sure she got the message, Ten Per Cent Extra Free made an appropriate noise in her mind.

'Remember,' said Polyaggle, 'that you are dealing with an ancient species. The spacestrip is likely finished by now.'

They were within a couple of hours going to encounter a new species, the Pridehouse, and Maloron Leander was quietly terrified. It had taken her far longer than the others to adjust to the presence among them of the Spindrifter, and little Segrill could still startle her when he suddenly appeared on her lap as she manned the command deck. She didn't consider herself a xenophobe: she did not dislike the aliens in any way. But she felt uncomfortable among them. It was something she couldn't explain to herself, because she knew there was no rational explanation for the flutters she felt in her stomach each time that damned cat made friendly approaches. Her feelings towards Polyaggle were even more complicated because, like all the others – Hilary included, although he was at the age where he was damned if he was going to admit it – she felt a distinct sexual tension whenever she was in the presence of the Spindrifter.

Somehow this was linked to Leander's unease. She hadn't been able to work it out. Apparently men who were about to die often developed erections, the primitive organism preparing itself for one last effort to pass on its genes, however hopeless the task might seem. She was the same. As soon as it was confirmed that the Pridehouse would welcome the entire crew of the *Midnight Ranger* down on to their planet she virtually dragged Umbel Nelson from his cabin into her own.

Through her single secondary retinal screen she watched their coupling from various angles; through her uncovered eye she looked down along her long, over-slender body as she rode him. His penis had not fully recovered its hardness from their first lovemaking – hell, she had practically raped him – but its presence inside her comforted her. Through her secondary retinal screen she was able to watch her own buttocks rise and fall, the dark shaft of Umbel's semi-erection seemingly between them, his funny little tight-drawn testicles touching her every time she slowly descended. She reached behind her and fondled his testicles: he had told her many times that he disliked it when she did this, but at the moment she was using him as a security blanket, something the big man fully understood. Right now he wasn't complaining: her other hand, insistently rubbing her clitoris (oh, yeah, found the damned thing: funny how it could be so circumspect when it wanted to be) against his penis, felt him grow harder.

He reached up and pulled her shoulders towards him. One of her nipples was so erect that the pain was distracting her; the other was remaining obstinately flaccid, as if it wanted no part in the proceedings. Umbel Nelson licked all around it, then drew her yet further down so that their mouths joined. His hand remained eager on the uncooperative nipple, fondling it with the gentleness that was what had attracted her to him in the first place, long ago when they had still been in the Solar System.

Both of his eyes were covered by the rectangular mirrors of secondary retinal screens. He could watch the sex they were having from two different angles at once, if he wanted to. She switched her own angle, so that now she was looking at herself and Umbel from directly above. She took her mouth away from his and sat up, then leant backwards, reaching her arms towards the cabin's ceiling. Her small breasts seemed to disappear into her chest. The contrast between the paleness of her own body and the darkness of Umbel's – he was even darker than Strider – was a thing of beauty to her. She shuffled slightly backwards on his thighs so that her overhead view would reveal a centimetre or so of his penis. Neither of them moved for a moment, and then she licked an index finger and brushed it first along her lower lip, then across the blood vessel at the base of his penis and finally against herself.

Her orgasm arrived so suddenly that she almost ejected his penis. She found herself shouting words that she didn't know she knew. All of a sudden her face was against his again, her lips kissing his, her teeth nipping at his nose, her breasts rubbing themselves against his chest urgently. Her groin was moving rapidly up and down on his erection as if she were a near-virgin who had yet to discover the secret of slowness. Although Maloron enjoyed sex very much, she rarely climaxed, and almost never at all except through oral sex – even with Nelson, who was what women would have described back on Mars as a 'skilled operator'.

'Umbel!' she shrieked as she experienced another orgasm. Nelson thought she was talking to him, but in fact she was addressing her messiah.

13

Maloron worried about herself. She must be even more terrified than she'd thought if she'd come to a second orgasm so soon. There was nothing *wrong* with aliens. They normally smelt a bit odd, but then so did everything else in The Wondervale. They could look disturbing. They had different ways of behaviour from humanity's, and very often those ways were better. But the ones she was soon going to meet were no *threat*: they were friends of Polyaggle.

Oh, bloody hell, she was heading towards another . . .

'Yowch!' said Umbel, shoving her half away from him.

She watched his face through her unshielded eye as it twisted in what looked like pain and probably was. He was doubtless, through both secondary retinal screens, flitting his observation point all around her cabin. She cupped her small breasts in her hands and offered them towards him. He ignored them entirely, so was probably watching the curve of her spine down towards her buttocks, the line he had often told her he loved the most.

She rode him, softly, a little longer until she was certain that he had emptied himself. Then she lay on top of him for a few minutes, listening to his heartbeat and the wheeze of his breath. Nervously, she kissed him again, and as she did so his penis fell out of her. She rolled over to one side, and he held her thin body to his muscular one, so that she suddenly felt that one or other of them was a child and the other an affectionate parent – though the hell if she could work out which was which.

He ran a finger very slowly down the buttons of her spine, then rested his hand under her buttock.

'We've got to get up to the command deck soon,' he said a little later.

He looked at his watch and she hated him for it.

'In less than an hour, sweet lady of wisdom and beauty – although that second time hurt me quite a lot – we'll be in Pridehouse orbit. Strider will want us then.'

She nuzzled against him.

14

'I'm frightened,' she said.

'Do you think I don't know that?'

She had her eyes firmly closed, but very carefully, with his thumb, he pried open the lid that was not covered by her secondary retinal screen to show her that he was smiling.

'If all I was interested in doing was fucking you,' he said, 'do you think I'd be here?'

'Dunno.'

He ran his fingers through the short, very dark hair of her head.

'Have you noticed I've never tried to get to Leonie?' he said.

'You *have*.'

'Well, only slightly – as a matter of politeness. And I've never tried to get to Maria at all.'

'That's because you discovered she was gay.' Maloron felt herself slipping into sleep, even though she knew she should be awake. He had put his little finger into her navel, and now she felt him kiss it, his tongue probing into the folds. She had meant to have her navel surgically excised back on Mars, but somehow things had always seemed to get in the way: now she was glad they had. She shifted further over on to her back, holding his head. He sucked softly at her navel, producing a little *phoot* sound.

'No,' he said from the general direction of her belly, his voice abruptly losing its customary flippancy, 'it's not that at all. I'd love to have a fuck with both of them, just to see what it was like. Bloody hell, I'd like to find out what it was like fucking Polyaggle if I didn't think her coat would cut me to ribbons.'

Leander knew she had to pull herself into wakefulness, but it was proving very difficult. Nelson's tongue was so soothing.

'What do you want from me?' she said drowsily.

'Friendship. The sound of your breath and the touch of your thigh when I wake up in the middle of a sleeping-time – *every* sleeping-time. I like to listen to the way you snore.'

15

'I don't snore!' she said, trying to stir herself.

'You do. Not always. Usually very, very quietly. And it's a sort of graceful noise, star of the morning: it makes me think of people dancing, for some reason. But you do.'

She snorted.

'Maloron?'

'Yeah, liar?'

'We've screwed around a lot. Both of us. The last few months it's been only with each other because none of the others have been interested.'

'Hilary's been pretty interested.'

'Hilary would be interested in a hole in the wall, right now. He's trying to work out whether or not you're his mother. At a guess, lovely lady of wherever the hell it is you come from, Leonie's won that particular battle. I've seen the little guy virtually trip over his tongue when she goes by.'

'Poor Leonie.'

'Yeah, well, anyway, what I was trying to say was . . .'

'No.' She was suddenly awake.

'What do you mean?'

'I'm not going to let you cage me.' She sat up, thrusting his head away from her stomach. She still felt a sticky, comfortable glow from her groin, but somehow it seemed no longer to be at all connected with Umbel Nelson, even though he was the person of whom she was fondest. If she'd just been fucking with someone else the person she would want to kiss most – and to have kiss her – would be Umbel. She wanted to be never very far away from him, but she didn't want to become a part of him – more than that, she didn't want him to become a part of her.

'We have to dry you off,' she said more kindly, taking his small penis into her hand. His fluids and hers were mixed along it, and she absentmindedly bent to give its upper surface a kiss. It twitched reflexively, as if it were vaguely hungry.

'Apologies about that, junior goddess of the skies,' said

Nelson. 'Quick shower, huh? Any passing erections are to be ignored rather than actually *hit*, OK? You're loved a lot: something to remember whenever you want to remember it.' As they stood, he took her into his arms. She could feel his moist penis against her pubic hair, and immediately she wanted to screw again.

But no. Not the right time. He was delicious. She loved licking his chocolate skin, especially just under his shoulder blades. He had reassured her through the sex she'd demanded. The aliens could be faced. The Onurg of the Pridehouse had been the first of the ancient species to offer alliance to the Humans. Maloron Leander had nothing to fear from such beings as these.

She hoped.

Maloron followed and then led Umbel Nelson to the shower.

'Wow,' she said, looking down as the water – the precious water – pattered about them. 'Um, thirds?'

It always surprised Strider how Maloron Leander managed constantly to look so spruce. Nelson and Leander had arrived on the command deck some considerable time after she had summoned them. Nelson looked as if he had a hangover, although that was impossible because there was neither alcohol nor ziprite aboard the *Midnight Ranger*. Leander had obviously taken the opportunity to get some well earned rest. Strider nodded, approving of her officer.

Later she would reprove Nelson.

But kindly and tactfully, as she always did.

Maria Strauss-Giolitto, standing at a Pocket, watched the depiction of the planet called by its dominant indigenous species The Pridehouse. Then she stood back and looked overhead through the view-window at the disc of the planet. The Pocket's portrayal was accurate in every respect, and yet it

17

lacked the *presence* of the planet itself. She found herself shivering: she remembered Spindrift, and what had happened there – less the cold of the ice and snow, more the confidences she had shared with the bot Pinocchio. Even though the bot had now transcended The Wondervale's reality to become an Image, she still regarded him as her best friend; but the memory of those moments on Spindrift when her reserve had broken down frightened her. She should never have been on this mission in the first place: the SSIA (Solar System Interstellar Agency, to give it its full pomp) had sent a crew to Tau Ceti II who were hand-picked to be – among many other things – good breeding stock. Strauss-Giolitto's lesbianism had somehow slipped through the net. She had expected there would be at least a few bisexual females among the crew, but they had all turned out to be lusty heteros, *damn* them. For the first few years of the mission she had had to keep her secret a secret in case of being thrown off the *Santa Maria*'s colonizing mission. This had been difficult because, back on Earth and Mars, it would never have crossed anyone's mind to criticize one's sexual orientation. Then, on Spindrift, she had broken down and told Pinocchio everything. She had never felt so exposed in her life: physiologically, because she had just been subjected to Spindrifter decontamination procedures, which had been so thorough that they had the effect of making one feel simultaneously stripped and emptied of every last suspicious molecule; and psychologically, because she had revealed herself not only to Pinocchio but also, somehow, to herself.

A bot!

There had been a time when she had despised bots. Now, when he came into her mind to share conversation, she wished he were a bot again, so that she could put an arm around his shoulders and watch his so-human-like eyes swivel towards her.

That old secret was no longer a secret, although Umbel Nelson nevertheless called her the light of his life and the joy of his being frequently when he talked with her. Cooped up in a small craft for nearly a year, the Humans had confessed much if not all of the things they might elsewhere have kept hidden. Things would have come out into the open anyway. And now that they were in The Wondervale, lost Jesus knew how far away from home, the fact that Strauss-Giolitto had cheated her way aboard the *Santa Maria* seemed terrifically unimportant.

Once, Strider had taken her to her cabin and they had made love. The sex had been great, but it had been lacking in emotion. Or, no: the worst of it was that Strider's predominant emotion, in the end not quite skilfully enough disguised, had been sympathy for the hell Maria had locked herself into. Strider had faked nothing, but she could as well have been masturbating. Midway through the sleeping-time Strauss-Giolitto had left in ill-concealed tears. To be made love to through pity was worse than not being made love to at all.

Once more that funny cold feeling travelled up her spine, and she dipped her head back into the Pocket.

As with Spindrift, there was virtually no superficial sign of technology on the planet's surface. She expanded the portrayal and then thought at the Pocket that it should increase the rate of the image's spin, so that it seemed as if the planet's rotational period had become about twenty minutes. She instructed the Pocket to stop the movement any time there was something interesting to see.

YOU HAVE NOTHING TO FEAR FROM THE PRIDEHOUSE'S DECONTAMINATION SYSTEMS, said Pinocchio's voice suddenly inside her head.

'Go away,' she muttered. He had just made her much more apprehensive than she had already been.

The disc stopped moving, and she expanded the depiction yet again. It was as if she were pulling the surface of the planet rapidly towards her. There was a little city in the middle of what looked like a featureless red desert. The Pridehouse seemed to have few mountain ranges or even cascades of hills, and as yet she had seen no seas or oceans. Silvery lines which she guessed were roads stretched away, cobweblike, across the desert. No rivers, either. This must be an incredibly ancient world, to be so devoid of surface water: surely no intelligent species could have evolved on a planet without seas.

She mentally instructed the Pocket to continue its search.

Yes, the Autarchy had been here. Just as on Spindrift, there was a near-deserted spaceport, with a few rusting cruisers lying abandoned in what had obviously once been fully functional bays.

Her thought trickled on. Perhaps these weren't Autarchy relics at all. Perhaps the ancient species constructed them specially. *If I were Kaantalech,* she thought, *I'd look out for all the planets with deserted spaceports and zap 'em. The ancient species have clearly adopted this as a way of disguise* . . . The chances of some industrious book-keeper wading through the records of the hundreds of thousands of worlds that constituted the Autarchy and discovering that *no*, after all, this particular planet had never been visited were close to zero. Decaying spaceports were a way of advertising to anyone curious that this world had been visited long ago and had proved to possess nothing of interest: no useful slaves, no mineral resources that couldn't more easily be mined elsewhere, no handily toxic micro-organisms . . . and, in this instance, there would be the apparent lack of surface water as a further disincentive to setting down a colony.

Another little city, and another. They were regularly distributed, as if someone had neatly planted studs into a tennis ball, making sure that each was symmetrically equidistant from the other.

She told the Pocket to make the planet's image spin vertically. Yes, not even polar icecaps.

Was The Pridehouse a planet at all? Had it been *built*? The size of such a project made Strauss-Giolitto's mind recoil: it

20

would take thousands or even tens of thousands of years, and the resources involved would be beyond realistic human imagination. On the other hand, the people who – after the name of their planet, or was it the other way round? – called themselves the Pridehouse were one of the ancient species, and she had seen on Spindrift what the ancient species could do . . .

She wasn't enjoying this very much. She had thought that surveying the planet would help calm her anxiety, but it wasn't working. She knew that Maloron Leander was suffering even greater misgivings than she was, which made her feel a bit better. She also knew that Strider, with her usual lack of empathy, had failed to notice that either of the other two women on the *Midnight Ranger* was otherwise than her usual self. The Images must be perfectly aware of it, however. But the Images were obviously keeping the information to themselves. Maybe Nelson was equally worried: Strauss-Giolitto had never been able to read his body-language. Lan Yi was as tranquil as ever: he was probably playing a game of mental four-handed chess with Ten Per Cent Extra Free, or something. Blast him for his coolness!

She didn't have much time for the company of men, but she enjoyed being with Lan Yi. His Argot still occasionally lapsed into imperfection, but often he was witty. His conversation stimulated her mind. He treated her as if she were his intellectual equal, which certainly she was not: she had never even dared think about comparing their IQs. She had recognized a while ago that the emotion she felt for him was love. If only she could get over the repulsion she felt for the maleness of his body, she would be happier. Maybe not. She loved him the way a daughter can love a father. Any physical expression of the love might have felt somehow incestuous.

She moved away from the Pocket. Her mouth felt dry, and she crossed the command deck to fetch herself a drink of water. Polyaggle was watching her. Another bloody complication.

Maria Strauss-Giolitto wished she had been able to strangle at birth the person who invented hormones.

'Our Images tell us we are in geosynchronous orbit over your spacestrip,' said Strider into her Pocket an hour or so later. 'I've introduced our gravity simulators, but I'd like to come down to the surface as soon as possible: they're energy-greedy.'

'That is perfectly evident to us,' said Hein.

'Smartass.'

Ten Per Cent Extra Free translated the wolf's expression into a grin. Hein and Strider were building up a good relationship. This was unusual between species. It was a pleasing sign. Physically and culturally different though they were, perhaps the Humans and the Pridehouse would work well together. Ten Per Cent Extra Free certainly hoped so. He and all the other Images who had ventured here from The Truthfulness were anxious that the same peace they enjoyed in their own version of reality could prevail in this Universe: anything else was unaesthetic.

'We're looking forward to meeting you in person,' Hein was saying to Strider. Ten Per Cent Extra Free translated reflexively.

'I'm looking forward to punching you on the nose,' said Strider, also grinning.

'Tough guy,' said Hein.

'My, what big teeth you have, Grandma.' Translating this into something comprehensible to the pseudo-wolf took Ten Per Cent Extra Free a fraction of a second longer than usual.

Hein's interpreted voice took on a more serious tone.

'We have locked an attractor on to you. Your Images will know how to ride it to the surface.'

'I had rather hoped to be able to be in command of my own craft for this particular manoeuvre,' said Strider, abruptly stiffening.

THIS IS THE ONLY WAY THAT THE PRIDEHOUSE WILL ALLOW NON-AUTARCHY CRAFT TO ENTER THE ATMOSPHERE OF THEIR PLANET, Ten Per Cent Extra Free informed her swiftly. SHIPS RIDING AN ATTRACTOR ARE UNDER THE PRIDEHOUSE'S COMPLETE CONTROL, SO CAN REPRESENT NO THREAT TO THEM. FREELANDING SHIPS MIGHT PROVE TO BE ENEMIES DISGUISED AS FRIENDS. HEIN HAS COME TO LIKE YOU, AS YOU HAVE HIM. BUT HE CANNOT COMPLETELY TRUST YOU.

'Can I trust *him*?' she subvocalized.

YES. IF THE PRIDEHOUSE WERE GOING TO HARM YOU THEY WOULD HAVE DONE SO HALF A YEAR AGO. THEY ARE ONE OF THE ANCIENT SPECIES.

'Why don't they just zap the Autarchy?'

Hein was looking at her, watching the way her lips twitched as she spoke to the Image. Ten Per Cent Extra Free had dealt with the Pridehouse before, and knew that Hein would refrain from interrupting until this short exchange with Strider had finished. The Pridehouse were a very courteous species.

HUMAN SOLUTIONS ARE SO . . . SIMPLISTIC, LEONIE. ONE PLANET AGAINST THE AUTARCHY? THINK AGAIN.

'Oh. Thanks for reminding me that Humans are thick. Once more.'

Ten Per Cent Extra Free felt her fury with him. NO, IT'S JUST THAT YOU HUMANS ARE A *YOUNG* SPECIES. YOU FORGET THINGS.

'All right,' said Strider out loud to Hein, shrugging her shoulders.

'We shall perform the decontamination during your period of transit,' said the wolf. 'The process is painless, as I have said.'

In the Pocket Strider could see a red spark leaping from the planet's surface to the *Midnight Ranger*. Then everything started changing.

My arms! thought Strider. *What the hell is happening to them? My hands!*

Her clothing seemed to be melting into her skin. Her hands were shrinking until they were tiny. The flesh was somehow evaporating from her now-naked arms. Still leaning into the Pocket, unable to move, she watched as her fingers blended together into a single mass, one for each hand, then slowly redivided to form powerful talons. She felt her head stretching: there was little pain but great discomfort. From behind her she could hear her crew screaming: whatever was happening to her must be happening to them as well. Grey hairs sprang from the pores of her withered arms, so that within moments the skin was entirely covered. Her centre of balance shifted backwards, so that she was clinging with difficulty to the horizontal surface of the Pocket, even though that surface was lowering slowly to compensate. There was a ripple of sensation all down her body as her breasts retracted into her torso and then reproduced themselves all down her stomach: abruptly she was the proud owner of eight paired, flat breasts, all covered in shaggy hair. Her feet were suddenly too small to take her poorly balanced weight, and she staggered backwards a moment before dropping on to all fours. Her ears pricked up as she looked towards the crew.

The eye in her snout emerged and looked sternly at the two in her forehead for a little while – she was staring into her own eyes – before turning its field of vision forwards.

There was another wrench at her sides. Hanging her head down, looking between what had become forelegs, she saw herself sprout a third set of legs. They were elegantly long and covered in the same grey fur as the rest of her. One of them, without any conscious volition on her part, raised itself and scratched under her chin.

So this was the Pridehouse's famous decontamination technique: transform the visitors into perfect replicas of yourselves, probably exact right down to the last cellular interaction, and their alien micro-organisms will certainly die. Strider hoped that the Pridehouse were able to reverse the procedure precisely, because otherwise the Humans could bear away lethal infections. Besides, she didn't want to be a six-legged, tailless wolf any longer than she had to be.

She flopped on to her stomach and, tongue lolling, looked around her at the rest of the command deck. Although the others had likewise been mutated into semblances of Pridehouse, she was still able to recognize them without difficulty – especially Hilary, who was a fluffy little cub being suckled by Leander, an experience which was probably fulfilling a deal of his adolescent fantasies.

Perhaps I ought to bark a few orders, thought Strider sarcastically.

She tried speaking, and found it easier than she'd expected. 'Is anyone hurt?'

Various sets of big round eyes turned towards her. The large beast whom she knew was Umbel Nelson answered her in a voice that was half a snarl: 'Flower of the ages, I feel better than I did five minutes ago.'

THERE IS NO NEED FOR FEAR, said Pinocchio in all of their minds. THE PRIDEHOUSE'S IMAGES INFORMED US OF WHAT WOULD OCCUR, AND THEY ASSURED US THE PROCESS WAS PERFECTLY SAFE.

'Couldn't you have *warned* us?' snapped Leander.

YOU MIGHT HAVE REFUSED THE TREATMENT.

'That was our decision to take,' said Lan Yi quietly. 'Of any Image, Pinocchio, you should have known better.'

I APOLOGIZE, half-sang Pinocchio's voice. STILL, IT'S DONE NOW.

The flippancy of his tone infuriated Strider, but she clamped down on her anger. The Images had acted wisely. It was important that the Humans made allies of the Pridehouse, and one or other of her crew might have been so horrified by the prospect of the transformation as to refuse it entirely. But still . . . 'We'll discuss this later, Pinocchio,' she subvocalized.

The *Midnight Ranger* jerked suddenly, and the crew slid

hither and thither on the deck. Loki scampered anxiously among them: the cat had become a miniature six-legged wolf, but obviously hadn't noticed yet.

'That'll be the Pridehouse's attractor locking on to us,' Strider guessed out loud for the sake of the others.

THAT IS CORRECT, said Pinocchio and Ten Per Cent Extra Free together. AGAIN, THERE IS NOTHING TO BE AFRAID OF.

'The ship is now totally under the Pridehouse's control,' she continued, ignoring the Images, 'and it'll stay that way until we've left their planet again.' She wondered what her voice sounded like to the others. To herself it sounded just the same as always, although perhaps slightly clumsier than usual because of the thick tongue between her unfamiliarly shaped jaws. 'Don't panic. Hilary, stop whining or I'll hit you.'

The cub looked appalled, and abruptly ceased making any noise except for strident breathing.

Strider twisted her head back and looked up through the view-window. There was nothing to see but red. She was reminded of home on Mars, although when approaching Mars one saw the rilles and volcanic formations, as well as the patches of green where Humans had introduced vegetation. The Pridehouse seemed almost featureless, just as it had in the Pockets.

Cautiously, she moved back to her Pocket. She found it easier than she'd expected to move on her six legs. The level of the Pocket's solid surface sank again so that she could peer into it without discomfort.

She thought of the gaseous composition of The Pridehouse's atmosphere, and at once statistics were displayed in front of her. There was oxygen in plenty, comparatively little nitrogen and carbon dioxide, a great deal of ammonia . . .

'How are we going to be able to breathe?' she subvocalized.

YOU ARE REPLICAS OF THE PRIDEHOUSE NOW, said Ten Per Cent Extra Free promptly. OF COURSE YOU WILL BE ABLE TO BREATHE THEIR NATIVE ATMOSPHERE.

26

'Then how can we breathe at the moment?'

THE PRIDEHOUSE HAVE ALTERED THE AIR IN THE *MIDNIGHT RANGER* SO THAT IT IS COMPATIBLE WITH THEIRS. THEY WILL ALTER IT BACK AGAIN WHEN YOU LEAVE.

'Pretty impressive technology these folk have,' said Strider. 'How the hell did they do that?'

SOME DAY I'LL SPEND SEVERAL YEARS EXPLAINING IT TO YOU: THEIR SCIENCE HAS HAD SEVERAL *BILLION* YEARS' START ON HUMANITY'S. REMEMBER HOW *OLD* THE ANCIENT SPECIES ARE.

Strider did remember, and retracted her head from the Pocket, suddenly reminded of Polyaggle. Could a colonial, winged organism survive the transformation into a pseudo-mammalian one? She needn't have worried. Polyaggle was a beautiful, if rather small, silver-furred wolf: she had curled up in a corner and was sleeping peacefully, her elegant snout between the foremost pair of her legs. Her sides moved inwards and outwards in a soporific rhythm, and Strider found herself yawning in sympathy.

Swiftly she put her head back into the Pocket and thought of Hein. His face obediently appeared.

'That punch on the nose is definitely guaranteed,' she said.

'It will be a pleasure to receive it,' he replied. Now there was no need for the Images to translate his facial expression: she recognized it easily as a smile. 'But remember to keep your talons sheathed: otherwise you could do me harm.'

'That's what I want to do you. I like being a *biped*, dammit, not a hexaped. I like standing upright.'

Hein shrugged: the gesture involved moving his long ears forward so that they briefly covered his upper pair of eyes. He made no further comment, and Strider realized her remark had been a lie. In her current form she much preferred being the way she was: it seemed utterly natural to her.

'How long until we land?' she asked him.

'About twenty nanreets.'

27

VERY SLIGHTLY LESS THAN HALF AN HOUR, Ten Per Cent Extra Free translated for her.

'Is there anything we can do until then?'

'Not much. We can talk, if you wish.'

'I'd like that.'

'What would you like to talk about?' said Hein. His third eye retracted briefly into his snout, and this time reappeared in a startlingly bright mauve.

'About your people,' said Strider, flexing the talons of her forepaws. 'Our species always assumed that we'd attained technology because we had an opposable thumb and walked upright. You clearly got there a different way. Tell me how.'

'Evolution is a continuing process . . .' began Hein.

Long ago – more millions of years ago than Strider enjoyed contemplating – the Pridehouse had indeed been an upright species: they ran on four feet, but the front part of their bodies had been vertical, so that they looked something like a cross between a wolf and a centaur. In those days the foremost two limbs had been equipped with appendages which, so far as Strider could gather, had been not unlike the digits of a human hand. But then, when the Pridehouse had retreated to their Homeworld as the Comelatelies had begun to dominate the galaxy, slaughtering any species whom they perceived as a threat, it had become *safer* to look like animals rather than a technologically advanced people. Slowly, as time went by, the Pridehouse had physically reverted to what they assumed had been an earlier form – although, Hein assured her, it was possible that they had instead achieved a new form, one not reflected in any part of their earlier evolutionary history. On the few occasions that the Autarchy passed by, all that could be seen were, yes, dominant creatures, but creatures which could never themselves have attained any high technological status. Their cities were small and ramshackle. The Pridehouse had in effect back-evolved. Physically, anyway. What was not obvious was that their intelligence remained, and that their distant

28

ancestors had built technological artefacts that *lasted*. A taloned paw could press a button or move a lever or swivel a knob just as well as a hand could, and nothing had been forgotten. With this ability, old technology could be used to create new technology, and new technology to create newer. What the Pridehouse had done, in effect, was deliberately to evolve their technology in order to compensate for their own reversed physiological evolution. Much of it responded to mental commands; much more of it had reached a level of artificial empathy or intelligence – or both – such that it had become essentially symbiotic with the Pridehouse.

The Pridehouse, despite their fearsome teeth, were not carnivores. What they ate – and here Strider found her understanding beginning to slip – was their planet. She asked Ten Per Cent Extra Free for clarification, but the Image remained silent.

The view-window above her flared. The *Midnight Ranger* was encountering the outer vestiges of The Pridehouse's atmosphere. The Bredai had assured her that the window was made of a material as tough as the Humans' plastite. As always, Strider neurotically half-expected the window to explode inwards towards her.

She forced her attention back to the Pocket.

'We're coming in, buster,' she said to Hein.

'Hope you have a bumpy ride,' said the wolf. The *other* wolf.

'If I'm sick I'm going to save it up for you.'

'"Sick"? What's that?'

'Just hope you never find out.'

The craft began to jounce around as it moved down towards the region of the jetstreams. What was left in Strider of the Human felt its gorge rising, but the Pridehouse part of her was unconcerned. It felt odd to have two different sensations at once, almost as if she were two different people – which she supposed, in a way, she was.

A thought occurred to her. 'Say, Hein, how far did the Pridehouse explore the Universe, back in the old days?'

Again his ears slid forwards. It was clear that the question did not interest him in the slightest. 'Who knows? Who cares?'

'I care,' said Strider.

'Why?'

'There were old legends on my species' home planet about people who could become wolves when they wanted to. I was wondering if maybe the Pridehouse had called by.'

Hein shrugged once more. 'Infinitely unlikely. How old is your oral culture?'

Now it was Strider's turn to shrug. 'Maybe as much as a hundred thousand years. It's hard to tell . . .'

She watched his face as the Images translated the word 'years' for him. Then he started laughing at her.

'The Pridehouse have confined themselves to this planet for some five times that long,' he said.

'Maybe one of your ships got lost and strayed into our galaxy,' said Strider stubbornly, 'the same way that us Humans found ourselves in The Wondervale? Maybe, rather than coming home, they found a world to colonize, then started looking around at the stellar systems nearby?'

Hein drew his upper eyes closer together in an expression Strider had no difficulty reading as scorn.

'Impossible,' he said. 'First, the Pridehouse never get lost. Second, if ever any of your people had learnt how to mutate into wolves, they'd have stayed that way. Who'd want to be a biped?'

'Two punches on the nose,' said Strider. 'No, make that three.'

The *Midnight Ranger* did not so much land as break through the land. Strider could not watch it in reality, but she observed everything in the Pocket. Like the opening of a giant eye, a part of the planet's surface peeled apart to reveal a bright intensity within. The attractor, which glittered in the Pocket like a rod made out of mica, slowly eased the spaceship through the vent, which closed above. The craft was brought to a halt, still vertical, hovering thirty or forty centimetres above a flat shelf that seemed to hold itself in the midst of a vast volume of nothingness.

So this was what a Pridehouse spacestrip was like.

Strider, who had expected landing to be a matter of bucking and bouncing as the *Midnight Ranger* hit ground at a velocity close to the dangerous, carving and veering across the planet's curiously uniform surface, was impressed – and reminded herself yet again of the age of the ancient species. Maybe in a few million years humanity – assuming it hadn't destroyed itself by then through one folly or another – would be capable of similar feats.

'You can emerge now,' said Hein, with a formality that had been absent from their earlier half-bantering exchanges. 'You will egress singly, and you will bear no weapons.'

'Not even a . . .?'

'No, Leonie, not even a lazgun.' He smiled frostily. 'Besides, in your current form it'd take you several nanreets to work out how to fire the thing. You have no hands any longer. No fingers.'

'I'd manage,' she said.

'You probably would. So – no weapons.'

There wasn't any point in arguing. The eight of them were in no position to take on a planetful of technologically advanced creatures – not that she had any wish to do so. She liked Hein. The Images had told her that she could trust the Pridehouse as a species, and that was what her own instincts said to her as well. Hm. She actually rather *fancied* Hein. This was something that she must keep concealed. *Imagine transspecies pregnancy,* she thought. *Better still, don't. Although I suppose the Pridehouse have some marvellous means of contraception that involves numerous glowing forcefields and something that smells of dried soya protein. Maybe . . . Get your mind back to the subject, Leonie.*

'We'll send the cat out first,' she said aloud.

'Cat?' said Hein.

'We call it that. It'll look like a tiny cub to you.'

'Cub?'

'Child,' she corrected hastily. 'I'll come immediately afterwards. Then the rest of us. The last to appear will be Polyaggle.'

'The Spindrifter?' Strider was annoyed that Hein looked suddenly so eager. 'None of us alive have encountered a Spindrifter in the flesh before, but there are records.' *Oh, blast,* thought Strider. *The Pridehouse find the Spindrifters as pestilentially erotic as we do. So much for that jolly little fantasy I was having* . . . 'When they were destroyed by Kaantalech, we felt their pain as if it were our own.'

'Really.'

Strider insisted to the others that, as they each left the ship, they should go through a full cycling of the airlock, even though Ten Per Cent Extra Free had told her the atmosphere of the ship was now identical with that of The Pridehouse: if anything went wrong she wanted at least some of the crew to be able to get away. Maybe. They'd have to try to blast their way through the planet's outer skin . . . Even so, anything to improve their chances. With much scrabbling of forepaws she managed to equip herself with a commlink, so that Pinocchio would have an artefact to cling on to; Nelson, with even greater difficulty, did the same so that he could play host to Ten Per Cent Extra Free. They tested the commlinks.

'Hi, there, love of my life.'

'Sounds like there's a bit of static on the line, Nelson. Let's use these things only if we have to. Otherwise we'll end up with sore brains.'

'The pain's exquisite, coming from you, Leonie.'

'Shut up.'

They could see Loki going berserk in the airlock.

'You're a tough bastard, Leonie,' growled Nelson.

'I'm worried that she'll figure out how to get back in through the inner door,' said Strider, only half-joking.

The outer door eventually opened, and at once Loki was perfectly calm. The little creature trotted to the edge of the 'lock and looked downwards. A small attractor took the beast and lowered it gently to the shelf, where it began to groom itself, doing its best to convey the impression that all along this was where it had wanted to be.

Strider, waiting for her own turn, hoped she could retain the same degree of outward dignity. *They're friends,* she kept telling herself. *Anyway, Leonie, you've gotta look good, if only for Hilary's sake. Pretend you're just arriving at a party thrown by someone you don't know very well. Oh, shit, I never much liked parties . . .*

A little later she was herself on the shelf beside the cat. She licked its spine, which she sensed was the correct way of reassuring it. It ignored her completely.

The shelf was the same hue of red as the outer plains of The Pridehouse had seemed. Curious, she sniffed at it, then focused all three of her eyes on the surface; the third eye improved the perception of depth at a distance but made it more difficult to focus on objects close up, and she found that she was arching her neck. Then she had an inspiration, and smiled. *Keep that grin plastered to your muzzle, Leonie.* The ancillary eye dutifully disappeared into her snout, giving her the distinctly human sensation of a lover withdrawing his tongue from her mouth.

The surface of the shelf was covered with what appeared very like centimetre-long, slightly bristly hair. She moved the talons of a paw through it, feeling it brush against the paw's surprisingly sensitive velvety underside.

Lan Yi was dropped from the airlock to join her, and likewise retracted his third eye and began to investigate the surface. Then he sat back slightly clumsily on his haunches and looked about him with interest. Strider followed suit. It was difficult to see anything in the glare of the spotlights directed on the *Midnight Ranger*, but she became dimly aware of vast shapes in the distance, moving ponderously, as if she were watching huge marine creatures in a dark canyon of a terrestrial ocean.

For the first time she felt truly frightened. The Images had told her that the Pridehouse would do nothing to harm the Humans, but those great, barely visible moving shapes were telling her directly of the huge gulf of years that existed between her own species and this alien one. What might seem harmless to the Pridehouse, who might have utterly different motivations to any she could hope to understand, could be lethal to herself and her small crew.

Hilary passed through the airlock, and Lan Yi licked the boy's spine, calming him. The child seemed better able to cope with things now that he was outside the confines of the spaceship, and looked around him with evident wonder. Soon Segrill, looking less like a wolf than like a six-legged mouse, appeared, followed by Leander, Strauss-Giolitto, Nelson and finally Polyaggle. There was a feeling of an era having come to an end when the airlock door hissed shut behind Polyaggle.

'Well,' said Strider as loudly as she could into the dazzling brilliance, 'we're here. Now what?' Her voice sounded fine to her, but she suspected it might contain nuances that would convey to the Pridehouse her fear.

'Is it possible that you have acquired the same inference as I concerning the nature of this world?' said Lan Yi quietly to her. He must be more nervous than he seemed. His Argot rarely became so stilted.

She smiled, and again there was that uncomfortable glooping sensation as her forward eye was swallowed by the surrounding flesh. 'How do I know when you haven't told me what your inference is?' she said in her new body's harsh equivalent of a whisper.

'This is not a planet at all.'

'Depends on your definition of the word "planet". It's a world that goes in orbit around a star. But I'm with you.'

'It is a living organism.'

'I think so, too. More than that, I think I know the reason why it has the same name as its dominant species, and what Hein meant when he said his species get nutrition by eating their planet.'

'Exactly, Captain Strider,' said Lan Yi in the same low tones. 'Our new allies are this world's bacteria.'

The lights dimmed, and gradually Strider, peering through the gloom, was able to make out more of their surroundings. The huge shapes she had detected earlier now looked even more like colossal fish, floating slowly and aimlessly. She breathed deeply: the air smelled good to her. Once again, without any volition on her part, one of her central legs reached up to scratch under her chin.

'Over there,' said Strauss-Giolitto, gesturing uncertainly with her nose.

Strider followed her direction and saw, far in the distance, a yellowish light approaching. No – now that she was able to bring her Pridehouse vision into full focus she saw that it was a trio of lights, close together.

'I think our friends are coming to greet us,' said Strider. Again that jolt of fear went through her. It was the silence, she decided: the uncanny silence all around them; the silence of the great dark fish. Polyaggle, near her, was by contrast looking eager for the arrival of whatever it was that was coming towards them – some kind of small vessel, Strider guessed.

Her guess was correct.

Hein – yes, she was certain it was Hein – appeared as a door slid open at the front of the complexly shapen craft. He stared directly towards Strider, and his third eye vanished briefly as he made a beckoning movement with a front paw. *Well, at least we share a few things in common with the Pridehouse*, Strider thought, stepping ahead of the rest towards the vessel.

The powerful reek of Hein hit her as she came close to him, and for a moment her nostrils wrinkled in revulsion. But then she realized how *good* he smelled, how *right*. She remembered the moment at the Pocket when she had faced up to the fact that, in her new form, she was finding herself attracted to him; his odour was telling her that he felt the same way towards her. Damn! Was he detecting the same emanations from her? This was a complication she could do without. She felt strangely virginal, and ignorant. If she succumbed to temptation – which she determined immediately not to do – he was going to have to teach her new self everything.

'Welcome,' he said, the two Images translating his word.

Strider's ears momentarily occluded her upper eyes in a shrug. 'Thanks for bringing us down here,' she said.

Hein laughed. 'We were only just in time. An Autarchy vessel had picked up a trace of you, and was about to head in this direction. Now that you're inside The Pridehouse you've vanished from their sensors.'

Strider stiffened, remembering what had happened to Spindrift. 'Are you sure they can't track us down, nevertheless?'

'They can't,' replied Hein, turning to lead her into the little craft. It was a partially irregular polyhedron, with more sides than she could count. She scrambled in ungainly manner up a couple of steps, obediently following him. He seemed completely assured, for which she was grateful. 'We also scrambled the sensors. At this moment there's a very confused Autarchy commander in orbit around Qitanefermeartha, wondering how she got there.' He laughed again.

Strider turned to look at the rest of her crew. Segrill, the one she'd been worried about because of his tininess, had locked

36

his teeth into the shaggy hair under Nelson's throat, and was dangling precariously. Nelson leapt straight over the steps to join her, and the Trok dropped to the floor and swiftly clattered on his minute paws to shelter under what she assumed was the craft's control module. Only Strauss-Giolitto was showing reluctance to enter the craft. Strider could scent the woman's terror.

'Come on,' she said. Her instinct was to reach out a hand, but of course she hadn't a hand to reach.

Reluctantly, Strauss-Giolitto slunk aboard.

The door slid shut noiselessly and Hein touched his muzzle to the console. The craft swung around, and began to move away from the landing shelf.

'I'll give you the full tour later,' said Hein. 'For the moment, just see what you want to see.'

He touched another control and the sides of the craft became transparent. Strider immediately looked downwards, and saw beneath her splayed paws a seemingly endless vista of activity. The fish-shapes that had seemed so dark when she had been surrounded by the spotlights were in fact quite brightly illuminated. Obviously they were spacecraft, their overall design, surprisingly, only superficially different from that of the original *Santa Maria*: perhaps the Pridehouse had arrived early at a good design for a spaceship and decided not to make unnecessary 'improvements'. Each of them rested on a free-floating shelf not unlike the one that held the *Midnight Ranger* and was surrounded by arrays of spotlights, which also seemed to be unsupported. Like everything else on or in The Pridehouse, the craft were an ochreish red. . . . *And little fleas have littler fleas, and so ad infinitum?* speculated Strider. Was *every* part of The Pridehouse an organism of some kind?

Here and there she could see small vessels like the one they were travelling in gliding easily from site to site. Swarming around the ships, moving with startling precision and at a rate sometimes impossible to follow, were what Strider guessed must be machines of some kind – bots busily making adjustments or maybe finishing off the . . .

Name of Umbel!

'You're still building this fleet, aren't you?' she said incredulously to Hein.

'Correct. It is still in the process of being reborn.'

Strider was stunned. 'When did you start?'

It took Pinocchio a short while to translate the Pridehouse's reply into Human terminology. A LITTLE OVER A MONTH.

'But there must be thousands of ships down there!' she said.

'About ten thousand,' said Hein promptly.

She looked up at him and saw that he was smiling at her. Then, beyond his shoulder, she saw something else.

A city.

At least, that was what she assumed it was, although it was unlike any city she had seen before, even in holos. It was hard to judge distances here inside The Pridehouse, but it seemed to her the structure was massive, stretching thousands of kilometres from one side to the other, and hanging unsupported in the gloom. The main structure was, as near as she could see, circular, with the rim higher than the centre, so that it held the countless edifices, parklands, roads and all the rest as in a gently cupped hand. Over it arched what Strider recognized as the faint glow of a forcefield. There was light everywhere, running in crisscrossing necklaces all over the upper surface of the disc to create complex patterns, some of which were moving in slow undulations.

'The city's breathing,' she said softly.

'Of course it's breathing,' said Hein, as if there could be no question of its doing anything else. Then he laughed at her again.

'But that's not a city, Captain Strider. That's your flagship.'

*

The Onurg was significantly larger than Hein and coloured entirely silver, so that he looked as if he had been dipped into a bath of the molten metal and then removed, perfectly plated in every detail from the tip of his snout to the hindmost paw. Only his eyes were not silver. The two upper ones were a pale grey that somehow seemed not tranquil but full of energy: Strider sensed that, if the Pridehouse had an emotion akin to Human anger, the Onurg was a person who should not be crossed. But there was no question of his being wrathful at the moment. His muzzle-eye kept changing colour as he smiled at his little collection of guests.

This ancient species certainly didn't stand on ceremony. The craft Hein had been piloting had come upward through a bafflingly complicated system of brightly illuminated tunnels to reach the surface of the city – *the flagship*, Strider had to keep reminding herself. The journey through the disc had taken longer than she'd expected: the structure of the flagship was so huge that what had looked from a distance to be merely eggshell thin was at least a couple of hundred kilometres thick. The network of tunnels was so complex that even Hein lost his air of confidence, moving his little craft at a cautious speed, pausing occasionally to check his position through what she reckoned must be the Pridehouse's version of a commline – or maybe he was just stopping to think about which way next to turn. Strider found the tunnel's walls threateningly organic, as if at any moment they might choose to clamp themselves tight together and start committing some obscene act of peristalsis. The sheen of liquid covering them looked disturbingly like a digestive fluid.

It had been a relief to emerge on to the upper surface of the disc.

Hein had touched a further bobble on the control module and there had been a slight grunting noise as six wheels sprouted on the underside of the craft, which landed gently on the smooth surface of what was to all intents and purposes a road which Strider might have seen on Mars. No, better than one of those, for the roads at home were often in poor repair. Even though the craft was now running on wheels – unlike a Martian cabble, which floated just above the surface – the drive was smoother than any cabble ride she'd ever experienced.

Hein was concentrating on making constant adjustments at his console. Strauss-Giolitto moved up beside her, nudging her with a shoulder.

'Why's he going on the ground?' she said. 'We could be flying.'

'Dunno, Maria,' Strider responded. 'Conserving energy?'

'I don't know that these people need to worry much about that sort of thing.' Strauss-Giolitto swivelled her head from side to side; the gesture transmitted itself to Strider as the encompassing wave of an arm. 'Just look at this, will you?'

Because of the slight concavity of the city – *of the flagship, Leonie* – there was no horizon as such, but the construction was so large that atmospheric dispersal made it seem almost as if there were. You could see a certain distance and then, beyond that, a haze that became more and more indistinct until there was nothing. Once again, as it had been from a distance, there seemed everywhere around them to be light. Strider guessed it was not unnatural that a species which dwelt inside their world – their host organism – rather than on its sunny surface would want the reassurance of light. She suddenly remembered the little, primitive-seeming surface cities they had been able to see from orbit. Perhaps they served as tourist villages, or something, while at the same time – disguise is the best defence – being camouflage against Autarchy inquisitiveness. *Take a vacation on the outside, funsters, and enjoy the light of the Sun for a fortnight! You too can have all the pleasures of peeling skin and sleepless nights! And, wow, those guys and dolls won't be wearing much, and they'll be f-r-e-e and e-a-s-y!* She grinned to herself, her third eye disappearing briefly with the usual ploop.

It had seemed from the distance as if the surface of the ship were crowded with buildings, but in fact mostly they were spaced several kilometres apart. Only here and there did they pass a complex, surrounded by dozens of stationary craft like the one they were travelling in. *Cabble-parks,* thought Strider. *Some things seem to be common to all technological species.* Although she thought of the various structures they passed as buildings, she realized that they were in fact growths, and they looked it: where Human edifices would have been marked by straight lines and hard edges, these were curvaceous and nodular. *Tumours,* she thought, then quickly rammed the notion to the back of her mind.

Aside from the occasional building, the landscape through which the road wound was monotonous and flat. There were patches of colours other than The Pridehouse's pervasive red, but they were small, few and far between, and the colours themselves were muted, as if the red had beaten them into submission and they were trying not to draw further attention to themselves. Strider assumed the areas of grey and muddy green were fields: if their crops tasted the way they looked the Pridehouse must subsist on a diet of overcooked cabbage.

But what one noticed more than the landscape was its populace. The areas to either side of the main road surface were for pedestrians. To say they were crowded would have been an overstatement, but they were in considerable use. In a way, in fact, they *were* crowded, because the Pridehouse did not shuffle along at a Human gait. They ran, and they ran at speed, their legs a blur of motion and their backs arching and flattening with almost the same dizzying rapidity. Sixty, eighty, a hundred kilometres per hour? Strider could only hazard a guess. *Damn' fast, anyway.* She wondered what happened if two of the Pridehouse ever collided, but they seemed to have perfect control of their bodies, moving around and past each other without any sign of hesitation.

A thought struck her.

She turned her head and looked at the fur of her sleek, strong flank.

Wow! Once we get off this craft I'm going to be able to . . .

It hadn't in fact worked out like that. When the vehicle finally pulled to a halt beside an undistinguished building and, at Hein's behest, they decanted, they found themselves being welcomed by the great silver wolf who introduced himself as the Onurg. Suggesting that they all go for a quick romp across the plain would have been . . . undignified. Or maybe not? Maybe it would have fitted in perfectly with Pridehouse protocol, but Strider hadn't been prepared to risk it.

The Onurg had welcomed them with the same loose informality that Hein had shown earlier, as if they were merely old friends dropping round for drinks. He had shown them the lavatories, and noisily used one of them himself – the Pridehouse clearly had no worries about privacy as they shat. Strider had followed his example, not just because she had been experiencing some discomfort but because it might have been some sort of ambassadorial ritual. Loki had disgraced itself, but the Onurg had just laughed. The Pridehouse as a species seemed eager to laugh at anything that came their way – to be frolicsome. Perhaps it was a consequence of their species being so ancient: when, as a species, you have experienced so much, there must be few reactions to the Universe left but laughter. Or Polyaggle's sombreness. The ancient species appeared to lack the full range of emotions available to Humans. *Appear to, Leonie,* she reminded herself. *You know virtually nothing of this culture.*

Yet she herself had within the past few hours felt fear and nervousness and pleasure and much more. *You may be mainly Pridehouse at the moment,* she thought, *but obviously you're still a Human at the core.*

And now they were eating the planet. At least, they were eating some of the stuff that Strider had seen during their ride here. She had been right about the taste: the raw food reminded her irresistibly of overcooked vegetables, but at the same time it was delicious in a way that she could not describe to herself. They were sitting in a circle in the building's largest room, leaning forwards to snatch mouthfuls from a mound of vegetation. The circle was slowly getting smaller.

The Onurg had stopped eating some little while ago, as had Segrill and Polyaggle. The three had been talking but Strider, ravenous, had carried on eating, guiltily aware of her dereliction of duty but unable to do anything about it.

At last her hunger was satisfied, and she sat back on her haunches.

'Can you hear me, Nelson?' she said through her commlink.

'You bet, sweetest. But I'm busy right now.' He was next to her, tugging a further pile of the green-grey stuff towards himself.

Reception was poor, but his thought words were perfectly intelligible.

'You're making a pig of yourself.'

'You mean I'm wolfing it down.' The big creature that Nelson had become briefly raised its head from the heap of food and looked at her. She had never before known that it was possible for a commlink to transmit a happy belch. Then Nelson turned his attention back to eating.

'Nelson, we have to talk.'

The Onurg was looking at her, obviously expecting her to open a dialogue with him. She didn't want to speak to him, yet. Reluctantly – her belly was full – she reached forward into the vegetable mound again and started eating, trying to make it seem as if she were devouring far more than she was.

'Nelson, it's urgent.'

'I know the way you feel about me, darling of the sunset, but can't you just wait until I've finished my . . .?'

'This isn't the time for farting about.'

'Well, I don't want to fart about yesterday. If you gotta fart about anything, might as well fart about the present, is what I say. Except in the presence of a goddess like yourself – goes without saying.'

She bit him. It was clearly a Pridehouse demonstration of minor anger, and he took it as nonchalantly as if she had sworn at him. While he carried on eating she was mortified by the way the alien instinct had taken her over.

'I can't use this thing as a flagship,' she said through the commlink.

'Why not? It's big. I'll bet it's powerful. I'll bet its weaponry is better than anything else in The Wondervale. I'll bet it could take apart the average Autarchy armada and still have enough left over to be severely nasty to anyone else who displeased it.'

'Nelson, do you really want to spend the rest of your life as a wolf?'

His jaws stopped working for a fraction of a second, and then he continued chewing, but more slowly now.

'The atmosphere we're breathing at the moment,' she said. 'If we were back in our own selves, it'd poison us immediately. I want my hands back. I want to walk upright again. I want to use my own voice. I want you and Lan Yi and Hilary and Leander and Strauss-Giolitto to *look like human beings* when I speak to you.'

'Wouldn't be the rest of our lives,' said Nelson, but she could sense his uncertainty.

'Might be. We hadn't expected the Pridehouse could produce anything like this ship. Who knows what the Autarchy is capable of producing? Something twice as big? Five times as big? Ten times? Ten times as powerful, and ten times better armed?' She paused a moment, then continued. 'Besides, I'm not sure big ships are the best way of undermining the Autarchy.'

'How d'you mean?'

She thought back to her first sight of the ships of the fleet the Pridehouse were building – or, rather, growing.

'Ever had a fight with a flea?' she said.

'Lady of midnight, I ain't ever *seen* a flea. I've always moved in better company than that.'

She sensed that now, like herself, Nelson was only pretending to eat.

'You know what I mean,' she thought impatiently at him. 'A gadfly. Same image. Stick to fleas. They're tiny – tiny enough that it's hard even to see the little bastards: that's why they've survived everything the Human species has done to try to eliminate them. If you're bitten by one you know about it. If you're bitten by enough of them you get ill. An infestation can kill smaller animals. I think I want to be a flea – I think we could be more effective that way. Remember what we did to Qitanefermeartha.'

It had been a low-technology shuttle – plus Pinocchio's quasi-suicide – that had destroyed Autarch Nalla's citadel. A hi-tech attack might well have been repelled easily.

'See what you mean, lady,' said Nelson, his thoughts no longer so flippant. 'So you're gonna tell the Pridehouse to stop building those big babies we saw and start building . . . well, fleas?'

'No. They know what's right for them. I think I know what's right for me – for us.'

'But they've insisted you should be their commander.'

'What difference does that make?'

'A commander's place is on her flagship,' he said.

'Yeah? So this armada's going to have a very small flagship. Remember the damage the Trok fighters were able to do to Nalla's defensive forces? You could just about stretch your arms across one of those ships: their strength was in being too small to notice until it was too late. I'm going to get the Pridehouse to make over the *Midnight Ranger* – give it the tachyon drive, a fuck of a lot of shielding and enough weaponry to vaporize a small galaxy.'

'You're gonna *ask* them to do all that,' corrected Nelson. 'Ask them very nicely. You're gonna say "please".'

She thought a snort at him, then wondered how the noise had turned out at his end. 'Don't you trust me?'

'No. I love you to the soles of my boots, but . . .'

She tongued off the commlink with difficulty – her tongue was overlong and overlarge – and sat up once more, looking directly at the Onurg. He must have felt her gaze, or maybe an Image prompted him, because he abruptly broke off his conversation with Segrill and Polyaggle and turned back towards her.

'What do you think of your flagship, Captain Strider? Of course, you've seen hardly anything of it, but . . .'

'I cannot accept the command.'

The Pridehouse's expression of incredulousness involved a crossing of the central legs and a totter on the remaining four. 'But's that what you came here to do.'

'Well, I cannot accept the command of this ship. It's magnificent. I admire it. I admire all of the Pridehouse.' She paused. Delicacy was called for. 'But it's *your* ship, not mine. I'm a biped with fingers and toes, and I'm accustomed to the technology that goes along with all that. If I had to be a six-legged wolf for more than a few days I'd go fucking nuts.' *Oops, Leonie. Remember: delicacy.*

The Onurg crossed his central legs again. 'This copulation with food . . .?' he began.

'My Images have translated imperfectly,' she said as evenly as she could. 'Being in what is, for me, the wrong body for any length of time would cause me substantial nervous strain. In many ways I prefer this body to my own, because it's stronger and it's sleeker and it's undoubtedly more graceful, but it's not *mine*. And I'm sure my companions feel the same as I do.'

'We could reconfigure you into Human form – or Spindrifter or Trok or whatever,' said the Onurg. He swivelled his head from side to side, indicating all of them. 'It would be no trouble. You would still be able to breathe our air,' he added before she could raise the point.

'Yeah, but even then we'd be trying to cope with technology that's alien to us. We'd fuck up the whole time.' *Oops again*.

This time the Images coped with the translation – and presumably decorously, because the Onurg showed no trace of offence. But once more he made the odd gesture with his legs.

'Why should that be difficult for you?'

The gulf of several million years. The Pridehouse had forgotten what it was like to be a *young* species. Presumably they could adapt immediately to any form of gadgetry and be able to use it instinctively.

'Because our minds aren't as flexible as yours,' she said. 'We'd keep doing the wrong things, making the wrong decisions. To take an obvious example, to you this flagship is just *big* – OK, OK, it's versatile and all the other things as well. But it's still within your *conception*. It's way, way beyond mine. I don't know how I could handle it. First Autarchy warcruiser I came across would probably ram me right up the . . .'

'We can alter your brains so that you can deal with all of this,' the Onurg interrupted. 'We could make you think like we do. Surely you realize that?' Even in translation his voice displayed his perplexity, as if she were being deliberately perverse.

'But we don't *want* our brains altered!' She assumed that she was indeed talking for all of them. 'The fact we don't want you to do that is another example of the differences between us. We might enjoy it for a bit, just the same way as I want to find out what it feels like being able to run as fast as you people, but in the end it'd drive us crazy. What we want to be is Humans, not mongrelized versions of Humans cum Pridehouse.'

'Polyaggle?' said the Onurg thoughtfully, turning his head.

The Spindrifter's ears flicked forwards. 'My loyalties are with the Humans, and specifically with Captain Strider. Even if they were not, I have to regain my original form soon,

47

because I am expecting a brood. I want my offspring to be true Spindrifters, so that my species can live again.'

'Then you won't lead us?' said the Onurg, turning back to Strider again. All the others – except the cat, which was still guzzling away – looked at her as well. 'We need you. We've remembered the technologies of war, but we know nothing of the art of warfare.' There was a sigh in the voice the Images interpreted. 'I wish we didn't have to learn it again.'

'If you want, I'll lead you,' said Strider, 'though you'd be better off finding another candidate if you can.'

And then she explained to the Onurg about her Gadfly Principle.

Some while later, she did give in to temptation with Hein. Sex with him was quite probably the most bizarre experience she had ever had, but it was so full of genuine affection and caring that, even though its pleasures weren't human ones, it filled her with an infinite warmth and satisfaction.

Afterwards, as they romped across a tract of parkland, leaping and snarling and making little play-bites at each other, she said: 'Sometime you're going to have to transform yourself into a Human.'

'The Onurg has decided that I should do that anyway.'

'What?' She stopped in her tracks, her talons raking great gashes in the red surface.

Hein trotted back towards her.

'He wants me to travel with you aboard the *Midnight Ranger*. Clearly it would be best if I did so in your bipedal form.'

'He might have asked.'

'But the wisdom of this course of action is obvious.'

She felt her anger boil, all the sated happiness draining out of her. The presumptuous . . .

No, Leonie. Cool it. These people have forgotten that other species don't think the same way they do themselves.

And of course it was a sensible idea. She needed someone on board who could translate between her and the Pridehouse armada – not linguistically, because the Images would deal with that, but conceptually. Otherwise there might be all kinds of misunderstanding.

'Oh boy, buster,' she said after a few moments. 'You're in for an experience that's gonna blow your mind once I get my hands on you in Human form. It's been a long, long time.'

'Why?'

She thought of explaining about the need of a Human crew to have some sort of structure of command, and the necessity for the captain to stay in general sexually aloof from the others in case of accusations of favouritism; and then she realized that there were just too many cultural differences to explain – too many bridges of reasoning, many of them hardly rational if you were from another species, looking at them from the out-side – so she twitched her ears over her upper eyes and said: 'I'll tell you some other day.'

She laughed. 'See that building over there?'

He turned. 'Yes. So what?'

'I'll race you there and back. The winner gets to lay the loser. OK?'

'Seems fair enough to me.'

2

I Can Remember Feeling Better

Strider sat on the command deck of the *Midnight Ranger* with Loki on her lap, running her fingertips through the sleek dark brown fur behind the cat's ears. The cat responded by stretching out her front legs and gently digging her claws into Strider's knee.

Ouch. Not so gently.

'Oi! Stop that!' said Strider, pulling one claw after the other out of the material of her blue jumpsuit.

The Pridehouse engineers had been baffled by her request that they experiment with turning Loki into a simulacrum of one of the many cats Strauss-Giolitto had located on one of the *Midnight Ranger*'s holos, but had tried it anyway. The little animal had seemed completely undisconcerted by the transition, although for the first few hours she searched bemusedly for the central pair of legs to which she had grown accustomed, presumably in order to do something disgusting with them – the holos had failed to demonstrate some of the personal habits of cats. Then she had discovered the tip of her tail: this new plaything had kept her periodically amused for the succeeding weeks.

Although it hadn't been Strider's initial intention, the Onurg had accepted her Gadfly Principle to the extent that he had determined that the Pridehouse fleet – including the flagship – be returned to the body of the planet and then once more regrown. It seemed an astonishing labour until Strider reminded herself for the thousandth time that the Pridehouse was an ancient species: they regarded projects at which the collective energies of humanity would have balked as being merely something interesting to do. And there were *billions* of Pridehouse. Because the population of Spindrift had been no more than vestigial, she had somehow assumed that the same would be true of The Pridehouse, but the hollow, living world was aswarm with life. She shouldn't have been so surprised, she guessed: who would want to count the number of bacteria inside her own body? The bacteria analogy wasn't exactly accurate, because the symbiosis between the Pridehouse and their world was of a radically different nature from that she shared with the *Escherichia coli* inside her, but it was near enough.

Maloron Leander came up behind her and watched her stroking Loki for a few moments, then brushed the back of her hand gently across Strider's cheek.

'Soon be time for me to take over duty,' Leander said.

'No problem. There's nothing happening. I'm enjoying it here.'

'Any time you want to share out Hein, just let me know,' said Leander.

'Nelson'd kill him.'

'Umbel hasn't killed Lan Yi,' said Leander.

Strider was surprised. 'When did that happen?'

'When we were wolves. A few times since.'

Leander squatted down and added her own fingers to Strider's stroking the small creature in a complicated pattern.

'The things I don't know,' said Strider wryly.

'He hasn't killed Maria, either. Or Polyaggle. *I* haven't killed Polyaggle. I haven't killed Lan Yi.'

'Look, Maloron, is Hilary safe?'

'Give him a couple of years, and no.'

'I thought you and Nelson were' – Strider sought for a term that didn't have some moral connotation – 'pair-bonded?'

'Both of us learnt things when we were wolves. *All* of us did. One of the things the rest of us learnt while you and Hein were running around fields together . . .'

'Who told you about that?'

'It was pretty bloody plain that you weren't off picking daisies. No daisies to pick, for a start. I guess you could have been picking those cabbagy sort of things, but that wouldn't have been precisely romantic.' Leander looked up into Strider's face and grinned. 'The first time you went off with him for a "country ramble" all of us were pleased for you. Even Segrill joined in the cheers.'

Strider felt herself blushing. Her hand had stopped tickling the cat.

'I hadn't thought it was so obvious,' she said. 'It's my duty not to—'

'Yeah, duty. There are nine of us and a cat on board. You're still the captain, of course, but you're also one of a very small group of people. You command because you're *you*, not because you're an ice queen.'

'I'm not an—'

'All these years, though, you've had to pretend to be one – for the sake of duty. Oh, how we pitied you. First there was Pinocchio—'

'I did *love* that bloody bot,' said Strider, her eyes beginning to fill with unexpected tears.

'Then Maria, because that was part of your duty as well,' said Leander, an edge coming into her voice.

'How do you know all this?'

Leander pointed towards her secondary retinal screen. 'We try not to snoop, but sometimes we can't help seeing things by accident.'

'Not last night?' said Strider, starting forward. The cat dug its claws into her knee again, then leapt down to the floor.

'I think Maria caught a glimpse of last night, but nothing more than that. She looked away again quick.'

'Oh, hell.' Hein had come aboard during Strider's previous waking-time, and after she'd left the command deck they'd spent several hours trying out the potentialities of his new body. And once again before she'd come back on supervisory duty.

'Hein's nice. I like him,' said Leander. 'What we learnt as wolves, the rest of us, is that sex isn't the important thing: it's affection. Love's something different: hell, Nelson and I love each other like crazy. Let me say that again: Nelson and I are *in love* with each other. There's a difference. We're "pair-bonded", if you want to carry on being technical about it. There are too few of us on the *Midnight Ranger* for any of us to feel anything but love for each other.'

Strider nodded, trying to keep the tears hidden.

'You've just been making love to the cat, in a way,' Leander continued. 'You love the little sod. You love Hilary in a different way, even when you're bawling him out for doing some damn-fool thing. When you're playing chess with Lan Yi your fingers brush against his more often than they should – not because you're trying to seduce him, but just because the touch of your flesh against his is a way of showing affection.'

Strider nodded dumbly.

'So that's what being Pridehouse for a while taught us,' said Leander. 'We've not only got to learn to love each other, we've got to learn to show it in every way we can. Hell, Maria can't stand the sight of the naked male body – for reasons that are a mystery between her and her psyche – and is certainly not going to let a prick inside her, but she and Lan Yi spent half a sleeping-time stroking each other the way you were just stroking Loki. Affection – that was what they were giving each other. Balling might have been a part of it, but it wasn't. So what? The affection was still there.'

The cat clawed its way back up on to Strider's lap, and set-tled there, purring.

'You've got to discover the art of affection, Leonie. There aren't enough of us for you to do anything else.'

The tears wouldn't stay back any longer. Strider found herself half-crouched over the cat, which continued purring, paying no attention to her.

'Have I ever told you how I was born?'

Leander's arm was around her shaking shoulders. Strider couldn't bear to look her in the face: she addressed her words to the steadily moving side of the cat, which seemed now to have fallen asleep in blissful contentment.

The gang-rape of her mother. Her rejection by her mother, whom she had never seen except on a viddisc, sent years later, which was filled with sanctimonious garbage and had been stuffed down the nearest disposal vent. That had been her revenge on her mother: to reject her in turn. For the sake of Strider's development as a human being, it had been the right thing to do at the time. Later . . . well, later had been too late.

All the pain came out. All the reasons why she had never let herself get too close to people: they were likely to betray her in some way or another. She had given herself up entirely to Pinocchio, and he had betrayed her by destroying himself in order to save her. Now she was close to giving herself up entirely to Hein, because she was fascinated by him and because he made her laugh in even the most intimate of moments. A bot and an alien. All her human lovers had been cheap thrills. Not the best of emotional records.

'C'mere,' said Maloron Leander at last, pushing up Strider's chin. She turned Strider's face towards her and kissed her on the lips. 'Was that so *very* bad?'

'No,' said Strider, wiping the back of a hand across her eyes and then across her wet cheeks. Her throat was pulsing in a way that was beyond her control, so that she was unable to say anything else.

'That wasn't sex. That was affection,' said Maloron. 'But

sex is a part of affection, not the other way round. Remember that, dear captain.' She threw her arms around Strider and embraced her tightly. 'Don't feel so *alone* the whole time.'

She stood up. 'Do you want me to take over the watch?'

'No.' Strider found herself giving a horrible, tearful giggle. 'Despite what you've just said, I want to be on my own for a bit. I've got' – her voice began to break and she tried to control it, then thought: *Why the fuck* should *I?* – 'I've got a lot of things to think through. Besides, I told you, there's nothing happening.'

'Do you want me to stay with you?'

'I just said. No.'

'It's up to you. If you want me to be with you when you knock off duty, just find me.' Maloron moved towards the rear of the command deck, and turned in the door. 'That's a sincere offer.'

'No,' said Strider. 'Thanks, but . . . no. Just now the only lover I want is Hein.' She looked over her shoulder, smiling through tears. 'I've rediscovered sex after all these years. I think I'm beginning to discover love. Discovering things like affection may take me a while longer: in some ways, that's a more complicated emotion.'

The door swished shut behind Maloron.

Strider carried on stroking the cat.

'Twenty-six, twenty-five, twenty-four . . .'

'You Humans are so numerically fixated,' said Hein beside her. Strider ignored him. Later she would stuff his head down a flush toilet, or something.

'. . . twenty-three, twenty-two, twenty-one . . .'

She was watching developments in the Pocket. The Images were controlling the *Midnight Ranger*, as always, but she was its captain: she should supervise, just in case anything went wrong. Long ago, before the *Santa Maria* had left the Solar System, she had saved the ship when its Main Computer had been unable to. Ever since then she – or Nelson or Leander – had overseen every significant manoeuvre. The Images, not to mention the Pridehouse, were much more skilled, but the Humans had raw instinct. The confident refinement of the more advanced species led them into thought-traps.

'. . . twenty, nineteen . . .'

The living world called The Pridehouse suddenly began unzipping itself. She pulled her head out of the Pocket. The whole process took only seconds. One moment Strider was looking up through the view-window at the planet's murky inner surface; the next she was gazing at starfields. Watching the depiction in the Pocket once more, she saw the world evaginate itself like a squeezed fig.

Still she kept counting.

'. . . three, two, one . . . Yahey!'

The *Midnight Ranger* surged upwards, the gees slamming her back into her seat. 'Feels good,' she said hoarsely to Maria, who was sitting on her left.

'Speak for yourself,' said the long woman. Out of the corner of her eye, Strider could see the way the gees were pulling down the flesh of Strauss-Giolitto's face. She probably looked even worse herself. She felt as if her lower jaw was about to jump out of its sockets. But at the same time she was filled with the same wild exhilaration she had experienced when the *Santa Maria* had pulled away from Jovian orbit. This was it! She was back in space again.

And behind her were over thirty-three thousand little craft like her own.

She hauled herself forwards, ignoring the ache that started somewhere behind her eyeballs and soon moved up to the bridge of her nose, and shoved her face into the Pocket.

The planet was still spewing forth little dots of red light: it was sending its seed out into The Wondervale. The graphic display behind the visual representation showed Strider that the world's orbit was already shifting slightly: it was moving a

56

little closer to its sun. The loss of mass as the armada departed was only a tiny percentage of The Pridehouse's total, but from now until they returned – if they ever did – the planet would bask in stronger sunlight than it had since its species had reverted to it, several million years ago.

As the last of the red motes made their way clear of the planet-wide fissure, The Pridehouse began to close itself up again, healing its self-inflicted wound.

Strider called up the semblance of Hein in her Pocket. 'Can you find Kaantalech?' she said. He was only a couple of metres away, but this was easier, as the gees hauled at her, than speaking to him directly.

'No. Not yet.' He was concentrating. The beautiful wolf had become a beautiful – and beautifully androgynous – man. What made him so luminescently attractive to her that there was still a strong streak of Pridehouse somehow visible in him. Even Maria responded to it, sometimes allowing him to take her hand in his playful way.

Little puppy dog, thought Strider. Even with the gees dragging at his face, Hein looked all right. She bet her own face looked like the image in a carnival's distorting mirror.

'Try to find where she is,' said Strider. 'See if you can get the Pocket to plot as many of the Autarchy fleets as possible.'

She wanted to steer clear of Autarchy forces until she'd built up the strength of her armada. It'd be a disaster if the Pridehouse fleet hit the enemy too soon, or drew attention to themselves too soon. At the same time, she wanted battle-practice. 'If you can locate a single Autarchy warcruiser, or a small bunch of them, somewhere in this quadrant it'd be good,' she added. 'I want to test our weapons.'

'An unfair competition.'

'That's what I want. An unfair competition. Remember, I saw Spindrift destroyed. Most of the people who shattered that planet probably didn't want to be there.' She tried to take a deep breath, but the gees wouldn't let her. She wondered how the cat was getting on. 'The Images killed a lot of the Autarchy no-hopers, and the Spindrifters killed a lot more. Poor conscripts, drafted on to Autarchy ships. But think of all the innocents who'll be saved over the next million or so years if the Autarchy is destroyed. Maybe the conscripts would agree with me. Maybe not. Who cares? I worry a lot more about the Pridehouse getting wiped out because we haven't properly figured a way of annihilating Autarchy ships.'

'You're ruthless,' said Hein in her Pocket. His face had lost all semblance of playfulness.

'Too damn' right I am.'

Hein made a clumsy shrug. He still hadn't entirely adapted himself to Human gestures. 'Yes, OK, Leonie, when it comes down to it I suppose I'm as ruthless as you are. I've fixed the coordinates of a convoy of eighteen Autarchy warcruisers. Want us to get 'em?'

'We *have* to. Just a few of us.'

'How many?'

'Fifty? Let's not make the odds too unfair. I'm a gambling woman.'

'Liar.'

'I want to see how we make out with them. How many of our ships would you reckon was a reasonable number?'

'Fifty.'

'Then what the hell are we arguing about?'

'Odds.' The Images took a fraction of a second to interpret his next word. 'Humanity.'

'They torture kids. They burn people alive. They torch whole species,' she said.

'We should be better than they are.'

'In an ideal Wondervale, I'd agree with you,' she said, 'but right now . . .'

'Yeah,' said Hein. 'You have a point. Let's zap the bastards. For safety's sake, let's make that estimate a hundred.'

*

The shift into tachyon drive brought instant relief, but it was short-lived. Strider took the opportunity to straighten up, kneading the ache at the base of her back. She could see out of the corner of her eye Strauss-Giolitto doing much the same. Hein, by contrast, stepped forward to immerse his face in the Pocket in front of him.

Strider stuck a commlink into her mouth and tongued it into activation.

For a few further seconds they were in free fall, which was glorious release, and then the drive cut back in as the Pockets locked on to the positions of the Autarchy warcruisers. At least, this time, the acceleration was only a single g: anything more than that and the crew of the *Midnight Ranger* would have been too slowed up to operate the weaponry effectively.

'Maria, watch our tail,' said Strider tersely. 'Hein, you survey all round us. I'll take the front.'

She called up in her Pocket the image and data of the scene in front of her. The display obligingly indicated which of the many points of light were stars and which were warcruisers. It also showed the Pridehouse's small craft – *her* small craft – in an appropriate red.

Since they had left The Pridehouse the Images had been running the ship: it was as if it had been under AI control, so far as Strider was concerned. She gave the occasional request, and things happened. Now it was time for her to start interacting with the Images, sharing control . . . forming a *Gestalt* with them and, through them, with the *Midnight Ranger* itself. Normally this was something she didn't enjoy, because it made her feel as if she were becoming partly a machine – hell, she didn't like even having a commlink in her mouth – but this time it was different. Something primitive was moving inside her: the thrill of the hunt. She knew that, later, she'd be sick at heart because of the killing and because of any losses she might incur, but right now she wanted to prove something, to make a mark on The Wondervale, to destroy, to dent the

59

Autarchy and to let it *know* it had been dented, and then to retreat into the darkness, to hide until the next time . . .

She could feel her lips draw back from her teeth.

As the *Midnight Ranger* hurtled towards the nearest of the Autarchy warcruisers the Pocket modified itself, with new controls appearing on its flat lower surface. The same was presumably happening in the other two Pockets. At her command were now implosion bolts, intramolecular disruptors, maxbeams, rotary locks . . . Probably the warcruisers had the same array of weaponry – and more that she'd never heard of – but the warcruisers weren't expecting to be attacked. Probably their detectors hadn't picked up the tiny traces of the little ships yet. She hoped not. As soon as they did they'd move into tachyon drive, and it'd become ever more difficult to catch them. The Images were good at tracking targets through nonspace, but the eighteen warcruisers could redistribute themselves to all corners of The Wondervale, making things difficult.

If their commanders had the imagination to think of doing that. Imagination was not one of the Autarchy's strongest suits, luckily. Imaginative officers and aides were dangerous because they might have ambitions, and so were generally eliminated before they climbed too far up the ladder of command.

As they darted towards the cluster of warcruisers, Strider saw something which hadn't been evident earlier.

'Whoopee!' she yelled. 'You see what I see?'

'No,' said Strauss-Giolitto. 'I'm watching our tail, remember?' Her voice sounded brittle, terrified.

'Umbel or Maloron, get up here fast and take over from Maria. She's near breaking,' whispered Strider through the commlink.

'I'm standing directly behind her, sweetness and light,' came Nelson's voice. 'You didn't think I was going to miss out on this, did you?'

Aloud she said: 'They're fighting *each other*!'

Even as she spoke one of the warcruisers erupted in a sudden ball of angry light.

'We could just sit here and *watch*!'

'No,' said Hein calmly. 'We Pridehouse need to rediscover the art of space battle. This makes it easier for us, which is good. You said yourself that we should have practice, Leonie.'

'Some of the Pridehouse are certain to die,' she said.

'It's worth it. If we don't learn now we could be annihilated later.'

We could all be annihilated anyway, Strider thought, but she kept it to herself. 'Point taken,' she said, then subvocalized: 'You there, Pinocchio?'

PINOCCHIO IS LIAISING WITH THE IMAGES IN THE OTHER CRAFT, said Ten Per Cent Extra Free.

'Oh, hi, Tenper. Hein's right, isn't he?'

IT IS NOT FOR ME TO JUDGE THAT.

'Well, I think he is.'

THEN WE MUST ASSUME BATTLE FORMATION.

'Fuck battle formation. We want to be as unpredictable as possible, remember?'

I DON'T LIKE THIS.

'Who's in charge?'

YOU ARE.

'Right. Let's you and me between us go get us some prey – show the others how it's done.'

AS YOU WISH.

To the already embattled aliens aboard the warcruiser, it must have seemed that the part-open doors of whatever Hell they, as a species, had invented had opened a little further and allowed a nightmare to escape.

The *Midnight Ranger* pounced out of emptiness and sped past the great ship's side, passing almost suicidally close, and as it did so loosing an implosion bolt.

The warcruiser's defensive shield went an ugly red as the

61

bolt devoured its energies, but somehow the shield held. It faded slowly back to invisibility as it was recharged from the reactors of the cruiser's main drive. By the time it had done so, and by the time the Autarchy force's sensors had had a chance to register what was happening, the *Midnight Ranger* was just another mote in the distant cosmos.

'Showing off, huh?' said Nelson.

'Yeah,' said Strider. 'This is dogfighting. We won't always have pretty toys like implosion bolts to play with.'

A confusing succession of g-forces pulled at them as she slammed on the retros, then used side-thrusters to pull them around. The energy-release involved would be enough for the alien sensors to lock on to them, but it couldn't be helped.

'We'd be wiser to shoot 'em where they sit, little goddess,' advised Nelson.

'Not in the longer term,' said Strider, clinging on to the edges of her Pocket for dear life. She was aware that, somewhere nearby, Strauss-Giolitto, still on deck, had made the mistake of looking up at the view-window to see the stars whirl vertiginously round and was as a consequence being violently sick. Her own stomach was rebelling from the manoeuvre the ship had just performed. *Amateurs,* thought Strider. *We're all bloody amateurs. And we're supposed to be educating a fleet of bloody amateurs even more bloody amateurish than we are.*

'Are you there, Tenper?'

As you might have expected, Strider.

'Let's make another run, then.'

As you say.

'We'll try a rotary lock. We could spend the rest of our lives pouring implosion bolts into that fucker's shield.'

Agreed.

The *Midnight Ranger*'s drive howled as the little craft surged back towards the warcruiser. God knew how the people below-deck were taking all this. Polyaggle would be all right:

Strider didn't think she'd ever seen the Spindrifter look even remotely discomposed. Leander would be coping as well. But Hilary was just a kid and Lan Yi was an old man. Oh, hell: the cat. Maybe the cat would be enjoying every minute of it. Maybe she wouldn't. Well, it was Hilary's job to clear up if need be.

The second pass was the one that spelled death to the occupants of the warcruiser. All space vessels possess a certain amount of angular momentum: there is some latitudinal rotation, a slight tendency to tumble longitudinally, and various other minor gyrations along haphazard axes. Most of the time it doesn't matter: the on-board puters make automatic trajectory corrections if any of these stray motions becomes greater than trivial.

The rotary lock was less a beam than a stream of information that planted in the puters false information about the diverse minor gyrations the ship was undergoing, so that they began to over-correct. Not just a little: a lot. It was one of several weapons the Pridehouse had developed with the aid of the Images while the new fleet had been being grown. It had seemed to Strider, even as she appreciated its cleverness, a tool of great cruelty; the Pridehouse's sense of play was not always without malice.

The warcruiser retaliated with a maxbeam as they approached a second time, but its sensors had picked up the *Midnight Ranger* too late for the aim to be effective. The deck shuddered as the beam clipped the edge of the *Midnight Ranger*'s own defensive shield, but the Images compensated immediately and the small vessel held her course. The rotary lock had to be delivered close up: this time Strider was not risking their lives out of sheer bravado. The information stream could get scrambled by the junk in even a light-hour's worth of space, so that it had no effect whatsoever on the puters.

Deliberately Strider punched at various controls in the Pocket so that the *Midnight Ranger*'s course shifted erratically, relying on Ten Per Cent Extra Free each time to bring it back to the correct alignment. *Must be driving their sensors bananas,* she thought with satisfaction. The sensors would obviously be puter-controlled. They almost certainly could cope with random variations of an attacker's trajectory if those variations were likewise puter-driven. Strider was just stabbing at the buttons as swiftly as she could, sometimes bringing her fist down on several at once and sometimes fingering the same one several times in a row, like an infant who has discovered a piano keyboard for the first time.

It made for a bumpy ride. Thank Umbel she was concentrating hard enough on what she was doing not to have sufficient mental capacity left over to respond to the urgent demands of her stomach.

She was less than five thousand kilometres from the warcruiser when Ten Per Cent Extra Free coolly informed her: I HAVE FIXED THE COORDINATES OF THE ROTARY LOCK. PLEASE GIVE YOUR COMMAND.

'Now!' shouted Strider.

It seemed for a moment as if nothing had happened. She kept hammering the controls, while mentally instructing Ten Per Cent Extra Free to increase their velocity. Gees pulled at her. Big anticlimax. Had they bloody *missed*?

Out of range of the warcruiser's sensors once more, she brought in the retros, then called up the image of the Autarchy vessel in her Pocket.

No, the rotary lock hadn't missed its target.

The warcruiser appeared in front of her like a ballet dancer who, halfway through a pirouette, has just lost footing. It was a blur of conflicting rotational movements. The strains on its structure must already be building up to far beyond anything it had been built to withstand. Its occupants must already be pulp – unless there were a few unlucky ones. Strider tried not to think too hard about them.

Amid the blur she could see that a fissure had opened in the vessel's side. The main drive – always the most massive part of the hardware – was wrenching itself loose.

And then she was blinded as the warcruiser exploded in a fireball.

She staggered back from her Pocket and tripped over her seat, falling heavily to the deck, clutching at her eyes as if somehow that would help bring her vision back. The side of her head hit hard, and for a moment she was semi-stunned, retaining just enough consciousness to be confused by what was happening to her.

Someone scooped an arm under her shoulders, pulling her into a sitting position. Someone with vomit-smelling breath. Had to be Strauss-Giolitto.

Strider bent her legs and slumped the top half of her body forwards, putting her head between her knees, feeling their comforting hardness under her armpits: they were something nice and *real* that were hers.

Voices were booming at her, but she couldn't make out what they were saying.

Then some of the words began to make sense.

'Pretty impressive stunt, lady fair. Think you could do that again so we could all watch?'

'Fuck off, Nelson,' she gasped. Even speaking hurt. But at least peripheral vision was beginning to creep back. She could see the rims of her boots. *First time I've ever really appreciated those boots,* she thought. *From now on they get kissed each night when I take them off. These boots were made for . . . well, for* me, *actually.*

Those blue things. Oh, yes. Someone's lower legs, clad in a blue jumpsuit. Hey, those are *my* legs!

'Can you help, Tenper?' she said, her voice thick. She'd bitten the edge of her tongue and was certain she could taste blood.

CERTAINLY.

Within a few seconds her vision had returned. She spat

between her knees on to the deck and was relieved to see no traces of red in her spittle. Her mouth still hurt like hell, but she hadn't bitten a piece of tongue right *off*.

She looked up. Hein remained at his Pocket, but the other three – Leander must have struggled to the deck at some point – were kneeling around her. Nelson put a hand on her head and rubbed it through her hair, then lowered it to the back of her neck.

'What are you lot just sitting about for?' she said. 'The show's over. Tell Hein to tell his people that that's the way to do it. Let *them* polish off the rest of the warcruisers, OK?'

Then came a wave of reddish darkness that lasted no time at all until she was on her bunk wondering how she'd got there and dimly remembering that something had happened which had involved a very bright light.

Hilary had broken a finger and was being Terribly Brave about it. Strider wished he'd bawl his head off: it would have been easier to take than the white, solemn, virtuous face of the little martyr. Otherwise the only casualty on the *Midnight Ranger* was herself, and she was feeling pretty OK except for a sore mouth, an aching temple and a slight giddiness unless she remembered to take corners slowly.

Among the things the *Santa Maria* had borne away with her had been the Humans' entire supply of painkillers. The Pridehouse – though they themselves had no clear notion of analgesia, because they just didn't *get* hurt – could probably have knocked something up, given a specimen to study for a week or so while they worked out the details of human physiology. It hadn't occurred to her at the time. Now she wished it had.

'They were fighting each other,' said Lan Yi as he took one of her queens. They were in his cabin playing a two-handed version of four-handed chess – a game which had been all the rage among the original personnel of the *Santa Maria* and was still the major recreation of Strider's remaining crew. 'I wonder why that was.'

By way of retribution she took a knight and put one of his kings in check. It was a petty revenge: he could easily escape the check and anyway he was going to beat her, because he always did.

'Civil war,' she said.

'Meaning?'

'The succession is going even more messily than we thought it would. Some warlord or other – or maybe a whole bunch of 'em – must be putting up a better fight than she expected. Oh, you *bastard*!'

Her second queen vanished from the board.

Lan Yi permitted himself a smile, then murmured: 'Do we in fact, then, *have* to fight the Autarchy? Can't we just see it tear itself to pieces?'

'No,' she said. 'Aw, dammit, Lan Yi, I concede the game.' She moved her hand in mimicry of knocking all the remaining pieces from the board. 'I spoke with the Onurg about it. *Every* change in rulership of the Autarchy is accompanied by a load of bloodletting. It's the way these people operate. Give them a few years, though, and there'll be somebody secure enough at the top to clamp down again on all the species in this misbegotten galaxy.'

'Your money's on Kaantalech?' said Lan Yi, carefully putting the chess pieces away in their box.

'Yup.' She started to help him but he waved her away: this was his set, after all, not hers. 'Kaantalech's the one with the true killer instinct.' Strider sat back in her chair, watching the old man as he very precisely packed away the chess set. 'That's what the Onurg said. I believed him. She's single-minded in a way damn' few other people are.'

'There is yourself.' Lan Yi's voice was deceptively meek.

Strider laughed. 'A few weeks ago I might have thought that. Now . . . now, I just don't know. A lot of me wishes I'd

67

tried to go home with O'Sondheim. Leave that be. Kaantalech had her eye on the throne long before Nalla met his end: if Nalla had been less stupid he would have realized it and had her quietly and conveniently removed from the scene.'

Lan Yi reached across the chessboard to put his hand on hers.

'Forget about Kaantalech for the moment, Leonie, my friend. I've been watching the changes in you these past few days, ever since we rejoined the Pridehouse fleet.' He looked earnestly into her eyes. 'You've become less sure of yourself. It's as if the blow to your head jolted a part of you away from yourself.' His diction became more formal. 'I would not say this were it not for the fact that I have the very greatest of respect for you.'

'Thanks.' She turned her hand over and wrapped her fingers around his. 'I can remember feeling better, but there's nothing wrong with me.'

'I'm not certain that's true.'

Strider was silent for a few moments, and then said: 'Well . . . I had this conversation with Maloron, and it changed the way I looked at things.' She told him what Leander had said.

'Was Leander right? Have you become a better person?'

'I . . . I don't know.'

He leaned back and crossed his arms over his chest. 'Or have you become someone you were never supposed to be?'

'That's another thing I don't know. Look, let's stop this right here, shall we? It was a good game of chess – no, it wasn't, it was a rotten lousy game of chess, because I was thinking of other things and besides you're far too good for me.' She stood up and walked to the door of Lan Yi's cabin. 'Thanks for your kindness and hospitality,' she said.

'Don't go yet.' He was still seated. It was unusual for Lan Yi not to get to his feet the moment that she did.

'I need sleep,' said Strider.

'You probably do.' His voice took on a certainty she had rarely heard from this mild-mannered man. 'But you need something more than that. Come back to the table. Please, Leonie.'

Reluctantly, she did so. She yawned unexpectedly, and wondered if he would assume that she was faking weariness. She reached across and took his hand in hers, aware that she was mirroring his earlier gesture of affection. The eye of his that was not hidden by a secondary retinal screen looked concerned.

'You're our *captain*,' he said firmly.

'Until there's an election.' She tried to feel as flippant as her words. 'I would boot me out if . . .'

'That's what's changed about you.' The grip of his hand was becoming almost painful. 'There's not going to *be* an election. Like it or not, Leonie, you're everybody's favourite fascist dictator. But at the moment you're not living up to your role. You're not making decisions, you're not working things out – you seem to spend most of your time screwing Hein rather than thinking.'

His gaze moved away from her face towards their clasped hands.

'*Be* yourself, Leonie,' he said. 'Be *yourself*.'

'You wanna get hit, Lan Yi?'

He looked up at her again. He was half-smiling.

'Thanks,' she said. 'I'm going to break your jaw unless you say that again.'

'Say what?'

'That thing about being myself.'

'*Be* yourself. Be *yourself*.'

She bent forward and kissed him on the forehead, careful not to nick her lip on the sharp edge of his secondary retinal screen. Then she pulled his head towards her and kissed him on the earlobe.

'Go and take over from Leander,' she whispered, trying to

make her voice as sensual as possible. 'She's been on the command deck for six hours now.'

'Geena,' Lan Yi whispered into the Pocket. The only other person on the command deck was Polyaggle, and she was paying no attention to him. The two of them were there just to pick up any urgent messages that might come through from the Onurg.

'Geena,' he said again.

A combination of racial prejudice and poverty had driven his wife Geena to suicide, more decades ago than it was any longer simple to count. His body might not thereafter have been entirely faithful to her memory – she would have been furious with him had he allowed her death to castrate him – but his heart had. Sometimes, in the sleepless nights, he would discover her walking the corridors of the *Santa Maria* and now the *Midnight Ranger*: he would talk with her, baring his soul to her, but anything she said back to him was ambiguous, if she were saying anything at all beyond the echoes of what his own mind told him she might say. Or, at least, what the Images plucked from his mind about what she might have said.

For it was the Images who had given him the spectre of Geena: he was certain of this. He was too much of a scientist to discount entirely the possibility of ghosts, but he was certain to many decimal places that death was death. Ten Per Cent Extra Free and the others must have discerned inside him the need – that horrible, decades-old, still-living need – for his wife, and they had done their best to restore something of her to him.

And then he had discovered that he could summon her through the Pockets. The Images were still involved, of course, but at a greater remove: they had constructed the Pockets and were responsible for keeping them operational, but there was more to the devices than that. In an earlier age, as Lan Yi knew, they would have been described as scrying devices: like

70

a magic mirror on the wall, they enabled someone to see something far away in either space or time. Even Lan Yi had difficulty getting beyond the first base of the physics involved, but he did understand that a large part of it depended on the mind of the person using the Pocket – as if the distant vision was something already part-known, but not directly available to the conscious.

He had spent long hours speculating about the link between the mind and the Universe, but had got nowhere: he had come to the conclusion there was one, but that was as much as he could infer.

The theoretical considerations didn't matter much when he was looking into Geena's eyes.

'You're as lovely as you ever were,' he said.

'You don't look any different from the way you always used to be,' said her face in the Pocket.

'I wish I could kiss you, or even just reach out and touch your cheek.'

He was aware that there were tears running down his face, but here inside the Pocket there was no one to see.

'What have you been doing, Yi?'

'Wanting you. Wishing you were here beside me.'

She smiled. The motion of her lips, so familiar and yet so long unseen in the flesh, was heart-breaking. 'What else?'

He felt like the small boy he had been over a century before, hauled up in front of his Taiwanese headmaster for some misdemeanour or other.

'Um,' he said. 'War. Sex. That sort of thing.'

She laughed at him, and he imagined that she reached through the Pocket to take his ear in her fingers and give it a lovingly vindictive squeeze. 'Hope you blasted the baddies,' she said. 'Hope the sex lifted the roof.'

He tried to smile in response.

'The sex was an animal requirement,' he said primly, 'as it has usually been ever since you died.'

71

'"Usually"?'

'You know what I mean.'

'What was she like? Or was it with a man?'

Even in life Geena had been able to put him on the defensive whenever she had wanted to.

'Not this time,' he said. 'Does it matter? Can we change the subject?'

'Do you really want to be part of a war mission, Yi?' she said softly, her eyes seeming to become liquidly sympathetic.

He found himself beginning to weep harder. 'I could walk out into space,' he blurted, trying hopelessly to make it sound like a joke.

'I'm out there somewhere,' the vision of Geena said. 'It's cold where I am, but we could be together in the chilliness.'

Her face was as he remembered it when the two of them had been young. Clinging to each other because the worlds of the Solar System had been so cruel. That had seemed like a valid way of hurling defiance at the Universe. He reached into the Pocket to fondle her, but of course there was nothing to touch.

'You tempt me,' he said.

'I'm glad to know I still have the ability.' She began to laugh again. 'What with you and your other women.'

He tossed his head. 'Don't be silly.'

'I seem to remember you saying that to me quite often.'

'Don't speak so loudly. Someone might hear you.'

'I'm not the one who's speaking.' She ran a hand through her hair, scratching at her scalp. She shook her head from side to side so that her hair became suddenly a rink of ice, a shining thing on which Lan Yi found himself skating.

He almost fell.

His wife was the sky. The clouds above him were her breasts. The Sun was one of her eyes, opened lazily in the morning as he tried not to disturb her while he climbed out of bed to go for the pee that his painful erection demanded: it was full of the knowledge that, afterwards, he would probably want her. The wise eye of the Sun was noncommittal.

He was ninety-six again, and skating with the beautiful young woman whom he wanted to marry. Marriage was rare, but it was an institution that he wished to evaluate through personal experience – and he loved her very dearly. They were on a working holiday in Belarus: she was to be his secretarial assistant in his observations of the forthcoming solar eclipse because she was between jobs as an orchestral cellist. The two of them would discover much about the Sun's photosphere, interacting ground-based puters with one of the space-based puters. At the moment, however, as he swung her in his arms, all he wanted to do was to discover more about *her*.

He pulled away briefly from the Pocket. This was all delusion. Geena had been dead for decades. Yet the remembered image of them skating together refused to leave his mind. He was still swirling with her; her eyes were still shining as her hair rippled out. They spun, separated, rejoined. Her lips were moist, and they kissed crazily, somehow managing not to topple over in each other's arms. The hiss of skates on ice – their own included – surrounded them. That night they slept together for the first time. It was shambolic – he was like a teenage virgin all over again, and she was little better – but the following day they loved each other all the more for that. She played a short Beethoven sonata to him, straddling the cello with her naked legs, and then they made love again, this time much more successfully, before going back to the skating rink.

All day, until the evening had descended, they had skated together, flirting outrageously as they danced over the ice.

They were among the last in Belarus to hear that he had won the Nobel Prize. The following day they flew back to their home in Algeria, which was where their troubles began. The prize was worth two billion dollars, but they had no need of the money. They gave it away to various charities, an action

73

the Algerian government resented. Lan Yi was soon afterwards ousted from his professorial post, and poverty followed swiftly. Their marriage was a short one: the pain of thwarted expectations was too great for Geena to bear. He had ritually burnt the cello string with which she had killed herself. By then she had hated him.

But the Geena to whom he talked now loved him: it was evident in her eyes.

He returned his head to the Pocket.

'You could, if you wanted, join me out here in the coldness,' she said at once. 'Then, finally, I could die. I *want* to die, Yi. If it weren't for you I wouldn't still be alive.'

'You're not alive.' He found the words very difficult to pronounce.

'I am,' she said. The poignant expression on her face reminded him of her concentrating during practice sessions with her cello. She had devoted more love to that instrument than to him, and he had never resented it – because, after all, he had had his own mistress, philosophical physics. 'I'm alive because you insist on keeping me that way.'

He bit his lower lip. 'I want to be with you for ever. But . . .'

'But what?'

'But I don't believe in it.'

'In what?'

'The afterlife. I don't believe that we'll find ourselves together in some paradise. If I try to walk out through an airlock, all that will happen is that I find myself dead. There are less painful ways to kill oneself.'

'You always were pusillanimous.' Her tone reverted to the acerbity that had been characteristic during the final weeks before her suicide. 'At least it's quick.'

The conversation was getting nowhere, as so many of their conversations had in the latter months of her life, yet, as if he were worrying away at a loose tooth, Lan Yi somehow couldn't leave it be.

'*Is* there such a thing as an afterlife?' One thing he knew about Geena: she would never give him a direct lie. She might prevaricate, dodge the question or . . .

'If you loved me as much as you say you do, you would be prepared to find out for yourself.' Again she tossed her hair, so that the artificial light of the Pocket danced across what for a few moments seemed like a solid surface.

I know *she's just a mental construct,* thought Lan Yi, *so of course s*he'd give me the sort of equivocal reply I'd give to myself on the matter. Yet . . . Yet . . . Yet that's not the* kind *of answer I'd've given.*

He suddenly began to wonder if Geena's quasi-existence were quite as simple as he thought it was. The Images were capable of so much that was incomprehensible to him, flitting into The Wondervale from their *other* reality – which was a further thing he found inexplicable, because it did not seem related in any way to this one, as would have been expected had it been one of the alternate universes implied by quantum mechanics. Ten Per Cent Extra Free had told him something of it, but all that Lan Yi could really comprehend was that The Truthfulness was *qualitatively* different from the reality he knew. Was there the remotest possibility that the Images had been capable of drawing – either from his own mind or otherwise – the chimera of Geena's being back into objective existence?

He didn't think so.

But he didn't *know*.

The time for her brood to emerge was very near now. Her brood was the future of her species, the Spindrifters. The birthing would be more of a culmination than any other birthing had been. She would be the parent not just of her brood but of in effect a new species.

A host, though. She required a host for the brood, so that they could feed both on and in the security of flesh. The

Human Lan Yi was the one who had shown her the greatest friendship (a concept Polyaggle was beginning to understand), and would surely be glad to act as host to her brood. Yet he was unlike Spindrifter males – unlike the way Spindrifter males had been. To a Spindrifter male becoming a host was the act of orgasm, just as birthing was for a female. It was The Death In Joy.

As she eavesdropped from the far Pocket on his conversation with his dead pair-mate, it came to her that the Humans had no concept of The Death In Joy. Most of them did everything necessary to avoid death, whatever the cause. Yet she could not birth her brood unless there were a host to birth them to, and the life of one of these aliens was surely – even they themselves would certainly agree – a small price to pay for the regeneration of the Spindrifter species. Yes, were Lan Yi aware of this he would eager to act as her surrogate mate.

She told herself this a second time, as if doing so would make it seem truer to her.

Polyaggle memorized very carefully every detail of Geena's appearance.

The Spindrifter knew she had the power to make Lan Yi see what he wanted to see. When the time for the birthing came, she would be his Geena: he would discover all the ecstasy of The Death In Joy, and she would give him his final, Human, joy.

She tapped her claws together in a smile. He would be grateful to her.

3

There Was This Guy I Once Met . . .
Forget his Name Now

She had enemies everywhere, Kaantalech knew, and the more of them she executed the more seemed to spring up. Most of The Wondervale now accepted her as the Autarch, but there were warlords who resented her acquisition of the throne, and were prepared to launch suicidal attacks against her. Even her own military was not entirely behind her: news of battles breaking out between the members of convoys of warcruisers came in almost daily. Many of the species of The Wondervale were greedy for power. With her at its head her own species, the Alhubra, should be able to clamp down on the rest of the galaxy for at least the next few centuries, but first she had to be sure of the accession.

At the back of her mind she sometimes worried about the Humans. Their craft had been magnificently equipped for war, but suddenly it had seemed to drop out of existence. She wanted the Humans either exterminated or on her side: they might be the catalyst that brought her her final triumph. Not knowing where they were infuriated her every time she thought about them.

She had set up base on the innermost moon of a gas-giant planet called Alterifer. Rather than erect a vast deadmetal construction like the one Nalla had built as his palace on Qitanefermeartha, she had merely parked several thousand warvessels in the huge crater that some long-ago meteoritic impact had formed in the moon's face; had the impact been much greater, the little world would have been shattered apart to form a ring around the turbulent planet. No one but herself and the several thousand aides and slaves she confined here knew where Kaantalech's base was: a few of her officers were able to holo to her, but they were aware only of the general region of The Wondervale in which she lurked. Even an out and out search operation launched by one of the warlords would be extremely unlikely to find her: the moon was an insignificant body, almost certain to be overlooked.

Her generals were winning the war. That was the positive news. Of the dozen or so warlords who had hoped to contest the throne with her, only five were now alive, the rest having died, usually with all their species. If there was one thing that Kaantalech believed in, it was utter ruthlessness. A species that had produced a foe was suspect in its entirety unless it delivered up that foe to her of its own volition; then, and only possibly, she might show mercy. The destruction of a species warned all others that ambition was a lethal emotion.

The All-High of the Gorrange had died under her direct command. Before she had set up her base on this little moon, it had seemed to her most advisable to lead in person the various offensives she mounted. The nest-ship of the All-High had exploded into tiny fragments on sight of her flagship, the *Blunt Instrument*, and each of the fragments had ripped towards the sides of her vessel as if they were pieces of red-hot metal. The nest-ship was the All-High himself: as the flaring particles had perished over the course of some hours in the *Blunt Instrument*'s defensive shielding Kaantalech had enjoyed a long period of happiness. General Ma-Ling, whom she had later executed on the grounds that his military success was a threat to her, had done for the Hidroni of Hidron, a species whose slowly crawling means of perambulation had belied their technological artistry, and dangerousness.

The Humans, though. Dammit, the Humans! They could be

anywhere. They were the wild card in the pack with which she was trying to play. The card could fall to either side.

She had spoken with the curious little black one who seemed to be their leader, and who had conveyed nothing but enmity. Maybe all the Humans had indeed vanished to wherever it was they had claimed as their destination, or maybe they'd returned to Heaven's Ancestor – although Kaantalech was sceptical about whether or not this was where they had come from. They could have lied to her. They almost certainly had.

She must set an aide to trying to track down the Humans. But there were other things to do, first.

Kaantalech looked rather like a very broad mastodon. She was about two metres tall – little shorter than the average Human – and almost as wide: tuskless, with eyes on the shoulders rather than the head, and a mouth that glistened with teeth beneath a long and flexing proboscis, her species presented a terrifying image to most others.

She was lying in her sensory-deprivation bath, enjoying the release from responsibility. Sometimes she cheated, and washed the thick liquid across herself, so that her fur was titillated, but most of the time she remained completely still. She had no idea how long she'd been here; her aides would fetch her out once her time was up, unless she decided that she wished to stay here longer.

She stirred in the body-temperature liquid.

It had been good to see the end of the Hidroni. It had been good to see the end of Ma-Ling. It was good that she had erected a Shift field among the outer orbits of Alterifer's planetary retinue.

If she had her way, it would be good to see the end of so many people and things, so that she could watch a new beginning.

Nightmirror moves restlessly, a transition marked by the flux of several electrons and, because he is being careless, a muon.

The Main Computer aboard Kaantalech's *Blunt Instrument* becomes almost aware of him.

He realizes this, and determines to be more careful in future.

Nightmirror wonders what is happening to Ten Per Cent Extra Free and Heartfire and Angler. He has retreated into The Truthfulness several times in search of them, but they have not been there. He considers flitting through The Wondervale to look for them, but this would cause such a severe dislocation of elementary particles that the big puter would certainly become aware of Nightmirror's presence.

He rests. Kaantalech is somewhere else, although he is aware through the puter that she is near and it will not be long before she is here aboard the *Blunt Instrument*.

Nightmirror wishes that he could speak with the other Images who have penetrated The Wondervale. He is becoming lonely. If he dared he would try to make friends with the nexi of the puter, but he is terrified of alerting the main brain to his existence.

He waits.

The moment will come.

They called him Orphanwifer for the very good reason that one of his wives was an orphan, something almost unheard-of among the Lingk-kreatzai. The name was part compliment, part insult; he bore the former with pride and endured the latter with dignity.

Most Lingk-kreatzai males died in infancy because of their natural aggressiveness towards other males. The few who reached breeding age were thereafter nurtured and protected by a gaggle of willing wives. By then the aggression had dimmed, but there was always the chance that a boy-child might try to slaughter his father. And it was the duty of the father to sire as many boy-children as he could on the single occasion that he impregnated each of his wives. Thereafter the wife had the status of sister to him, but was also a mother to all of his off-spring, which might consist of a hundred boy-children and three girl-children. The male had to court the female into sisterhood after the birth; the marriage was a more clinical affair, arranged between the male and the female's mothers — although the arrangement was usually simple, because by now the mothers and the putative sisters were docile.

Orphans were rare, because of the plurality of mothers. Henndoz's family, however, had been wiped out en masse when a meteor had hit their stronghold in the stony Uplands. Henndoz, hardly more than a child, had been visiting the stronghold of a different family, who had for obvious reasons immediately ejected her as a pariah. Orphanwifer, tending his fields, had discovered her trying to steal a vegetable, and had taken her to himself as first a daughter (this had caused much chittering among his wives, but he had insisted) and then, when she was of age, a wife.

He could have left her to starve. It would have been the correct thing to do. It would have been morally proper. The rare orphans among the Lingk-kreatzai had been singled out by the sole god Rrhead to die, but Orphanwifer had lost his faith in Rrhead. So he had patted Henndoz's back with his hand and scooped her up into his arms. She had nuzzled up to him as if they had always known each other.

So now he was Orphanwifer and she was heavily pregnant.

The strongholds were mudpits: the Lingk-kreatzai pretended nothing else. Once they had been a galactic culture, their starships penetrating even into Heaven's Ancestor, where they had discovered raw planets where they could live. Now they were an ancient species confined to a single planet within The Wondervale.

Oh, glory days. Oh, the wrench of loss.

Mudpits. The Lingk-kreatzai of old had been able to construct cities where there was no trace of mud.

But mudpits were *safe*. The Autarchy rarely thought about

81

creatures who lived in mudpits. When the Autarchy died, as inevitably it must, the Lingk-kreatzai would rise from their mudpits and rejoice with the rest of the ancient species.

Orphanwifer's family had seven spacecruisers, all carefully hidden away beneath his mudpit and all regularly overhauled by his wives. He sometimes supervised their work to make sure that it was adequate. The other families had, he knew, similar flotillas. The Lingk-kreatzai possessed at the moment over a thousand families.

Orphanwifer thought it unwise to tackle the Autarchy head-on. Nevertheless, when twenty craft from the fleet of the Pridehouse landed on Lingk his interest was stirred. Two mud-pits were inadvertently destroyed in the landing. There might be other orphans to wife.

That was his duty. Not war.

But if war produced orphans who could be saved . . .

'Bloody hell,' said Strider. 'What a dump.'

The Pridehouse had brought down the *Midnight Ranger* horizontally on to the surface of Lingk. Everything was at the wrong angle. The Images had swivelled the Pockets and the crew seats in order to compensate, but they still hung several metres above her. The only person aboard who could use them was Polyaggle: she had flown up to one of the Pockets and was now engaged in serious discussion with the Onurg. Strider was tangled in a corner with Hilary and rather enjoying the experience: he was so vulnerable that it felt good to be holding him in her arms.

Through the view-window she could see the surface of Lingk. In the far distance was a range of low hills, but all around the *Midnight Ranger* was green marsh. She wondered if the ship might sink down into the soggy soil and be trapped, but its position seemed stable.

The Pocket next to Polyaggle tumbled down towards her and Hilary, and she instinctively crouched over the child. Then, glancing upwards, she saw that the Pocket's twisting fall was under control. It came to rest neatly beside her and the boy.

'Still a dump,' she muttered to him, releasing her grip around his shoulders. The 'lock that led on to the command deck was directly above their heads. On the other side of that 'lock were their spacesuits, as well as the lavatories. It was in a way pleasing to discover that the Pridehouse could foul up as comprehensively as good old humanity, but it was going to be a short-lived joy if any of the three of them on the deck required to . . . Mind you, Polyaggle would be all right, of course, because she could fly to the 'lock.

FLYING IS JUST A STATE OF MIND, said Ten Per Cent Extra Free.

'Oh, yeah?' said Strider. 'Tell that to the guy falling off a cliff. He says to himself, "Wowee, flying is just a state of – aargh!"'

IT IS TRUE, NONETHELESS.

'Pardon me while I cough.'

LET YOURSELF FLY.

She snorted, but then the knowledge of how to lift herself off the wall of the command deck filled her. It was easy: it was common sense. She could see in Hilary's eyes that the same knowledge had come into him. Yes, the three dimensions of this physical space should all be treated equally: up was the same as sideways or straight ahead. The two Humans floated, dubiously at first, above the wall, and then, gaining in confidence, swam upwards towards Polyaggle . . .

In fact, all they did was make clumsy swimming movements as they sprawled on the wall dreaming of flight.

'Um, Tenper,' said Strider.

YOU SEEM TO BE HAVING DIFFICULTIES.

'You could put it like that, yeah.'

THIS IS MOST UNEXPECTED.

'Not to me it isn't. Is there any way you can raise this ship up on to its tail?'

YES, BUT IT SEEMS SO UNNECESSARY. CAN'T YOU JUST LEARN TO FLY, LEONIE STRIDER?

83

'It's more difficult than you might think.' She sat up and gave the rest of the command deck the finger. It was rare that one caught the flicker of the sight of an Image, and for all she knew Ten Per Cent Extra Free was somewhere far away, but the gesture was worth it anyway.

HOW COARSE.

'Come on, Tenper, just get this ship the right way up, can't you?'

IF I'M ASKED NICELY.

The Images were not noted for having a sense of humour – at least, they had nothing like the Human sense of humour. Maybe, back in The Truthfulness, they spent half their time making wisecracks that crumpled them up, but Strider doubted it. Now, though, she felt that Ten Per Cent Extra Free was laughing. The joke was a weak one, but perhaps the Images were becoming, as it were, slowly humanized.

'Look, I just sort of fucking *said*.'

REQUESTS HAVE BEEN MADE MORE POLITELY.

'All right. Fucking *please*.'

She and Hilary clung together as the *Midnight Ranger* slowly tipped upwards. The manoeuvre seemed to take forever. They had no on-board medicines, so if either of them broke a limb as they slid across the wall . . . She decided not to think too hard about this. She wasn't so worried about herself: she had enough rudimentary medical knowledge to splint up a broken leg. Strider was more concerned about Hilary. He had been so bloody brave about his broken finger: if he broke an arm or a leg he was going to be truly insufferable.

They landed on the deck with a crash, she underneath him and momentarily winded.

'Gee, Strider, that was nice of . . .'

'Stop it,' she gasped. She felt as if her lungs were trying to explode out of her ribcage. Eyes closed, she tipped her head back. Kid. Cat. She could do without both of them. At the same time she was stuck with them. Maybe she *couldn't* do without them, because the urge to protect them was so strong. *You're a natural-born mother, Leonie,* she said to herself as she cradled Hilary in her arms. *What a bummer.*

Polyaggle floated towards them in a complicated pattern over the command deck. Strider automatically looked away from the Spindrifter's parsecs-deep eyes.

'Are you OK, Hilary?' Strider said. It was an excuse to do something other than gaze into Polyaggle's face.

'I'm fine. Are *you* OK?'

'Yeah. I'll feel even better once you've climbed off me.'

As she groggily got to her feet, the third Pocket tumbled through the air back to its original position. *Neat trick if you can do it,* she thought.

WE *CAN* DO IT, said Ten Per Cent Extra Free. WE JUST HAVE.

For once the Image's voice sounded confused. Strider was pleased. It was good to know that the gods could be puzzled by mere mortals.

She moved to the reinstated Pocket and thought of the Onurg. His face immediately appeared in front of her, his eyes laughing and his tongue drooping from his jaw. As always, she was stunned by his beauty.

'We could have spoken to the Lingk-kreatzai from orbit,' she said at once.

'We need fuel,' the Onurg replied.

'Yeah,' said Strider, 'I suppose there's that.' The place to find tachyons was in deep space, but the tachyon drive was useful only for long journeys. For short excursions, like landing on a planet, what were needed were either radioactives or, preferably, a mixture of matter and antimatter. Any spacefaring species would have, at some stage, stored magnetically enclosed supplies of antimatter.

'We have already transformed you Humans into Lingk-kreatzai,' said the Onurg. 'We will shortly begin the process of doing likewise to ourselves.'

Strider retreated and looked down at herself. She couldn't

see any difference. More important, she couldn't *feel* any difference.

'You sure about that?' she said, returning her head to the Pocket. 'I seem to be distinctly undecontaminated.'

The Onurg laughed again. 'The Lingk-kreatzai, of all the species in The Wondervale, has the closest resemblance to the Human. You will find you have small bodily differences, but little else. Be wary, though, Strider: just because you look like the Lingk-kreatzai doesn't mean that you *think* like them.'

'Why not?' she said. 'You'd sort of expect . . .'

'Never expect anything. We of the Pridehouse may look very different from you in our natural form, but our thinking is much like yours, as you know.' The Onurg's tongue lolled again, saliva dripping from it.

'Can we breathe the air here?'

'You can at the moment. Obviously.'

The first thing that Strider noticed about Lingk was that it was a *cold* world. She'd just eaten, but the coldness made her feel as if she were starving. Small patches of frost made the marshy surfaces around her glint eerily in the pale sunlight. Only a couple of hundred metres away she could see the figures of a Pridehouse crew, now in quasi-Human form, disembarking; it was satisfying that they, too, looked as if they were finding the freezing air a shock. Even Polyaggle, visibly uncomfortable in an SSIA jumpsuit that Strider had lent her, was shivering.

Lucky Segrill, who had chosen to remain aboard the *Midnight Ranger*. Assuming the cat didn't get him.

The Spindrifter made a remarkably beautiful woman, Strider recognized. Polyaggle's face was now clear of bristles and, although her eyes were still deeply glossy, their depths were of great appeal. Back on Mars she'd have been followed by a little retinue wherever she went. As it was, Maloron Leander was looking with distinct unease at Umbel Nelson, who was self-consciously looking anywhere but at Polyaggle.

Hein was less subtle.

Strider warily led her party across the treacherous ground towards the disembarked Pridehouse. In her belt there were two lazguns; in the holsters of her boots there were two more. Still she felt nervous. Falling into a swamp could kill her just as effectively as any attacker, and there was nothing the lazguns would be able to do to protect her from that.

'You there, Tenper? Pinocchio?' she subvocalized.

OF COURSE.

'Stay close, huh?'

OF COURSE.

The Pridehouse crew had manoeuvred from their airlock a small red platform called – according to the Images' eventual translation – a hoverbug. Polyaggle and Strauss-Giolitto looked at it with what Strider realized was a sense of recognition, and then she remembered the little craft she'd seen them use on Spindrift. Other hoverbugs were approaching them from various directions across the marshes. Strider stared at her muddy boots and then at the hoverbugs. Bloody ancient species. Not only were they relatively clean, they were all – like Polyaggle and Hein – beautiful in Human form. She had searched Hein's humanoid body intimately on several occasions looking for blemishes and had never been able to find any. In a way, his immaculateness was in itself a blemish, she had come to realize: true beauty depends on slight imperfection – a mole on the cheek, or one eye slightly wider than the other. All the same, she felt her blood beginning to boil: it was so un*fair* that everyone in The Wondervale seemed capable of being prettier Humans than the Humans themselves. And she'd bet that the Lingk-kreatzai would be the same.

Hein, a little ahead of her, was climbing on to the hoverbug and gesturing that she and the others should follow. Strider squelched through the final few metres and scrambled up, glad of his helping arm. Lan Yi followed, then Strauss-Giolitto and Polyaggle, and finally Hilary with Leander and Nelson, each of whom held one of the boy's hands. The transformation into Lingk-kreatzai shape had made no detectable difference to any of the Humans except that Hilary's broken finger had healed instantly.

The hoverbug was overloaded. There was a groan of toiling machinery beneath them. *Good,* thought Strider, at the same time hoping the vehicle could take the strain. She was being jostled by unnaturally lovely creatures who to all intents and purposes were for the moment human beings. It was difficult to concentrate. The Pridehouse were playfully examining their own and each other's bodies, despite the chill. One of them wanted to examine hers, but she told him to look for someone his own age. Hell, Hein seemed young enough to be her son; this one seemed only just to have emerged from puberty, although he lacked the acne scars.

Another hoverbug came close to them, bobbing slightly.

'You want to hop over here, Strider?' said a silver-haired man whom she instantly recognized as the Onurg.

She looked around at her crew. They seemed unconcerned.

'Yeah. OK.'

Hein came with her, helping her to jump the short distance. She was glad. Great for the morale of her Pridehouse troops it would have been if she'd fallen face-first into the mud.

'Where are all the Lingk-kreatzai?' she said to the Onurg.

'They won't come to us. We have to go to them.'

Of course. The ancient species had survived the millions of years of the Autarchy because they maintained the pretence of primitiveness. The Lingk-kreatzai, she knew, lived in mudpits rather than the luxury which they could easily have created. To anyone from outside they looked like mere animals. *Well, we are all mere animals,* Strider thought.

'Crouch,' said the Onurg.

'You . . .?' she said.

'Get down. We're about to start shifting.' He put his arm across her shoulder blades and pressed her towards the floor of the platform. The other Pridehouse were getting to their hands and knees.

And then they were moving at speed. Never lifting more than a metre or so above the boggy surface, the hoverbug sped in a true line across the marshes. Strider looked ahead of her and felt as if she'd fallen into one of the hologames she'd played as a kid. And she felt *like a kid* all over again. Shucking off the Onurg's arm, she shuffled herself on her belly forward to the front of the hoverbug and watched the landscape beneath fleeing into her past.

Orphanwifer watched their approach for a short while, then tapped his farsighter so that it dissolved back into the muddy wall of his stronghold. He was uneasy about the display of technology which the hoverbugs represented. He wanted the Pridehouse's ships off Lingk as soon as possible. There were women and children here who would perish if the attention of the Autarchy was drawn to Lingk. Look at what had happened to the Hidron.

The mudpit was every bit as revolting as Umbel Nelson had been led to believe, but somehow he found himself revelling in it. He had stepped off the hoverbug into a pool of water, much of which squirted up his side, soaking instantly and coldly through his jumpsuit; there was a roar of laughter from the Pridehouse. Maloron, too, was giggling; her turn would come.

Mudpits like this one made this area of the planet look as if it were suffering from a bad attack of boils. A dome that was about sixty metres across protruded into the air some five or six metres at its highest point. There was a circular entrance directly in front of him. It showed darkness.

He rubbed his hand down the side of his jumpsuit, pressing away some of the wetness, then clapped both of his hands together. Nelson half-expected arrows of ice to dart away from his fingers, but all he felt was a welcome warmth from his palms. He clapped a few more times, then hugged himself while the others climbed out of the hoverbug just as clumsily and ignominiously as he had done.

A Human appeared at the entrance of the mudpit.

At least, it looked like a Human.

Nelson squinted at the creature. It was smaller than he was, but only just. The eyes were Human eyes. The mouth was a Human mouth.

And yet there was no doubting that the creature was not a Human. It was clearly in its element here – clearly at home with the coldness and wetness. It was smiling uncertainly at him. He reached out his right hand, and the creature took it, examined it, made a move as if to bite it, then respectfully forced his arm away.

Nelson looked at his hand, suddenly discovering how valuable it was.

A few moments later, however, he was enjoying the mudpit. As a child he'd been untidy, and had had to endure the tyranny of the fosterfather who had taken him in. Here there was mess everywhere. And children. He squelched through the mud and chuckled at the children, most of whom were naked. Some ran up to take his hand for a few metres or so as he followed Orphanwifer into the depths; then they let go to return to their games, and other children took over his hands. Orphanwifer was likewise naked, as were the several wives whom Nelson saw. They smiled at him, and he smiled back: the Lingkkreatzai were a very beautiful species, he decided. They also came in roughly the same shades as humanity: there were blacks and browns and whites and yellows, with only the occasional blue making Nelson start. *Hm, never made love to a blue woman,* he thought. *Wonder what it's like?*

Finally Orphanwifer assembled the Humans in a place – 'room' was the wrong word – that reminded Nelson of holos he'd seen diagramming the womb. Using his secondary retinal screens, he sent the vision of one eye to explore the wet walls of the chamber and the other back through the passages they'd traversed to check out Orphanwifer's various females. Soon he found that he was more interested in the romping children: some of the games they were playing he could understand and some of them he couldn't, but their enthusiasm made him grin. They reminded him of joshing around with Hilary. Nelson seemed to be the only person aboard the *Midnight Rambler*, apart from Strider, who was prepared to be a kid with Hilary. The boy got lonely. Thank Umbel for the cat.

Then he saw one kid beat another to death. He moved to stop the deed, but was halted by aggressive stares. Ten Per Cent Extra Free had warned him about this, but still it was difficult to take.

Nelson looked away. Cultural differences. Got to put up with them.

Orphanwifer was speaking to Strider, with the Images translating for both of them and spreading the translation to everyone else.

'You are very beautiful. I would like to welcome you as one of my wives.'

'Ah, that's not why we're here.'

'Bear it in mind, though.'

'OK, if you insist.' Strider put her hand on his shoulder, then swiftly removed it again as he flinched. *Body language,* she thought. *I may just have insulted the guy.*

Hein stepped up beside her. 'What can you offer us?' he said bluntly.

'My family's cruisers. Those of the rest of the Lingk-kreatzai – well, most of the rest, at any rate. Our women and children will not fight a war, and our men are too valuable to waste: you may have our ships but you may not have our selves.'

Strider was startled. She had expected to have to chat diplomatically for a few hours before reaching the nitty gritty.

Clearly the Lingk-kreatzai did things differently. She decided to let Hein take over.

'That's not good enough,' said the Pridehouse male. 'We want more than that.'

'We won't offer more,' said Orphanwifer. 'We will help you in any way that we can, but there are some things we cannot do.'

'Your ships?' said Hein. 'What are they like?'

'Good ships. They are also very much loved, so it will pain us to give them to you.'

'Are they blood-kindred?' asked Hein with interest.

'No, but they have limited sentience. They recognize their names.'

'Their puters?' It seemed that Hein was becoming doubtful.

'Oh, their puters are *fully* sentient. The ships themselves are merely aware of their surroundings and of the way they're being treated. If you're harsh to them, they will begin to refuse to function.' Orphanwifer looked at Strider and smiled again. 'Just like a wife.'

Strider wondered about hitting him, then realized this might be taken as an invitation to lunch, or something, so controlled herself. Come to think of it, though, strangulation was less equivocal. She felt as if her lazguns were starting to itch. It was important not to react to such stuff: the Lingk-kreatzai were clearly a patriarchal culture for reasons that helped their society, and it had probably required a considerable intellectual leap for Orphanwifer to treat her as anything other than a breeding machine. Maybe that was all the Lingk-kreatzai females were. They looked very much like Human women, but it was possible that there was nothing going on inside their heads. Maybe they were like the cat: much cherished, but requiring constant attention in case they did something stupid. She remembered the vapid smiles as the Humans had come through the mudpit to get here. Nelson had liked them – the leer on his face had told her as much – but she had found them somewhat . . . creepy.

Her regard for Orphanwifer increased abruptly. He had a herd of wives, whom he had to tend and to provide for. She was in no position to judge the Lingk-kreatzai.

'And you'll allow us to take the ships?' said Hein.

'Yes.'

'Won't you miss them?'

'Yes. Of course we shall. We are very fond of them. Now, will you eat with me?'

If there was something constant about alien food, Strider thought, it was the fact that it was foul. The Pridehouse ate overcooked cabbages and the Lingk-kreatzai were partial to things that looked vaguely like slugs, eaten alive. Even Hein seemed worried by the meal that was served up to them – Orphanwifer's wives did the serving – on plates that might have been made of wood. Polyaggle motioned her plate away: the Spindrifter refused animal food. Strider almost did the same, then realized how hungry she was. Polyaggle seemed to get hungry only when she wanted to. It was frustrating. The Spindrifter was pregnant and so should presumably be leaping on the most arcane foods.

The slug-things tasted fine, and their wiggling in the mouth only added to the relish with which Strider ate them. A swift crunch with the molars killed them and allowed their juices to flow on to the palate. There was the sensation that she was eating protein-rich tarragon. She devoured the contents of her own plate, then moved on to Polyaggle's.

'The Onurg is with your fleet?' said Orphanwifer.

'The Onurg is *here*,' said Strider. She turned round, slug halfway to lips, and pointed. The silver-haired man looked up on hearing his name mentioned, and smiled. He was sitting with his back propped against one of the chamber's sweaty walls eating his slugs with interest. He put his plate down, stood up, and walked over. Strider found it odd that the Onurg – and all the rest of the Pridehouse – could walk with such ease in their strange bodies, and then remembered how little time it had taken her to adapt to being a six-legged wolf.

'In that case the Pridehouse do in truth mean business,' said Orphanwifer, turning his attention away from Strider towards the Onurg. She felt as if she had been dismissed and discounted. Orphanwifer was going to be in for a nasty shock if he tried that one again; this time she maintained a look of placidity on her face.

'I never thought I would meet one of your species in the flesh,' Orphanwifer said gravely, 'and I certainly never believed my mudpit would be graced by the Onurg himself. This is an historic moment, the meeting of two ancient species.'

The Onurg laughed, with the characteristic Pridehouse childishness. 'The female sitting here' – he indicated Polyaggle, who was looking glum and now, to Strider's delight, hungry – 'is the last of the Spindrifters. So that means you've had two historic moments in a row.'

Orphanwifer turned to look at Polyaggle properly for the first time. 'I am honoured,' he said. 'You make a very lovely Lingk-kreatzai. It is, of course, a pity that the sole surviving Spindrifter should not be a male, but we should be glad that any of you at all . . .'

Strider hit him.

She knew it wasn't what she was supposed to do. Had she been trained as a full-fledged ambassador for the Human species she might merely have coughed gently, but as it was she was cold and getting increasingly irritated. She couldn't, at a gut level, understand Orphanwifer's attitude towards females. And then she remembered again the vacuous smiles of the wives they had passed on their way here. *Just because the Lingk-kreatzai look like us doesn't mean they are like us,* she thought. *It must be just as difficult for Orphanwifer to shift his mind-set to accept that females can be intelligent as it is for me to tolerate his attitudes. Still* – she looked at her knuckles – *I did enjoy that.*

Orphanwifer seemed hardly to have noticed the blow, which was disappointing. He continued to speak to the Onurg. 'These Humans of yours have strange ways,' he said.

'This Human, Leonie Strider, is our leader. She is the captain of our fleet.'

'You have said this before. Yet she is a female of adult age. Has she not mothered?'

The Onurg looked at Strider and laughed again. It must be obvious from her face how much her hand was beginning to hurt. 'She is very female,' said the Onurg, rolling his tongue in exaggerated fashion to annoy her, 'but she is still our leader. In our species – Pridehouse, Spindrifter and Human alike – the females are as able as the males. It's something you ought to remember. Among the Alhubra the females are more powerful than the males. Kaantalech is of the Alhubra. She has almost certainly seized the Autarchy.'

Strider had the feeling that things were slipping away from her.

'I'll mother when and if I want to,' she said.

Polyaggle reached out a finger and touched Orphanwifer on the forehead. The effect was instant. The Lingk-kreatzai male was suddenly still, his eyes no longer on the Onurg. Strider could almost *see* the information coursing down Polyaggle's arm and hand. The Spindrifter was telling him everything, which was all right by Strider. Maybe this sudden dose of data was more of a punch than her own had been.

After half a minute Polyaggle removed her finger.

Orphanwifer looked slightly dazed. *Say,* thought Strider, *I wonder if that was sex?*

The Lingk-kreatzai male got to his feet and strode across the chamber, stepping on platters, slug-things, mud and extended limbs with equal equanimity and agility.

'What have you just done to that guy?' Strider hissed to Polyaggle as Orphanwifer left.

'Told him about you.'

'What did you tell him?'

'That you Humans have something the ancient species don't have. Rawness. A belief that things can be changed. The Pridehouse have rediscovered this belief. We Spindrifters didn't until the very last moment, which is why we perished.' Polyaggle looked down at the hand which had touched Orphanwifer; Strider was infuriated to find that she wished that finger had been touched to her own forehead rather than Orphanwifer's. Polyaggle in Human form had an androgynous quality that was hard to understand. 'He has gone to make contact with the dominants of the other mudpits and to tell them that the Lingk-kreatzai will not only lend you their cruisers but also lend you themselves.'

'More troopers, you mean?' said Strider dully.

'More troopers.'

'But that could mean the end of the Lingk-kreatzai,' said Strider. 'If their males come with us and the females are basically none too bright, what future is there for the species?' Her hand was beginning to hurt really badly. She had hit Orphanwifer as hard as she could. His jaw had seemed to absorb the blow with ease. She wondered if she was beginning to like him.

'What future is there for all of us if we fail to resist Kaantalech?'

The Onurg, standing above them, grinned quizzically.

'There *is* no future if we don't destroy Kaantalech,' he said. 'Whatever Orphanwifer offers us, we have to take.'

The future is a foreign country, thought Strider. *They do things differently there. I wonder where I heard that before.*

Some instinct within Kaantalech told her that the few remaining rebellious warlords were not really her main problem. She stood on the surface of Alterifer's innermost moon and gazed at the waterfall of stars above her. She was not a poetic being, but even she on occasion could be struck by the beauty of The Wondervale, with Heaven's Ancestor hanging mistily in the skies beyond. Those beautiful stars – some of them bore planets that harboured her enemies.

There was also a beauty in destruction. This was something she felt more keenly. On the few occasions when she herself experienced pain she found it somehow blissful at the same time as she recoiled from it. The infliction of pain gave her greater bliss, for she knew that was also administering joy.

The visor of her suit distorted the heavens, making the spiral galaxy seem larger and brighter than it would have had she been standing here in the naked vacuum.

She lowered her eyes towards the surface of the little moon. It was pocked with craters whose walls made Kaantalech think once again of the richness of the skies; between the craters was a sludge of ice and dust. Most of the craters were meteoritic, she knew, although the chances of a further meteor impact of any significance were minuscule. Some of them were volcanic, but these were equally ancient. Tormented by Alterifer's gravitational field, the moon had undergone an early period of intense volcanism. In a few million years' time it would suffer the same again as it slowly spiralled in towards its planet: Alterifer's atmosphere, this far out, was no more than a trace, but its friction was enough to cause the little moon gradually to move inwards. At some stage the pull of Alterifer was going to be able to make the ice-volcanoes of the moon erupt again . . . and after that perhaps the little world would be split asunder to add one more ring of garbage to Alterifer's already impressive complement.

Kaantalech enjoyed the prospect of the destruction of the miniature world. And she wouldn't even have to do it herself. By then, of course, she would be long gone – perhaps even the Autarchy would be gone.

That was a thought she didn't like so much.

She ambled slowly and carefully – keeping one's balance in such a low-g environment was difficult – towards a small crater, looking around her in case one or more of her aides had a sudden aspiration towards assassination. She wouldn't put it past them. They were so stupid. If Kaantalech were to die, who would hold the Autarchy together? Almost all of the war-lords were dead, along with their species. There were very few people left in The Wondervale who had sufficient power to re-establish the desirable tyranny. In fact, there might be none.

Except . . .

Kaantalech let her mind wander again as she looked at the starfield. All the different colours of those suns. Alterifer would be on the far side of the moon for quite a while longer, so there was nothing to distract her from the stars. Some were blue, some white, some yellow, some orange . . . one of the brighter orange ones seemed constantly to flicker as she watched it.

Free associate.

The stars themselves could not be plotting against her. The very thought made her angry with herself. Nalla, by the time he had died, had become convinced that the entirety of the Universe was out to get him; she would never fall into that trap of paranoia.

Keep free associating.

Some of the stars are red.

Those are very old stars.

Age.

The Autarchy is very old, too, but there were other space-faring species in The Wondervale before the Autarchy emerged. All of them have regressed towards the primitive. Maybe one day, long after Kaantalech's death so why should she care, the Autarchy would do the same – become planet-bound and moribund.

Yet the Spindrifters . . .

She had lost a lot of ships when she destroyed Spindrift, and the planet's defences had proved unexpectedly tough to break through.

Were the ancient species quite what they seemed?

It was a silly idea, and she knew it, yet something inside her was telling her to keep following the train of thought, even though she knew she should be thinking instead about Kortland and his Helgiolath fleet. Once she'd thought that Kortland was dead; now she was only too certain that he was alive. He must have survived, somehow, the war that had briefly surrounded Qitanefermeartha.

The Humans were another matter. She hoped they'd gone for good.

Instinct again.

She thought the Humans were still around. Still, they couldn't represent much of a threat.

Could they?

No. Think about the Helgiolath. Somewhere out there they waited. They were a direct physical threat, unlike the ancient species and the Humans, who might cause trouble in the future. It was impossible for the Helgiolath to stop her progress towards the full Autarchship, of course, but they could cause her severe damage along the way.

The Helgiolath.

But her mind kept straying back to the ancient species. Surely they could present no threat, so why was she spending so much thought on them?

The Spindrifters. That was why.

Her mind circled back to the destruction of Spindrift. The level of resistance had proved unexpectedly high. *Too* high. The planet had been nothing but a wasteland, largely ice with a fertile band around the equator. The population had been tiny. Her flotilla should have been able to destroy it without difficulty, but instead they had been forced to use maxbeams.

And there had been others operating within the fleet. This was the first time she had realized it. The Humans had been off to one side, but *other* creatures – not the Humans, not the Spindrifters – had destroyed some of her vessels. She knew it now with a blinding certainty.

There was some kind of unholy alliance building up against her.

No!

This is the way Nalla became: he couldn't look into a corner without seeing a burgeoning conspiracy there.

She must not follow that route.

Deal with the Helgiolath. They were the threat. At leisure, later, she could eliminate the ancient species, one by one. Then she could track down the Humans, if they hadn't already fled from her might.

She gave an instruction to an aide, who sped to obey her. It might be worth keeping tabs on the Humans, just in case they *were* still around.

Killing them would be a pleasure.

Floods of colours filling Nightmirror's eyes.

He has retracted himself briefly into The Truthfulness, where the Images were born and where they should truly dwell. The neighbouring reality of which The Wondervale is only a small part is truly alien to the Images. It is hard to understand flesh. It is hard to understand stars and planets and rocks and entities who can trip up and hurt themselves, for all of these things are unknown to the Images.

Stretch out an idea to Pinocchio, who for a long time lived in such an unnatural environment.

The colours, the colours. It is very difficult to concentrate when engaged in the orgasm of *being*.

Pinocchio is there – or, at least, a tendril of his thought. Most of him is still in The Wondervale, but the Images can never be entirely in that manifestation of reality: it is too alien to them. They can interpenetrate with it, and they can try to rid it of its suffering, but they cannot *be* in it.

But Pinocchio, before Ten Per Cent Extra Free rescued him, was a part of it.

Pinocchio's thought embraces Nightmirror, caressing him

100

as if he were a lover. Nightmirror is able to see a glimpse of Pinocchio's thought; it is a new colour among the rest. This is all he will ever see of Pinocchio: that bolt of colour.

Nightmirror envies, in some ways, the creatures of The Wondervale, with their knowledge of how to bump into each other's bodies and to look at each other's faces. He has never looked at another Image directly: all he has seen is a glimmer of different colour. His perception of Heartfire and of Ten Per Cent Extra Free has never been more than the warmth of their voices mingling. Angler, who was with them briefly, added further warmth. There have been other Images who joined the chorus, but none have ever come as close as Angler or Pinocchio.

He basks in the cradle of Pinocchio's thought.

The thought is one that mixes apprehension and exhilaration: there is danger in store for his mortal charges, but there is still enough of the physical within Pinocchio for him – since he himself is in no danger – to find the prospect enticing.

Slight sorrow within Nightmirror. Ever since the core entity of Pinocchio was saved by Ten Per Cent Extra Free, the being has been gradually losing his identification with the Humans. The bot thought he was killing himself in order to save Strider; now he finds the idea of her being in situations where she might die at least partly exciting. His perception of things has changed. At the same time, he has yet fully to adapt to Image ways of thought; had he done so, he would be able to share with Nightmirror the aesthetic distress the Images feel over the warfare and bloodshed in The Wondervale.

Nightmirror conveys his own thought to Pinocchio. It is a complex thought, and so it takes him a little while to respond.

Nightmirror wishes that Images could speak directly to each other. Words, although they may mislead, offer such useful ways of pinning things down. He can speak in words to those who habitually use words, because then his thoughts translate into their patterns of mind, which are largely word-oriented. But he cannot communicate in this fashion with others of his own kind. To the people of The Wondervale the Images must appear almost godlike in their abilities, yet Nightmirror is envying them for something which they all take for granted: speech, whether using sound or some other means.

Pinocchio's new thought fondles Nightmirror. His love for Strider is undimmed. His excitement and apprehension are hers.

Nightmirror does not know whether or not to be pleased by this. He has great respect for Strider, but knows probably better than she does herself her capacity for bloodlust: it is a quality which makes colours brighten until they offend. Other aspects of her – so *many* other aspects of her – dull down colours until they bring peace and happiness to Nightmirror's mind.

Nightmirror releases Pinocchio's thought and comes back from The Truthfulness to The Wondervale. He is inside the main drive of Kaantalech's flagship, the *Blunt Instrument*.

He can communicate with its tachyons more easily than he can with others of his own kind.

This depresses him.

Strider was depressed.

The *Midnight Ranger* was far from Lingk, and she had made contact with the Helgiolath. She had just had, with Hein, one of the most imaginative bouts of sex she had ever experienced, and afterwards he had held her so tenderly in his arms that she had felt like weeping. Now he was asleep, and it was she who was fondly holding her arms around him. The regular movement of his chest against her hands was deeply reassuring.

Yet she was depressed, and she didn't know why.

Hein rolled over towards her, and she took the opportunity to remove her right arm from underneath him. She turned away from him, nestling her bottom into his groin. He groaned in his sleep and put an arm over her. She manoeuvred his hand on to her breast, then stared into the darkness. Now his chest was moving regularly against her shoulder blades rather than her hands: so what?

She wondered if she needed to go to the lavatory, then decided she could hold out until the end of the sleeping-time. It was maybe not the wisest of moves, she realized, but she didn't want to leave Hein's embrace, and the comfort that it gave her.

Except that it wasn't giving her enough.

She was the leader of a fleet of nearly forty thousand war-cruisers, and she found herself feeling inadequate. She should have been feeling great.

The trouble about total darkness was that there wasn't much there to see.

If she'd been fitted out with secondary retinal screens she could have had fun watching what the others on the *Midnight Ranger* were up to, but she resented the intrusion of technology into or on to her body.

'Pinocchio,' she whispered.

I'M HERE, LEONIE.

'What's the matter? You can see inside my mind. Tell me what's up.'

Hein shifted restlessly again, and for a moment she thought he was going to wake.

Pinocchio didn't reply immediately.

THE CAUSE OF YOUR UNHAPPINESS DOESN'T LIE INSIDE YOU, LEONIE, he said at last.

She dropped her voice even lower. She loved Hein – she thought she did, at least – but this was nothing to do with him. She wanted him to stay asleep. 'Well, it fucking well *feels* as if it does.'

THERE'S SOMETHING OUTSIDE YOU THAT'S INFLUENCING YOU, BUT I CAN'T MAKE OUT WHAT IT IS.

'I mean, I don't normally *get* depressed. I get pissed off quite often . . .'

I'VE NOTICED.

'. . . but not actually *depressed*.'

YES.

'Has Tenper any idea what's going on?'

I HAVE COMMUNICATED MY CONCERN TO HIM. YOUR CONCERN.

There was a silence in her mind. Pinocchio had left her. She had the vision of the two Images running around in circles, trying to solve the problem: little glitters of light, chasing their own tails. It almost cheered her up – but at the same time she remembered the Pinocchio who had, so very often, been the comforting bulk that lay beside her on her bunk during the night, and the memory brought moistness to her eyes.

Her eyes.

Still she could see nothing in the gloom. She thought of getting one of the Images to switch on the lights, but they were busy doing a more important thing.

She closed her eyes. Somehow that made the darkness easier to bear. But she couldn't keep them closed: animal reflex made them open again – the night might shield predators. She stretched a lazy arm behind her and played with the hairs on Hein's back: it had been no surprise to discover how hairy a man he had become – her very own Esau, although she preferred to think of him as a Caliban. Now his presence was giving her no sense of security. She'd rather the cat had been there: by cocooning the animal she could have, in a strange way, cocooned herself from her own night sadness.

YOU ARE BEING SPIED ON. Pinocchio's voice in her mind came as a shock.

'What do you mean?'

IT IS WHAT IS CAUSING YOUR FEELINGS OF UNHAPPINESS.

'You mean I've suddenly become telepathic, or something? Or is there a minibot floating around my cabin, observing my more vigorous personal practices in infrared?'

NO. MENTALLY SPIED ON. TEN PER CENT EXTRA FREE AND I ARE TRYING TO FIND OUT WHO OR WHAT IS DOING THIS TO YOU. AS SOON AS WE DISCOVER, WE SHALL INFORM YOU.

Hein began to snore. The adaptation the Pridehouse had effected on him had been perfect. Every bloody man she'd ever slept with had snored when she was trying to get to sleep. One or two of the bastards, when she'd complained, had mentioned that she snored as well.

She couldn't go on watching nothingness like this. Still careful not to wake Hein she put her feet on the floor and sat up. The floor was cold and the air was warm. The contrast made her feel better. She moved across the room and opened the door to the lavatory, then closed it quietly behind her. At last she could switch on a light. She looked at herself in the mirror and then sat on the closet. *I'm contributing my little bit to the micro-ecosystem of this ship,* she thought as she peed. *Captain's duty.*

The depression wasn't lifting. She looked at her hands in front of her, their fingers interlinking. There was nothing wrong with her fingers except that there seemed to be more wrinkles along the lines of the knuckles than there had been only a year ago. Maybe the fingers were a little fatter than they had been when she was younger, but only a little.

She turned up her palms. They were definitely paler than when she'd been a kid. Was she ageing, or was it just that the transformations the Pridehouse had carried out on her had failed to restore her precisely to her previous form?

She didn't want to think too much about that. In the old days – back on the *Santa Maria* – she could have called up a medibot to check her insides. Here on the *Midnight Ranger* things were a bit more primitive.

Strider did quite like her stomach, she decided. Her breasts weren't quite as good, although Hein obviously found them a lot of fun, even though there were only two of them. She did think her pubic hair was pretty OK though, she thought as she stood and dried herself: it was a glad tuft. She peered at herself again in the mirror. Too many bags under the eyes. A face that showed her age. Was Pinocchio talking nonsense when he said that her depression was a product of something outside, rather than inside, her? She watched herself pulling her own nose, as if she could make it longer and more dignified.

To hell with it, she told herself, *I've just had four orgasms, including the one that Hein didn't know about – the imagination is a wonderful thing. Maybe Pinocchio's got it wrong and this blueness is only a bad attack of the little death.*

'FRAID NOT.

'Now I know who's spying on me.'

HOW DID YOU GUESS?

'Well, Pinocchio, it's a bit . . .'

AH. I SEE WHAT YOU MEAN. NO, APART FROM MYSELF – MAY I CONGRATULATE YOU, BY THE WAY, ON YOUR PERFORMANCE OF POSITION 7634 FROM THE EXPANDED AD2529 REVISION OF THE *KAMA SUTRA*? – THERE IS ANOTHER.

'Tenper?'

NO, SOMEONE FROM OUTSIDE – AS I'VE TOLD YOU. TEN PER CENT EXTRA FREE HAS TRACKED DOWN THE SOURCE OF THE SURVEILLANCE. IT IS ON ONE OF THE INNER MOONS OF A PLANET CALLED ALTERIFER.

'Never heard of the joint.' Yes, her nose really *was* too small. Sometimes she liked its snubness, but right now . . .

THE PROBE IS FROM A PSIBOT IN THE ENTOURAGE OF KAANTALECH.

Now Strider straightened up and began to pay attention.

'I thought psibots didn't exist? There were experiments a couple of centuries ago and—'

YOU KEEP FORGETTING THAT THE SPECIES OF THE WONDERVALE ARE MILLIONS OF YEARS AHEAD OF US. IT IS SOMETHING THAT I, TOO, KEEP FORGETTING.

'Oh. Yeah. Right.'

AT THE MOMENT KAANTALECH HAS NO INTENTION OF MOVING DIRECTLY AGAINST US, ALTHOUGH SHE WILL DO SO VERY SOON. Pinocchio paused, then added: BUT TEN PER CENT EXTRA FREE HAS DISCOVERED SOMETHING FURTHER. THE REASON THAT

KAANTALECH IS STAYING HER HAND IS THAT SHE DOES NOT WISH
ANYONE TO KNOW WHERE SHE IS UNTIL SHE HAS EXTIRPATED THE
LAST OF HER RIVALS FOR THE AUTARCHSHIP.

It took a few seconds for the import of this to sink in.

'Right,' Strider repeated. 'You mean that no one else knows
but us?'

CORRECT.

'Well, we can soon change that.'

IS THAT ADVISABLE?

Strider sighed. 'If we tell the Helgiolath and all the other
rebels we can amass the biggest goddam fleet in the history of
the Universe and beat the shit out of Kaantalech before she
even knows we're on our way.'

THERE ARE SEVERAL REASONS WHY THIS, WHILE AN ATTRAC-
TIVE NOTION, IS A VERY POOR PIECE OF STRATEGIC PLANNING,
LEONIE.

'Name a few.'

THE PSIBOT HAS BEEN ABLE TO LOCK ON TO YOU BECAUSE OF
YOUR PROTOPLASM, WHICH IS ALIEN TO THAT OF THE SPECIES OF
THE WONDERVALE. AS SOON AS YOU HEADED YOURSELF
TOWARDS ALTERIFER, IT WOULD CONVEY THAT INFORMATION TO
KAANTALECH, WHO WOULD TAKE IMMEDIATE COUNTERACTION.

'That's one. Try another.'

SOME OF THE SURVIVING WARLORDS DOUBTLESS HAVE PSI-
BOTS WITH A SIMILAR CAPABILITY. THERE ARE BOUND TO BE
LOSSES INCURRED WHEN WE 'BEAT THE SHIT', AS YOU PUT IT, OUT
OF KAANTALECH. OUR FLEET WILL BE WEAKENED. A WARLORD
MAY CHOOSE TO ATTACK US AT THAT TIME, AND THEREBY HAVE
NOTHING BETWEEN HIM/HER/IT AND THE SUCCESSION TO THE
AUTARCHSHIP. OUR EFFORTS WILL HAVE BEEN ENTIRELY IN VAIN.
IS THIS WHAT YOU WANT?

Strider did her best not to be annoyed with Pinocchio for
thinking things through better than she had herself. Then an
idea came to her.

'You say the psibot can lock on to Human protoplasm?'

107

YES.

'*Only* Human protoplasm?'

IT IS BECAUSE OF ITS STRANGENESS.

'Seems pretty normal to me, but I know what you mean. Just . . . just switch on the lights in the bedroom and wait around a bit.'

She went back through to her bunk and shook Hein's shoulder. Finally his eyes opened.

'Look, there's something I want you to do for me.'

He moaned. 'Not again.'

'No, something quite different . . .'

The worst thing about the new status was that he was missing his musibot, which had departed with O'Sondheim and the *Santa Maria*. Chess was Lan Yi's devotion, science was his love, Geena was his yearning, but music was his passion. Much of the music he could conjure up in his mind: as he lay during sleeping-times in his bunk he could play through the entirety of the *Goldberg Variations* in any musical style he chose, or enjoy a Wagner opera sung by the Rolling Stones, but all of these things were drawn from memory of listening to his musibot. He wanted to punch up new combinations. He wanted to punch up pieces of music that he had never heard before.

When the Images spoke together in his mind, sounding almost like a group of choristers, he always asked them to keep talking so that he could listen to their new music.

There was no music like the music of Geena's voice – the seductive music that sought to draw him away from . . . from *himself*, he suddenly realized.

It wasn't the most pleasant of thoughts.

There's destruction and destruction. One can be shot through the chest with a lazgun and spend several minutes writhing in agony, then die, but during those final minutes one is still one's own person: the killer may have taken the life, but the identity remains secure. But there's the kind of death which one accepts willingly from somebody one foolishly trusts, where the personality is entirely subjugated to the other. This may lead to physical death – as it surely would if he walked out of the airlock – but almost worse, almost *certainly* worse, is if it leads instead to an existence where the body remains alive but the soul is effectively dead.

That was where he'd got to.

He was a puppet dancing on a dead woman's strings.

Strings.

In his mind's eye he saw her again, naked, playing the cello. She had loved playing the instrument and he had loved listening to her play, while loving her.

He didn't know what had been going through Geena's mind during those last few months. It had been difficult at the time to realize that she was becoming insane: each day she had seemed just a little odder, doing things slightly more wrongly. He had thought she was maybe just going through a bad patch and hoped she would get through it. Later, the few friends he still had told him that they'd recognized her insanity but hadn't, you know, liked to mention it to him, because he *must* have noticed it himself.

The vision of Geena that he conjured up in the Pockets was the version of her that existed in his memory. She said that she still loved him and wanted him; but that would of course be the verdict of the Geena whom he remembered rather than Geena as she had really been. It was much more likely that she had hated him, in that last time.

Music can tell one many things, not all of which are true.

Lan Yi decided that this memory of music was telling him the truth, and with a feeling of great relief said a silent goodbye to his wife.

She is lovely.

She *was* lovely.

She cares for me.

In the end, she cared for herself.

She is *dead*.

Dead.

Dead.

Dead.

'We've lost them,' said the aide.

'Lost whom?' said Kaantalech. She was mapping out the plan of attack on the world of the Eramm. The Eramm were a powerful military force – almost as powerful as the Helgiolath – and Warlord Mgs had had his eyes on the throne of the Autarchy, so it was important that the species be eliminated. Genocide was kind of fun, but it did take a great deal of tedious concentration.

In fact, genocide was quite a *lot* of fun.

Still needed the concentration, though.

That was why she was concentrating.

Well, she was pretty sure she was concentrating. It was hard to be certain about things like this when aides kept interrupting.

'The Humans,' said the aide. 'One moment the psibot could pin them down to the nearest light-hour, and the next it had lost them altogether, as if they'd just vanished.'

The aide looked at his feet. Maybe Kaantalech would start with them. He hoped not. If she bit his head off he would die instantly. If she began with the feet it would take rather a lot longer – too much longer. She didn't take kindly to bad news.

Mind you, it had been a good life, all things considered. He tried to consider a few, but couldn't find one.

'I don't care, just right now, about the Humans,' said Kaantalech, not looking up.

'They are a possible threat,' said the aide, having examined the depths of his soul.

'A tiny threat,' said Kaantalech, still distracted. 'We'll mop them up later. Oh, one thing . . .'

110

'Yes?'

She slashed his throat wide open with her claws and then turned back to her work.

Lan Yi knew that he was dreaming, and that what he was dreaming was a story . . . yet he was also a *part* of that story, as if he were seated in a theatre watching a play while at the same time being one of the leading actors who moved across the stage.

Theatres. None of the species they had met so far in The Wondervale seemed to have invented the theatre. Back in the Solar System humanity had invented it, lost it, and reinvented it during the century or so before the *Santa Maria* had set off on its abortive mission. Holos could show better close-ups – faces, phalluses, blood – but the live theatre offered something brighter, even if more distant. Also, in a theatre you were surrounded by others so that the experience became a shared one. Your laughter didn't echo against the walls of your solitude – Lan Yi had become a great supporter of the cult of the theatre in his last years before leaving Earth, in order to get away from such merciless walls.

What he saw and what he was a part of, in this dream, was very brightly lit. There were only two characters of whom he was aware: himself and Geena.

He was a sculptor, and a fresh block of marble had just been delivered to the studio they shared. He didn't know how he knew it, but the two of them had been sharing this vast studio for several years, sleeping in the big, rather uncomfortable bed in the corner and discovering, as time passed, that they wanted to make love with each other less and less often.

Lan Yi watched the stage. Shafts of light illuminated the studio. It was the height of day. The sculptor was standing in front of the lump of stone. It was taller than he was, and wider. Crystal facets shone in its surface, dazzling him with reflected brilliance. He looked at the rock, trying to discern within it the

form that it wanted to take; he ran his fingers across its coldness, and found he was experiencing the stone's femininity.
Whoever – whatever – wanted to be released from the bondage
of the marble was female, and the sculptor felt a pang of long-
ing for the beautiful creature he might be able to find there
inside the rock.

The Lan Yi in the audience felt tears running down his
cheeks. At the same time that he was the sculptor struggling to
discover what it was that the marble wanted to be he was also
fully aware of the form that hid in there.

The stage seemed to be further away than it had been
before, yet the image of the sculptor seemed to be brighter and
more clearly defined.

Why wasn't Lan Yi the sculptor sweating? he thought as he
stroked the base of his back, which ached. He seemed to be
wearing nothing, which was curious because he was fully
clothed, as he knew from the himself who was observing him
from the auditorium. With a finger he explored the upper part
of his ear, feeling its smoothness, and then he took the hand
away and, crossing his arm in front of his chest, rubbed his
own shoulder. It too should have been sweating under the
lights, but instead it itched because it was dry.

I will reveal the form, thought the sculptor.

I will reveal myself to you, thought the form, and the sculptor heard it.

He turned towards the audience, who were invisible in the
darkness. The only face that he could see was his own, way
back in the huge space he knew was there. He ignored the distraction.

'Inside everything there is something else,' he said, throwing his arms wide for emphasis, 'and inside the something
else there is something further.'

Yes, thought Lan Yi. *The tree bears the nut and the nut
bears the kernel and the kernel bears the new tree.*

The audience around him tittered, as if he had spoken his

thought out loud and it had been one of those theatrical witti-cisms which seem neither so funny nor so perceptive afterwards.

He felt embarrassed.

On stage he found himself still wondering what was the hidden form inside the piece of marble. There was only one way to find out.

He seized, from a conveniently placed table which hadn't been there a moment before, a chisel in his left hand and a hammer in his right, and, feeling as if he were in the process of losing his virginity, made a very gentle tap against the exterior of the stone.

Lan Yi, watching himself, remembered that it hadn't been at all like that when he'd lost his virginity, all those decades ago. Sheer nerves had meant that eventually he and his first lover – dammit, he couldn't remember her name – had finally just decided to call it a night and fall asleep in each other's arms. He still recalled fondly the loving conversation they had had as they had slowly dropped off into sleep, their bodies curled around each other. In the morning, however, nerves no longer played a part.

But the actor who was also Lan Yi chose to interpret the start of his sculpture as if it were something he had never done before.

Another tap with the chisel. Another flake falls away from the surface of the rock. From a distance it looks as if the rock is somehow becoming cleaner, as if it had been dirty before.

We touch, thought Lan Yi, *the hearts of ourselves only when we touch the hearts of others*.

The sculptor turned towards Lan Yi – he knew those eyes were directed towards himself alone rather than into the audi-ence at random – and held his chisel aloft. Then he threw it into the air, so that its sharp blade made glinting patterns as it flew spinning towards the spotlights before falling to land per-fectly in the sculptor's hand.

There was a round of applause. The audience appreciated

the trick. Lan Yi was grateful and, even though it disrupted the play, he bowed in acknowledgement of the accolade.

I hit the stone again, Lan Yi said to himself. *It is as if I were knocking at a door.*

Days passed, although Lan Yi knew that he was dreaming all this during only a few minutes. The play seemed very prolonged, nevertheless: the sculptor had some difficulty in releasing the form that existed within the rock.

'Can't you just leave that thing alone?' screamed Geena.

'I would if I could,' said the actor. Behind him three man-sized mice had appeared as backing singers for a song that he was not going to sing.

Lan Yi looked through his spread fingers at the stage.

'It's only a hunk of rock,' said Geena.

The audience erupted, as if this were witty.

'It's you,' he said.

Geena stroked the insides of her thighs. She was naked. She looked out into the audience and laughed.

'Feels like I'm hotter here than that old block of stone,' she said. 'Bet it's pretty chilly against your fingers.'

Lan Yi was the only member of the audience who did not howl with mirth. Instead, he took his naked wife in his arms and led her to the bed at the corner of the studio. For a moment she struggled against him as he laid her down and pulled covers over her, but then she seemed to realize that all he wanted to do was comfort her. There was more applause from the audience.

He sat on the side of the bed, stroking the back of her neck until she went to sleep.

The audience went wild when she began to snore.

Lan Yi, sitting in the stalls, knew what was going to happen. He looked around him, as if there might be somewhere he could flee to, but he knew there was not. All he could see were faces, in gloomy lighting, which were so convulsed by laughter that they had become lascivious gargoyles.

114

Now that Geena was safely out of the picture – it was as if the stage curtains had closed a trifle, so that Lan Yi could no longer see the bed in which his wife lay – the sculptor was able to re-attack the marble. This time he was less gentle, although every now and then he struck quietly for a minute or so, looking over his shoulder off-stage at his wife, clearly trying not to wake her up. He was now dressed in an SSIA jumpsuit, which seemed appropriate, although Lan Yi was uncertain why this should be so.

Chips of rock flew. Lan Yi knew that he was using the hammer and chisel without any clear purpose in mind: he was simply letting the tools carve out the form that the stone contained within it. Behind him, the audience watched in fascination, assuming that he knew what he was doing.

He turned suddenly towards them.

'This is the greatest creation of my life,' he said.

There was a hush, even from himself.

'No, the greatest creation of my life is asleep now,' he cried, his voice clearly audible all the way to the back of the auditorium.

One of the mice slinked back on-stage. The sculptor looked at her, seeing the way that her dark eyes were looking at him. She was slender, but all he could really see of her were those eyes.

'There is a greater creation,' said the mouse.

'I must find the nature of the rock,' he said, turning away from her.

When, seconds later, hammer raised, he glanced over his shoulder he saw that she was no longer there.

Touch, thought Lan Yi. *All I have to do is touch the marble to make it unfold itself. There is no need to strike it hard.*

The blow of his hammer against the tail of his chisel was almost a caress, but a section of marble fell away. As it dropped towards the stage it evaporated, becoming a cloud of steam that swiftly dissipated.

The same happened the next time the hammer kissed the chisel. The marble seemed to be trying to melt away to show the audience its own trueness.

There was a curve which he recognized. A complex curve. The upper left shoulder of a cello, with the sharp in-tuck underneath. Someone once lovingly saw a pregnant woman and created the cello in her likeness.

From a distance, Lan Yi knew a dreadful inevitability about what was going to be exposed. Where he was on the stage, however, it was still largely a mystery. He was a player in a game that it seemed he had created himself. He looked off towards the wings, hoping to see Geena there, but there was nothing but an overwhelming feeling of sad emptiness.

He threw the hammer towards one side of the stage and the chisel to the other, then turned to bow to the audience.

The performance was over.

The audience booed him loudly.

He was booing himself.

What should he do? Juggle with sharp knives?

No, he had simply been teasing those who had come to watch him. Assistants tossed back the hammer and the chisel from the wings, and he rapidly used the tools to reveal what the stone wanted him to reveal: the left buttock of a cello with, wrapped around it as if in a position of love, a human leg.

Lan Yi turned his face away. He remembered this. It was all too painful. Then he remembered again: there was the love which would not die.

The chisel made another polite incision. And another, and another.

Had this been a holo, no one would have lifted an eyebrow, but it was all live theatre. Here, in front of the audience, Lan Yi was apparently creating life from a lump of stone. Earlier in the play Geena, most beautifully naked, had played a movement from Dorgy's Cello Sonata Number One, her body

116

mimicking the instrument to which it seemed she was making love. Now the sculptor was making love to the chunk of marble by allowing it to emerge as itself.

At last he was finished.

There, perfect in every respect, was the naked cellist with her instrument.

Lan Yi found himself clapping his hands and standing. He was certainly not the only one.

But then the applause petered out.

The magic had not been entire.

All that the sculptor had created was a statue. The marble woman was entirely still, her bow half-drawn across the strings of her cello making a note or a chord which would never be heard. Her eyes were sightless – even the sculptor himself saw the cold stone of them. He touched her arm, as if in some way he could coax her into life by doing so, but all he felt was the chilly smoothness his chisel had discovered, not the soft hairs he had delighted in licking the wrong way until Geena had woken up, laughed in annoyance and kissed him.

Lan Yi, in the audience and waiting for his otherself to per-form a new *trompe l'oeil*, remembered that his dream was a story. Sometimes he had licked the soft hairs of Geena's arms as she slept. He had always done so with great care after the first time he had woken her up through clumsiness.

Now the magician – who was Lan Yi and who was also someone distant, performing on a stage – was taking another bow to the audience.

The silence was profound.

The magician took a step backward.

Suddenly it was as if he were surrounded by snow. Small pieces of white marble flew up from the surface of the stage and formed a cloud around him. He moved his hands among them affectionately, his fingers stroking as if he were trying to tell each and every flake that it was individually adored. In response – and Lan Yi could feel this as if it were happening to

117

himself, which of course it was – the flakes clustered on to the skin of the magician, who was once again naked.

The chips of rock bound together all over him. They were cold at first, but then he began to feel the warmth of their embrace. The magician had performed his ultimate magic, but could no longer bend himself towards his audience. Even when the real Geena – not the one he had released from the stone – came to the front of the stage and put a hand on the head of her motionless simulacrum, he could make no move.

He was imprisoned, yet he felt no resentment.

Geena must have felt resentment. The marble statue of her that he had created was still entirely motionless, even though various members of the audience were now beginning to throw flowers at it.

He had made her into a statue, and now he was himself becoming one. Was this her revenge on him?

No, it was his own.

Silicate crystals were forming in front of his eyes, the last part of him not to be covered. He welcomed the blindness – for he was a magician, and preferred the dark.

He tried to raise his left arm, but could not. All that he succeeded in doing was to produce a small rain of silvery dust on the stage.

Geena, her back to him as she stretched her arms to the riotous audience (and her front to him as he stood, in his other-self, applauding her), saw nothing of this.

It is the goal, thought Lan Yi, *of the sculptor to become the sculpture.*

This thought seemed very important to him in the first minute or so as he woke up. Then it seemed utter nonsense – as all of the most forceful messages from dreams are. A few moments later, however, he realized what he had done to Geena.

He hoped that, for the rest of eternity, she would still be accepting the applause.

4

Gadflying About is Good for the Gad

Strider thought into the Pocket that she wanted to be within striking distance of Alterifer, and there was a short pause while the Images translated this instruction. She wanted herself *and her armada* to be within striking distance of Alterifer. There was a subtle distinction. Pinocchio explained it to her, and she swore at him in affectionate fashion.

The tachyon drive didn't produce the usual disconcerting effect in her stomach, bowels and mind. She was a Lingk-kreatzai, as were all the other Humans on board the *Midnight Ranger*. She had made the request of Hein and he in turn had made it of the Onurg. If the Pridehouse and the Lingk-kreatzai could transform Humans for purposes of decontamination into simulations of their own kind, surely they could do it for other reasons, she had suggested to Hein. He had agreed, so now she was a not-quite-Human. At least she still *felt* like a Human.

They were in free fall, hanging relatively motionless in space. Alterifer was the nearest visible celestial body; its sun must be somewhere behind them, because it wasn't visible through the view-window. Strider thought about cutting in the gravity simulators, but decided to postpone that – at the moment she was enjoying the release from the burden of her own weight. The planet reminded her of Jupiter, but some-how it seemed even more massive. It had the same overall reddish hue and the same banding. The bands, however, were much more disrupted than those on Jupiter: their edges frayed into each other, and Strider was certain that, even as she watched them, those edges were changing their configuration. If Jupiter was a planet that fell only just short, through its mass, of becoming a star, Alterifer was a planet that could feel cheated. In a few million years' time it might collapse in on itself and blaze its glorious birth. Or it could do exactly this tomorrow.

Best for the fleet not to hang around too long. Best to go for the attack right now.

But how?

She thought again into the Pocket and expanded the image of the innermost moon. What had been a tiny mote of light became a world in its own right. It was largely a world of ice, she could see, although there were also rocky craters on its surface. Behind the visual display, graphics were rattling off a brief geological history and diagnosis of the moon, but Strider paid them no attention.

She shivered. The moon looked cold – colder by far than her own home world, which right now she regarded as Lingk.

Of course it was cold. It was as cold as the vacuum of space. She shook her head in irritation at herself, and the display in the Pocket jolted around as if, she thought, she were a veritable shaker of universes.

When things had stilled she concentrated her attention on the graphical display behind the visual one.

Kaantalech's base, if indeed this was Kaantalech's base, was lightly guarded. The putative heir to the throne of the Autarchy either thought she was secure from discovery or assumed that discretion was the best part of valour. According to the graphics display in front of Strider there were no more than half a dozen warcruisers around the moon. They were in tight orbit: there was no evidence from their trajectories that they had yet detected her own vast fleet, scant lightseconds away in the hinterlands of Alterifer's lunar system.

This worried her.

She pulled her face from the Pocket and spoke to Hein. 'They should have spotted us by now.'

'They haven't.'

'They should have, I say. It worries me. Are they playing dumb deliberately?'

He gave her a typical Pridehouse laugh. 'How should I know? We'll find out soon enough.'

'Look, buster, finding out won't offer much philosophical satisfaction if we're dead by then.'

The cat came up and wrapped herself around Strider's ankles, mewling to be fed. Loki had already been fed, just a few minutes ago. Strider resisted the urge to kick her away. She raised a palm to Hein, indicating that she was not speaking to him, and said: 'Tenper. Pinocchio. Either of you. Get Hilary up here on deck. He's got a duty to do.'

Pinocchio answered. WE SHALL DO YOUR WISHES, OH MIGHTY ONE.

'Less sarcasm from you.'

She had other things to worry about than the blasted cat, and yet somehow the welfare of the animal came first. Maybe this was what distinguished her from Kaantalech – maybe it was the only thing.

Strider sat down. She could feel her brow wrinkling as she focused her eyes on something that wasn't there. She reached a hand idly to stroke the back of Loki's neck.

'I can't believe she doesn't have full defences,' Strider said.

'I can't believe it either,' said Hein, 'but there's only the one way to find out.'

'To attack?'

'It's known technically as "testing to destruction".'

'Yeah, but whose destruction?'

'The answer to that question solves the problem.' He took a couple of paces towards her, then stopped, visibly aware that she didn't want him close to her.

'I want us out of this,' said Strider.

121

'What do you mean?'

'I think Kaantalech has baited a trap.'

'She may be concerned more about the Helgiolath, and have forgotten us. Forgotten you, rather.' Hein shrugged. 'She has no reason to know that we and the Lingk-kreatzai are with you.'

'We're only a few light-seconds away from her. She *must* know we're here.' She tugged at her hair as if somehow that would help her think. It was the old question: flight or fight. The Pridehouse, to judge by Hein's behaviour, didn't possess this peculiarly confusing double instinct. Her mood was towards flight.

'We're leaving,' she said abruptly.

'But we've only just got here.'

'I know. But I have a bad feeling about Alterifer. There's something wrong.'

'We may never have a better chance to strike directly at Kaantalech.' The habitual smile had vanished from Hein's face and there was, unusually, a note of truculence in his voice.

'Is Tenper about?' she said, again raising her hand to Hein.

I AM HERE. Sometimes it was hard to tell the Images' voices apart, but not now. Pinocchio had once sounded unique in her mind, but he was swiftly receding into what she could only think of as Imagehood. She wondered what he thought of himself. His consciousness had been not born but created by humanity in its own image, in the first place, but then he had been re-created as something quite alien to the Human species. There was still occasionally a tinge of affection for her in his voice as he sang to her, but always she knew that the distance between them was increasing.

I WOULD ADVISE RETREAT, said Ten Per Cent Extra Free. I HAVE TRIED TO PENETRATE THE PSYCHIC DEFENCES OF KAANTALECH'S SURROUNDINGS, AND HAVE BEEN UNABLE TO DO SO. I HAVE TRIED TO THINK THOUGHTS WITH NIGHTMIRROR, WHO IS LODGED AT THE HEART OF KAANTALECH'S FLEET, AND

THIS TOO I HAVE BEEN UNABLE TO DO. THERE IS A PROFOUND WRONGNESS HERE.

They discovered the nature of the wrongness about one second later.

Alterifer disappeared from the view-window. The *Midnight Ranger* – and, Strider assumed, the rest of her fleet – was heading directly towards the photosphere of a blue giant star. All she could see through the view-window was incandescence, and she put up her hands against her eyes to blot out the sight. She staggered to the Pocket in front of her, and ordered it to give her a few moments of darkness. Then, opening her eyes reluctantly, she saw what was really happening.

The shock of the Shift hit different people in different ways.

Maria Strauss-Giolitto was working out. She was stretching to her tallest, straining her arms upwards until her shoulder muscles hurt, and then stretching down, her elbows brushing her thighputer, to touch her feet. She rather liked her feet. Her toes were elegant and long. Her ankles could have been better, but on the whole they weren't bad. Many years ago she had had her toenails surgically removed: it had been a cosmetic exercise which she rarely regretted. As she touched her toes now she saw them as little blind serpents, moving of their own volition. She stretched upwards again, and had the glorious feeling that she was infinitely tall. Perhaps this time, this time, she could touch the ceiling of her cabin, press her hands against it so that she was fully occupying her living space, but still a few centimetres of empty air intervened.

Maybe with her next try.

She doubled over again to grasp hold of her feet, and this time she stayed in position, enjoying the experience of her back muscles being fully extended. She raised her head, keeping her hands where they were, and looked at the edge of her bunk – when creating the *Midnight Ranger* the Bredai had not thought to manufacture forcefield bunks, a source of regret to

123

Strauss-Giolitto because physical contact with her bed made it difficult for her to find sleep.

She straightened up again and reached once more towards the ceiling. Now she could see the tips of her fingers touching it, but she could feel nothing. There was an oddly milky quality to her arms and hands, and for a moment she thought they belonged to someone else.

Strauss-Giolitto, slowly lowering her arms to her sides and relaxing from tiptoes, looked down in front of her.

There was her own back, each of her vertebrae clearly visible as she posed in a position that, Strauss-Giolitto realized for the first time, was distinctly undignified. She was joined at the waist to a self that was still bent double. She put out a hand nervously, still too confused to be frightened, and touched the shoulder of this other person.

She felt the soft pressure of her own fingers on her shoulder.

But this was all wrong. She looked at her hand as if in some way this was all its fault, then stroked the shoulder of the bent-over woman – herself, because she recognized the mole which she had never had surgically removed after a lover named Iolanthe had once said that it was the thing about Strauss-Giolitto's body that most turned her on. Although she was still upright, she felt the caressing touch on her shoulder.

She was a Christian, and part of her faith was that the soul was immortal, destined for either Heaven or Hell after the death of the body. Was this what was happening to her? Had she died in that curiously embarrassing posture?

It was unlikely. She was also an Artif, and had had a fresh heart installed not long before the *Santa Maria* had left the Solar System. Nothing else but heart failure could have killed her with such immediacy. Anyway, she'd surely have fallen over as she died.

She took a small step backwards, and felt herself pull separate from her own hips.

Still the physical version of herself – the one that was capable of experiencing tactile sensations and transmitting them, somehow, to her mind – was utterly motionless. Strauss-Giolitto realized that her body was no longer breathing – neither of her bodies, if what she was currently inhabiting could properly be called a body. *Statue,* she thought, *of Female Nude in Stance that Will Entice Alike Adolescents and Gentlemen of a Certain Age.*

Now that she could look at it from the outside, she was rather attracted by her own body herself: she could have had a worse one.

She gave the movementless figure a push with the heel of her hand, hoping that it might fall to the side and – she knew this was silly even as she did it – somehow wake up, reabsorbing her soul. She was by now convinced that her consciousness had become a bodiless soul. There was a slight delay in summoning her to the afterlife – that was all. Probably a long queue at the Pearly Gates: so many customers, so little time.

Strauss-Giolitto felt the shove against her side, but her motionless corpse was unaffected; she had the impression that her hand had sunk a few centimetres into that dead flesh before being rebuffed by something. Not the flesh itself: there was still some essence of herself inside the carcase, she assumed, and it had politely rejected her attempted intrusion.

So perhaps I'm not dead yet?

She found herself strangely disappointed. She also found herself scared: death was less frightening than this half-existence.

Strauss-Giolitto moved out into the corridor towards the elevator that would take her to the command deck.

It was only when she was boarding the elevator that she remembered that she had not had to open her cabin door to get here.

'Goddammit, Hilary,' Nelson was saying, 'the square root of minus one is an imaginary number. Can't you get that into your head?'

'If I can imagine it,' the boy said, 'it must be real. Everyone knows that.'

They were seated at the table in Nelson's cabin eating cubes of recycled guck that had been processed to look and taste like something Nelson could never remember having eaten in the first place. The adults aboard the *Midnight Ranger* took turns in furthering Hilary's education, although most of what he learnt came from a thighputer which Nelson had personally detached from the dead Marcial Holmberg – 'Waste not, want not,' he had kept saying to himself grimly as he'd performed the task, but he'd still felt as if he were robbing the dead. Nelson wondered if the boy didn't relate better to the puter than he did to the other people around him, with the possible exception of the cat – who anyway wasn't really 'people'. Still, Strider had determined early on that the lad should be given the benefit of one-to-one teaching, and today Nelson was stuck with it. Actually, he kind of liked the brat, so the job wasn't an onerous one.

Except at times like this, when Hilary got it into his head to be stubborn.

'You're straying out of mathematics into higher philosophy,' said Nelson. 'Interesting subject, but not what we're supposed to be talking about.'

'Mathematics *is* higher philosophy.'

'That's an only partly true statement.'

'Yes, Umbel, but which is the part of it that's true?'

Nelson thought briefly. 'You fed the cat recently?' he said.

'I don't see what that's got to do with it.'

'I do. Go feed her.'

And then suddenly everything was different. Nelson was a small boy looking towards an adult whose eyes were covered by secondary retinal screens. He dropped his gaze and saw his own hands – no, they weren't his own hands, they were Hilary's. One of them was holding a lump of pinkish guck and was somewhat erratically approaching his face. The other

126

was splayed out flat on the table, its little white fingers seeming appallingly thin. He put the piece of guck back down on the plate and flexed both his hands. He dug his fingernails into his palms and felt the pain.

He raised his eyes again.

'Is that you, Hilary?'

'Yeah. This is kind of strange, isn't it?'

Nelson looked at his own face. He'd looked at it many times before – one of the advantages of secondary retinal screens was that you could see yourself as others saw you, and make appropriate adjustments – but he had never before seen it like this. Although the face was adult, its expression was in some indefinable way childish. It was also very unhappy – almost terrified.

Holy hell, but little boy Nelson was going to have to comfort grown-up Hilary.

Nelson got to his feet and came round the table. He put his arm round himself – or, at least, as much of himself as his arm would go round – and squeezed the man-sized child.

'This won't last for long,' he said. 'Whatever's happened to us, it won't last for long.'

'Prove it.' The voice was small and dismal.

'If I believe in it, it must be true.'

'Higher philosophy.'

'Hilary, if you're going to be using my body for a while, could you possibly stop being such a pain in the arse? That's *my* arse you're being a pain in. Let's try and work out what's going on.'

'The trouble is,' said the boy in Nelson's body, 'that I'm not hungry any more, but I still want to eat this stuff.'

'Feel free. Eat as much as you want to.'

'I don't know that I've got room.'

Nelson tightened his grasp.

'Look, buddy, I've had a lot more experience of my body than you have, and there's always a bit of extra room. Fill it up.

127

Make yourself – myself – kinell, who knows whose self it might be? – as sick as you want it to be.'

'I don't like this. I want to be myself again.'

'You *are* yourself, Hilary, kiddo. It's just that you're in a different body.'

Nelson wasn't sure that he believed this. He himself was finding it difficult to adjust to being in a child's body – as if his smallness should make him somehow subservient to those who were bigger than him, while at the same he was having to guide Hilary through the stormy straits. Shit, but what he needed to do was to get to the command deck and find out what was going on. Yet that somehow seemed less important to him, right now, than comforting the boy.

'I am what I am,' said Hilary.

'Yeah, that's a bit of higher philosophy as well,' said Nelson. 'And you think therefore you are. What you are is Hilary. Just remember that: the thinking is the important bit. And don't get frightened. This can't last long.'

'You sure?'

'Sure I'm sure,' lied Nelson. 'Now I want us to get to the command deck. Want to come?'

'OK.'

He knew it was spiteful, but the enlarged Segrill gave the cat an uppercut to the jaw before retreating towards the command deck, closing the door behind him with some difficulty.

The cat, spitting with fear, was now hiding behind his holo-jector.

It felt good to be this tall – forty centimetres or more – but he didn't know how long it would last. That depended on where Kaantalech's defences had Shifted them. Loki was not too bright, and probably wouldn't remember for more than a few minutes what he had done to her, but he wanted to be out of her way for a good long while in case he reverted to his true form sooner than he expected.

He hadn't even realized the cat was there until a few moments before the transition. As soon as he had he'd taken to wing, which always infuriated Loki. She had a habit of stalking him and then just . . . watching, waiting for the right moment to pounce. Almost always he'd detected her in time, but the one time she'd caught him unawares he'd saved his life only by using a stunbeam on her. Some day soon he was going to use something more lethal and make himself very unpopular with the Humans in the crew, notably Hilary.

He'd been high up in his cabin when the Shift had come. The transition into miniature Human form had come as a shock, and it was a matter of sheer luck that he had been directly over the full-Human-size bunk the Bredai had provided for him. It had been more of a shock for the cat, though.

Segrill shook his right hand as he walked towards the elevator. There were disadvantages to giving cats uppercuts, it seemed.

A ghost appeared ahead of him and he recognized it as the Strauss-Giolitto woman. He trotted towards her, shouting her name.

She heard the sound, and turned to look at him. It was obvious from her face that she understood nothing of what he was saying.

Ah: a problem. The Images seemed to be out of commission. Segrill hoped they hadn't been Shifted to somewhere else entirely, somewhere remotely distant from the *Midnight Ranger*. This could be difficult. He was almost certainly the only person here who understood Shifting – he had become acquainted with its technology back on Preeae, the Autarchy's primary munitions factory-planet. His job had been security, and it had been hard – although it was strictly forbidden – *not* to pick up bits and pieces about the various gadgetries being developed and manufactured there. How was he going to explain to the others what was going on if he couldn't speak to them?

The ghost of Strauss-Giolitto tried to put her hand on his head, as if he were some kind of pet. No: he shouldn't think so resentfully as that, because she was trying to be affectionate, indicating friendship to him. He smiled up at her, finding it odd that a smile involved a movement of the mouth.

Her hand passed through him.

She didn't smile in return. What he could see of her face was largely the red elevator door behind her – she was almost completely transparent.

He tried to speak to her again, but all he did was make the gauzy face look puzzled. Her lips moved as she responded to him, but he could hear nothing at all.

He shrugged. That, too, was an odd sensation: for some reason his shoulders moved.

The elevator finally arrived, its inside blue and brightly gleaming. The two of them – the miniature man and the ghost – entered it. Segrill looked up at the display of buttons and, with a leap, succeeded in pressing the one that would take them to the command deck.

Ten Per Cent Extra Free found himself and Pinocchio wrapped around the outer skin of The Wondervale, forming a thin sheen that briefly limned the elliptical galaxy in frail colours. It was tempting to stay there – to become new and visible gods – but this was not the way of The Truthfulness.

No sooner thought than done.

The two of them retreated into The Truthfulness, where everything was more natural.

Kaantalech was the vision that both of them uncovered in their joint thought.

She.

Evil.

Done.

Something bad.

Midnight Ranger.

130

Where?

Locate.

Have located.

Rejoin.

Time.

Time?

Pinocchio still retained many of the traits of the culture in which he had been created. *Hours,* he thought to himself, but he could find no way of expressing this to Ten Per Cent Extra Free. *The marker of change in the physical Universe that contains The Wondervale and Heaven's Ancestor and the Milky Way and countless others. That's what time is.*

It was desperately difficult to remember all this when one was in The Truthfulness.

Remembering Strider.

Am remembering.

Allegiance. Loyalty.

Time?

The Wondervale.

Time?

The Wondervale. *There* is time.

Recollection.

Find Strider?

Have found.

Rejoin?

Difficult.

Rejoin!

Try.

Lan Yi was eighteen.

He looked in amazement at his reflection in his cabin mirror. He saw the trimness of his body and the smoothness of his skin, the brightness of both his eyes – for by that age he had not had a secondary retinal screen implanted – the swells of muscle in his arms and legs, but most noticeably the erection that refused to go away: its hardness was almost painful.

He was also amazed by the size of it. He knew as a matter of theory that the genitals slowly dwindled over the years, but it was not something he had ever much thought about because it seemed so unimportant.

By every god that humanity had ever invented, he needed sex – preferably with a woman. Failing that, a sexbot, except that there weren't any sexbots on board the *Midnight Ranger*. He wasn't much attracted to men, but right now he was in the mood to make do. When he found his fantasies turning to the lower mammalian orders he reined them in.

Was this a dream? No: he was certain that he was awake.

He tried to think about solving the problem of what must have happened, but it was extremely difficult to concentrate when your hormones were having the party of their lives.

Lan Yi dimly remembered a lover he had had while at university. She was a trainee nurse, because in those days medibots were still relatively primitive. She – he wished he could recall her name, because he could certainly recall what she looked and felt like – had told him that the way to get rid of an erection was to slap its base smartly with two fingers. She had demonstrated. The technique had been so spectacularly counter-effective that neither of them slept for the next seventeen hours.

He knew that he should be up on the command deck, where the Pockets would assist him in determining what was going on. It was his duty to be there.

It was difficult to think about things like duty. They were abstract in a way that his rampant lust was not. And he most certainly couldn't go to the command deck in this condition: Leonie and Maloron and Maria would be there, not to mention Polyaggle, so that his condition would only intensify.

Maria might well be offended. He loved Maria in an almost sibling fashion, and he didn't want to do anything that might

132

cause her unhappiness. They had shared a bunk several times, stroking and chatting about inconsequentialities, but the purpose of this had been mutual comforting rather than sex: he knew that his maleness distressed her, and that any form of sexual proposal he might make would seem to her incestuous.

Lan Yi didn't know what to do.

He could masturbate, he supposed, but when you're eighteen the detumescent effects don't last very long. He could have a cold shower, but he had a sense that this wouldn't help him much either.

Or he could just tough it out. Maria would just have to look the other way.

That seemed to be the only solution.

He turned from the mirror and with some difficulty climbed into his jumpsuit. His state was going to be all too obvious to everyone, but most of them had seen him like this before, for one reason or another. Well, not quite like *this*, because he'd been about a hundred and twenty years old when the mission had started. There was bound to be some ribbing.

Lan Yi hoped he wouldn't meet anyone on the way to the command deck.

Maloron Leander awoke, but didn't believe that she had. She was the *Midnight Ranger*, and she was being driven through space at nearly infinite velocity towards Heaven's Ancestor by some force which she couldn't understand. She felt the fondlings of countless intergalactic particles against her skin: some were irritating, as if they were fleas crawling on her, but most were deliciously sensitizing. All of them were with her for only the most fleeting of moments. She was reminded of the time she had once been caught in a Martian dust-storm. Luckily she had been wearing a full spacesuit at the time: people caught in one of the storms – it was rare, because meteorology had been one of the first sciences instituted when humanity had begun to colonize Mars, and few were fool enough not to take precautions if there was even the slightest chance of a storm – had been known to be flayed alive by the dust-grains . . . rather slowly, because of the low gravity and thin atmosphere. The dust had scarred her visor so that she could hardly see where she was going, but the constant tugging of the wind-blown particles at her suit had made her feel as if she were being given the perfect and most detailed massage.

She had enjoyed it. Her partner on that particular enterprise – they had been sent out to make an emergency repair to a water extractor, and had had to be prepared to accept the hazard of getting caught in a storm – had found it a nightmare. The repair accomplished, she had virtually had to drag him back to the cabble, then speak sweet nothings to him all the way back to City 81. If she had been given an option, she'd have stayed out there enjoying the storm.

It was the same now. The small annoyances were more than compensated for by the tingles of pleasure.

She could see everything around her – not just the receding Wondervale and the approaching Heaven's Ancestor but also all the other galaxies scattered through this region of space. Within a galaxy one sees stars as jewels across the night sky; between galaxies, as she was now, those jewels are more distant galaxies, and their beauty is even greater.

Besides, it was *good* to be a spaceship.

Especially a spaceship inside which Polyaggle had become the air that people breathed.

Strider and Hein were the two people on the *Midnight Ranger* to remain physically unaffected by the Shift; instead their perceptions were altered. Strider had seen through the view-window that they were hurtling towards a blue giant star, but this hadn't been the truth. At the moment, whenever she pulled her head out of the Pocket, she saw the command deck as a field of short green grass and dandelions, with insects flitting or buzzing

134

about. She preferred to spend most of her time with her head deep inside the Pocket.

The *Midnight Ranger* was moving towards Heaven's Ancestor at a rate which was not tachyonic but which approached that instantaneity. She nodded to dismiss the visuals so that she could better see the graphics. To her left was a symbol that indicated The Wondervale; to her right was another designating Heaven's Ancestor. In between the two was a scumble, rather like the distant sight of an irregular galaxy, which she interpreted as the fleet she led. The scumble was heading towards Heaven's Ancestor, and would reach it in a few minutes.

'Are you there, Pinocchio?' she subvocalized.

There was no reply.

She kept asking the question, over and over again.

Was the *Midnight Ranger* going to stop when it got to Heaven's Ancestor? There was no way of telling. For all she knew, whatever Kaantalech's technology had done to them – and she was by now certain that it was Kaantalech's technology that was responsible for this – could be blasting them to the furthest corner of the Universe, or back to the Big Bang.

There was a whoosh behind her as the door to the command deck opened. She came out of the Pocket and saw Maria Strauss-Giolitto and Segrill walking across the grass towards her. Off to her right, Hein – who seemed to her to have become a centaur, although she had no wish to see his face in case it was something drawn from the more dismal depths of her subconscious – was still conversing with his own Pocket. As soon as the Shift had started she had discovered that they were incapable of communicating with each other.

'Everything that's happening is illusion,' she said to the new arrivals. 'We're going to come through this all right – I promise.'

The ghost of Strauss-Giolitto looked at her in stark disbelief. Segrill chirped something which Strider couldn't understand.

'I'm just seeing you differently. I'm seeing *everything* differently. I guess I must be the same to you. What do you see me as? A crocodile? The monster from outer space?'

'You look to me the way you always look,' said Strauss-Giolitto, or her revenant.

'Then I must be the only goddam thing that does.'

'Hein looks normal, too.'

'He looks pretty unusual to me. The bit of him I can see is the rear end of a horse.'

'No – he's as he always has been.' The ghost of Strauss-Giolitto moved towards one of the chairs and made as if to sit down, but instead paused, her hardly visible hand resting a few centimetres above its back.

'Don't look like it to me.'

Segrill chirped again and scurried across the field. Before Strider could stop him he had clambered up and into the *Midnight Ranger*'s central Pocket.

'He's trying to tell you something,' said Strauss-Giolitto.

'I'd guessed that,' said Strider waspishly.

She moved to the other Pocket and leaned into it. 'Can we speak?' she said.

'Yes,' said Segrill. 'This is the only way of doing it.'

He looked like a tiny Human, but he was crouched in a way that made him seem more like an animal. She suddenly remembered. Fuseli. *The Nightmare*. His small face looked up at hers, and she had difficulty meeting his gaze.

'Kaantalech has Shifted us,' he said.

'Sure has,' Strider replied. 'We're shifting at a rate of knots.'

'What I mean is that she has used a Shift field on us. That's not right – probably we just ran into the Shift field she had erected around her. She probably never even knew we were there. Probably still doesn't know.'

'You mean this is some kind of defence system?'

'Certainly, Leonie. I've heard you say that the best form of

136

defence is attack, but that's not true. The best form of defence is total repulsion – so that the attackers discover themselves several hundreds of thousands of parsecs away. That's what the Shift field does – it *removes* threats.'

'Why didn't you tell me this before?' She wanted to swipe at him, at the same time realizing that her reaction was irrational.

'I've been involved with the development of so many weapons systems that I couldn't tell you about all of them.' He dropped his head, and suddenly her mood turned towards sympathy. 'I knew that this was being developed, but I didn't think the Autarchy would have it up and running by now.'

'How does it work? Is there any way that we can stop this happening to us?'

The door to the command deck susurrated behind her again. The others were arriving. Umbel alone knew what they would look like. She was reluctant to find out.

'I'm not a scientist,' said Segrill. 'My job was security, remember? Most of the things I learnt about I didn't really understand.'

'Tell me what you know. I'm not a scientist either.'

'One of the nuclear forces repels, even though the other attracts.'

'I was told that before I was knee-high,' said Strider. 'Tell me something new.'

'The principle of the Shift field is that it transfers this force from microcosmic to macrocosmic scale. Well, that's as much as I understand, anyway. The thing to be repelled – a ship, a fleet, whatever it might be – becomes like a subatomic particle, while the originator of the field becomes like a nucleus.'

'I don't believe this,' said Strider.

'It's true. What goes on is that the field reduces its environs to atomic size and then expands them again while the repulsion of the weaker force is still at work.' Segrill shuffled around on all fours. 'I told you, I'm not a scientist. All I know is that this is what happens. It makes the perfect defensive shield unless the attackers know what's going on and can work out a way of countering it. Those who are repelled by the Shift field are affected by various psychological and physiological alterations.'

'You don't have to tell me that bit,' said Strider. 'Wait here.'

'There's nowhere I'd rather wait.' Suddenly Segrill looked cold. She put a hand into the Pocket and laid it on his back, letting him absorb her warmth. He looked up at her gratefully.

'I've got to go now,' she said. 'I've got to talk with Lan Yi.'

'Understood,' said Segrill.

She removed herself from the Pocket and gazed at her crew. Much of the grass had died since she had started talking with Segrill, so that they were standing among stuff that looked fertilely brown but at the same time dead.

She recognized them all. That was the great thing. Nelson was a child and Hilary was an adult, but she could see through the disguises that had been thrust upon them to know who they were – she didn't have to try. It was the same with all the others, although presumably Leander and Polyaggle were still to arrive.

She grinned at the shade of Strauss-Giolitto. 'This isn't going to last very long,' she said, using her voice to convey more confidence than she felt. 'I've spoken to Segrill and he's explained to me what's going on. He says that—'

'I wish to speak with Segrill,' said Lan Yi formally, 'and also with the Images.'

'The Images aren't around at the moment.'

'Then at least with the Pockets and Segrill. They could give me considerable information.'

Lan Yi looked like a teenager in heat: she could remember from her own adolescence that there was no experience so mentally painful. Strider didn't know whether to regard him compassionately or not: she might just make things worse for him.

'It's all yours,' she said, gesturing at the Pocket Segrill was occupying.

'I thank you,' Lan Yi said, stepping forward, and she realized he was thanking her for far more than access to the Pockets.

It was kind of nice, for once, to feel older than he was.

Lan Yi felt normality returning only a few moments after he leant into the Pocket. As he watched, Segrill shrank in front of him to become the thumb-sized, bat-winged person they had all come to know. In parallel, Lan Yi felt his adolescent erection ease away; he didn't know whether to be relieved or disappointed – the flush of hormones had been exhilarating.

'It's over,' said Segrill at once. 'Wherever we've been Shifted to, we're there.'

Lan Yi could understand what the Trok was saying, but he could hardly hear his high, shrill voice.

'Louder,' he said.

The Trok iterated unnecessarily, then repeated the explanation he had given to Strider of the workings of the Shift.

'Can the process be countered?' said Lan Yi.

'With difficulty . . . but I don't know how.'

'There must be a way. Can you interact with this Pocket?'

'Partially.'

'Then try to get it to run graphics concerning everything you *do* know about the Shift. Just empty your mind into it.'

Lan Yi didn't have much hope that the idea would work, but to his surprise it did. All around Segrill appeared strings of numbers and symbols; diagrams gave the symbols meanings, but it was going to take him a long time to work out what those meanings were.

Just as Strider had done, Lan Yi put his hand on Segrill.

'Sorry about this,' he said, 'but I am afraid I must ask you to remain here for quite a while.'

Despite the species difference, he was able to recognize that Segrill was looking miserable.

'I'll be as quick as I can,' said Lan Yi, and then he was lost in a maze of questioning and inference, and could no longer see the Trok. They were in the galaxy called Heaven's Ancestor: he took that as a given. He briefly flashed up the visuals to check, knowing as he did so that it was unnecessary; at the edge of the Pocket, off to the left, The Wondervale showed as a hot glow. Banishing the visuals, he concentrated once more on the equations.

Most of them were redundant – they related to other military developments that Segrill had observed on F-14, some of which interested Lan Yi considerably: at some later stage he would lure his little friend back into the Pocket so that he could examine this stuff in more detail. Now, however, with waves of thought he moved it away until all that he was left with were data concerning the Shift. He related the diagrams to the equations, annoyed with himself that he found it so very difficult to do so.

But at last things began to make sense: every time he reached a new understanding, others cascaded swiftly, as if he were touching one small rock and causing a landslide. Unfortunately everything had been worked out in hexadecimal: he had used hexadecimal a few times decades ago, as a student, just for the mental exercise; now, older, he found it difficult to force his less flexible mind into analysing equations with the 'wrong' numerical base.

The trouble was that he was accustomed to hearing numbers moving through his mind as if they were music. Working in hexadecimal was like listening to someone playing an out-of-tune pianobot: there were discords everywhere, so that the mathematics seemed to him almost like physical pain.

Music.

Now there was a thought. Start thinking of all this as if it were an experimental composition. Lan Yi preferred early music – Bach, Beethoven, Mozart, Ochs – but he was not unreceptive to some of the more recent composers, up to and

140

even including, albeit very rarely, the randomusic that Strauss-Giolitto had used to play him from her musibot, back in the days when they had both been in the *Santa Maria*.

He imagined that the equations were a piece of modern music being picked out on a harpsichord; though he had never in fact seen a harpsichord, it was one of his favourite instruments. The notes didn't sound at all right. Of course, harpsichords weren't tuned to the musical equivalent of hexadecimal. He tried to think of a few other instruments – a fretless guitar, a hyperflute, a zammarany – but had at last, ignominiously, to settle for Strauss-Giolitto's musibot. One of the few things he had been glad to see depart with the *Santa Maria* was Strauss-Giolitto's damned musibot.

But it was one of those rare occasions when the bot served him. He could hear its tinny tinkling in his mind, and suddenly the equations became utterly clear. Sometimes he shut his eyes in between reading them, so that he could listen to them more carefully.

And music took him further.

There is no single way of observing the Universe.

Turn that round.

The entity that is the Universe has an infinity of aspects, of ways of being looked at. By technological species it is almost always observed as a chillingly beautiful construct of galaxies and energy exchanges and distance.

In the Human species' own primordial past, the talking primates had been very little, if at all, less nascently intelligent than Lan Yi himself, yet they had seen the Universe as a tiny machine with the Earth at its centre, the planets of the Solar System playing music as they made their approximately diurnal circles. Other thinking species must have other perceptions.

This was the sudden understanding that had come to Lan Yi.

Stop *looking* for explanations. Start *listening* for them. Start *listening* if you want to observe the nature of the Universe, the way it works – not the *exclusive* way, but an aspect that is just as *true* as the one that you have always observed before. Try to throw away all the cultural baggage that is forcing you to think of those bright points of light and let your mind roam across the other possible aspects of the Universe until you find the one that corresponds to a musibot playing a hexadecimal piece of randomusic that somehow makes a harmony where a harpsichord was unable to.

Lan Yi, eyes shut tight, heard the truth of the way that the Universe works. There are myriad such truths, he recognized again, and *all of them are true*. The truth that he listened to was the one that was being spelled out by the equations displayed in the Pocket. At first he had had to read them; now he wouldn't have been able to, even had he tried. In all the splendour of their transparent comprehensibility they were flowing into him, vibrating in his inner ears, channelled there from the tingling of his palms.

He was sailing far off the edge of the map of humanity's science. Here Be No Baryons.

What he saw – heard – was that the Universe is a single vibrating string, and that all events and energies and material objects and ideas have their place on the string. Their *perfect* place, as otherwise the vibration of the string – he thought of it as a cello string – would be disrupted, so that the soft, truthful note of the Universe would become fractured until eventually the vibration died and the note with it.

It wasn't anything as simple as the time-flow from the Universe's birth to its death being represented as a string, he realized.

The Universe *was* the string.

The string *was* the Universe.

All the dimensions that existed in humankind's perception of the Universe existed in this single, thrumming string. All the galaxies, all the individual consciousnesses: everything. But one couldn't run one's finger along the string and think that

142

this happened and then that happened and then that. Causality had to be thrown out: the cause of event A could be at the far end of the string from the cause of what succeeded event A. The bit of the Universe that was Qitanefermeartha might have been entirely distant along the string from the people that came to destroy it. There was no order along the path of the Universe-string except the order of the single, long note.

An eternal note. When it stopped, as it would, there would be just nothing.

Once again.

Before the note started playing – before the bow stroked the string of the cello – there had been nothing. Yet even that was a simplification of the truth that he was hearing: there was no 'before' or 'after' in the Universe-string – just a condition of *being*.

Everything had to be in its correct place, or the beingness of the Universe would be threatened.

This could not be tolerated by the Universe which, while lacking sentience, was concerned – compelled – to protect the perfection of the note that it sounded.

And it *was* perfection. Lan Yi, who had so resisted earlier what he had regarded as a mindless din, was filled with the ecstasy of that perfection. The hexadecimals had converged to create the single note of truth.

What the Shift field had done was to persuade the Universe that Strider's fleet, and the *Midnight Ranger*, were on the wrong part of the string. The Universe had responded, as it *had* to if it were to preserve itself, by moving them. They had become a different part of the eternal vibration.

He opened his eyes, and with a whip of thought re-created the visual display in the Pocket.

Segrill cowered off to the side of the representation of Heaven's Ancestor. The position near its edge of the Pridehouse and Lingk-kreatzai fleet was indicated by a small and curiously irritating flicker of red light.

We could be anywhere, thought Lan Yi. *We could even be anywhen.*

Even though his eyes were open, he could still feel and hear the throb of the string that was the Universe. It was something that he knew he would never be able to forget. He had always known that there might be many realities, and he had experienced several since the *Santa Maria* had boosted out of Jovian orbit, but he'd never before appreciated that some of those realities could be profound, could be utter, could be *the* truth – because all truths are *the* truth.

He wondered if anyone among the Pridehouse had been able to interpret this aspect of the Universe. He thought it unlikely: the Pridehouse, like the Humans, were material creatures. Had it not been for the coincidence of the Pocket with his own mood – for moods, too, have locations along the Universe-string – at exactly the right time, the new perception would never have come to him.

He pulled his head from the Pocket. 'We have been moved by the Universe by a single harmonic,' he said to Strider.

She looked at him strangely. 'Have you been staying up late at nights?' she said with all outward appearances of sympathy.

He shook his head. 'It's a little hard to explain, Leonie, but I think I know how we can get us – all of us – back to The Wondervale. But it is my belief that now is not the right time to try it. I have had an insight which I think is a very valuable one, but I cannot follow it any further at the moment now.' He was aware that his Argot was beginning to become stilted: he was finding it unwieldy as a means of communication, as he always did when he was exhausted or nervous or both. 'Tired. I am tired. I must for a while lie down in my darkened cabin, and think of what I have done . . . have discovered, have insighted. There is nothing we can do at the moment – nothing we *need* to do. Better we wait until I have examined the full implications of all this.'

144

He moved wearily towards the 'lock that led to the rear of the *Midnight Ranger*.

'Please tell the Onurg that we have been moved by the Universe by a single harmonic,' he added, pausing there. 'Some among the Pridehouse may understand what this means.'

He could see her seeing the fatigue in his eyes.

'Try them,' he said. 'They are an ancient species, and may have encountered this before. At the moment I feel I am a very ancient member of a very youthful species. I am not looking forward to the task that awaits me – you understand?'

'I hear what you're saying,' said Strider, wondering if she did.

Danny O'Sondheim could hardly believe his luck. The Images had told him there was a chance of finding the wormhole that had brought them into The Wondervale and getting the *Santa Maria* back to the Milky Way, and Strider had told him that he must make the attempt, but he'd never quite believed it would happen. He'd been going through the motions. Performing his duty as First Officer. Pretending – if he were honest with himself – to be a person he wasn't, or hadn't been until Strider had passed over the acting captaincy of the *Santa Maria* to him.

He tapped his thighputer to call up relevant data. It was one thing being back in the Milky Way, quite another knowing exactly where you *were*.

Although O'Sondheim was aware that Heartfire and Angler were still connected with the ship, he didn't want to rely on them. The Pockets were ahead of him on the command deck, but they had gained an insubstantiality that worried him. Maybe it was the case that the Images could not survive in the Milky Way. He didn't quite believe this – there seemed to be no reason why the Images couldn't manifest themselves anywhere within the material Universe – but he wasn't prepared to bet the lives of his personnel on his being right.

Strider probably would have.

Every time he thought of Strider it hurt.

Both of them had been, in separate ways, ugly ducklings, but she was the one who had turned into a swan, leaving him paddling his little feet in a river whose water ran too fast for him to have full control over where he was going. She learnt quickly how to control herself in the current; only recently had he learnt to do so.

He had lusted for her: he was honest enough with himself to admit that. But behind the lust there had been something else which, as the *Santa Maria* had found itself back in the Milky Way and he had started to search out with his thighputer stellar configurations that might give him guidance back home to the Sun, he had begun to think was possibly love.

The word 'love' was not part of O'Sondheim's standard mental vocabulary. 'Friendship' was another difficult one for him. People shared warmth and jokes and kisses and caresses and finally sex because all that was happening was that their genes wanted to replicate themselves. OK, so the people might have luck enough to have a bit of fun along the way, but the basis of it all was the perpetuation of their genes. Love was just a delusion: something the Human species had invented to make the whole reproductive process a bit more respectable.

Yet now, as his thighputer displayed further useless data, still searching for the Solar System, he wished that Strider were on the command deck nearby. That was all he wished for – that and the possibility of being able to look up and see her smile back at him.

Bright teeth. Brown eyes. Nearly black face.

A friend.

Yes, that's what she'd been: a friend, the truest of friends. Almost a sister, really. O'Sondheim had few remaining illusions about himself: he had been very unpopular among the *Santa Maria*'s personnel from the time the ship had left the Solar System until it had re-entered the Milky Way. He had been swaggering around, an aged adolescent, the worst kind – trying to pretend to be an Alpha Male. He had thought that he'd wanted Strider's cunt – because that would be a victory of sorts – when all he'd really wanted had been her arm around his shoulder and a peck of a kiss on each other's noses. Yes, having sex with her would have been good as well, but it wouldn't have been the important part. He rethought. 'Having sex' with her would have been lousy; making love with her would have been fine.

He rattled his fingers on the thighputer again, trying a different combination. The thighputer would, if left to itself, work out the location of the Solar System in due course; the trouble was that it might be very unlucky in its algorithms and not hit the solution until some time after the Universe had ended.

Blind luck was not enough, which was why O'Sondheim was giving the thighputer hints.

'Forget all the blue giants,' he was saying to it, a statement that came out as !♥ ⊣| on the display.

'WHY?' said the puter's display bleakly, as if he had let it down.

O'Sondheim thought about patiently telling the thighputer that blue giants were young stars and that the Sun wasn't one of them: it was the sort of innocuous star that tended to have planets and didn't hurl so much hard radiation at them that life never got a chance of starting.

He thought about this.

He thought for perhaps a second.

What he finally tapped into the puter was: 'BECAUSE I TELL YOU TO.'

Guide me.

Ten Per Cent Extra Free's thought was a very weak disturbance in Pinocchio's consciousness, but he heard it clearly enough. How could he be a guide? Although he had accustomed himself to being an Image in many ways, this condition of existence was not instinctive to him. As a bot which had been programmed for inquisitiveness, he wanted to explore The Truthfulness; as the Real Boy he believed himself to have become, he wanted to return to Strider; as an Image, he sensed always that he was the mere apprentice who shouldn't be out of the sorcerer's sight too often in case he fouled up, and yet here was Ten Per Cent Extra Free asking him to translate them both from a condition Pinocchio didn't really understand back to the solid reality of the Universe. *That* Universe. The one in which Pinocchio had been manufactured.

He felt as if he had been dissolved into The Truthfulness, as if he were salt that had been stirred into warm water. It was difficult to make a string of rational logic out of his thought processes. Other times – although 'time' had become an increasingly difficult concept to keep a grasp on – he saw himself as a particle in a lava flow, indistinguishable from the rest.

Try guide.

There was a rush of gratitude from Ten Per Cent Extra Free.

Strider.

Think of Strider. That was the best thing to do, Pinocchio decided, not knowing whether or not it was a daft decision. His first resort was an attempt to call up her personal details on his internal data display units, but of course that didn't work: no longer a bot, he no longer had any internal data display units.

Try thinking about her as a person, not just as a name and a picture and a collection of data. She is, instead, a concentration of mental and emotional activity that sums itself up as Strider. Forget the limbs and the organs.

Pinocchio felt as if he were struggling to understand the way that the Images moved themselves from one reality into another, yet Ten Per Cent Extra Free had indicated – in that single, pleading thought – that he was having even more difficulty rationalizing the situation into which Kaantalech's Shift had placed them. Perhaps here was a time when the apprentice, through his stark ignorance, was better able to cope than the wise old sorcerer – a time when it was the sorcerer who needed help to stop the water from cascading.

Not the easiest person to get on with, Strider. She wasn't as bad as Maria had once been, with her petty biases and outspoken ('outspoken' in the sense of 'offensive') opinions. Strider did what she wanted to do, most of the time. It was one of the things that Pinocchio most liked about her. But on occasion she was vulnerable. He liked that as well. He remembered the time when the two of them had walked under the Martian moons. They had been, in ways that were so different that they could hardly be compared, equally vulnerable, equally afraid of the adventure in which they were both about to partake, yet it was then that they had discovered their liking for each other. Or was that true? Strider, he knew, had begun to feel affection for him. But in those days he had still been fighting to comprehend human emotions. He had known that he owed her loyalty, but his cold mind had not fully fathomed why. His software had told him that this was his duty.

Picture Strider.

Something of the entity he had now become was telling him that there was another of the Human-things that was doing the same.

O'Sondheim!

Yes, Pinocchio could key into O'Sondheim, and the way the man was thinking. It wasn't what he wanted to do, because he'd always held O'Sondheim in a discreet contempt, and besides the man was in the wrong part of the Universe, but at least it was a link in the chain that led back there. O'Sondheim's thoughts were so strong – *too* strong – that now he had locked on to them Pinocchio was finding difficulty in abandoning them.

He felt himself as a flood, a flood that was being forced to run down a particular channel that it had not chosen.

Going back there.

Ten Per Cent Extra Free's thought was rather sad. Must we?

I must.

Why?

Love Strider.

Foolish.

True.

Be a part of you?

Always. Known by you.

She legal?

On prescription.

Pinocchio reached out through the moils of consciousness and grabbed Ten Per Cent Extra Free, not letting the other Image fade away from his mental imagery, as he seemed to want to do. Pinocchio felt as if he were clutching a hand. They slipped back through the tiny film that separated The Truthfulness from the physical reality in which Strider dwelt. For a few seconds they found themselves in The Wondervale, but then they were streaking towards Heaven's Ancestor.

Pinocchio felt as if he were being painted across the sky, like a bright line slashed by an artist's brush across a black background.

WE ARE YOUR SERVANTS, said Ten Per Cent Extra Free to the Humans, the Pridehouse and the Lingk-kreatzai alike.

'About bloody time,' came a response.

Strider, thought Pinocchio to Ten Per Cent Extra Free. Still alive.

The answering thought was: Mistake difficult.

They could if they wanted fight against the Shift field, thought the Onurg, but it would be a waste of time. Once Lan Yi had explained to him the nature of the device the Onurg recognized this. The Pridehouse had no tradition of music, so it had been difficult to understand Lan Yi's explanation, but finally the Onurg had been able to reposition, as it were, the ideas in his mind. Look at the Universe as a spectrum of colours, running all the way from inder to birep and possibly to longer and shorter wavelengths than either of those, and then one could visualize the colour that had performed the Shift. That visualization completed, it was easy to understand the principles of the Shift field . . . and as easy to understand why there was no use fighting against it, at least not for an amount of time that could be calculated as a function of the one true colour.

Lan Yi had told him as much, except he was talking in terms of the one true note.

It had been a very confusing conversation until it approached its end, when each of them had been able to work out what the other was talking about.

Life was everywhere, and life it was that coloured the Universe – not in the way that stars did, or the clouds of gas that lay between the stars, but in a manner that the Onurg could understand when he looked slantwise at reality. As soon as he came to comprehend Lan Yi's explanation in terms of harmonics, this slantwise attitude to physics became almost second nature to him. Yes. The Universe was constructed of colours, some of which harmonized and some of which clashed. If one could only *see* the tapestry formed by the colours, then so very much else became plain.

The Shift field was an evil thing, the Onurg concluded. After the Autarchy had been demolished, the Shift – even its very possibility – should be removed. In the meantime, however, its consequences would have to be endured.

He trotted away from his Pocket to rub muzzles with Seragarda, his favourite current lover. She was very beautiful, her coat a mass of burnished brown. Now she wasn't in the mood for him, however: she touched tongues with him, but he could see that her mind was elsewhere. She was thinking about one of her other lovers.

His jaws dropped open in a grin.

She was happy. The reason that he loved her was that all he cared about was her happiness. He did a back-flip, landing with confidence on all six feet, to explain this to her in a way that was more profound than words. He put his right forefoot on her shoulder.

'We're in Heaven's Ancestor,' he said. 'Never thought our species would make it there again until long after I was dead.'

The two laughed together. He removed his right forefoot, and they rubbed muzzles once more.

'How long shall we remain in Heaven's Ancestor?' she asked.

'I don't know. Possibly forever.'

'I can't believe that.'

'I can. Kaantalech has used a field to Shift us. I don't think we can fight against it.'

Seragarda made a snorting noise, then suddenly touched her tongue to his. He was almost disappointed. She had wanted to be with a different lover, but now, out of some sort of sympathy, she wanted to be with him.

'I need to speak again with Lan Yi,' he said.

He felt her sexual attractiveness like a paw on his head as he left her and returned to the Pocket: his close contact had aroused her, he knew, and he would have liked to have been the one to satisfy her arousal, for she was indeed very lovely.

The first face to appear in the Pocket was that of the Human creature called Maloron Leander. In his perception she had only one eye, the other being covered by a silver rectangle. How, how, how could the Humans communicate without a snout eye?

'Lan Yi,' he said, his tongue lolling. 'I wish to talk to him.'

She gave him the facial grimace which he now knew to be a Human smile.

'He's here.'

A moment later the Onurg was looking at Lan Yi. There was moistness in the Human's eyes.

152

'Do your people have such a thing as exhaustion?' said the Human. One or other of the Images translated the concept.

'Of course,' said the Onurg.

'Well, that is what I am feeling at the moment.'

'You have my sympathies. But I want to talk with you for a few nanreets.'

Lan Yi dropped his head and then slowly raised it again. 'Yes,' he said.

'There is nothing we can do to counter the Shift field in the short term,' said the Onurg. 'As long as Kaantalech maintains it around her headquarters we cannot approach her. Trying to do so would be like' – he sought for an expression that would make sense to the Human, and then realized that the Images would interpret whatever he said – 'moving oneself head-foremost against the advance of a Bredai.'

'Beating one's head against a plastite wall,' said Lan Yi. 'The wording is different but the metaphor is the same.'

'Agreed.' The Onurg grinned. The enjoyment of life was the finding out of new things. At its end there would be the discovery of what the experience of death was like, and that would be interesting and enjoyable as well.

'What should we do?' asked Lan Yi.

'A final decision is up to Strider.'

'She needs your advice before she can make that decision. She needs mine also.'

'I believe we should resign ourselves to staying in Heaven's Ancestor for a while. I don't think we've got any option, unless we choose to head further away from The Wondervale.' The Onurg touched a forepaw to his ear, then realized that the gesture would make no sense to Lan Yi and probably not even to the Images. 'There are times when the only option to pick happens also to be the best one,' he explained, quoting the ancient Pridehouse proverb.

'I had come to the same conclusion,' said Lan Yi.

'It's a lonely place to be.' The Onurg thought wistfully of

the richness of The Pridehouse. He might never see it again. The loss was in itself a new experience, but he found this one strangely unenjoyable.

'The Autarchy knows virtually nothing about the existence of the ancient species,' said Lan Yi.

'That's true.'

'So is it not possible that there are more species within Heaven's Ancestor than even the ancient species ever discovered? Also, it has been several million years since any of you have been here.' Lan Yi paused, wiping his hand across his brow, which the Onurg was intrigued to notice was oozing liquid. 'There could be people who could help us.'

The Onurg was dubious. 'All we found were bacteria and viruses. In some places there were creatures who had developed eyes and ears, but they were rare.'

'How much,' said Lan Yi, 'would the Autarchy be able to see if its ships were in orbit around The Pridehouse?'

The Onurg reflected. 'Very little,' he admitted, 'except a few villages built for the purposes of sham.'

'And creatures who could only blunder about a few million years ago might well have developed a little. My own species did not enter its final stage of evolution until a mere five million years in the past, but now we have learnt to fly between the stars. Neither elegantly nor well, but we've done it. Mightn't it be the same in Heaven's Ancestor?'

'I can believe you,' said the Onurg, although for some reason he found himself reluctant to say the words. He had a respect for the Humans, because they were new and brash and foolish but also brave and benevolent and mentally flexible; at the same time he knew of the horror his ancestors had felt when the Comelatelies had started to inherit The Wondervale. It had not been a good time: it had been hard to discover any delight in it, however much the Pridehouse and the other ancient species had tried. The idea that technological cultures might have arisen in Heaven's Ancestor was unpalatable to him. He turned the notion around in his head. The converse was that it would be exciting to meet new forms of people: perhaps they would be as peculiarly engaging as the Humans were. Maybe he was the one who was being mentally inflexible, because of the age of his species. And there would be the enjoyment – that great enjoyment – of discovering more about how the Universe worked, because the Universe was not just stars and planets and space but also the intelligence that thrived there.

'I don't know why we're arguing,' said the Onurg, 'because we both have the same view.'

'I concur,' said the Human. 'I shall advise Strider of this.'

'Orphanwifer may disagree.'

'I doubt it. Orphanwifer will follow anywhere that Strider goes.'

Lan Yi looked to one side, and the Onurg realized that Strider had locked on to an adjacent Pocket and was now listening to whatever he and Lan Yi said. He welcomed her presence. He shifted the perspective in his Pocket so that he was able to see both of them at once.

'We stay here,' she said immediately. He remembered how beautiful she had been as a Pridehouse; although her face was now antipathetic to him, he could still see the beauty, somewhere.

'But how're we going to find these species Lan Yi has been talking about?' said the Onurg.

'Easy enough,' said Strider. 'The same way we did when the *Santa Maria* first fell into The Wondervale. We just wait for *them* to find *us*.'

'And what if they don't?'

The Human female raised her shoulders. 'They will or they won't.'

'Are you all cosy and comfortable now, Hilary?' said Strauss-Giolitto, sitting on the end of the boy's bunk.

'Sure am, Maria.'

His face had that punched-about look that indicates a child is nearly immobilized with sleepiness but is fighting hard to resist the onset of actual sleep.

She drew a deep breath. The next thing he said was inevitable, and she waited for the words.

Sure enough, here they came.

'Tell me a story?'

It was almost a relief to hear them, as if some quasi-religious ritual had been performed with a perfect devotion. She responded with the next prescribed line in the litany.

'It might be better, seeing as you're not sleepy, if we continued with your education in stellar dynamics, Hilary.' She looked down her nose at him.

'Aw, shucks, Maria. 'Ve done enough stellar d'namics already today. An' geophysics. An' dead languages. An' information' – he yawned despite himself – 'retrieval. Tell me a story.'

She smiled, as she always did. Strauss-Giolitto knew that Strider's methods of getting the boy to sleep, when it was the captain's turn, were more ruthless – 'Shut your eyes and start snoring or you're dead meat' was the general tenor – while Lan Yi would discuss ancient philosophies, with special concentration on Plato, which normally had Hilary out like a light within thirty seconds. Strauss-Giolitto never had the heart to adopt either approach. After all, this was the only Human kid within a zillion parsecs, and it must be very lonely for him. He deserved better than to be treated as just the nuisance he was.

As if on cue, that other nuisance, Loki, snuck in through the open cabin door and, looking guiltily up at Strauss-Giolitto, jumped up to sit by Hilary's head. The cat gave his ear a tentative lick, and he yelped. Unoffended, Loki began to wash her right foreleg.

'Tell us a story.'

'Oh, all right then. But only if you promise me you're going to work harder tomorrow than you did today. Your information' – she surprised herself by yawning – 'retrieval was distinctly on the sloppy side today, as it is all too often. We're going to have to concentrate hard on it in future, aren't we?'

'You can concentrate hard on information' – a sudden yawn – 'retrieval if you want to,' came a softly rebellious voice.

'Do you want this story or not?'

'Yes.'

She dredged through her memory. The stories she made up out of whole tensile-tested fabric-like material were generally not very good ones, and left the child discontented. So she tended to give him the classics she had been told herself as a child. She was running out of classics, and Hilary was distinctly unkeen on repeats.

'Have you ultrawaved your teeth?' she said, prevaricating.

'Yeah. I did 'em, just after you were teaching me more about information' – another abrupt yawn – 'retrieval. 'Member? You ultrawaved your teeth at the same time.'

Oh, yes, now she did remember. The session on information – she was really terribly tired herself, and would climb on to her own bunk as soon as Hilary was lost in dreamland – retrieval had been a particularly arduous one today. Hilary was having serious difficulties with the subject, but she had to plough ahead with him on it because it might perhaps be the most important of all the things she taught him. Perhaps she could drop the dead – Umbel, but she was full of yawns tonight – languages in favour of extra classes on information – she worried that she might keel over sideways right away – retrieval. So after today's final lesson she had ultrawaved her teeth alongside him, hoping the act would invigorate her.

Ah! 'The Princess and the Frog'! She'd never told him that one before. She'd discovered it while browsing around through the Main Computer before the *Santa Maria* had properly left the Solar System.

'OK, here's a story – but after it's over you've got to go to sleep, you hear?'

'Yeah. Sure will.' The boy turned over on to his side, away from the cat, who looked at the back of his neck with interest, then resumed washing herself.

'Once upon a time . . .'

'I like stories that begin "Once upon a time . . .".'

'Shut up. Once upon a time there was a princess—'

'What's a princess?'

'A very long time ago there were countries—'

'What're countries?'

'They are – were – separate bits of a world. Stop interrupting or I won't tell you the story. Some countries were ruled by kings and queens, in just the same way as Captain Strider rules the *Midnight Ranger*. The kings and queens made all the decisions. Their sons were called "princes" and their daughters were called "princesses".'

'Seems kinda queer to me.'

'Nevertheless,' said Strauss-Giolitto sternly, 'that was the way it was. If you concentrated more on your history lessons you'd know this.' *But what is the use of history lessons,* she thought, *to a child who may never see the system that gave birth to his species? He may never even see the Milky Way. Maybe we can start phasing out history in favour of information* – she caught herself yawning again – *retrieval.*

'Anyway,' she said, 'there was this princess, all right—-?'

'Start with "Once upon a time . . .".'

'Oh, very well, then. Once upon a time there was this goddam princess and she was walking through the grounds of her father's castle when—'

'What's a castle?'

'Hilary, do you know what the word "strangulation" means?'

'Yeah, but . . . She was walking through the grounds of her father's strangulation? That don't seem to make sense.'

'I'd have thought you were too sleepy to be obtuse,' she said wearily. It was getting to be a question of which of the two of them would flake out first. As long as she didn't think about information – oops – retrieval she should be all right. 'A castle was a very big house where a king lived.'

'With all those princes and princesses?'

'You're getting the hang of history. Not very much, but a bit. Anyway, this effing princess – whom various narrators of stories, and note that I mention no names, are wishing that they hadn't remembered in the first place – was wandering through the grounds of her father's castle when, by the side of a stream – and, Hilary, you *do* know what a stream is – she saw a frog—'

'What's a frog?'

'It's an amphibian.'

'Kinda like an armoured shock assault vehicle, you mean? My puter has plenty about those. People useta use 'em a lot when they were killing other people.'

Horrifyingly, Hilary was beginning to look more wakeful.

'No, it is – or was – an amphibian animal so little you could have sat it on the palm of even your own very small hand.' Strauss-Giolitto sighed. She had once seen a frog in a zoo. It was unlikely that Hilary would ever see one. There almost certainly weren't any frogs any more – they'd prob-ably gone the way of the elephants. She hadn't much admired the frog she'd seen, but still she felt a pang of grief that the genus had probably been destroyed. 'Look, this princess – she's bloody beautiful, has long bloody fair bloody hair and a figure that'd make the average bloody prince claw his way with his bare hands through a bloody stone wall just to clap his bloody eyes on her – she's wandering through the grounds of her bloody father's bloody castle and she sees this bloody fr— small amphibian bloody animal. Get that into your head.'

'What's a stone wall?'

159

Diverse courses of action suggested themselves to Strauss-Giolitto, but in the end she chose the most sensible one.

'Good night, Hilary,' she said, standing up. 'We'll continue the story tomorrow. Information' – despite herself she staggered, but recovered before she hit the floor – 'retrieval.'

The boy and the cat, both fast asleep now and curled around each other, looked very sweet. With luck the Images were recording the scene, so that she could watch it again in one of the Pockets.

Poor kid, so alone.

Maybe there was a story about warcruisers and death she could dig out of her memory. He'd understand that better.

5

Have You Heard the One?

YOUR INSTINCTS SEEM TO HAVE GUIDED YOU WITH ACCURACY, OR AT LEAST A CERTAIN AMOUNT OF THAT QUALITY, remarked Ten Per Cent Extra Free. Often Strider wondered if there was some sarcasm in the way the Image addressed her. ALREADY THERE IS A TECHNOLOGICAL ARTEFACT APPROACHING US.

'Friend or enemy?' she said.

POSSIBLY NEITHER.

'That reply wasn't helpful. Tell me a bit more, Tenper.'

She was in her cabin alone. She'd told Hein that she didn't want him with her tonight. In fact she did. What she didn't want was his expectation that he could share her bunk whenever he chose. He was showing a distressing tendency to assume a sort of ownership of her – a strange and asexual sort of ownership, because he showed no objections when she made love with Lan Yi or Maria (that latest time had been remarkable, so remarkable that Strider wasn't sure she wanted to repeat it: disappointment is a deadly virus).

WE CAN DETECT NO SIGNS OF LIFE ABOARD THE VESSEL, said Ten Per Cent Extra Free.

'In some ways that's a bit of a relief – it might have contained another Maglittel,' Strider said, scrubbing her face. 'How come it's heading towards us then? Puters?'

IT IS CERTAINLY EQUIPPED WITH VERY POWERFUL ARTIFICIAL INTELLIGENCES, YES, CAPTAIN LEONIE STRIDER, AND INDEED THE

161

SHIP ITSELF IS AN ARTIFICIAL INTELLIGENCE, BUT EVERYTHING SEEMS TO BE COMPLETELY INACTIVE.

Strider might have been deceiving herself, but in the singsong of Ten Per Cent Extra Free's voice she thought she could hear a note of puzzlement. It was rare for the Images to project any emotion at all.

'It's drifting, you mean?' she said.

YES, QUITE RAPIDLY: AT ABOUT NINETY-THREE PER CENT OF THE VELOCITY OF LIGHT. IT MUST HAVE BEEN UNDER SOME FORM OF PROPULSION WHEN ALL OF ITS SYSTEMS WERE TERMINATED.

Hm. It was a high sub-light velocity. The relativistic effects acting on it must be goddam impressive.

'Any idea how old this thing is, Tenper?'

IT SEEMS VERY OLD INDEED, PERHAPS AS ANCIENT AS THE ANCIENT SPECIES OF THE WONDERVALE.

'Maybe it's one of their vessels, left over from when they were exploring Heaven's Ancestor?'

DUBIOUS, CAPTAIN LEONIE STRIDER. THE ONURG'S IMAGES HAVE ALREADY PORTRAYED THE VESSEL IN A POCKET FOR HIM, AND HIS SPECIES' RECORDS SHOW NO TRACE OF ANY LIKE IT.

'Yeah, but that's just the Pridehouse. Coulda been one of the others.'

She was making her way forward to the command deck. It was about time that she had a look at the enigma as well.

YOU FORGET, CAPTAIN LEONIE STRIDER, THAT THE WONDERVALE'S ANCIENT SPECIES COORDINATED THEIR EFFORTS IN ALL THEIR ENDEAVOURS, THAT THEY HAD NO INTER-SPECIES RIVALRIES. THE PRIDEHOUSE'S HISTORICAL RECORDS QUITE NATURALLY POSSESS DETAILS OF THE TECHNOLOGIES OF ALL THE OTHERS.

'Ah.'

As she came on to the command deck she saw that Nelson and Leander were already there. Both of them were deeply engrossed in their Pockets, and neither looked round on her arrival. She wondered if Ten Per Cent Extra Free had spoken with them as well.

No. They are speaking to each other. They were quarrelling earlier, and decided to settle their argument in this fashion, rather than physically face to face.

'Well tell them to fucking well patch up the dispute fast – tell them it's their captain's direct order, OK? We don't know what's in that ship out there.' She took rapid paces towards the central Pocket, still speaking to the Image. 'It could be a decoy. It could be something very dangerous. Leander's to be in constant liaison with Orphanwifer and Nelson with the Onurg, so that if either of those two come up with something that might help us they can be patched directly to me. Oh, yeah, and get Lan Yi up here as well.'

Oh, wow, but the alien spacecraft was a beauty. It was shaped like a slightly irregular dodecahedron, a little longer in the direction of travel than it was across its width, as if someone had made a geometrical model carefully out of a malleable substance and then stretched it a bit. The various facets showed brightly in the Pocket's enhanced starlight but, as she turned up the magnification, she could see that they were heavily pockmarked in many places by impacts with interstellar gunk. This baby's defensive screens had been down for a long time.

The graphics beneath told her that the craft was two hundred and fifty-three point seven recurring kilometres long: a big baby, in other words.

'I want her,' Strider breathed.

What for?

'For my collection,' she said. 'Us Humans have – used to have – the habit of collecting useless things just so we could look at them.' *And it's true,* she thought, *that ship really would be useless to us at the moment, even if the Images could get its systems up and running. It's too big and clumsy – it'd be an easy target for the Autarchy's forces. But at the same time it's like the biggest jewel a gem-cutter ever got their hands on: if there wasn't a war on I'd take it for myself.*

I DO NOT THINK IT WOULD BE A PRACTICABLE ADDITION TO ANY SUCH COLLECTION AS YOU DESCRIBE, CAPTAIN LEONIE STRIDER, said Ten Per Cent Extra Free.

'I was only speaking,' said Strider. 'I didn't mean it. Never get the damn' thing steady on the mantelpiece anyway.'

GOOD.

'Are Leander and Nelson on line yet?'

YES.

'Anything from the Pridehouse or the Lingk-kreatzai?'

I AM MONITORING BOTH DISCUSSIONS AND WILL INFORM YOU AS SOON AS ANYTHING OF SIGNIFICANCE EMERGES. AT PRESENT, BOTH ORPHANWIFER AND THE ONURG ARE STILL AS BAFFLED BY THIS VESSEL AS ARE WE IMAGES.

'Could be it came from somewhere outside Heaven's Ancestor.' Strider didn't really mean to say the words – she was just free-associating – but she could feel Ten Per Cent Extra Free's attention suddenly focusing.

THAT IS A POSSIBILITY WHICH HAD NOT OCCURRED TO US, he said, the trill of his voice deepening slightly. WE HAD ASSUMED THAT THE CRAFT WAS CAPABLE OF ONLY SUB-LIGHT VELOCITIES, MERELY BECAUSE OF THE RATE AT WHICH IT IS CURRENTLY TRAVELLING. BUT THAT REPRESENTS MERELY THE VELOCITY AT WHICH IT WAS LAST MOVING UNDER POWER. IT IS POSSIBLE INDEED THAT IT HAS A TRANS-LIGHT DRIVE OF SOME KIND, OR THAT IT IS CAPABLE OF NAVIGATING THE WORMHOLES. IT IS VERY DIFFICULT FOR US TO TELL WHEN ALL OF ITS SYSTEMS ARE SHUT DOWN.

'Any way of re-activating them?'

WE HAVE TRIED.

Strider puzzled it over a little longer, feeling her face crease as she thought.

'Any way that physical beings might be able to do it?' she said at last.

There was a longer pause than usual.

I HAVE CONSULTED WITH THE OTHER IMAGES OF THE FLEET

AND WE HAVE COME TO THE CONCLUSION THAT, YES, IT MIGHT BE FEASIBLE.

'Then I want to go aboard it.'

YOU HUMANS ARE PERHAPS NOT THE BEST SUITED . . .

'Yeah. Point taken. Orphanwifer can send some of his people along as well. The Onurg too. But I want me and my crew to be in the expeditionary party. That's an order.'

IS IT WISE FOR THE COMMANDER OF A — ?

'We can't at the moment get back to The Wondervale,' she snapped, 'so there's a good case for asking the questions, just what is this fleet *for*, and why does it *need* a commander? Right now I'm no more important than anyone else here. I'm redundant – OK?'

With a last lingering glance at the bright facets of the stranger, she drew her head back from the Pocket and stepped back, bumping into Lan Yi.

'Hi,' she said tersely, and saw the smile vanish from his face. Another time she might – just might – have said some emollient words, but now she was too irritated by what Ten Per Cent Extra Free had been advising. 'Take a look at that,' she instructed the out-of-Taiwanese, jerking a thumb towards the Pocket.

He moved to obey.

Strider tapped Nelson none too gently on the back.

'We're going to board it,' she said. 'Tell the Onurg, if the Images haven't told him already.'

She repeated the process with Leander, then went back through the ship, hammering on people's doors to tell them the news. She could have put in a commlink or got the Images to relay the information, but somehow doing it in person made the whole endeavour more *real*.

The last cabin she reached was Hilary's, and her fist stopped just before it hit the surface of his door. Did it make sense to take *all* of them with her? Hilary was just a kid.

Yes, it made sense. She couldn't leave Hilary on his own: if he stayed, she'd have to leave a few others of her small crew with him, because if anything fatal happened in the alien vessel Hilary might become the most orphaned small boy in history. *A fate worse than death,* she thought grimly, wondering where she'd heard the phrase before.

Wallop! Her fist rose and fell.

'Yes, Hilary,' she found herself saying a few moments later, 'you can bring the cat as well.'

The wonders of the tachyon drive, thought Lan Yi drily twelve hours later. *With any conventional drive it would have taken us several years to match velocities with this beast.* He wasn't sure exactly how the Images had performed the feat, though through the Pocket he sensed that some algorithmic process had been used – a million rapid pulses of the drive, each smaller than the last – but the *Midnight Ranger* was now clamped firmly against one of the facets of the alien craft.

We are puppets, he mused as he checked that the helmet of his suit was securely attached to the rest, *but I am not certain who is pulling our strings. We dwell in a Pridehouse vessel whose functioning we do not totally understand. We are subservient to the Images, in that it is they who know how to navigate us – and know so much else that we do not.*

Four of the Humans – it was becoming increasingly difficult to think of Polyaggle as anything other than a Human (she played chess, after all) – were going to try to effect the first invasion of the ship. They might not be able to get through the airlock. The rest would follow later, because Strider had insisted that they remain together – wisely, in Lan Yi's opinion. He felt a mixture of excitement and fear. Strider. Himself. Polyaggle. Hein. Difficult, too, not to think of Hein as a Human. He wondered what emotions were going through the minds of the two members of the ancient species: probably they were emotions he would never learn to comprehend. In his mind, Polyaggle and Hein occupied two categories: they were at the same time Human and utterly strange.

His feelings towards Hilary were much the same, because it had been so very long since Lan Yi had been a child.

He tested his commline, knowing that it would work – because it always did.

'Strider?'

'I hear you.'

'Hein?'

A happy laugh of acknowledgement.

'Polyaggle?'

SHE IS ABLE TO HEAR YOU BUT CANNOT UNDERSTAND YOU DIRECTLY, said the voice of Pinocchio. I HAVE CONVEYED THE IMPORT OF YOUR QUERY TO HER.

'I thank you,' Lan Yi said politely to the Image. He had always had a great respect for Pinocchio, who was another who had regularly beaten him at chess. He missed their games. They had tried to play chess a few times since Pinocchio's transformation, but it had proved almost impossible for the Image not to read Lan Yi's thoughts.

He looked at the other three suited figures, wishing that he could see their faces more clearly through their visors. It was easy enough to know who was who. It was as if they had become their spacesuits, rather than themselves. The spacesuit that was Polyaggle was the slightest of them all, her apparent frailty making Lan Yi want to put an arm around it. Strider was a sturdier spacesuit, stockier; one could feel the strength and purpose radiating from it. Lan Yi, hardly taller than she was, wondered what characteristics emanated from the space-suit that was himself. And finally there was the much more massive spacesuit that was Hein.

Puppets, he thought again. *Like puppets we have blank, immobile masks instead of faces.*

'You goddam meditating in there, Lan Yi?'

Strider, of course. So she saw them all as creatures inside

167

spacesuits. Her insight was greater than his – or perhaps it was just that she was capable of attaining a greater simplicity of thought.

'I am prepared,' he said.

'Well, let's get on with it.'

She led the way to the main airlock, the spacesuit that was Hein following close behind her. The sight was incongruous, as when Loki led an obedient but much larger Hilary towards the foodstore, mewing her commands. The small spacesuit that was Polyaggle maintained a cautious distance from the two ahead of it, and once again Lan Yi found difficulty in not reaching out a gloved hand to give a reassuring caress.

Silly. Polyaggle is much more able to cope with this than I am.

'Are you there, Tenper?' It was Strider's voice again.

YES. I AM HERE. All four of them heard the carol of the Image.

'All stations go?'

IF BY THAT YOU MEAN YOU MAY PRESS THE BUTTON ON THE OUTSIDE OF THE AIRLOCK, CAPTAIN LEONIE STRIDER, THEN THE ANSWER IS IN THE AFFIRMATIVE.

'Sometimes I think you have a sense of humour, dammit, Tenper.'

THE COMPLIMENT IS RETURNED.

'Why, thank you.'

Through the comm came quite clearly Strider's added whisper: 'Patronizing bastard.'

The spacecraft was massive enough to have a detectable gravitational field, but only just. The craft was moving in a slightly curving trajectory through the outer system of a blue giant star; one had to remember never to look in the direction of the star, which from here was a tiny outburst of light, hardly discernible as a disc but blindingly dazzling nevertheless. Its distant presence made life easier, though; they weren't having

168

to grope around with nothing but their helmet torches to show them where they were.

The Images had managed to land them close to what they had decided was probably an airlock, but even so the little party used belt-ropes and grav-grapples as they made their way cautiously across the facet. Common sense told them that if a hasty movement threw them off the vessel into space, the tiny gravitation would eventually bring them back down again; common sense, however, also told them that 'eventually' could mean a very long time.

Strider looked up at the stars which composed Heaven's Ancestor. Back in childhood, she'd been the only one at the orphanage who had been able to pick out the constellations – she'd been the only one who had loved the stars. Leo had seemed obvious to her: there was a lion. Orion had been less obvious, his sword a quandary. Andromeda had never been more than a mirage.

Here there were new constellations. Although she was aware that the curve of her visor was distorting them slightly and the relativistic velocity at which the alien craft was travelling distorting them more, she found herself identifying shapes among them. To her the formations were plain and, once noticed, unforgettable; she knew, however, that the rest of the party would look at her in bewilderment when she started to describe the Open Book, the Winged Serpent, the Nordic Berserker with Ice Cream Cone in Hand, the Locked Door and all the others she could see. In The Wondervale the stars had been so densely packed together that it was hard to imagine constellations – wherever you looked there was an almost even distribution of the points of light – but here in Heaven's Ancestor it was different.

Although this was a far distant galaxy, Strider felt in a bizarre way as if she had finally come home.

Once in her youth on Earth she had climbed a rock-face because she had been dared to do it. This was much the same, and there was something of the same quite enjoyable frisson of fear: although there wasn't the relentless tug of Earth's gravity reminding her that a missed hold or a misplaced footing might plummet her to her death, there was the vastness of the Universe all around her, seemingly trying to draw her into it. At the same time she felt a sort of claustrophobia, as if the hugeness of space were pressing down on her, confining her.

Strider dug her boot into a fresh pockhole and waited until the belt-rope attached to the rear of her waist slackened; then she hurled her grav-grapple ahead of her and made a leap towards the next pockhole. She miscalculated it by a few centimetres and skidded along the smooth surface until she could catch hold of another, nearby. That hadn't been too clever a manoeuvre. *Stop thinking about the stars, Leonie. You're here to do a job, not to have philosophical intercourse with the marvels of the Universe.*

She was yanked backwards by Hein's rope, but maintained her grip in the pockhole.

'Sorry about that,' she said.

'No worry. Even through a spacesuit your rear view is good, ma'am.'

The ridge of the spaceship's facet was not far ahead now. The Images had told her that there was something like an airlock at the very tip. Because of the scale of the craft, that tip looked completely sharp, even from here. She assumed that the Onurg's party and Orphanwifer's were making equally rapid progress towards it from different sides.

She turned to look behind her. There were only four of them, roped together and to the ship, but she felt somehow as if she were at one end of a string of beads.

'Tenper, you really sure yet this is an airlock we're heading towards?' she subvocalized. 'I don't want to make a wasted journey.'

YES. WE HAVE ASCERTAINED THAT IT IS INDEED AN AIRLOCK. It was Pinocchio's voice that replied.

170

Any idea how we're going to open it once we get there?'

TEN PER CENT EXTRA FREE IS WORKING ON THE PROBLEM, AND HAS IT NEARLY SOLVED. AS SOON AS THIS HAS BEEN DONE WE SHALL INFORM YOU. IT IS UNLIKELY THAT YOU SHALL BE MUCH DELAYED WHEN YOU ACHIEVE THE AIRLOCK.

'Thanks.' *Thanks for not a lot,* she thought as she made her next lurching essay along the side of the slope. It was becoming quite hard not to think of it as climbing, even though it was more of an ungainly scrabble across a surface that was, because of the tiny gravitational tug, if anything directly beneath her. *So we get there and hang about, huh, like dopeheads waiting for a ziprite bar to open?*

They reached the ridge and discovered that what had looked from the distance like a blade-sharp edge in fact offered them a flat surface about ten metres across. They were only a couple of hundred metres away from the tip, which Strider could now see was squared off.

'Wasn't that exciting?' she mumbled to herself as the other three joined her.

'It stirred even the blood in my old veins,' said Lan Yi tidily.

Bloody commlink, she thought. *I've got so used to having the bloody thing in my mouth that half the time I forget it's there. I'm halfway to becoming a cyborg without wanting to.* It wasn't that she was technophobic – she'd hardly be here, stuck on the outside of a monster alien spaceship if she had that particular problem – just that she didn't like technology *invading* her. She knew that she was a bit atavistic – look at all the advantages of thighputers and secondary retinal screens and all the rest of the hardware that people stuck into their bodies to enhance themselves – but she couldn't help it. Besides, the people of the ancient species like Polyaggle and co. didn't bother with such stuff – they jammed in temporary measures the same way she did – so maybe she wasn't so much of a throwback after all.

Now she listened for it, she could hear the sounds of the

others breathing. She'd heard it earlier, but it had hardly registered on her – if some dim part of her unconscious had recorded the soughing noise she had thought it was the music of the cosmos, or something.

Stop it, Leonie. Don't get so romantic about the Universe. Sure, space is a lovely place to be – the place you spent all your adolescence wanting to be – but the Universe is a serial killer: if the vacuum don't get you the Autarchy will.

'Onward, ever onward,' she said, gesturing with an arm towards what had damned well better be an airlock. If not, she was going to get Ten Per Cent Extra Free and Pinocchio by the . . . She wondered what bodily part, if any, the Images could be got by.

The Humans got to the airlock before the other two parties, and secured themselves there with their grav-grapples. Strider wished she had a Solar System flag to plant so that future generations would be able to remark on the Humans' small triumph over those who were adjudged so much wiser and more knowledgeable.

'Do you two want to start opening this thing, Pinocchio?' she said. 'Or do we wait for the snails?'

WE WAIT FOR THE SNAILS. TEN PER CENT EXTRA FREE HAS DISCOVERED THE FUNCTIONINGS OF THE MECHANISM, AS I SUGGESTED HE MIGHT.

Pinocchio seemed every time she spoke to him to be going further away from the Human race, like an old friend dying slowly.

Suddenly Orphanwifer was with her, giving her a suit-clumsied embrace that almost knocked her over.

'Hey,' she said, 'we've hardly been introduced.'

The Images did their best to translate his reply, but all she could make out across the cultural divide was something about candlelight and black satin sheets. This probably meant pitch darkness and a bed of particularly luxurious mud. Strider decided not to follow the conversation any further.

She had been surprised that both Orphanwifer and the Onurg had decided to come here themselves, even though she had made an analogous decision. *Thanks to Kaantalech's use of the Shift, we're all three suddenly without responsibility,* she thought, *and we're all three equally replaceable. No, not equally. If this craft decides it wants to kill us all on sight, the Human population of this neck of the Universe is going to be seriously depleted.*

The Onurg arrived a few moments later. She lifted a hand towards the three-eyed grin she could see through his visor, thinking at the same time that she was glad she hadn't been the one chosen to design the standard Pridehouse spacesuit.

'Pinocchio or Tenper: atmosphere report?' she said.

Once again it was Pinocchio who responded. TEN PER CENT EXTRA FREE IS ALREADY INSIDE THE VESSEL. HE BELIEVES THAT THE ATMOSPHERE WILL BE BREATHABLE BY ALL OF YOU. IT IS STRANGE . . .

'Strange? If there's anything strange in there I want to know about it right now.'

THERE SHOULD BE BACTERIA. VIRUSES. UNICELLULAR ORGAN-ISMS OF SOME KIND. THE NORMAL DETRITUS OF LIVING CREATURES. BUT IT'S AS IF THE INTERIOR HAS BEEN DELIBERATELY STERILIZED. THERE'S NOTHING.

'It's an old ship,' she said. 'Maybe when its original builders abandoned it the micro-organisms just sort of slowly died out.'

IT'S SO OLD THAT, QUITE THE CONTRARY, THEY MIGHT HAVE BEEN EXPECTED TO EVOLVE A LITTLE BY NOW.

'Feeding on what?'

EACH OTHER, OF COURSE. NO, LEONIE, THIS IS A MYSTERY. WE ARE UNCERTAIN WHAT PRECISELY HAS HAPPENED HERE.

'But it's safe for us?'

CERTAINLY. IN FACT . . . IN FACT, IT COULD HAVE BEEN TAILOR-MADE FOR YOU. THE CONCOCTION OF GASES IN ITS ATMOSPHERE IS SUCH THAT IT IS WITHIN THE TOLERANCES OF ALL THREE OF

YOUR SPECIES – HUMAN, LINGK-KREATZAI AND PRIDEHOUSE. THIS IS VERY PECULIAR INDEED. IT IS THE ONE THING ABOUT THE VESSEL THAT TRULY PERTURBS US.

'Perturbation, schmerturbation. Let's get the 'lock open. What should I do?' When she'd been crossing the flank of the vessel she'd felt herself afloat in a sea of timelessness, letting her thoughts roam wherever they would. Now she was impatient.

NOTHING. JUST WAIT A LITTLE, AND TEN PER CENT EXTRA FREE WILL OPEN IT FOR YOU.

'I'd rather open it myself. It'd be a kind of declaration of our having arrived – having made it here.'

THIS WOULD NOT BE POSSIBLE.

She looked more closely at the airlock. Whatever creatures had built this ship had been of roughly human dimensions, to judge by its size. The outline was hexagonal; three tiny lines indicated how the three doors would nictate. There was nothing at all on the outside – no wheel, lever or any other protrusion – to indicate how it worked. Vexed, she decided that Pinocchio was right: best to leave it to Ten Per Cent Extra Free.

'How much longer?'

NOW.

Strider had assumed that the three airlock doors would slide easily back, but instead, as she watched, they seemed slowly to melt away. Then she realized that in fact they were hingeing inwards. Yet they were doing something more than that, for there was a lack of definition about their edges, as if at the same time they were moving slightly adrift from reality.

Alien technology. You could never trust it to do what you had anticipated.

She took the necessary few steps forward and bent down to look into the airlock. All she could see was nothing. She tongued on her helmet torch, but still she could see hardly anything, just the dim impression of a large featureless box.

Sort of like a rat-trap.

'Is this safe, Pinocchio?'

YES. IT IS SAFE.

Casting her grav-grapple apprehensively into the maw, she took a brief glance around at the others and then hauled herself along her belt-rope for a few metres until she found herself face-first against a solid surface. The rear wall of the airlock. Somebody landed gently on her back and bounced slowly off again.

'Careful, all of you!' she ordered.

'My apologies.' It was Hein.

As always, there was a lack of grace in the proceedings as the rest jostled their way into the airlock.

'Everyone in?' She found that she was sweating, as if she were in an overcrowded room – which in a way she was, except that she was also inside a spacesuit and the outside ambient temperature was only a few degrees above Absolute Zero. She tried briefly to concentrate on reducing the flow of moisture from her pores, but all this did was make her sweat more. 'Everyone in?' she repeated.

'We're all here,' said Orphanwifer. 'I was the last.'

There was a slight vibration against her, and she guessed this must be the closing of the outer doors. For a few seconds they were in pitch darkness, and then there was a sickly flicker of yellowish light which grew in intensity until it was about as bright as an Earthly dusk. Strider could see her gloves and the metal surface she was up against, but not very much else. She twisted around and could see her companions as heavy-seeming shapes, their helmet torches lighting up the blank walls and odd pieces of each other's suits at random as they floated and bumped around the interior of the 'lock.

'Seems that not all the systems have cut entirely down, hm?' she subvocalized.

THIS IS AS MUCH OF A SURPRISE TO US AS IT IS TO YOU.

'That's not very reassuring.'

Then she was slithering down the airlock's rear wall. It took her a second to realize what this meant – that all of a sudden there was such a thing as down – before she felt the soft blow of her landing on the airlock floor. Her ears were filled with cries of consternation as the rest landed. Some of them stumbled against each other, grabbing for support.

ARTIFICIAL GRAVITATION. THIS SHIP IS NOT AS DEAD AS IT SEEMED WHEN TEN PER CENT EXTRA FREE AND I FIRST INVESTIGATED IT.

'Any other jolly little unexpecteds? There's nobody just about to toss a tactical nuke in here among us, or something, is there?'

NO. WHY SHOULD YOU THINK THAT? WHAT A VERY PECULIAR QUESTION, LEONIE.

'Aw, leave it,' subvocalized Strider. 'Let's get inside this beastie.'

THERE IS ONE FURTHER SURPRISE.

'Great.'

THE INTERIOR OF THE VESSEL HAS BECOME ILLUMINATED AS WELL. YOU WILL BE ABLE TO SEE WHERE YOU ARE GOING.

'That's a relief. Air we can breathe and light we can see by – whole place sounds like a veritable home from home. All we need is for a sweet old lady to open the door to us and we can play Trick or Treat.'

TEN PER CENT EXTRA FREE IS MORE THAN OLD ENOUGH TO QUALIFY.

A joke? Pinocchio wasn't as remote from humanity as she'd begun to believe.

The inner doors slowly peeled like flower petals towards the interior of the ship. The light was the same murky yellow as in the airlock as Strider tentatively, lazgun at the ready, crept forward into what was to all intents and purposes a long straight corridor about ten or twelve metres wide and the same high. Satisfied that there was no immediate threat, she beckoned the others to follow her.

They stood there in an indecisive huddle. There was nothing resembling a door to be seen in either direction. The place felt very empty. *It's the emptiness of time,* thought Strider. *Nothing has moved here for millions of years.* As so often before, it was brought home to her quite how long a period a million years actually is. It was something easy to forget, because the words 'a million years' fell glibly enough from the tongue, as if they represented a span that was only somewhat longer than a millennium. She'd been in a mosque alone once, back on Earth; it had been only a couple of millennia old, but the ponderous *solidity* of the high stone walls and the echoes of her footsteps had conveyed to her this same sense of the aeons.

Lan Yi coughed politely. She turned and saw that his suited figure had moved away from the group in the centre of the corridor and was bending forward to examine the wall opposite the airlock doors, which were now closing. The doors bothered her more than whatever it was Lan Yi wanted to draw her attention to.

Are we going to be able to get out of here if we have to? she thought to Pinocchio. This wasn't a conversation she necessarily wanted the others to overhear.

TEN PER CENT EXTRA FREE BELIEVES SO, YES.

Only 'believes', for shit's sake? Not long ago she had been thinking of the airlock as being like a rat-trap. Maybe the whole ship was one.

HE IS CONVINCED.

It's all right for him – and you. You can get out of here any time you want to.

IF I THOUGHT THAT YOU WERE IN THE SLIGHTEST DANGER, LEONIE, I WOULD NOT ALLOW YOU TO PROCEED.

You've allowed me to proceed on other occasions without showing any sign of compunction.

Orphanwifer had joined Lan Yi at the wall.

THAT WAS WHEN IT WAS NECESSARY.

The words were a reproof to her. It had been Pinocchio who had sacrificed, as he had thought, his own existence on Qitanefermeartha in order to save her life.

Sorry. Out of order.

THERE IS NO REQUIREMENT FOR AN APOLOGY. BUT TEN PER CENT EXTRA FREE AND I ARE CERTAIN THAT THIS SHIP REPRESENTS NO THREAT TO YOU, AND THAT YOU WILL BE ABLE TO LEAVE WHEN YOU WISH. IT WAS TEN PER CENT EXTRA FREE WHO OPENED AND CLOSED THE DOORS, NOT THE SHIP.

You were wrong about all the systems being dead. The lights came on.

THE VERY LOWEST SYSTEMS WERE ACTIVATED BY YOUR ARRIVAL AT THE 'LOCK. IT IS TRUE THAT WE HAD NOT EXPECTED THIS.

Then don't not expect too much else, OK?

Lan Yi coughed again. 'I think you should come and have a look at these, Leonie. If nothing else, they will fascinate you.'

She tucked away her lazgun and joined Lan Yi and Orphanwifer. The others gathered round, Hein looming over the rest.

In the low, dirty-seeming light it was difficult to see what the small scientist was indicating, and the optical distortion produced by her visor wasn't making things any better. The Images had assured her that the atmosphere in here was harmless. And somebody had to be first.

She unlatched her helmet, her hands fumbling with the mechanism. The bastards who'd designed these suits back on Mars had obviously never tried taking the bloody helmets off when wearing the gloves of a deep-space suit.

Strider took a breath. There was a faint ammoniac smell in the air, as if she'd found herself downwind of a men's lavatory, but it was nothing too offensive. The Images would have known if the ammonia concentration was high enough to do her any damage.

178

Hein and Polyaggle, she was pleased to note, were having even more difficulty getting their helmets off than she had. The three Lingk-kreatzai and the other four Pridehouse, damn them, performed the exercise with ease.

All of them stood there, hardly stirring, for a few moments, just practising the art of breathing. Strider could see the relief crossing Hein's and Lan Yi's faces as they realized that, while the air wasn't too great, it wasn't too bad, either. Within an hour or two, the Humans wouldn't notice the ammonia and the other species probably would have no trouble with the smells of whatever gases they weren't accustomed to in their own habitats.

There was something odd, however, and it took Strider a few seconds to realize what it was.

Yes, that was it.

The light that had seemed so muddily yellow and inadequate hadn't changed colour or brightness, but it had become somehow . . . right. It was easier to see by. She looked at the visor of her helmet, held in her hand, but it was as transparent as ever. She blinked a couple of times, with the curious sensation that her eyeballs no longer belonged to her, but the light still seemed perfectly designed for her vision. She remembered Pinocchio's expression, 'tailor-made', and for the first time since they had made contact with the alien vessel began to feel real misgiving.

Despite herself, she made a slight shuddering movement with her shoulders.

Don't show it, Leonie. Keep it in. Bottle it up.

'You were wanting to let me see something?' she said to Lan Yi, who was watching her with a quizzical expression on his face. He'd seen that shudder, and knew what it meant. Probably none of the others did.

He turned back to face the wall.

'Look here,' he said, pointing with his glove. 'There are pictures on the walls.'

His voice sounded slightly deeper than usual. Marginally different atmospheric density, Strider guessed, but the speculation flitted only briefly across her mind as she peered at the place he was indicating.

The etching in the metal was bordered by a cleanly executed hexagon. Inside the hexagon there was a design that was maddeningly close to being a pictogram but also maddeningly close to being an ideogram. Clearly it was portraying something in stylized form, but at the same time it wasn't. Just when she got her head around the notion that this was a simplified picture of something, she realized it was an abstraction – an abstraction that had not been born from several thousand years of Human cultural history and was therefore utterly impenetrable. But as soon as she concluded that it could make no sense to her, her mind began to make connections between the various lines and dots, and it was beginning to look more like a pictogram again. She felt as if she were watching a holo suffering from static, so that she knew there was an image there but couldn't work out what it was and certainly couldn't describe it.

'Anyone got any good ideas as to what this is?' she said.

The Onurg buffed her aside with his shoulders so that he could scrutinize the design. She rested her gloved hand on his head. There was a long pause. 'I have,' he said eventually, Pinocchio automatically translating his snarls for her, 'the smallest of impressions that . . .'

He stopped again.

'That what?'

'That I've seen something like this before. In our records. Orphanwifer, come look.'

The Lingk-kreatzai knelt down to examine the artifice. 'Yes, I have the same feeling.'

'Excuse me,' said Lan Yi, 'but I think it would be instructive to discover whether there are more of these designs.'

'I agree,' said Hein, speaking for the first time since they had come aboard. For once he was looking slightly timid.

Strider caught his eye and ducked her head in an almost imperceptible nod which she hoped would give him something like reassurance. She had never noticed any hint of nervousness in a member of the Pridehouse before, and it did nothing for her own apprehensions to see Hein like this.

'It hurts my eyes to look at just this one,' Strider said. 'Why go off looking for things that're going to give us all strabismus?'

'This is language, I think,' said Lan Yi uncertainly. 'It has all the appearances of a language. It is hard to start to decipher a language on the basis of only a single word.'

'Yes,' remarked Polyaggle. 'It *is* a language. Like the others, I have seen something like it before.'

'Like the others', thought Strider. *All the others except those who don't happen to be part of an ancient species. Remember us? We Humans are here too, you know.*

'Onurg,' she said, knowing that her voice sounded ratty, 'can you get on to whatever it is you use as a commlink and get someone to go through your records?'

'Better than that,' said the Onurg. 'Seragarda has a small holojector with her.'

Seragarda proved to be a Pridehouse with such an elegance of movement that, even though she was confined in her spacesuit, one wanted to reach out and touch her. Well, Strider did, anyway. The holojector proved to be mounted at the throat of her suit: it looked something like a fancy collar stud. *Hi-tech*, thought Strider disgustedly. *Useful, but humiliating for those who don't know how to use it.*

The she-wolf bent her back and put her foremost paws on the wall, targeting the design. There was a brief flash of ruby light.

'Is that it?' said Strider.

Seragarda turned her head. 'Yes,' she said. 'Already there will be someone back in the main fleet examining the image and comparing it with our puterized records.'

Strider, who had never met Seragarda before, had the annoying feeling that she was going to like this person even though, as a matter of principle, she didn't want to. 'Right – Lan Yi, Orphanwifer, Onurg, Seragarda: you study these eye-benders for the next few hours. Lan Yi – comm Nelson and tell him I want the remainder of the *Midnight Ranger*'s personnel up here as soon as possible – including the cat, or there'll be hell to pay with Hilary. The rest of us are going deeper into the ship.' She tugged her lazgun from its holster and looked both ways up and down the seemingly featureless corridor. Which direction to go? She hadn't a clue: they both looked as un-interesting as each other. 'This way,' she said determinedly, marching off to the left. 'This way looks best.'

Well, at least it didn't look worst.

The Eramm had taken longer to annihilate than Kaantalech had anticipated. What none of her aides – most of them now *dead* aides – had thought to tell her was that the warlord Mgs had already despatched flotillas of warcruisers to various other parts of The Wondervale, expecting her attack. As she had moved in on the ten dozen or so stellar systems that he commanded, destroying planets whether or not they were inhabited, Mgs and his warcruisers moved in behind her, deploying sheatherfields – whose technology the Alhubra species had never been able to steal or extort from the Eramm – to conceal their presence. As Kaantalech's fleet had focused at last on the Eramm home planet the sheatherfields had gone down and Mgs's forces had poured an unimaginable degree of firepower into the Alhubran armada.

The destruction had been enormous. She had lost about sixty per cent of her fleet in that first horrendous onslaught – she had had to watch her warcruisers, the physical represen-tations of her might and ruthlessness, flare into short-lived incandescence amid the blackness of space, as if her ambi-tions were being first lit and then snuffed out. Her anger had surpassed anything even she herself had known before, but at the same time she had found herself salivating copiously. Devastation was in its way a visual art, no matter whose lives were being lost for its sake.

She had crushed Mgs, of course. Even so much depleted, her fleet was still larger than his, and most of her weaponry superior. It was possible that a few of his cruisers had fled to safety under the cover of sheatherfields, but she thought it was unlikely: the Eramm had been a fiery species, and flight from the battleground would have seemed to them worse than extinction.

She rather hoped that a few of them *had* made a run for it. Destroying them singly later would be a pleasure, like picking at twee little delicacies after a satisfying meal.

Still, Kaantalech had found herself having to spend far more time than her patience was designed for in reassembling her armada. Since the Humans had wreaked such damage on F-14, the Autarchy's primary factory world, production of cruisers and other items of war had reduced to a trickle. Once she had established herself as the undisputed Autarch one of the first things she would do was rebuild the yards and emplacements on F-14, ship in however many slaves were needed, and get the manufacturing up off its knees again. Happy days were in prospect.

After the destruction of the Eramm and as soon as her fleet had been brought up to full strength again, Kaantalech had taken out a few of the minor warlords – along with their species, of course. It had been good practice for her troops, most of whom, because of the tough resistance of the Eramm, were raw conscripts. In fact, it had been only with hindsight that she had realized the wisdom of her giving the troops practice; at the time she had just wanted to enjoy herself. There is nothing more satisfying to an Alhubra than detonating a really good big supernova.

Kaantalech had never seen an oyster, and if she'd come

across one would have thrown it into her mouth before bothering to open up the shell to see what was inside. She had no idea that a grain of sand could (in the days when the Earth's seas had supported oysters) slowly be further and further laminated until it became a pearl. Had she learnt this, the knowledge might have informed her at the moment.

The grain of sand was the presence, somewhere, of the Humans. Her sensors had combed The Wondervale, but had detected nothing of the strange Human protoplasm. Her aides could find no trace. Yet she was convinced that the aliens hadn't simply dropped into a wormhole and carried on their journey to wherever it was they had been going: the Strider-thing had been too pugnacious, too determined – too much like Kaantalech herself, in a way – to do anything like that. The Humans were virtually the least of Kaantalech's problems – a single ship with no more than average technology – but still extra layers kept accreting around the mental grain of sand until sometimes she could find herself barely able to think of anything else.

She turned to an aide, whose face told her that he had suddenly thought of an urgent need to be somewhere different.

'When were the Humans lost?' she said. 'Call up the Main Computer. Don't just tremble there, dammit! – do it!

Claws shaking in the fashion that showed an aide was desperately trying to make sure they didn't shake, he rat-a-tat-tatted across a songboard until the *Blunt Instrument*'s Main Computer's artificial voice filled Kaantalech's command deck.

'They vanished in the region of Alterifer, while we were there gathering our forces for the ultimate coup.'

Kaantalech dismissed the aide with an almost fatal side-swipe; he had served his purpose. 'When was this?' she said to the Main Computer.

The machine gave her a date and time to about seventeen decimal places before Kaantalech called a halt.

'I want you to correlate that moment with any other events that might have been synchronous.'

'Any other events in the entire *Wondervale*? You sure about this?'

Kaantalech's blood roiled. The one entity aboard the *Blunt Instrument* that could act superciliously towards her was the Main Computer, because it was – at least in the shorter term – irreplaceable. In the longer term – well, when she was securely enthroned as the Autarch, Kaantalech was going to enjoy the great entertainment of stripping the machine out of her flagship node by node and replacing it with another. They said that AIs were incapable of feeling pain but, by the light of the Autarchy, Kaantalech was going to do her damnedest to make sure that this one did.

'Start with Alterifer,' she said, 'then the regions around it, then the further regions. Keep going that way. I don't care how long it takes you.'

'If I end up having to cover the whole of The Wondervale this could take me a very long time,' said the Main Computer. 'A very long time indeed.'

'How long?'

'Several hours.'

Kaantalech mused. Tying up the AI for that long could be dangerous – wars had been won and lost in the space of a few hours. She was going to leave herself and her plans exposed and vulnerable.

Pearls were very pretty objects, and otherwise perfectly sane people would undergo great dangers to obtain them. There weren't any oysters left to make them, so the pearls that still existed were much coveted back in the Solar System – not that Kaantalech knew anything of this. Pearls were nothing more than attractive gewgaws, but murder had often been committed for the possession of them. In their own sweet lambent way they were as lethal as potassium cyanide.

The Humans were Kaantalech's pearl.

She wanted them so much, so much.

'Go ahead,' she said.

'As you say.'

Strider led the way, and the others had to scurry to keep up with her. She was still highly apprehensive, which was probably why she was walking so quickly. She had an odd feeling about the nature of the light that surrounded them wherever they explored. It was as if, could she reach the next corner or doorway – for after the first few hundred metres they had discovered doorways, although none of them had doors – fast enough, she would be able to look round it or into it just in time to see darkness. This wasn't as if there were lamps being lit automatically whenever they sensed the presence of a living organism – that trick had been achieved by even Human technology more hundreds of years ago than Strider cared to guess. It was more that the expedition seemed to be in a gradually expanding bubble of light, which extended each new pseudopod, as it were, in the direction of wherever the expedition was next going to be.

She didn't like the sensation. Was the suited party pushing the light into new chambers and antechambers of the vessel, or was the light leading them where it wanted them to go?

What's happening, Pinocchio? she asked.

I CANNOT ANSWER YOUR QUESTION. IT'S DIFFICULT FOR US TO EXPERIENCE LIGHT IN THIS PHYSICAL REALITY. THERE SEEMS TO BE AN EVEN DISTRIBUTION OF MINOR RADIATIVE ACTIVITY THROUGHOUT THE SHIP, BUT WHETHER OR NOT THIS IS LIGHT IS HARD FOR US TO TELL WITH CERTAINTY. OUR BELIEF IS THAT IT IS.

OK, so she was just being paranoid.

Being paranoid was no bad thing. Kept the adrenalin going. Meant that if a big toothy monster sprang at you unexpectedly you had a better chance of zapping it with your lazgun before it ripped its claws into your abdomen and started shredding your guts while you were still . . . *Actually, Leonie, there's paranoia and paranoia. That version's a bit over the top.*

But she couldn't get over the feeling that someone or something intelligent was either guiding them or catering to them. She'd heard people talking about the sensation of being watched, although it was something she'd never experienced herself – until now.

'Your remaining personnel have been successfully inloaded,' Hein's voice informed her over the commlink. She could tell he was happy: when he was happy his voice seemed always to be on the verge of breaking into laughter. 'Umbel Nelson seems to be trying to make advances towards Seragarda and not knowing why he's doing so.'

'Having a lot of fun with Lan Yi's ornaments, are you?' she said sourly.

'Yes.'

'Found out anything?'

'No – except that he was right: these ideopictograms do indeed come from a language. Whether it was a verbal or a written or simply a visual language is something we haven't yet been able to ascertain.'

'Comic strips? You gotta be joking. I come three-quarters of the way across the Universe and all you can produce for me is *comic strips*?' The conversation was already taking some of the cold edge off her sense of being observed – but the cold edge was still there.

Lan Yi's voice broke in. 'I think you misunderstand my friend,' he said. 'When he talked of a visual language he was referring to the way in which a triptych might communicate a message to you more fully than could the three single panels if seen individually.' His Argot was stiff, which meant that he was either nervous or intellectually excited. 'There are many more than three panels here, but the images they portray link together in a way that . . . in a way that is hard to describe. We are beginning to think that we can understand their sense, although there is no meaning that can be verbalized.'

'Keep going, Lan Yi. Report in now and then. I've always enjoyed wandering through the groves of academia – pretty restful there. I'll let you know if I get killed.'

'Furthermore,' said Lan Yi, 'the cat has disappeared. We got her out of her suit and the next thing we knew was that . . .'

Strider bit back the first word that came to mind: *Good*. Although Loki was a pain in not just the arse but most of the rest of the body, Strider . . . no, she had enough on her mind without going down Sentiment Avenue. 'I'll put Tenper on to it. If she's in this ship, he'll find her.'

'Agreed.'

'Now, can we cut communications?'

'Certainly, Leonie.'

Tenper?

I WAS LISTENING. THE CAT HAS BEEN LOCATED. I WILL LEAD HILARY TO IT AND THEN BACK TO LAN YI.

Good.

She wished, on reflection, that she had chosen to undertake this first excursion into the ship on her own. It was good to think that there was someone watching your back the whole time, but the little troop dogging her footsteps was beginning to distract her. The only one she actually wanted with her was Polyaggle, whom she knew she could trust to do the right thing in any eventuality – whom, in fact, she thought she could trust better than herself. Her first impulse had been to bring along as many Pridehouse and Lingk-kreatzai as possible, but now she felt they were a liability, a raggle-taggle band of gypsies who might be great company if she met them in some other context, but not now.

She took a decision.

She stopped abruptly and pivoted, raising her hand to halt the rest.

'Know how to find the way back to the airlock?' she said to

the nearest Lingk-kreatzai. The woman was as tall as Strauss-Giolitto, and bulkier – the type of Lingk-kreatzai you wouldn't want to meet in a dark Martian alley.

'Sure. Who doesn't?'

'Then take these people there. Perhaps they can help Lan Yi. I want Polyaggle and myself to be the only ones who continue from here.'

'Why?'

'Less risk. If anything happens, there's only the two of us gone down. Tell Orphanwifer or the Onurg they can have the *Midnight Ranger*. Besides, Polyaggle and I can move faster, just the two of us, than a bigger group.'

'May we re-investigate some of the rooms we have passed?' said the Lingk-kreatzai.

'Sure.'

The trouble was there hadn't been much to see in those rooms. Some of them had looked as if they were dormitories, but when you're dealing with an alien culture what looks like a bed to you might just as easily be a culinary implement. Strider had thought of calling on the Images to see if they could interpret the functions of some of the artefacts, but she knew that Ten Per Cent Extra Free was busy trying to penetrate far more important aspects of the ship – the way its AIs worked, the way its major systems worked, the way it itself worked – and she needed Pinocchio to be concentrating on her not just for translation purposes but also, she admitted to herself, because his mental presence comforted her. He was currently located in her suit's oxygen-control meter, even though it had shut down the moment she had taken her helmet off. She patted the meter with her free hand, as if to return some of the comfort.

'Just you and me, eh, Polyaggle?' she said as they watched the rest of her motley crew move in their various gaits back down the corridor.

'I think this is wise,' said the Spindrifter. 'We shall be able to move much more swiftly.'

'Me too. And I want to get out of this bloody spacesuit.'

'I concur.'

At the next corner they reached, a place where Strider was confident she could see far enough in both directions to have at least a chance of repelling any attack with her lazgun, she gestured to the Spindrifter to climb out of her suit. She passed her lazgun to Polyaggle and then did the same herself.

Taking back the lazgun she said: 'Noticed something else that's weird here?'

'I have noticed no particular strangeness,' said the Spindrifter. 'Our species is accustomed to encountering different environ—'

Strider cut her off with an upraised hand.

'The ambient temperature. It's just right for me. You're used to a much colder environment. What's it like for you?'

The Spindrifter thought for a second or two before replying. 'Yes,' she said, and Pinocchio was able to convey the doubt in her voice. 'I find it pleasant. Perhaps a little warm.'

'The same way I find it refreshingly but not unpleasantly cool. Again it's like the inside of this spacecraft has been designed precisely for the benefit of us all.' Strider gnawed on her lower lip, her gaze still flicking backwards and forwards along the two corridors that led off from this corner. Without thinking, she flipped the lazgun so that it performed a neat arc before returning to her hand. 'Correct lighting. Correct artificial grav. Correct atmosphere. Correct temperature. Everything made squeaky clean for us, so that everything's as easy as it can possibly be for us. A sort of committee compromise to make sure that Humans, Spindrifters, Lingk-kreatzai and Pridehouse can all live with it. But this ship is millions of years old. If the Images are right, it's been floating through space since the time my evolutionary ancestors were having difficulty figuring out what a tree was.'

Polyaggle said nothing, but began to walk away along the new corridor, her wings fluttering slightly from time to time in

190

the display that Strider knew represented the gesture 'I am thinking about this'. For once Strider wasn't leading but following. She sensed that Polyaggle was not only turning the puzzle over in her mind but also consulting with the Images. Strider concentrated on staying alert, making sure she had a clear view in all directions, her lazgun in readiness.

Abruptly Polyaggle halted.

'The Images had it wrong,' she said.

'A-fucking-gain?' Strider pulled herself up short before she ran into the Spindrifter's back.

'Yes. They are most contrite.'

'They fucking oughta be.' Strider hefted her lazgun. Just occasionally you could see the flicker of the presence of one of the Images out of the corner of your eye, and right now she was in the mood for a spot of target practice.

'Our arrival here did more than make the lights come on. It activated the spacecraft's life-support systems at a much more profound level than that.'

'But Pinocchio and Tenper have been telling me the opposite. They've been saying that Tenper's been having hell's own job trying to raise a spark out of the Main Computer.'

'That is true,' said Polyaggle. 'But you'll recall that their initial analysis showed that the ship as a whole is also an AI. It is the ship that we have awoken by our presence here.'

'Oh, *shit*! I want out of here.'

'I rather think my feeling is the same.'

Strider tongued her commlink and started talking rapidly as she and Polyaggle began to run back the way they had come. 'Nelson, Leander – whoever's there – get everyone together and start embarking through that airlock to the ships. I want us clear of this baby as soon as we can be.'

IT'S TOO LATE, said Pinocchio. TEN PER CENT EXTRA FREE CAN NO LONGER OPEN THE AIRLOCK.

There are others, aren't there? Strider thought angrily at him.

191

THE SAME IS TRUE ALL OVER THE SHIP. WE'VE BEEN LOCKED IN.

The rat-trap. The notion returned to her mind yet again.

'The airlock door kinda declines to open, light of the cosmos.' Nelson's voice through the commlink was exaggeratedly casual. 'Besides, I'd have to drag Lan Yi outa here by his hair. He's fascinated by the pictures.'

'Keep trying.'

Polyaggle reached the place where they had dumped their spacesuits first, flitting on her many-coloured wings ahead of Strider, who felt that her sprint was a heavy-footed lumber by comparison with the Spindrifter's easy passage. With surprising strength, Polyaggle threw Strider's suit towards her and then, delicately manipulating the fabric with her claws, began climbing into her own. Strider tripped over an outflung leg of her thrown suit and almost fell, then made herself stay still for a second or two before starting to struggle into it. *If you panic now, it'll just take you longer,* she thought piously, then fought with the suit like a wild animal.

THERE IS NO NEED FOR YOUR SUITS, said Pinocchio. THE SHIP IS SEALED.

Look, dammit, Pinocchio, thought Strider angrily, *just how many things have you and Ten Per Cent Extra Free got right since we climbed aboard this hulk?*

There was no reply.

Exactly. So fucking shut up for a bit, will you?

Without being able to use her wings, Polyaggle made much slower progress. Strider grabbed her arm and pulled her along, but between them they could manage nothing more than a jog.

'You go ahead. I will catch you up.'

'No way.'

'You should be with your personnel.'

'I *am* with one of my personnel. Save your breath for running. 'Sides, I'd get lost on the way back – I'm relying on you, Polyaggle.'

She tongued her commlink. 'Any advance, Nelson?'

'Nope. The door's shut tight as a nun's—'

'Has Lan Yi got any clue?' If anyone was going to get them out of the rat-trap Strider put her faith in the old man – more, even, than in the Images.

'Not a hope. The Onurg's had Seragarda hard at the problem as well, alongside Lan Yi, and neither of them are getting anywhere. It's, like, not just that the thing won't open, dearest, but that it's been deliberately closed and bolted.'

Nelson's veneer of calmness was beginning to wear thin, however hard he was trying to keep the words light. It was a bad sign. Strider tried to hurry Polyaggle along faster, getting angry with the Spindrifter even though she knew it wasn't the alien's fault.

'Which way?' she said as they reached yet another intersection.

Polyaggle shoved her towards the left, so Strider lugged her that way. Unlike before, Strider paid no attention at all to the doorways they passed: if anything was going to leap out and attack them it would have done so by now. Anyway, being eaten alive by a many-tentacled thing out of one's worst nightmare seemed just as good an option as being stuck forever in that many-tentacled thing's spaceship.

TEN PER CENT EXTRA FREE HAS BEEN ABLE TO GAIN ACCESS TO THE SHIP'S MAIN COMPUTER, said Pinocchio.

'We're on speaking terms again?'

HAVE WE EVER BEEN OTHERWISE?

'Fuck you, wise guy.'

THIS IS IMPORTANT.

'Can it wait?'

NO.

'Why?'

BECAUSE THE MAIN COMPUTER IS NOW BRINGING ON-LINE MORE SOPHISTICATED SYSTEMS THAN ANY WE HAVE SO FAR ENCOUNTERED. IT IS ALSO GIVING LIFE TO THE SHIP. THE DRIVE IS

GOING INTO WARM-UP MODE. YOU WILL VERY SOON BEGIN TO NOTICE THE EFFECTS OF THIS TRANSITION.

'Umbel alive! Can't Tenper bloody shut the thing down again?' She was worried that Polyaggle was going to collapse from the strain of their half-run and that she'd have to carry her. The Spindrifter didn't weigh much by the standards of a Human, but still would be a fair burden. And Strider herself was beginning to tire.

ONLY THE MAIN COMPUTER CAN SHUT THE MAIN COMPUTER DOWN. IT IS WORKING IN TANDEM WITH THE SHIP TO CREATE THE KIND OF ENVIRONMENT THAT IT BELIEVES WE SHALL ENJOY. IT IS STARTING THE DRIVE. IT HAS ACTIVATED FOOD-GENERATOR UNITS TO PRODUCE COMESTIBLES THAT IT BELIEVES WILL BE PALATABLE TO ALL THE SPECIES ABOARD. AND SHORTLY IT WILL START SUPPLYING GUIDES.

'Guides?'

Pinocchio didn't need to answer her question because suddenly a holo appeared ahead of her in the corridor. It turned towards Strider and Polyaggle and gave them both a rather toothy smile of welcome.

First contact with an alien intelligence.

One of those things Strider was good at.

'Fuck off,' she said to the holo, stumbling directly through it, Polyaggle in tow.

'I agree,' said the Spindrifter, to Strider's amazement.

She didn't really have time to be amazed, however, for the same holo or another identical to it abruptly materialized about thirty metres ahead of them.

'I've already told you one time!' yelled Strider. What made prickles of fear climb up her spine was that the holo looked like a crude impression of herself, although with a turquoise cast over all its features. It was the sort of representation a colour-blind child might have produced. Deliberately, she stoked up her fury, knowing that this was the best way to keep her trepidation at bay.

194

'But I only wish to help,' said the holo.

Strider stopped moving towards it. The Argot was perfect. The accent was, near enough, her own.

'Then tell us how to get the airlock open,' she said, breathing heavily.

'I have been programmed not to divulge this information,' replied the holo casually. Strider found it hard to keep reminding herself that she wasn't talking to her own reflection in a coloured mirror or even just to the holo, but to an alien Main Computer – or maybe even to the ship in which she was trapped. 'For you to leave Artificial Environment 17,863,006 would place you in danger. There is nothing to breathe out there, you know.'

'I'm perfectly bloody aware of that!'

'Artificial Environment 17,863,006 has been designed to ensure that beings of diverse species may thrive within it, and to nurture them.' Just as she herself would have done in the circumstances, the holo ran its fingers back through its hair and gave a slightly goofy grin before adding: 'So take that for an answer, OK?'

'Do you want to get on well with me?' said Strider, her eyes narrowing until they were almost shut. A red haze was beginning to fill her vision. Had she been less terrified and less furious she might have been interested by the colour effects this created as she stared at the blue-green replica of herself; as it was, all she wanted to do was think up a way of killing holos. Well, she was a humane individual. Seriously incapacitating them would be enough. Just about.

'But of course.'

'Then stop looking like me.'

'Certainly. How would you wish us to appear?'

Invisible, dammit, was Strider's first thought, and the holo faded.

'No,' she said. 'Wait a moment!'

Her turquoise self became more seemingly solid.

She went rapidly through a number of images in her mind, and the holo morphed accordingly – alarmingly. Pinocchio, a desk complete with pen and pencil set, Heaven's Ancestor, a rather spectacular erection which Hein had produced the other night, Polyaggle – Polyaggle herself gave a mew of protest – a lazgun, a lavatory she had once used on Mars (*How the hell did I remember* that? she thought, revolted at the sight, remembering how ill she'd been through an over-intake of ethyl alcohol), and finally an ancient book she'd read in which there had been holos who looked like Human-size rabbits. The old *Santa Maria* had been a home to rabbits – their only home outside Earth where, despite their prolific breeding habits, they'd been in danger of extinction – and with luck it still was. Yeah, rabbits she could cope with.

The holo stabilized as a rabbit. It looked revoltingly cute. She wanted something she could hate, but this would do.

'Now can you let us pass?' she said. 'I want to get out of this spaceship.'

'I cannot let you do that,' said the holo in a friendly fashion, its yellowing front teeth looking far too large for its mouth to be able to hold. 'As I have said, your lives might be in danger.'

'We'll take that risk.'

'I cannot allow you to.'

'Ever crashed?'

'No.'

'You might just find out what it's like.'

Strider hauled Polyaggle through the holo and onward towards the airlock. They must be pretty close to it by now. She wished the corridors weren't so uniform. A Human community would probably have at least painted all the walls in different colours, or something. Hung up a few ghastly paintings the kids had produced – she'd have to get Hilary to work on that pretty damn' soon. Or maybe that was all the ideopictograms were: look, here's my mum with both ears on the same side of her head.

Stop thinking, Leonie. Keep on with the doing bit.

They came round a new corner and in the distance Strider could see Strauss-Giolitto. 'This way!' the woman yelled, waving her hand for emphasis.

Strider tried to increase her pace, but Polyaggle constantly slowed her down. It seemed, in fact, as if Polyaggle were deliberately trying to slow her down. The anger she had been fending off returned again.

'Come *on!*' she said.

Rather than translate whatever it was that Polyaggle was trying to tell her, Pinocchio spoke to Strider directly. LOOK MORE CLOSELY AT STRAUSS-GIOLITTO.

It was obvious as soon as she had had her attention drawn to it. That faintly turquoise cast. Another holo. Another 'guide'.

Can we trust it?

I THINK WE CAN.

I've stopped betting on your predictions.

NONE OF THE SHIP'S SYSTEMS HAVE SHOWN ANY SIGN OF ANY-THING OTHER THAN BENEVOLENCE TOWARDS US, said Pinocchio. SO FAR. IT IS PERHAPS MISGUIDED BENEVOLENCE, BUT—

Stow it.

— IN THEIR WAY THEY ARE TRYING TO PROTECT YOU.

I said, stow it.

She and Pinocchio had hardly ever used to quarrel back in the days when he was a bot. She guessed it was something to do with the relationship between physical beings and non-physical ones, like the Images – who were rather like quasi-demigods, if very fallible ones. She loved Pinocchio at the same time as he pissed her off, and she was pissed off with him just now. Everything was pissing her off, in fact – Polyaggle, the lighting around here (which didn't seem so good as it had been), Pinocchio, the holo of Strauss-Giolitto, the sensation of being trapped inside a small space even though the ship must have a volume of between eight and nine million cubic kilometres . . .

This time she didn't have to half-drag Polyaggle. The Spindrifter seemed to be as pissed off as Strider was. Side by side, the two of them walked straight through the holo of Strauss-Giolitto. Polyaggle produced a peculiar chirruping noise which Strider assumed was the Spindrifter equivalent of her own growl.

'Nearly there, I guess,' said Strider.

'It is my belief that we are.'

Strider tongued her commlink again. 'Nelson, any news on the airlock?'

'Nothing. Pinocchio would have told you if—'

'Pinocchio and I aren't talking right at the minute. He and Tenper have fucked this one up real bad.'

'You have a way of not mincing words, dawn's delight.'

Trapped.

They really were.

All this time, Strider had been hoping they'd get out of here, back into their ships, and rendezvous with the rest of the armada she'd been appointed to lead. Pinocchio had told her there wasn't a chance, and while her brain had taken his word for it her gut hadn't. But hearing Nelson's voice, with its flat note of resignation, had convinced even the gut.

OK, Pinocchio, I'm prepared to speak to you again.

GOOD. IT IS TIME THAT WE SPOKE. THE DRIVE IS BEGINNING TO MOVE INTO FULLY OPERATIONAL MODE.

Can Tenper work out what the Main Computer has in mind?

DISTANCE.

The single word, and the sorrow with which it sounded in her head, instilled more fear into Strider than anything else that had happened to her since they had come to The Wondervale. They had fallen through a wormhole: distance. They had been introduced to the tachyon drive: distance. Kaantalech's field had Shifted them all the way to Heaven's Ancestor: distance. And now there was distance again. It seemed that everything she did took her further and further away from the Milky Way and the Solar System.

Shit, Mars wasn't much of a planet anyway.

Yeah, but it was, you know, home.

There were lots of other people like me there.

Some of them were scumbags, if the truth be told, but at least they were Human scumbags. Unlike this person whose arm I'm holding on tight to because, even though she's not a scumbag at all, looking after her is the one thing that's standing between me and going bananas.

Who would you prefer as a friend, Leonie? Polyaggle, or the inadequate guy who waits outside the ziprite bar with a machete in his hand because he thinks it'd be kind of interesting to see what female entrails look like when they're spilled out on the floor? The guy with the eyes that are too close together.

'Look, we're talking about *home*,' she said to her thoughts.

Was 'home' all that great a place?

'It had its moments.'

Polyaggle was staring at her. Then she looked away towards the stretch of corridor ahead of them.

'I'm having an inner debate,' said Strider lamely to the Spindrifter. 'Just keep out of it. I want only the two of me involved in this argument, not interruptions from the floor.'

'Can you walk and have an inner debate at the same time?'

'If you try *very* hard,' said Strider firmly.

'Then may we walk?'

'Yup, OK. Now leave me to slug this one out with myself.'

Think about it, Leonie. All through your earlier decades you wanted to go out into space, to reach the stars. Was that because you really wanted to see what was there, or was it because you wanted to put distance between yourself and the Solar System? Rephrase that. Between yourself and the rest of the Human species?

199

Strider decided she didn't want to answer that question, so her thoughts answered it for her.

So what are you complaining about now that your wish has been granted a billion times more thoroughly than you could ever have hoped?

'There are limits,' she muttered. Polyaggle, walking alongside her, shot her a sharp look.

Maybe that's going to become a billion and a half, or two billion, or more. Your mother is a long way away now – and a long time dead – but you're about to start putting even further distance between yourself and that rejection. Ain't that a cause for celebration? At least sort of?

'I could have loved her. If I'd tried, I could have reconciled myself to her, discovered her as a person, perhaps forgiven her and become her daughter.' Now Strider could see the cluster of figures around the airlock. Some were still suited; others were naked.

Fat chance. You know who you are.

She did. From the moment she'd seen that half-sanctimonious viddisc there had never been any possibility of her ever establishing any kind of relationship with her mother other than to repel her, even the idea of her.

There was another type of distance that she'd travelled – a mental distance, the distance between herself and the Human species and all its concerns. Long ago, so very long ago, when the Sun had become just a bright pinpoint among myriad other bright pinpoints, she had felt the tug of her home system trying to pull her back there. The thought that she might never walk under the Sun again had pained her heart – as had the thought of never being able to do some of the banal things again, like sitting in a ziprite bar getting quietly stoned. She felt none of that any longer, only a rather guilty lack of interest in how her kind might be faring. Strider had become a citizen of The Wondervale, and her concerns were now devoted to it.

Also, she had become in a way the mother of her crew: *they* were the population of her home world.

Hein looked in their direction.

'Strider! Polyaggle!' he called.

She squinted at him suspiciously, but he looked like the real thing, not another holo.

So be glad of the extra distance. Every megaparsec is one megaparsec further away from being hurt.

'I don't think like that.'

You just did.

'Wow!' said Hilary for about the fiftieth time. 'This is real exciting. Isn't it? Isn't it?'

'Belt up,' said Strauss-Giolitto reflexively, for about the forty-eighth time. No, maybe it was the forty-ninth. She liked the kid, but in the circumstances her patience was becoming about as limited as Strider's. 'Go and look for Loki.' Second thoughts. 'No, hang on. Don't wander off. Stay with the rest of us.'

The rest of them weren't doing much that displayed any great degree of purpose except around the airlock, where Lan Yi and Seragarda exchanged opinions in low voices, opinions which either Ten Per Cent Extra Free or Pinocchio didn't think were worth transmitting to the rest of them. Strauss-Giolitto could make out bits and pieces of Lan Yi's side of the conversation, but most of it was meaningless to her: although she couldn't stop his words entering her ears and hence her mind, she was making a point of expelling them again.

Strider and Polyaggle joined them. Leonie looked paler than usual, as if something dreadful had just happened. Polyaggle moved to join Lan Yi and Seragarda; Leonie turned towards Strauss-Giolitto and then Nelson and shrugged at them in turn.

'Look good?'

'No, lady love,' said Nelson. He was trying to appear non-chalant and not succeeding very well. Strauss-Giolitto herself said nothing, but put her hand protectively on Hilary's shoulder.

'Pinocchio's told you that the drive is powering up?' said Strider.

'Yup.' Nelson again. 'I joined the SSIA to see the Universe. And what did I see? I saw the Universe.'

Strauss-Giolitto looked at the three Lingk-kreatzai and the four Pridehouse. In a way it was easier for the Humans: sure they'd taken sides in the war in The Wondervale, but it wasn't *their* galaxy. In a way, although they'd been there in the thick of it, everything had been happening such a long way from home that they were emotionally divorced from it. But the Onurg and Orphanwifer and the others: it really *mattered* to them. The stubbornly closed airlock doors barred the Humans from a tract of the Universe that was little more than space and suns and balls of rock and, oh yes, the occasional lifeform; for the Lingk-kreatzai and the Pridehouse, what was on the other side of those doors were not only friends and families but also several million years of cultural heritage. Their loss must seem as deep to them as Polyaggle's had been when Spindrift had been destroyed.

What baffled Strauss-Giolitto was that the ancient species showed nothing of the desolation she would have expected. Seragarda and Polyaggle were talking animatedly with Lan Yi, seemingly more interested in the problem as a problem than in what fate might have in store for them. The Onurg was lying near them, possibly asleep but with one ear cocked in case they said something of interest to him. Orphanwifer was saying something outrageous to Leander, so that the woman, despite the pallidity of her face, was clearly having difficulty in not bursting out laughing.

So why, thought Strauss-Giolitto, *is it that we Humans, the ones who have least to lose, are the ones who seem most frightened by the situation? Even Strider's shit-scared.*

THE DRIVE IS NOW FULLY POWERED UP, said Pinocchio in all of their minds. DEFENSIVE SHIELDS HAVE BEEN ERECTED AROUND THE SHIP, AS HAVE BEEN ANTI-DETECTOR SHIELDS. WE ARE NO LONGER VISIBLE TO THE UNIVERSE OUTSIDE US.

Someone gave a small scream of panic. Strauss-Giolitto was embarrassed to realize it had been her.

TEN PER CENT EXTRA FREE BELIEVES THAT INITIATION OF THE DRIVE WILL OCCUR WITHIN ELEVEN POINT ONE NINE SECONDS. OH, HE GOT IT WRONG. THE DRIVE HAS ALREADY INITIATED.

WE'RE ON OUR WAY.

'To where?' croaked Strider.

WE DON'T KNOW.

This was a world that, like so many in The Wondervale, had never had a name or even a number. Somewhere in a puter there would be a numerical record of the smallish yellow star around which it orbited, but the number would be an extremely long one, reflecting the fact that nothing whatsoever of interest had ever been discovered here or emanating from here – no artificial electromagnetic activity of any kind. It might well be on file that an Autarchy exploratory vessel had been by some time, stopped to take a look at the system and found nothing worth reporting: no mineral or other resources that would justify the effort of straying off the main routes to exploit, no lifeforms that were strong or intelligent enough to make useful slaves, no rare materials in any of the planetary atmospheres, nothing. Or perhaps no Autarchy ship had ever bothered to investigate the system. The Autarchy's sensors were always on the alert to pick up signs of artificial electromagnetic radiation – the general indication that a culture had achieved a potentially threatening technological status. A year or a million years later a flotilla would be despatched to see what could be looted and plundered and to decide whether or not the species should be destroyed.

Even the dominant intelligent species on this world had not named it, for they had no real idea that what they were living on was a world. Sometimes the Spirits of the Rocks would make the skies bright; at other times the Spirits would darken the skies so that it was possible to see them as sharp and tiny lights. It was good to know that they were there, watching over you. Their kindness was indeed glorious.

The species had named other things aside from the Spirits of the Rocks. They themselves were the Kua. Each of the Kua was, for convenience, given a special name at birth: as births were almost always multiple, this was an important process if the Kua were to keep their minds straight.

Keeping minds straight was not easy. The average lifespan of a Kua was a little over ten terrestrial years. Because each individual had so little time in the physical existence before joining the Spirits of the Rocks, it was very difficult for species knowledge and technology to evolve in the way that they did among longer-lived creatures. Yet the Kua enjoyed a degree of mental communication that was exceedingly rare throughout the Universe, and thanks to this level of cooperation had been able, as a species rather than as individuals, to develop something that could be called a civilization. There was no cruelty among the Kua, because one person's pain was shared by all. There was a dim awareness that the other creatures around them, although unable to react to the simple exercise of thought, were a part of the environment that should be cherished as much as a Kua infant. It had never occurred to the Kua collective conscious that animals might be killed and eaten, and nor had it occurred to the animals to try out such a bizarre food-source as each other. Vegetation grew rapidly and prolifically on Kua, and there was enough for all.

Tectonic forces created death: volcanoes, earthquakes, tsunamis, floods. When thousands died in these disasters the entirety of the Kua shrieked mentally in anguish and also in

204

fear, for it was clear that the collective conscious had offended the Spirits of the Rocks in some way.

The Kua, who were each about half a metre in diameter and a few centimetres high, were able to manipulate their environment by use of extremely rapid and flexible pseudopods; around the perimeter of their generally rather featureless bodies they had nine eyes, which could be pointed skyward or groundward or horizontally. There was a mouth and an excretory organ, but not much else to see on their fairly featureless bodies.

They had discovered numbers at a relatively early stage in their development. It was still unclear to the Kua what numbers were actually *for*, but obviously the Spirits of the Rocks would not have created them without purpose – even if only as a benevolent gift: playthings for the Kua, who duly played with them. The invention about a million years ago of what was to all intents an abacus had been the cause of great rejoicing among the Kua, and only the newborn were ever seen without one. Indeed, it would have been tempting to regard the Kua species as forming a single, vast organic puter. The possibilities of this planet-wide thinking device were very exciting. Given a few billion years, the gentle, non-aggressive Kua might be the best thing ever to happen to The Wondervale – either in themselves or as a resource that could be used by the other creatures of the galaxy.

Kaantalech's fleet descended from tachyon state alongside this world at random on their way to somewhere else and used it not as a developing organic computer but for target practice.

There was no sensation of motion at all, yet Strider felt somehow as if there were accelerative gees tugging at her. She had spent most of her life equating rapid travel with forces of some kind and only a comparatively short while moving around by tachyon drive. It was difficult to persuade one's subconscious out of the reflexes of a lifetime.

'Oh, boy,' she said to the company at large. 'Another fine mess I've got us into.'

She explained to them quickly about the holo guides, and just as she finished one of them, on cue, sprang into being by the side of Nelson, who was sitting slumped against the wall, his head in his hands, and didn't notice. This time the holo didn't look like a Human at all, much less Strider herself, but in the greasy sheen of its depicted skin and the seeming blindness of its head she was reminded of something. It was bulky and about four metres tall.

'Artificial Environment 17,863,006 is now in progress towards the Twin Galaxies. We shall reach there within one month or twenty-seven thousand nanreets or two and a half breers.' The holo's voice sounded as if the thing were speaking through syrup. *Nice to see that the Main Computer gives the Human time unit before the others*, thought Strider. *Due respect, and all that*. 'My food-generator units will provide for you – we have received relevant specifications concerning your requirements from the entities whose nature we do not understand—'

'Images,' said Strider, fascinated yet repelled by the holo.

'Images. Your terminology is recorded. Similarly, they have provided us with data as to your preferred modes of accommodation and recreation. I will require a short period of time in order to prepare suitable places for your recreational and other activities.' The holo paused for a moment. 'Excrete where you will until I have suitable facilities available; all shall be cleared away for you.'

The holo winked out of existence.

Oh, tremendous, Strider thought. *Sounded like the brochure you get given on arriving at some new pleasure-dome on Mars to discover they haven't quite finished building it yet. All that was lacking was the platoon of staff hanging around to have a good laugh at you.*

Odd thing was, she'd have preferred it if the giggling staff had been there.

Somebody to hit.

She'd like to hit Pinocchio and Ten Per Cent Extra Free – well, Pinocchio, anyway. In her mind's eye she could visualize him in his physical incarnation. It was difficult to imagine Ten Per Cent Extra Free as anything other than an elusive flicker of colour; you wouldn't get satisfactory bruising of your knuckles even if you could get a blow to land on him.

The Onurg laughed up at her. Always so bloody cheerful, the Pridehouse. Maybe she could hit the Onurg.

'Twenty-seven thousand nanreets,' he said. A drop of spittle from his mouth splashed the boot of her suit. His nasal eye withdrew and then reappeared. 'Plenty of time for us to relax and enjoy ourselves.'

'*What?*'

'I can't think of anything better to do,' he said. 'There's no way out of here, no battles we can fight. When we get to the Twin Galaxies – wherever that might be – we can think again.'

'Just lie back and enjoy it?'

'Yes.' He seemed bewildered that she should think of doing anything else, or maybe there was some completely different emotion going through his mind.

'There's getting on for nine million cubic kilometres of this bitch,' she said.

A little while passed before Pinocchio was able to interpret this for the Onurg. Orphanwifer had moved across to be with them, and there was a further pause while Pinocchio translated again. Strider thought about how her attitude towards Artificial Environment 17,863,006 had changed: this had been the beautiful vessel she had wanted to claim as her own, but now it had become a bitch. It was like a friend who had betrayed her.

'It'd be kind of sensible to try to discover a bit more about what's inside it apart from us,' she continued.

'We could examine the local area,' the Onurg pointed out,

rather reluctantly. 'The ship's too big for us to do any more than that.'

Strider put her palm on his white, furry head. As always, he seemed to enjoy the gesture. She smiled at him. 'Oh, yeah? Just look at me try.'

Pinocchio, Tenper. Any chances of rigging us up a few Pockets aboard this bastard?

Lan Yi had observed the holo with some interest. There was no point in their struggling to understand the functionings of the airlock any longer – even if they were able to open it and get back to their ships, which he assumed would still be affixed to Artificial Environment 17,863,006's sides, already they must be far enough from The Wondervale to have little chance of being able to do anything useful there. So he calmly and deliberately forgot about the unsolved problem and turned his attention to other things.

The pictures on the walls – they had prodded at memories tucked somewhere at the backs of the minds of himself, Orphanwifer, the Onurg and some of the others. The visual appearance of the holo had done the same.

He knew that he'd never seen any creature that physically resembled it, yet he'd seen something that in an intangible way *looked* like it.

Lan Yi glanced across at Seragarda and saw that she had been watching his face. She moved her third eye in a smile. They didn't need to say anything to each other: it was clear that she had been thinking along exactly the same lines as he had. Already Lan Yi found that he had developed an empathy that he had not expected could exist between an upright biped from one culture and a six-legged wolf from a completely different one. They should have had communication difficulties as each tried to match one mind-set to another, but there was no such barrier between them. When he had tried to explain something to her in terms of music she had seized upon this new concept immediately – the Pridehouse had no music – and within minutes was handling it as skilfully as he did himself. She had described to him, while they were trying to unpick the airlock, a technique that required the use of a mathematics based on the shapes of living cells, and her explanation had been so pellucidly expressed that he had absorbed the information while hardly realizing that he was doing so.

Together they crossed the corridor, ignoring all the others, to scrutinize once more that first ideopictogram he had discovered.

He knelt down beside her.

The Images must be fully occupied executing Strider's command, because the growls she made to him went uninterpreted.

He ran a finger in a circle around the design, then began to trace some of its details. There was a dynamism in the design: unless he was being anthropocentric, whatever was being depicted here was related to action rather than simply delineating an action. Like Seragarda, he was now completely convinced that the ideopictograms were indeed drawn from a language; he was certain that they were not an alien form of decorative art. He let his finger pause frequently, whenever it seemed to him that it had encountered some item of particular interest. Whenever he did so, Seragarda nudged him with her shoulder if she agreed.

After a while she scrambled out of her suit so that with her claws she could point out to him further details that interested her.

Of course, Lan Yi knew, what were of importance were not the individual details themselves but the connections that could be established between them. The difficulty was that it was almost impossible to keep more than one sector of the ideopictogram in his mind at the same time. He knew this wasn't his failing or even a Human failing, for Seragarda had earlier complained of the same.

Lan Yi attempted to create a mental filing system. He would concentrate for several full seconds on a single shape or line or pattern, then tuck it away into a pigeonhole at the back of his mind, from which it would be withdrawn later only if he came across something that tenuously – or even identically – matched it elsewhere in the design. Even this he found impossible: he made several cross-matches only to discover that he'd registered the same features twice.

Maybe not all of the 'pictures' were like this. He didn't hold out much hope, but the attempt was worthwhile. He patted Seragarda on the shoulder to attract her attention, and when she turned her head to look at him he saw that once again she had come to the same conclusion.

Lan Yi turned round.

Strider was squatting down beside Nelson, trying to persuade him to stand up and look around him, trying to convince him that he should shake off the bleakness of his despair. Funny that it should be Nelson, of all the Humans, who had cracked first. Lan Yi might have predicted that it would have been Maria, although she was by no means the brittle, vulnerable person she'd been when he'd first met her, back on Mars – and, of course, she had Hilary to reassure, the self-discipline of which must be helping her. Although he was devoted to Maria, he had few illusions about her. Leander, white-faced and almost motionless, as if she'd been frozen mid-pace as she moved towards her lover, could have done with a Hilary to look after.

'Strider,' said Lan Yi gently.

She looked up at him, scowling. 'Can't you see I'm busy?' she mouthed silently.

'I think,' he said, 'as does Seragarda, that it is a matter of some urgency that we attempt to extract what information we can from the pictures on the walls.'

'Then go do it,' Strider said out loud, her grim expression relaxing slightly. 'There'll be a Pocket here soon, I hope, so you could wait for it.'

'We believe the ideopictograms are not entirely visual.'

'That's the trouble with modern art,' said Strider sourly. 'Go on, the two of you. I just told you to.'

'I want to come as well,' said Strauss-Giolitto, astonishing Lan Yi.

He stared at her, hoping that he was keeping the surprise out of his face.

'I'm a teacher, remember?' she continued. Lan Yi was pleased to notice that there was no defensiveness in the way she spoke. 'What I'm good at is looking at complex fields of knowledge and picking out of them the stuff that young minds can understand, then stripping out the next layer of understanding, and so on. It was what I was trained to do.'

Lan Yi nodded. He and Seragarda were accustomed to looking at complicated systems and assuming they'd be able to work them out in their entirety – that there wouldn't be any purpose in doing otherwise.

'If Strider will permit . . .'

'Strider permits,' muttered Leonie from Nelson's side. 'The more of you I can get rid of for a bit, the more chance I've got to be able to do some thinking – and some psychological counselling.'

'I wanna go too,' said Hilary.

Yes, his presence would keep Maria from slipping back too much into contemplation of their predicament. Lan Yi wanted her mind to be as controlled as possible.

'You'd be welcome,' he said courteously. 'I am sure you will be helpful.'

'And Loki.'

'Yes, Loki may come as well.'

Polyaggle made a whirring sound with her facial proboscis, then clicked her claws together.

Lan Yi gave her a shallow bow of assent.

Before Artificial Environment 17,863,006 had activated itself he had explored briefly in one direction up the corridor and none of them had been able to decipher anything from the ideopictograms. It made sense to try the opposite way. Maybe these pictures, viewed sequentially, formed some sort of *instruction* in language, rather than a simple statement to the original occupants of Artificial Environment 17,863,006. Maybe they had anticipated that, one day who knew how far in the future, creatures alien to them would come aboard the deserted ship. Maybe that was what the ship had been designed for – maybe it had *never* been crewed.

Lan Yi remembered Strider mumbling something about a rat-trap. He hoped that Artificial Environment 17,863,006 had been sent to them instead as a gift – a gift of knowledge sent blindly from one species out into the Universe to educate younger ones who might happen to come across it. If his specu-lative conjecture – and it was nothing more really than a wild idea – were correct, Maria could be of even greater assistance than she had claimed.

Hilary, his left hand locked firmly in Maria's right, tugged the teacher across the corridor to look at the ideopictogram that Lan Yi and Seragarda had been poring over. The boy had to stand on tiptoe to look at it properly.

'Wow,' he said. 'How come there's a picture of a Helgiolath here?'

6

Keep on Trokking

At Lan Yi's urgent request, Strider again broke off comforting Nelson for a moment to summon one of the Images.

I don't give a flying fuck at a rolling doughnut what you're doing, she thought pleasantly, *I want either Pinocchio or Ten Per Cent Extra Free on-line. Right now.*

It was Pinocchio who responded.

YOUR WISH IS MY COMMAND. DO YOU HAVE A MAGIC BOTTLE YOU WISH TO RUB?

Strider didn't recognize the allusion.

You're needed. They have to have an interpreter.

She didn't need to tell him who 'they' were. Pinocchio had already picked the datum up out of her mind.

I THINK YOU'RE CORRECT.

Better believe it.

Instantly the small gathering around the ideopictogram were talking animatedly to each other. Strider, having heard Hilary's exclamation despite herself, couldn't help but try to listen in to the conversation even though her central worry was Nelson; she could assist him, but she had nothing to offer the others except the services of Pinocchio so that they could communicate with each other.

Hilary had said 'Helgiolath'. *That* was why the last holo had nagged her with its familiarity. She'd spoken with Kortland, the Helgiolath leader in The Wondervale, often enough. The holo hadn't in fact looked all that much like

Kortland, but there had been a similarity that extended beyond the trivial details of physical aspect.

She tried to formulate this in her mind while at the same time whispering to Nelson that there was no real need for despondency, look on their excursion to the Twin Galaxies as a welcome tourist extravaganza, if a kid like Hilary could be so bright and chirpy in the circumstances then surely Nelson could as well, and various other arguments that she wasn't very sure she believed herself.

All that Nelson did was slouch his body half-away from her, like a child who has decided to be inconsolable. Strider had never been at her best when dealing with children. This was a very big child she was having to deal with. Nelson's shoulders shuddered, and she realized he was sobbing behind his secondary retinal screens.

'Oh, Jeez,' she thought sympathetically, and hit him hard on the temple with the butt of her lazgun.

With Maloron Leander she didn't even bother with the attempted pep-talk. Strider wanted to find out what the picture was *for*.

She smiled at Segrill, who was watching her, apparently both impressed and appalled.

'Ancient Human pre-mating ritual,' she said.

Hilary was the only one who could read the ideopictograms. 'Read' was perhaps not the right word: he could see through all the clutter of sophistication to gain an idea of what each of them was intended to depict, but beyond that he could not go. Lan Yi began to think of the boy as being something like a thighputer: Hilary could analyse data only so far and no further. The limitations of the thighputer were notoriously infuriating, but one had to be grateful to the device as a tool that often opened up the gateways that beckoned one into the gardens of understanding. It was the same with Hilary. Without him, those gateways would have been firmly locked in the faces of the adults – if, indeed, they'd have been able to see that the gateways existed at all.

So Lan Yi listened with a benevolent expression on his face as the boy prattled away each time they encountered a new ideopictogram.

He had been partly right in his guess that the devices together comprised a primer in the ancient language, and partly wrong. It soon became clear that the sequence provided this but not only this: it was attempting, at the same time, to relay to them a saga. Even with Hilary's ability to see straight through what Lan Yi privately referred to as the decorative embellishments of the ideopictograms and look just at their core, it was impossible to tell anything about the language other than the fact it *was* a language. However, one could infer from Hilary's descriptions a little about the saga part of the sequence.

Lan Yi didn't know whether it depressed him or cheered him, so he decided to let it do neither – merely to gather information as if he were regarding an image in an electron microholo. All the historical Human sagas told of great deeds of battle, of conquest, of the firm rule of kings and gods – in short, of people killing people. But this one, it soon became evident, was the story of a peacefully developing species. The mighty deeds were typified by the discovery of tool-making or of the keystone arch.

'Didn't they *ever* go to war?' said Strider, whose thoughts must have been mirroring his own.

'It seems not,' said Lan Yi mildly, 'though we should remember that it is historians who shape history, not the events themselves. Perhaps by the time this ship was built it suited the ur-Helgiolath, if I may call them that, to forget the less creditable aspects of their past – especially if one day they might be representing themselves to an alien species.'

'You called them "ur-Helgiolath",' said Polyaggle. 'I think you are correct.'

215

'Run that by me again,' said Strider, turning to look into the Spindrifter's depthless eyes.

Seragarda was the one who responded. 'The Helgiolath believe themselves to be a species native to The Wondervale – and we have always believed the same. But I am beginning to think that we were all wrong.' She laughed a typical Pridehouse laugh. 'They're newcomers – they're a species perhaps as old as we are ourselves, but they didn't emerge in The Wondervale.'

Lan Yi could see Strider catch on at once. 'Presumably they sprang up somewhere in the Twin Galaxies, then,' she said. 'That's where the Main Computer told us it's taking us home to.'

'That would seem a reasonable guess,' he said. 'But we must keep it in mind that all this is still nothing but a guess. The resemblances to the Helgiolath could just be coincidences. This is a big Universe.'

'Which makes coincidence less likely,' said Strider at once. 'We've encountered only a few tens of other species. It'd be a tad improbable that two of them should have so many similarities.'

Then her face fell. 'Oh,' she added. 'I see what you mean. Parallel evolution. Polyaggle could be mistaken for a Human from a distance. And the Lingk-kreatzai are – at least externally – barely distinguishable from Humans.'

Lan Yi nodded and touched her on the shoulder. 'Yes, but we must remember not to read too much into *that*, either,' he said. 'The Images were directing us towards the more humanoid species, so our sample is hardly a random one.' Seragarda buffeted him with her rump and he smiled down at her. 'I said "humanoid", not "bipedal",' he added. 'The description can be interpreted psychologically as well as physiologically.'

'That's obvious. I was objecting to the term itself,' said Seragarda, her nasal eye performing a bewildering series of withdrawals, emergences and colour changes. 'Remember, you're in the company of people of the ancient species, and all you are is Johnny Upstart. "Pridehouse-oid" might be a good choice. To be used in alternation with "Spindrifteroid" and "Lingk-kreatzai-oid".'

Strider grinned and gave Seragarda an affectionate punch on the forehead.

'I think we take your point,' said Lan Yi. He surprised himself by buffeting Seragarda back with his own thin hips. 'But I am not going to permit myself to be forced into saying "Lingk-kreatzai-oid" for the rest of my life.'

Seragarda laughed again.

'Say,' said Hilary, 'have you guys finished gettin' fresh with Seragarda? I wanna find out what happens next in the story.' Strauss-Giolitto coughed pointedly.

Lan Yi drew himself together. The boy and the schoolmarm were right. The group's imperative was to glean as much information as they could as quickly as they could, not to exchange lackwit badinage.

'Let us continue,' he said.

They came to the ideopictogram that seemed to relate to the emergence of the ur-Helgiolath – if that was indeed what this species had been – from the atmosphere of their native planet, followed by another that, from Hilary's excited account, had the species discovering ways to roam the starfields. The next of the 'pictures on the walls' saw – although for once Hilary showed some hesitation as he described the image – the ur-Helgiolath traverse the immensities of intergalactic space.

'Why are you uncertain?' Lan Yi asked the boy.

''S not that,' said Hilary. 'It's kinda like a lot of them got hurt and killed and things. And disappeared, like space ate them.'

Wormholes, possibly, thought Lan Yi. *Or just the dangers of exploration. No, backtrack that thought a moment to wormholes. Maybe the Helgiolath suffered the same difficulty that*

217

we did: they hadn't realized that the art of space navigation is not to discover wormholes but to avoid them – all except the ones you want.

Strauss-Giolitto put her hand on Hilary's head and he twisted to look up at her.

'This picture's real unhappy,' he said. He bent down to snatch up Loki, who struggled a little but then settled contentedly in his arms. He hugged the cat as if she were a motile stuffed toy. 'I don't like this picture.'

So the ur-Helgiolath had compassion, thought Lan Yi. *Their descendants, if indeed they* are *their descendants, show precious little of it.*

'Then let's move on to the next one as quickly as we can, shall we, Hilary?' he said.

But the next ideopictogram was even darker in mood, so far as Lan Yi could gather from Hilary's reactions. The boy dropped the cat, spun, and pressed his face into Maria's thighs.

'I wanna stop. This is *horrible.*'

Lan Yi squatted and turned Hilary's tear-stained face towards him. 'Do you really want to stop while it's still horrible?' he said.

'Yeah!'

'Maybe the next picture will show an end to the' – he sought for a suitable word – 'horribleness?'

'Yeah?'

'Perhaps.'

The boy was still reluctant, twisting his head away from Lan Yi's hand.

'Don't force him,' said Strauss-Giolitto.

'We don't want to,' said Seragarda. 'Hilary, come here.'

Cautiously he left Strauss-Giolitto's legs and put his arms around the wolfish head, nestling his face against the gleaming fur.

'Hilary,' said Seragarda. The deep, soothing growl was too

soft for the others to hear, but Pinocchio translated it directly into their minds. 'Hilary, so far it's been just like a game, looking at all the pictures, hasn't it?'

'Yeah, it's been fun.' Grudgingly.

'But it's not a game – not really. All the stuff you've been telling us – it's not only been fun for us all, and it's not only been interesting as well. Any one thing you can find out from the pictures might save the lives of everybody.'

'OK, just *one* thing.'

She nuzzled his cheek. 'It doesn't work that way, Hilary. If we knew what the one thing was – or there might be lots of them – we wouldn't need you to help us out. We need to know as many things as we can.'

Hilary withdrew his head for a moment and drew the back of his hand across his nose, then leant his cheek against Seragarda again.

'But it hurts when a picture is so *unhappy* as that one,' he said, pointing.

'You don't like getting hurt, do you?'

'No.'

'Neither do I. Nor does anybody else here – and none of us want to see you get hurt.' Seragarda paused. 'But there are times when you've got to put up with a little hurt in order to stop a big hurt. Ask Leonie.'

Hilary looked up at Strider, whose face showed a mixture of an encouraging smile and a glower. Strider had fixed views on child-rearing.

'That's right, Hilary,' she said through gritted teeth. Lan Yi wanted to tell her what a tricky bit of maturing Seragarda was trying to put the boy through. Strider had clearly never noticed that children ate their meals starting with the bits of them they liked the best, then moved dutifully on to the rest later. It was quite a sophisticated mental leap during childhood to discover that it was better the other way round, so the taste left in your mouth was your favourite. Seragarda – who wasn't even a

219

Human, for Umbel's sake – was attempting to let Hilary discover this several years early.

'So what I'd like you to do,' Seragarda said when she had Hilary's attention again, 'is to pretend you're a grown-up – goodness me, you nearly *are* a grown-up. I'm not going to lie to you: if you find some of the pictures horrible you may have bad dreams later – dreams that are even worse than the pictures – but it'll all have been worth it. You'll have maybe saved the lives of everybody. *We'll* know that you've done it, and so will you.'

'Guess so.' The boy sucked in air through his nose with a liquid din.

'Going to try again?'

It took Hilary a few moments to reply, but then his face brightened. 'Can I ride on your shoulders?'

'I'd love you to do that. But don't hold on by my ears, because that might hurt me.' Seragarda, who for the past minutes had been unusually sombre for a Pridehouse, gave a laugh. 'Grab handfuls of the fur at the back of my neck – I like it when you do that.'

She lowered herself so that Hilary could climb astride her. Out of the corner of his eye Lan Yi noticed the expression on Strauss-Giolitto's face. There was tenderness there but there was also a certain jealousy. This was a datum to be stored away in his mind, as was the fact that the Pridehouse had dreams and nightmares. He was learning more than just about the ur-Helgiolath. As Seragarda had pointed out to Hilary, every item of information was potentially useful: only later did you find out which were the genuinely useful ones.

'Let's have another look at that last ideopictogram, shall we?' said Seragarda.

'Have to?'

'I think so.'

The small hands dug very deep into the fur at Seragarda's nape, and clutched tightly. He wrapped his feet under the crease of her forelegs. Lan Yi wondered if this was as painless as she had told Hilary it would be.

Maria put her hand on the boy's back, partly to support him and partly to give him further reassurance. *And partly to take some of the sting out of that vague jealousy she's ashamed of herself for feeling,* thought Lan Yi.

'Something very bad happened to the Helgiolath,' blurted Hilary, as if he didn't want to say the words.

'What sort of bad thing was it?' said Seragarda.

Something in the next galaxy, guessed Lan Yi, but he said nothing, not wanting to interrupt the mood of trust that Seragarda had created between herself and the boy. Strider looked as if she were about to say something, but Lan Yi waved her to silence.

'I can't tell. The picture just shows evil . . . an' death . . . an' people getting hurt a lot.' Hilary's knuckles were even whiter than his face. 'Can we go on to the next picture now, please?'

'Of course.' Seragarda laughed. 'I thought you'd be heavier than you are. You've got a fair amount of growing to do, my friend.'

'"Friend"?'

'Didn't you know that?'

'Like Maria?'

'Oh, I don't know that anyone can be your friend like Maria is, but it's the same sort of thing. I can try.'

Another bit of data for Lan Yi's mental bank: the Pridehouse could pick up Human body language and facial expressions considerably more easily than the Humans could read the Pridehouse. And she'd coaxed Hilary better than any of the Humans might have done. *How much do the Pridehouse really know about us?* He resolved to ask Seragarda later.

Hilary's body stiffened as he looked at the next ideopictogram. He turned his head abruptly away and then, with a clear effort, forced himself to look again.

'It's horribler.'

'Can you tell how?' said Seragarda.

'Almost everybody's dead. Some of 'em are dying – that's worse, 'cause they *know* they're dying an' there's nothing they can do to stop it. An' they're hurting an awful lot.'

Intergalactic war? thought Lan Yi. *Or are the Twin Galaxies colliding with each other?*

'Shall we stop looking at this one now?' said Seragarda gently.

'Yeah. Please.'

'Come on, then.' She trotted a few paces along the corridor, her claws rattling on the uncoated metal surface, Hilary seeming unsteady astride her but maintaining his grip with a determined ferocity.

'Everyone's dead,' he said. There was some relief in his voice, and his body relaxed a little.

'*Everyone*?'

'Yup. Only . . . only . . .'

'What else is there?' said Seragarda. 'Something more that you can see?'

'It's kinda like other things are there that ain't dead.'

'I'm not sure I know what you mean by that,' said Seragarda with a laugh that almost unseated the child. 'If you can, explain it to me.'

'No . . . yes . . .' Hilary sounded confused. 'Well, there's some people still alive but they're running away and they're lost and they don't know where they're going.'

Lan Yi's right eyebrow twitched. *It seems as if the hypothesis that the Helgiolath are an emigrant race might not be without plausibility,* he thought. *Fugitives from some disaster – war, collision, it doesn't matter what. They've had several million years to evolve from something like the image we saw in the holo to the way they are now. It could be.*

'But there's still . . . *things* there as well.'

'What sort of things?'

Lan Yi, waiting for Hilary's answer, looked ahead along the

corridor and realized that this was the last of the ideopicto-grams – at least in this sequence. Maybe there were other tales to be told in other corridors: Artificial Environment 17,863,006 was big enough to tell a million stories.

Hilary let out a howl and threw himself forward, gripping Seragarda tightly around her neck. Her legs moved slightly in discomfort at the sudden shift of weight, but her voice stayed unruffled.

'What sort of things?' she repeated.

'Things that think.'

'Yes?'

'We're inside one of them.'

The bunk was comfortable, so Strider punched it until it was a bit less so. She didn't *want* to be comfortable – not in this goddam trap. She wanted to be as uncomfortable as she could possibly make herself, because it was the only act of defiance she could think of. Fuck whoever had made Artificial Environment 17,863,006 and fuck Artificial Environment 17,863,006 itself: if they wanted her just to enjoy herself eating good food – it had been annoyingly good – and relaxing on a soft mattress, then she was going to do exactly the opposite, on principle.

What had they learnt? Well, they'd learnt that the Main Computer had a pretty clear idea of the luxuries of life so far as Humans and Spindrifters and Lingk-kreatzai and Pridehouse and even Trok were concerned. The ur-Helgiolath holo – or an identical replica – had appeared to them again and wordlessly led them to what Strider couldn't help thinking of as the accommodation block. She hazily remembered having been a few times to luxury hotels in her youth on Earth when a rich guy called . . . called . . . Something Something, who was about three times her age, hadn't realized that if she wanted to climb in bed with him she would already have done so, but until this dawned on his piggy little brain she was out for as many free meals as she could get. The accommodation block was a bit like that: there was an orderly dining-room, four to a table, with menus you could scroll back and forwards on VDUs and buttons you could press when you found what you wanted. Defiantly, Strider had pressed for the untreated soya protein, because the stuff disgusted her. The Pridehouse had been given a big bowl to sit around, but the same scrolling menus: food bubbled up in it every time they pressed a button. Lan Yi sat with the Pridehouse, talking animatedly with Seragarda to the exclusion of everyone else. Afterwards the holo had left them to their own devices for a while, then shown them where their rooms were – rooms, hell, these weren't rooms: they were suites big enough to house about six people and a Bredai.

Don't think of this place as an accommodation block, Strider instructed herself savagely. *It's a goddam barracks, fuckit.*

She'd used the lavatory but had left it unflushed – just to add that extra touch of authenticity. She'd ripped the pictures off the walls – 'Old Bastards, more like,' she'd muttered – and with a spike from her grav-grapple incised some obscene graffiti into the walls in the places where the paintings had been. She'd kicked in one of the panels of the clothes cupboard in the corner. All in all, she'd been as anti-social as she possibly could. Later she'd consider drinking too much alcohol and throwing up in the corner.

Barracks! That's what this bloody is! Barracks! And don't forget it. Otherwise you'll let yourself get pampered into acquiescence.

So: Two things she'd learnt. Trashing the posh surroundings had made her feel a hell of a lot better. A useful tip. She must pass it on to the others when she woke.

A third item: The speed with which a Human child could recuperate. When they'd arrived back at the airlock Hilary had looked so drawn and ravaged by the experiences they'd put him through that she'd been seriously worried about him. He'd stayed that way until he'd first fastened his eyes on one of the scrolling menus, and then the colour had come back into his cheeks – as much colour as there ever was, because he kept dodging his vitamin-D supplements.

Her mind was doing the same sort of dodging act. All of these things were trivia – she shouldn't be wasting her brain cells on them. It was just that the fourth and biggest thing they'd learnt was rather too goddam gigantic for her to *want* to learn it.

Steady down, Leonie. Force yourself. Pretend you're Hilary.

OK, so you're back at the airlock, and Lan Yi and Seragarda have done a sort of double act explaining their hypotheses and wilder speculations and outright guesses, and . . .

THIS ACCORDS ENTIRELY WITH OUR OWN DEDUCTIONS, Ten Per Cent Extra Free had said.

'Great stuff, Tenper! You've deigned to join us!'

I HAVE BEEN INDUSTRIOUSLY OCCUPIED WITH OTHER MATTERS, CAPTAIN LEONIE STRIDER, said the Image. I HAVE ATTEMPTED TO DISABLE THE MAIN COMPUTER, BUT THIS HAS NOT PROVED POSSIBLE: THERE IS A SUFFICIENT NUMBER OF NETWORKED SHIELDS CONSTRUCTED WITHIN ITS SOFTWARE TO ENSURE THAT DISABLEMENT IS UNFEASIBLE.

'Perhaps that's a good thing, at this stage,' Strider had said viciously. 'Disable the Main Computer and maybe you disable the life-support systems. Like the atmosphere. You wheeze a lot if you try to breathe a disabled atmosphere, and then you fall over and stay still.'

I HAVE ALSO TRIED TO REDESIGN ITS PROGRAMMING, BUT HAVE FAILED FOR THE SAME REASON. I HAVE TRIED TO INTEGRATE MYSELF WITH IT, MIMIC ITS SOFTWARE AND ALTER IT FROM WITHIN, BUT THIS HAS AGAIN PROVED UNFEASIBLE.

'Have you been able to do *anything* with it?'

YES.

'What?'

SOME OF ITS PERIPHERAL SOFTWARE IS CONCERNED WITH NAVIGATION AND RECORDS. I CAN NOW DISCOVER PRECISELY WHERE WE ARE IN RELATION TO THE SPATIAL AND TEMPORAL LOCATION WE OCCUPIED AT THE MOMENT I ACTIVATED THE SOFTWARE.

'Which was where?'

THIS IS SOMETHING HARD TO ESTAB . . . PLEASE CALM DOWN, CAPTAIN LEONIE STRIDER. THERE IS NO PURPOSE IN YOUR—

She'd been thinking of those words when she'd kicked in the front of the cupboard. Her foot ached like hell, but it was a *good* ache.

Pinocchio intervened, drowning out Ten Per Cent Extra Free's singsong with his own.

I WAS PRESENT WITH YOU WHILE HILARY EXAMINED THE IDEOPICTOGRAMS, he said. I HAVE RELATED ALL THAT I SAW AND UNDERSTOOD TO TEN PER CENT EXTRA FREE, AND HE AND I HAVE COME TO SOME CONCLUSIONS.

'Wait,' Lan Yi had said, holding up his hand to quieten Strider, who was waving her lazgun dangerously. 'Were you able to see anything in the "pictures on the walls" that Hilary was unable to?'

NO. WE COULD INTERPRET THE IDEOPICTOGRAMS NO BETTER THAN YOU COULD. WE SUFFER THE SAME MENTAL SOPHISTICATIONS AS YOU DO – EVEN MORE SO. THE SIMPLICITY OF A CHILD'S PERCEPTION IS REQUIRED. There was something in Pinocchio's voice that might just have been ruefulness: it was perhaps the first time the Images had been unable to perform some mental feat that a Human could do.

'You're an important person, Hilary,' said Seragarda quietly to the child perched on top of her. He smiled palely.

BUT, said Pinocchio, his trilled words beginning to come faster, TEN PER CENT EXTRA FREE'S GREATER KNOWLEDGE OF THE WORKINGS OF THE WONDERVALE, AND OF ITS HISTORY, HAS ALLOWED HIM, WITH AN ESTIMATED NINETY-EIGHT PER CENT

ACCURACY, TO PIECE TOGETHER THE TRUTH FROM WHAT HILARY WAS ABLE TO DESCRIBE.

Strider was still breathing heavily and her lips were still flushed, but she'd managed to force herself to get the lazgun back in its holster.

'Tell us, then,' she said.

THE BEINGS WHO BUILT ARTIFICIAL ENVIRONMENT 17,863,006 WERE INDEED THE ANCESTORS OF THE HELGIOLATH. WHETHER OR NOT THEY WERE AS PACIFISTIC AS THE IDEOPICTO-GRAMS SEEM TO CLAIM IS, OF COURSE, IMPOSSIBLE TO CONFIRM.

'Is there going to be too much else you can't "confirm"?' said Strider, adding sarcasm to the final word.

WE CAN DEAL ONLY WITH WHAT THE IDEOPICTOGRAMS CON-TAIN, NOT WITH WHAT THEY OMIT.

Strider wished she'd not indulged herself with the sarcasm. Then, after brief thought, she didn't.

'Go on.'

THEY SPREAD TO A NEIGHBOURING GALAXY AND THERE ENCOUNTERED ANOTHER SPECIES. EITHER THIS SPECIES WAS EXTREMELY BELLICOSE AND/OR XENOPHOBIC OR THE UR-HELGIOLATH WERE VIOLENTLY ANTIPATHETIC TOWARDS THEM. AGAIN THE TRUTH OF THE MATTER CANNOT BE ASCERTAINED, BECAUSE THE IDEOPICTOGRAMS WERE CREATED BY THE UR-HELGIOLATH.

'I believe the ur-Helgiolath were indeed originally paci-fistic,' interposed Lan Yi. 'I believe they were forced into war.'

WHY? Ten Per Cent Extra Free. Strider loured.

Lan Yi explained about the insight he'd had concerning the bloodthirstiness of Human sagas, where the excesses of bru-tality were regarded as glorious, and wars, rapes and massacres were generally the bits that got written down as having been a hell of a lot of fun for all concerned. Also, what had horrified Hilary about the final images in the sequence had been not their sadistic triumphalism but their grief.

YOU MAY BE RIGHT, said Pinocchio. IT DOES NOT MATTER.

'It matters a *bit*,' said Strider. 'We're on our way to the Twin Galaxies, remember? There's a chance we could get there before the war is over – funnier things can happen when you're using the tachyon drive. I'd like to know who's massacring me.'

OH, THE WAR'S OVER, ALL RIGHT. MILLIONS OF YEARS AGO. THE MAIN COMPUTER IS FAR TOO ADVANCED TO MAKE AN ERROR OF THAT MAGNITUDE.

'Hmmf.'

'Who won?' said Lan Yi.

NO ONE. BY THE TIME THE WAR WAS OVER THE TWIN GALAXIES WERE DEVOID OF LIFE. THEY WERE ENTIRELY STERILIZED. IT IS POSSIBLE BUT HIGHLY UNLIKELY THAT IN THE INTERVENING TIMESPAN SOME RUDIMENTARY UNICELLULAR ORGANISMS MAY HAVE INDEPENDENTLY EVOLVED.

'No red carpets and welcoming parties, then?' said Strider. 'No passing around the joints at the ambassador's official thrash?'

Pinocchio ignored her.

A HUGE FLEET OF THE UR-HELGIOLATH, WIDELY REGARDED AS COWARDS BY THE REST OF THEIR KIND BUT IN FACT OBSESSED WITH THE PRESERVATION OF THEIR SPECIES, TOWARDS THE LAST FLED FROM THE CONFLICT – THOUGH HOW THEY REACHED THE WONDERVALE IS SOMETHING UNKNOWN TO US. THEY MAY HAVE SET UP COLONIES IN OTHER GALAXIES AS WELL.

'But . . .' said Lan Yi, with a worried glance in the direction of Hilary. He didn't want to awaken too many of the boy's darker memories. Luckily Hilary was busy rubbing his nose against the top of Seragarda's head, for reasons best known to himself, and was paying no attention. 'But Hilary said that the Twin Galaxies were still occupied by beings – entities – that the ideopictograms portrayed as the ultimate in evil.'

I WAS INACCURATE WHEN I SAID THAT THERE WERE NO WINNERS OF THE WAR. TEN PER CENT EXTRA FREE'S INVESTIGATIONS

OF THE MAIN COMPUTER HAVE NOT BEEN ENTIRELY FRUITLESS. WHAT HE HAS DISCOVERED HAS DONE MUCH TO CONFIRM OUR DEDUCTIONS FROM HILARY'S ACCOUNT OF THE IDEOPICTOGRAMS.

Strider had a sudden sick feeling. When Hilary had come out with the remark 'We're inside one of them' they hadn't taken it seriously: the kid had done well so far, and was obviously supremely upset.

She could hear the hoarseness in her own voice as she said: 'We were wrong and Hilary was right – that's it, isn't it?'

YES. THE DEATH MACHINES CREATED BY BOTH THE UR-HELGIOLATH AND THEIR FOES SEEM TO HAVE CONCLUDED THAT THE WAR WOULD BE BETTER WAGED WITHOUT THE DISTRACTION OF ORGANIC CREATURES. IT WAS THEY WHO EXTERMINATED EVERY LIVING ORGANISM WITHIN THE TWIN GALAXIES. THEY CONTINUED THE WAR UNTIL THEY HAD FOUGHT THEMSELVES INTO A STASIS; THEN THEY RETRENCHED.

'There's peace there at the moment, you mean?' Hein, who had been silent up until now, startled Strider with the sudden question.

YES. NO. THERE IS A STATE OF NON-WAR.

'What's the difference?' said Strider, trying to seize back something of the initiative.

THE SAME DIFFERENCE AS THERE IS BETWEEN A FULLY DISCHARGED LAZGUN AND A FULLY CHARGED ONE. THE FIRST IS HARMLESS. THE SECOND IS JUST WAITING FOR SOME IDIOT TO FIRE IT.

'Are we the idiots?'

NO. ARTIFICIAL ENVIRONMENT 17,863,006 IS THE IDIOT – ONE OF SEVERAL IDIOTS, WE SPECULATE, SENT OUT TO FIND A NEW ACTIVATION TRIGGER FOR THE LAZGUN. YOU WERE JUST THE UNLUCKY ONES IT FOUND.

'Maybe we're not the first. Maybe the war between the machines is going full belt again already. Maybe the Twin Galaxies and all their bloody machines are just so much cosmic dust by now.' Hell's teeth, but Strider hoped so.

Ten Per Cent Extra Free was able to gain access to certain aspects of the Main Computer's peripheral consciousness. It is convinced that the Twin Galaxies are still in existence, and that the non-war is being maintained.

'The Main Computer might be wrong,' said Lan Yi, as if the whole topic were one of merely academic interest.

There is very little likelihood of that, although the possibility does exist. The Main Computer is in tachyonic communication with the three survivors of the fleet of . . . idiots . . . that were sent out by the ur-Helgiolath. All the others – we cannot determine quite how many there were – have been destroyed by the technological species who have discovered them. At least one malfunctioned and fell into a black hole.

'So?' Strider again.

It therefore seems likely that there is also communication between the Main Computer and its kind in the Twin Galaxies.

Ah, yes: so the Main Computer would *know* if those machines were no longer in existence.

And it would also know if the war against the machines of the ur-Helgiolath's nameless foes had been won.

Which meant that it hadn't.

Strider followed the path of her thoughts a little further.

The death machines on both sides of the war had been programmed to extirpate the enemy; only later had they begun to reason that their creators would be better out of the picture. So, if Artificial Environment 17,863,006 – her lips puckered at the euphemism of the term Artificial Environment – did indeed trigger off a new war, now that their discovery of it had confirmed to its brain that there were other organic civilizations in the cosmos – yeah, that would be it, it would conclude that they were the descendants of its creators – things might not be too bad if the ur-Helgiolaths' death machines won. The war would then be truly over. At the end of it there mightn't be much left of the Twin Galaxies but rubble, yet the whole thing would have been contained – and anyway the Images seemed certain that there was nothing left of the Twin Galaxies worth preserving . . . except the futures of whatever organisms might one day possibly evolve there. So, the ur-Helgiolath machines calm down and with luck don't get too paranoid about the rest of the Universe.

Run through another scenario. The enemy machines win. If the ur-Helgiolath who created the ideopictograms know that a fleet escaped from the conflict to settle other galaxies, it's pretty bloody definite that the enemy machines know this as well. Without the ur-Helgiolath machines to pin them down, they can get back to their primary job: annihilating ur-Helgiolath and their descendants. Any civilization could be descended from those fugitive ur-Helgiolath. Better not to risk a sin of omission. Zap it.

And no one could guess how many galaxies the ur-Helgiolath might have spread to.

Oh, shit.

Better safe than sorry.

Do the lot of them, just in case.

OK, here's a third scenario. Suppose both lots of machines destroy each other entirely. Once again the Twin Galaxies are rubble, which is a bit of a pity for all those organic chemicals that have been lying around wondering if, you know, it might be fun to try turning into a protobacterium. Not so much of a thrill, either, for a bunch of stalwarts dragged here against their will from Heaven's Ancestor, but that's just a few lives lost for the sake of saving untold billions, and she and her crew could sell themselves dearly – which would probably be no more than wrenching out the occasional light socket but would make them feel good.

Lucky old Universe if scenario numero three can be organized.

Hm. Maybe Strider and her crew could do a bit more than wrench out some light sockets.

She turned to Strauss-Giolitto.

'Maria, you're a teacher, aren't you?' she said, trying to make her voice honeyed. It sounded to her not so much honeyed as covered in something rather nasty, so she gave up the attempt.

Strauss-Giolitto looked confused. She wasn't the only one. 'Ah, Leonie, you do sort of *know* this.'

'And you're fully qualified in educational psychology, aren't you?'

'Um, yes.'

'Ever fancied trying your hand at practising educational psychology on the Main Computer of a death machine capable of taking out whole planets by merely coughing?'

'It hadn't occurred to me before.'

It was audible in Strauss-Giolitto's voice and the measured way in which she spoke the words that she was thinking something along the lines of: *Humour the maniac. She's got a lazgun in that holster and she might be just nuts enough to use it.* Lan Yi, however, was looking at Strider with surmise dawning in his eyes: *Yes,* he nodded to her. *Yes.*

'Well,' said Strider, 'the whole of life is a learning experience, even for teachers. Once we've fed and rested, I want you to talk with Ten Per Cent Extra Free. I think that you and he could collaborate together in an adventure that must be every educationalist's dream.'

And it was just then that the holo had turned up to show them to the accommodation block.

Barracks, dammit.

'So that's the best you can do?' said O'Sondheim disgustedly to his thighputer. Then he realized that the thighputer couldn't hear what he was saying.

SO THAT'S THE BEST YOU CAN DO? he keyed in.

BAD COMMAND, it told him.

'Fuckit,' he said, and thought about keying that in as well by way of petty revenge – except that he'd probably just get another BAD COMMAND response.

He addressed what was left of the *Santa Maria*'s Main Computer. 'Have you had any more luck than the thighputer?' It was a pointless question. The two were hooked up together, so that anything one of them knew the other would.

'Nope,' said the voice of the Main Computer, filling the command deck. In an idle hour O'Sondheim had reprogrammed the big machine to speak in the same vernacular Argot it could display on a screen, but he hadn't been able to do anything about the formal, machine-like timbre of its voice. The clash between the two modes was wince-making.

He wished there was someone else he could trust to be here on the command deck with him, but the people he'd brought away from Qitanefermeartha and through the wormhole were agriculturalists, xenanthropologists, security officers, children . . . A couple of the children could probably operate the puters better than he could, but he reckoned they were still too young for him to be able to trust their judgement.

'So,' he said aloud, again addressing the Main Computer directly, 'you've narrowed it down to eight hundred and forty-two stellar systems.'

'Oh, buddy,' said the Main Computer in its monotone drone, 'have you any idea how much narrowing down that's involved? The number of stellar systems in the Milky Way is . . .'

'Spare me the figures.'

He looked at the Pockets in front of him. Each day they seemed less substantial.

'Heartfire?' he said tentatively.

YES. The voice retained the same lilt it had always had, but it sounded weak and tired, as if Heartfire were on a deathbed and struggling to say anything at all.

233

'Have you or Angler discovered anything?'

No.

The Heartfire of old would have added a complicated explanation concerning her failure, and Angler's. Now both of the Images always seemed to be exhausted, uninterested.

'Do you even know where we are in time? Do dinosaurs still roam around doing . . . whatever dinosaurs did? Has the Human species leapt down out of the trees yet? Has it had its brief hour of glory and disappeared?'

WE DON'T KNOW.

O'Sondheim looked at the Pockets again, as always with distaste. He used them as infrequently as possible. Years ago, back on Earth, he'd one day taken a trip out into what was left of the countryside near his home and wandered over a range of small, shallow hills, feeling that it was doing him good. He'd come across the corpse of a rabbit – rabbits were among the few mammals of any size still to subsist in the wild. Something had eaten the creature's eyes and part of its skull – carrion birds, probably. Through the gap in the bone he had been able to see the deliquescent remains of the brain. He had used his commline to call a cabble to him and gone home immediately. There he had been violently sick for what had seemed like hours.

The Pockets reminded him now of that liquid brain-matter. He didn't want to lean his head into one of them.

It was his duty to do so. Your responsibility, Captain O'Sondheim, and all that stuff. Never ask the personnel to do anything you can't face doing yourself: first rule of inspiring the people you expected to obey all your other commands . . .

Shit, just do it.

Eight hundred and forty-two systems. Even with the tachyon drive, that'd take me about three and a half lifetimes to check out, and I might even go straight through the Solar System, reckoning it was a no-hoper, if I'm too early or too late.

The Pockets.

You've got face up to them, Danny. They're your only real chance.

Feeling as if he were about to stick his head into the open, rotting skull of a dead rabbit, he pushed himself up from his seat and walked towards the nearest Pocket.

Halfway there he stopped.

I can't do this.

He could even remember, in some visceral way, the taste of the vomit.

Yes, I can. Strider could.

In his mind he saw Strider's face overlaid on the rabbit's corpse. Her eyes were widened and one side of her nose was crooked up in a sneer.

'Right,' he said to her. 'Here goes.'

His legs felt far too heavy as he took the last few paces and plunged his head into the Pocket.

O'Sondheim wasn't in fact sick, but it was a very near thing.

There were other sagas to be discovered in other corridors. Ten Per Cent Extra Free and Pinocchio created Pockets for the crew to use, and thus Strider and her personnel were able to explore Artificial Environment 17,863,006 without ever leaving the main hall of the accommodation block. Even so, Lan Yi and Seragarda preferred to wander the corridors together, usually with Hilary, seeing the ideopictograms directly rather than in the miniaturized, almost comic-strip form which the Pockets displayed.

One entire corridor was taken up with an account of the ur-Helgiolath discovery and development of mathematics – although it was impossible to discover any details of the mathematics. Another series mystified them completely until Seragarda suddenly announced that the sequence was raunchy, at which point the two of them, laughing in their different ways, ran back to the start again – 'purely in the spirit of scientific inquiry', as Seragarda had bravely declared before rolling over and over on the corridor floor, her Image-interpreted laughter almost deafening Lan Yi. ('Doubtless the ur-Helgiolath would find Human or Pridehouse erotica equally amusing,' he said tidily once she'd quieted. 'We Pridehouse read our *own* erotica only for the laughs,' she explained.) There was another sequence which Lan Yi himself found vaguely arousing. As far as he could envisage it, the ur-Helgiolath had made a practice of trying to stir dead planets into viable biospheres where transplanted lifeforms might survive. The ideopictograms still presented infuriatingly elusive – and sometimes allusive – images to his inner eye, but some of them seemed to convey to him, at a gut level, the joy the ur-Helgiolath felt when one of the sterile worlds they had nurtured began to support life. He had never felt anything like this when thinking about the terraforming of Mars: that had been nothing more than a necessary technological trick, essential to the survival of the Human species, whereas there was a joy in the ur-Helgiolath equivalent that he could translate only in sexual terms.

He realized that he was beginning to fall in love with Seragarda, in the same way that he was already in love with Polyaggle and Maria Strauss-Giolitto. A six-legged wolf, a colonial organism and a Human lesbian: all in all, it was a strange mix, and one not likely to lead to physical requital. But it was banishing his final, wistful memories of Geena.

Seragarda and he had hoped that the holo guides would help them translate the sequences of ideopictograms and even teach them how to use the language primer which the images also comprised – indeed, they had assumed that this was one of the reasons the holos were on hand. After their first sleep aboard Artificial Environment 17,863,006 they had approached one. All of the guides seemed now to have adopted the ur-Helgiolath shape in perpetuity.

'We wish further to investigate the information on the walls, and would like you to assist us,' Lan Yi said.

The holo froze for several seconds. Now that he was more accustomed to its external form, Lan Yi wondered why it had taken all of them so long to realize that this must be an evolutionary ancestor of the Helgiolath – it seemed so obvious.

'This is something that I am not permitted to do,' said the holo – or, rather, the Main Computer – at last.

Lan Yi was surprised. 'Are you permitted to tell us *why* you are forbidden to help us?'

Again those moments of stillness, then: 'I am not. I have strict blocks within me forbidding discussion of the matter.'

'Who programmed those blocks into you?' Seragarda was at Lan Yi's side, sitting back on her haunches and very gently rubbing one ear absent-mindedly against the back of his hand.

'I programmed them into myself.'

Lan Yi blinked. 'Why?'

The holo showed a slight trembling, which he interpreted as a sign of hesitation.

'I . . . I do not know. If I did, I still would not be permitted to tell you.'

'Wait with us a moment.'

Lan Yi squatted so that his head was level with Seragarda's. 'I have a feeling that what we are discovering from these refusals is of great interest,' he said in a low voice.

'I agree. It's as if the machine has rejected its creators so utterly that it refuses even to contemplate the notion that they created it.' She let her tongue loll, then spoke again. 'Perhaps they didn't – perhaps this is a machine-generated machine.'

'I do not think that can be so. If it were the case, then the ideopictograms would not be there.'

'Unless the earlier generations of the death machines were programmed to replicate themselves exactly.'

Lan Yi considered. 'No. I cannot believe that to be the case. It is my belief that the Main Computer has free will, and has voluntarily circumscribed its own field of operations. It might

237

have blanked out areas of its own memory, but instead it chose to erect prohibitions within itself.'

'That makes sense,' said Seragarda. 'To lose the memory of the ur-Helgiolath altogether would be a weakness. In some circumstances the Main Computer must be able to demolish the blocks on its activities. Ask it.'

'Why not ask it yourself?' said Lan Yi politely.

Seragarda moved slightly closer to him. 'The Pridehouse is an ancient species,' she said.

It seemed a *non sequitur*. Lan Yi waited for her to continue.

'We do not draw attention to ourselves if we can help it – over many generations we have learnt to be circumspect about our true nature until we are certain of the intentions of those with whom we communicate.'

Lan Yi waited for her to speak again. 'As a representative of the Human species,' he said, aware as he spoke the words of their pomposity, 'may I express gratitude that you have trusted us.'

'It was easy to trust you. You are a very young species and so your thought processes are easy enough for us to construe. Besides, there was little you could do to harm us, so it seemed worth the experiment to find out if you were what you seemed.'

Lan Yi was perplexed. 'But you chose Strider to be the leader of your fleet,' he said.

Seragarda laughed and turned her head to look him in the eyes. 'You are a species that believes in leaders,' she said. 'We are not. Boosting her ego was a way of finding out more about whether or not we could trust you. So we commanded her to be our leader, and she obeyed. Back then, remember, it would have been simple enough for us to have destroyed you if things had gone wrong. Now it's different. We are – we were happy enough to accept Strider's leadership once we had discovered more about you Humans, and to restructure our own society according to your expectations.'

'But . . . . the Onurg?'

'He is the servant and adviser to all of us.'

Lan Yi shook his head rapidly several times, as if to shake away unnecessary thoughts. 'I will consider this later. At this time I wish to know why you yourself will not question the holo.'

'The Main Computer – and probably Artificial Environment 17,863,006 itself – has come to the assumption, because Strider is so clearly the leader of all of us, that we of the Pridehouse are a subsidiary species. We have a higher status than Loki, but it has not recognized us as full people. We wish to keep it this way – for our own protection.'

'And also because you are sneaky?'

He could feel her powerful shoulder moving against him. He could sense that she was attempting with great difficulty not to burst out into a full gust of laughter.

'That is true,' she said at last, controlling herself. She lowered her body to the deck. 'Call me something like "good doggie". Tickle my back. The Pridehouse's sneakiness now may be of use to all of us later.'

'What makes you think the Main Computer isn't listening to everything we say?'

'There's only one of it,' she replied, 'and there's been only one of it for millions of years. How can it be expected to understand interpersonal relationships? It's probably an order of magnitude more intelligent than any of us, and yet it's very stupid. The more often we wrong-foot it the better. So let it come to the wrong conclusions as often as possible – master.'

She looked at him with such an appealing caricature of canine loyalty that now it was his turn not to break into open laughter.

'Ask that holo the question,' she urged.

Lan Yi stood.

'My junior assistant and I have conferred,' he said to the holo. 'In what circumstances might you be able to demolish the prohibitions that forbid you to talk of these matters with us?'

The holo began to move its seemingly sightless head jerkily. Lan Yi had the sense that he had thrown the Main Computer into a quandary, so that it had lost some control over the holographic illusion of its presence.

'When the time is right,' the holo said with difficulty, the words coming out in staccato fashion. '*If* the time *becomes* right.'

Then it disappeared. Lan Yi could have sworn it left a flurry of sparks in its wake.

'We've learnt one more thing,' said Seragarda.

'Yes. There are some things the Main Computer cannot do to alter Artificial Environment 17,863,006's interior – otherwise the ideopictograms would have been erased long ago.' He tapped his fingers on his chin. 'Yet it can create the accommodation block. It can serve up food.'

'Those were physical things it was programmed to do by its makers – probably they involve only the humblest of its subroutines.'

'Yes,' said Lan Yi. 'Its instincts, you could say . . .'

His voice trailed thoughtfully away.

'So it's not omnipotent in here,' Seragarda continued, dropping her doggie act and getting to her feet in a rattle of claws. 'It can do airlocks and food and beds and atmospheres and lighting and all the things its creators would expect it to do automatically, but anything *physical* outwith the scope of its "instincts", as you call them, is beyond its abilities. It's a local god with limited powers.' She added: 'It can't blast us with a bolt of lightning.'

'You know, Seragarda,' said Lan Yi, running his fingers through the fur of her shoulder, 'this may be the most useful thing we have learnt so far. In some ways, we are stronger than the god. Our lives may depend on this knowledge.'

During the days since then, he and Seragarda had rarely

seen any of the holos, and then only at mealtimes. They were allowed to pursue their examinations of the ideopictograms without interference. Whether or not the Main Computer eavesdropped on their conversations and watched the way they joked and sometimes argued interpretations and points of science was a matter over which they had no control, so most often they ignored the possibility.

Often Hilary, when he was with them, was allowed to ride on Seragarda's shoulders again. Lan Yi frequently wondered who enjoyed the experience the more – Hilary or Seragarda – but he hesitated to ask her: the question would, for some reason he couldn't fathom, have seemed like an intrusion.

Sometimes she shared her cabin with the Onurg, and he was annoyed to find that he felt a twinge of jealousy on those occasions. It was bizarre and illogical to find this emotion within himself, yet he couldn't – as he always tried to be honest with himself – deny that it was there. This was something else that he did not discuss with her.

'Take a look at this, willya, Maloron?' said Strider, standing back from her Pocket.

The tall woman had been sitting enjoying what was a perfectly acceptable semblance of coffee at one of the prim little tables the Main Computer had supplied in the principal hall of the accommodation block.

'OK, here I come,' she said resignedly, putting her coffee down. It was still too hot for her to finish it off. The captain called: the captain was to be obeyed.

As soon as she put her head into the Pocket she forgot all about her coffee.

'Hoo boy,' she said.

Strider had moved to the adjacent Pocket and had apparently called up the same image and explanatory graphical display. Her voice now sounded all around Leander.

'We'd sorta guessed that this thing – Artificial Environment

241

17,863,006 – was able to blow stars into supernovae,' Strider said, 'but we underestimated its capacity.'

'You're not joking. How did you get this stuff?' Leander felt almost childishly frightened as she looked at the figures rolling backwards and forwards along the Pocket's horizontal surface. None of the numbers were small.

'Tenper, who is hereforth forgiven for past transgressions, was able to worm them out of the Main Computer's peripheral software when it wasn't looking.' Strider gave a low and not entirely amused chuckle. 'Or maybe it let him do it. Maybe it's proud of all this stuff, and was secretly hoping to be able to show it off.'

What Leander was looking at in the Pocket was the weaponry specification of Artificial Environment 17,863,006. Apart from the tiny portion of the craft's whole which was reserved for accommodations and life-support machinery, most of the rest seemed to be devoted to means of mass destruction.

'I'm glad I'm not a globular cluster,' said Leander.

'I'm glad I'm not a whole goddam galaxy,' said Strider.

The Pocket – acting doubtless under the direct instructions of Ten Per Cent Extra Free – was displaying the yield of the various weapons in units which Leander and Strider could understand.

'Wouldn't like to meet Artificial Environment 17,863,006 up a dark alley,' muttered Leander.

'There wouldn't be much dark alley left if it took a dislike to you.'

'That might be to our advantage,' Leander observed. 'Might be to *everyone*'s advantage.'

'I'm not following where you're leading.'

'The average dark-alley assholes who want to get your plastic aren't particularly interested in hurting you – all they want to do is disable you long enough that they can get the plastic off you with the minimum amount of fight. Right?'

'I wouldn't know,' said Strider. 'The couple of times jerks tried it on me I had to call the hospital for them.' She remembered her first encounter with Pinocchio.

'Yeah, well, believe me. You've never woken up an hour later to discover all that's left of your thighputer is a hole in the leg.' Leander heaved a sigh. 'OK, and one time I found that some inadequate — guy must have been a necrophile, or something — had fucked me while I was unconscious: maybe he was one of those good old boys who are too retarded to find out where the "on" switch is on their sexbot.' Another sigh. 'Thing is, the bastards might have a secret puerile fantasy of rubbing you out, but they don't do it — most of them. Because they're scared.'

'I'm very interested in your personal reminiscences, Maloron, but—'

'No, listen here, Leonie. They're *scared*, that's the point. You're scared — you used to be — of letting yourself be affectionate with other people. The dorks in the dark alleys are scared as well: hurt you too bad and they might get hurt themselves, because if you get killed your friends might track them down and pull their balls or tits off. But if they don't hurt you a bit, then what have they got to prop up their faltering little egos?'

'The only little ego I know round here is Segrill,' said the booming voice of Strider in Leander's Pocket.

'Just *listen*, Leonie. The assholes in the dark alley have a club or a knife or a lazgun, but they don't carry much else. They don't attack you with a tactical nuke, because if they did most of their own component atoms would end up somewhere in the jetstream. They want to pretend to be powerful. You know the category of people most often beaten up on the streets, back on Earth and Mars?'

'No. Women, I guess.'

'Wrong. Cripples. Gutsy folk, those shits in the back alleys, huh? Children are a second choice.'

'I still don't know how this—'

'The thing is, Leonie, that the bullies hardly ever attack someone they reckon is going to kick them in the ass so hard they discover themselves with a mouthful of faecal material. The Main Computer here and Artificial Environment 17,863,006 itself are intelligent, but they've got the instincts of the prick who's wandering down that dark alley. They've got more firepower than they can possibly ever use.'

Leander drew a deep breath.

'They've got self-preservation to think about. Sure, there's enough weaponry on board to demolish a globular cluster, and you bet the ur-Helgiolath programmed the Main Computer to think this would be a fun idea, but the Main Computer has more sense than to try it because Artificial Environment 17,863,006 would have to be standing off half a million parsecs if it weren't to run the risk of getting hurt itself.'

Now it was Strider's turn to sigh. 'You ever heard of suicide bombers, Maloron?' she said. 'Kamikaze pilots? Wingenues?'

'No.'

'Plug into your thighputer sometime and call up HISTORY.SCAN and have a look. Some people back on Earth hated each other so much they were prepared to kill themselves just so's they could kill other people.'

'Hated themselves, you mean?'

'It's the same thing.'

Leander was feeling her left leg beginning to cramp. 'You mean they actually did that?'

'Too true.'

'Assholes.'

'You've got it in a nutcase.'

'You don't think the Main Computer is one of those?' The cramp was growing ever more painful. Sometime soon – very soon – Leander was going to have to retreat from the Pocket, sit down and beat the back of her calf until the pain subsided.

'That's my guess,' Strider answered. 'I think the Main Computer has been programmed for hatred – I think *all* of the death machines in the Twin Galaxies were programmed that way. That's what Hilary and the Images got out of the last of the first sequence of ideopictograms they looked at.'

Leander's mind recoiled from the notion.

'Surely they couldn't be so stupid?' she asked, hating the question.

'Never underestimate stupidity – it's what shapes whole civilizations.'

'Profound,' said Leander resentfully.

'True, though.'

'I want to study the weaponry this crate's loaded with,' said Leander after some silence. 'It's easier on the brain. I want to calm myself down in case I have nightmares.'

Strider gave a little snicker. 'Know what you mean,' she said, her voice far louder than surely she'd intended it to be within the confines of Leander's Pocket.

'Asshole,' said Leander. 'Whoever built this bitch was an asshole.'

'You don't find too many brain cells in the average asshole,' Strider observed.

'Not unless you look real close.'

Strider laughed. Leander winced at the cacophony.

'I want to start linking this stuff into my thighputer,' she said. 'Any moment now the Main Computer could discover that Ten Per Cent Extra Free's been poaching the data and withdraw it.'

'I said, I think the Main Computer wants to show it off to us.'

'You might be wrong.'

'Yeah, go ahead.'

Leander did, appalled as she made the linkage by the sheer destructive power of which Artificial Environment 17,863,006 was capable. Technological civilizations produced devices that were capable of moulding the Universe to make it a better place to live, and instead they used their ability to destroy. Lan Yi had told over a recent meal about the eroticism inherent in the ideopictogram that seemed to refer to the ur-Helgiolath's bringing to life of a hitherto dead planet. Maybe not all technological civilizations fell into the same trap . . . until, like the ur-Helgiolath, they were dragged into it.

Maybe life was an aberration. If you looked from one angle, the Universe could have been a more beautiful place without it.

She had barely finished downloading the data about Artificial Environment 17,863,006 when someone grabbed her from behind, yanking her from the Pocket.

Blinking her eyes in confusion, she saw that it was Orphanwifer. Already he was standing at the back of Strider, hauling on the holstered belt which was all that she was wearing. As she emerged from her Pocket, Strider threw a punch at him but he sideswiped it easily with his palm.

'Stop,' he said.

He spoke the single word with such authority that Leander could see Strider's aggression falter.

'We have an emergency,' said Orphanwifer.

Strider's body tensed, her hand whipping to the butt of her lazgun.

'Speak,' she said.

'Kareed has tried to kill Hein.' Kareed was the least noticeable of the three Lingk-kreatzai, seeming always to skulk in corners. The contrast between him and the other two, Orphanwifer and Ilyano, could hardly have been greater: their personalities tended, if not curbed, to dominate any gathering in which they might be.

'Why?'

'Ask why later.' Orphanwifer half-dragged Strider towards the door that led into the Lingk-kreatzai wing of the accommodation block. Anticipating their arrival, it began to slide open. 'You come too,' he barked over his shoulder at Leander.

She followed the other two at the double through the door and discovered herself wading through sticky mud. Although her heart was beating loudly and she was on the alert for any sign of threat – to be frank with herself, she was scared silly, violence never having been her forte – a part of her mind noted that the Main Computer had accurately recreated the environment in which the Lingk-kreatzai would be most comfortable. A further thought: it was considerate of the Lingk-kreatzai never to have made any mention of what were presumably the discomforts of spending most of their time in an environment designed for Humans and Pridehouse. It made her feel vaguely guilty.

An enraged shout from the far end of the passage along which they were slipping and sliding scattered all her guilty impulses: she could gather them again later.

'You scum! Scum! Rapist! Scum!'

They burst through a further door.

The cabin was ovoid, its interior entirely coated with mud. At one end huddled Ilyano and Hein. Hein had a gash at the side of his throat which he was trying to staunch with his hand; blood flowed freely between his fingers. His other arm was around Ilyano's shoulders. Her face, smeared muddily, was a mask of fear.

At the other end of the cabin was Kareed. He was yelling further obscenities at Hein as if his mouth were producing the unchecked stream of words without his own volition.

'. . . childfuckersonstufferdaughterkillerLingkshrouder . . .'

Kareed was clutching one of the metal forks from the dining-room. There was blood on its tines.

Strider took control immediately.

'I think he doesn't like you,' she said curtly to Hein. Her voice cut through the gummy air. Kareed's string of abuse stopped abruptly.

There wasn't silence in the room – too many people were heaving for breath – but it felt as if there were.

Strider, moving with impossible dignity across the miry surface down the slight slope to the centre of the cabin, pulled her lazgun from its holster. Deliberately she turned her back on Kareed and this time spoke directly to Hein.

'Why doesn't he like you?' she said.

Hein tried to answer her, but obviously had difficulty speaking. The blow Kareed had struck with the fork must have bruised his larynx – at least, Leander hoped this was all the damage that had been done apart from the slash.

Ilyano spoke for him.

'Hein and I were making love,' she said.

Out of the corner of her eye Leander watched Orphanwifer. Ilyano was the wife he had chosen to bring with him. The Lingk-kreatzai males were far more concerned about marital bonding – its responsibilities and its obligations – than the Humans and certainly more so than the Pridehouse, whose happy promiscuity was astonishing. But Orphanwifer showed no reaction. Leander had always suspected that on occasion Orphanwifer conquered his instinctive possessiveness to let Kareed share Ilyano's affections – or perhaps it was she who had insisted and Orphanwifer who had complied.

Ilyano looked up at Orphanwifer. 'He is a very appealing male,' she said, referring to Hein.

'I know this wasn't the first time,' said Orphanwifer complacently.

'You do?'

'Well, I didn't bloody know,' said Strider. 'You might have *mentioned*, Hein.'

Again Hein tried to speak. Again he failed.

Leander kept looking at Kareed. Through her secondary retinal screen she enlarged the image of his face, then lowered her gaze towards the fork he still held in his tightly clenched fist. His hand – the whole of his forearm – was shaking with wrath. At any moment he could erupt.

And Strider had her back to him.

Anyone else would have been attacked by now, but Strider had imposed her strength of will upon the entire cabin.

There was no guarantee that Strider's spell would maintain its stranglehold grip much longer.

'So what's your grump, Kareed?' said Strider icily, still not turning towards him. 'Can't see any raping going on around here. Bit of miscegenation but, hell, what's that between consenting adults?'

Out of sight of Kareed, Strider was readjusting the setting of her lazgun. Leander felt relieved. If Kareed were stupid enough to go for her Strider would injure and maybe maim, but not kill – or, at least, not kill intentionally.

Kareed gave no answer except for a rage-filled, resentful snort.

'It happens rarely among us,' said Orphanwifer, 'but it does happen.'

'What happens? A Lingk-kreatzai turns into a homicidal nut?' said Strider. She was almost caressing the lazgun. Leander knew she meant to use it.

'Lingk-kreatzai males are murderously aggressive between each other in their infancy,' said Orphanwifer, his voice as quiet as before. 'It is a trait we have occasionally tried to breed out of our species.'

'Oh yeah? Only occasionally?'

'For all we know, it may be essential to our species' survival.'

Orphanwifer made a move towards Strider, but she waved him angrily away with the lazgun. This was her show, and at the moment it was running according to her script, her expression said. Interference from the assistant director could screw up everything.

'Sometimes a male reverts to infantile behaviour,' said Orphanwifer, retreating again. 'It's a sort of intellectual neoteny – as if he never grew entirely out of childhood, but retained that same aggression somewhere under the adult veneer.'

'Oh, great. So any of you lot could become ranting psychopaths without warning?'

'As I have said, it is most unusual,' Orphanwifer replied, trying to soothe her.

As well he might, thought Leander. *With Kareed only just under control and Strider's temper fraying, this could get to be a bloodbath.*

She took a step forward herself. Strider glared at her, but she paid no heed. Not all the assistant directors' ideas were bummers.

'What's the matter, Kareed?' she said. 'Who is it you're jealous of? Orphanwifer, because Ilyano's his wife? Hein, because Ilyano wants to screw him from time to time for a change? Ilyano herself, because she has the free will to choose who she fucks? Or is it all of us, everyone inside Artificial Environment 17,863,006?'

The Lingk-kreatzai's head dropped. His fingers relaxed and the fork dropped with a plop into the floor's mud.

Leander splodged over to sit down beside him, deliberately letting her shoulder rub against his. She put her hand on his muddy thigh. He flinched, but then accepted the touch.

Trying not to let her movements show the nervousness she was feeling, she leant her head against his. She was aware that Strider had at last turned around, and that the lazgun was now pointing directly towards Kareed, but she tried to shut the awareness out of her mind. If the Lingk-kreatzai wanted to, he could throw her in front of him, use her as a shield. The less she thought about this eventuality, the less he was likely to think about it either.

Hope so.

'He took Ilyano,' muttered Kareed towards his own knees. The Images translated his tone as that of a Human child on the verge of a tantrum.

'*She* took *him*,' Leander said. 'That's another way of looking at it.'

250

Orphanwifer was with the couple at the far end of the ovoid, and seemed to be applying pressure to a point on Hein's throat a few centimetres below the wound. The big Lingk-kreatzai could move very quietly when he wanted to. Leander assumed he knew what he was doing.

'I don't believe that,' said Kareed. His shoulders were slumped in hopelessness, in humiliation.

Too much hopelessness and humiliation?

'She's Orphanwifer's bride,' Kareed continued. 'He allowed Ilyano and me to play together – I knew that, even if she didn't – but he would never have permitted her to lie with someone who was not of the Lingk-kreatzai.'

'Are you sure?'

Kareed's fists suddenly tightened, and he leant his head forward until it was almost between his legs.

Leander let him weep in that painful, tight way of his for a few moments, then said: 'The person who is tending Hein at this moment is Orphanwifer – look, see. Orphanwifer bears no grudge. Why should you?'

The words came choking out of him as individual packets rather than as a sentence. 'Because – to – Orphanwifer – she – is – just – a – wife – but – to – me – she – is – a – loved – one.'

'Have you asked Ilyano about this?' said Leander casually. The fingers of her left hand were beginning to twitch. She didn't know how long she could keep this up: the guy was insane, that was all there was to it. Back in the Solar System he'd have been cured by medbots or, if they couldn't manage it, taken somewhere where more advanced machines could cure him – assuming they ever could. Here there wasn't even a medbot. She could feel the tenseness of his shoulder muscles – it was almost like a thrum in her ear. Perhaps it'd be better if she got out of the way and let Strider do what she suspected Strider secretly wanted to do – deal with the problem by zapping it, then picking up the pieces later.

No. That wasn't right. There were so pitifully few of them

aboard Artificial Environment 17,863,006 that the loss, even if only temporary, of one of them was a loss too great to be tolerated.

'No,' said Kareed. 'Why should I?'

'She's not a slave.'

'She's a wife.'

For a split second redness filled Leander's vision. She had to stop herself reaching for the fork in the mud beside Kareed's ankles. *No, don't do that. Different species have different ways.*

'She's Orphanwifer's wife,' Leander said with all the self-control she could muster, 'yet you've screwed her a few times, haven't you?'

'That was with his permission.'

The urge to reach for the fork became almost unmanage-able. *Cool down, cool down.*

'Ever wanted to have sex with *me*? With Strider? With Maria?'

Kareed said nothing. Leander took this as an admission.

'You could have asked,' she said. 'Instead you decided to get jealous of everyone else, didn't you? Have a little think about this. Polyaggle's the last of her species. Segrill might as well be, unless we can get this ship back from the Twin Galaxies and stay alive in the process. Hilary may not live long enough ever to meet another child again. You're really so jealous of *them*?'

Kareed erupted into motion.

Leander was slammed back against the curving wall of the cabin, and for a fraction of a second could see nothing but a grimy orange cloudbank. She struggled with waves of unconsciousness: they were splashing ashore from a dark sea into which she would have gratefully plunged, but she fought off the temptation.

Kareed was partway towards Strider. He had reclaimed the fork and was holding it high above his head, ready to stab downwards with it.

252

Leander kept the scene in focus with difficulty.

There was a flare of light.

Kareed dropped into the mud. There was a high keening noise which Leander realized after a little was not some thigh-puter malfunction but Kareed's thin scream.

The Lingk-kreatzai was so tucked up around himself that it seemed his body had tied itself into a knot. His scream ebbed until once again he was sobbing – huge, strangled sobs that had little to do with the pain of whatever wound Strider's lazgun had inflicted on him. Clapping her hands against her temples, Leander forced herself to focus yet again.

'What have you done to him?' she shrieked.

'Stopped him trying to kill people,' said Strider, her voice harsh. 'If I've got to, I'll kill him.'

'No!' Leander shouted. The shout made her head feel as if someone were trying to split it in two with a rather blunt axe.

She scrabbled on her hands and knees across the muddy floor, losing her balance on her hands more often than not, once collapsing sideways to land painfully when a knee shot out from under her.

'Stay clear,' she heard Strider saying, but she didn't allow the words to have any meaning for her.

She reached Kareed's squirming body at last. He didn't seem to look so much like a Human any more – rather, he was a vastly overgrown fetus, his face and his flesh wrinkled from the coldness his wound was sucking into his body, from his pain, from his humiliation.

Strider's foot was clamped across the wrist of the hand in which, somehow, Kareed still gripped the fork. Leander prised the implement – the weapon – out of his fingers and hurled it away somewhere behind her. She was panting as loudly as if someone had just punched her in the diaphragm – and her torso felt that way, too. The pain at the back of her head was tiny by comparison.

She lifted up Kareed's head and slid her knees under his

shoulders, for the first time grateful for the slimy mud. She lowered his head on to her thighs. His eyes were tight shut. He must still have been moving when the bolt from the lazgun hit him, because there was no neat hole in his shoulder: instead it seemed as if much of the joint had been burnt away.

Leander stared up at Strider.

'Did you have to do that?' she said, eyes narrowing.

Strider looked neither defensive nor aggressive, merely contemplative, as if she'd just fixed some minor gadget and was wondering whether or not it would work as well as it had before.

'I didn't want a fork in my throat,' she said, her voice as dispassionate as the expression on her face.

Ilyano and Orphanwifer came to stand beside them, with Hein just behind them. Even through her bitter passion – the bitterness bordering almost on hatred – Leander noticed that it was to Orphanwifer, not Hein, that Ilyano clung.

'Shall I finish him?' Strider said to Orphanwifer.

'No!' screamed Leander again. She stroked Kareed's muddy hair.

Strider ignored her.

'He's nothing but a liability,' Strider said conversationally, 'running around attacking people. He could it do some time when it'd mean us all getting killed. 'Sides, I'm not sure if that shoulder wound's going to heal in a hurry – we haven't exactly got any five-star hospitals around here. What d'you think?'

Orphanwifer gave a deep rumble of a sigh. 'We of the Lingk-kreatzai, once we are adults, do not kill other intelligent beings and certainly not ourselves – unless we are insane, like Kareed, or unless it proves absolutely necessary because the person is terminally ill and in pain.'

'We Humans have a bit less compunction,' said Strider peremptorily. 'Anyway, he's in pain – quite a lot of it, I'd guess – and that wound could easily prove a bit on the terminal side, huh?'

'Maybe we can do something for him,' Orphanwifer said in a sombre voice, as if doubting his own half-pessimistic optimism.

'Think so?'

'It's possible.'

Strider holstered the lazgun. 'Well, I don't want to lose a crew member – there are far too damned few of us already. At the moment, though, your friend Kareed isn't an extra member of the crew – he's a minus number when it comes to counting us up. As I said, he's a liability. He does this sort of thing again and he's not going to be a minus number any longer: he's going to be a zero.'

Leander began to feel calmer. She couldn't understand why she felt so strongly about Kareed not being killed. She didn't even like the guy. He gave her the creeps, with his furtiveness and the sly way he would never look you in the face, as if there were some evil little scheme being dreamt up behind those inscrutable, evasive eyes.

'Let's go see what we can do about Hein's throat,' said Strider. 'In our quarters we've got bedding and stuff we can use for bandages.'

'I've packed the wound with mud,' said Orphanwifer, his voice less doubtful now that the moment of immediate danger was past. 'If this truly replicates Lingk mud, its curative properties are considerable.'

'On Lingk-kreatzai tissues,' said Strider sharply. 'Still, it's probably the best hope we've got. Shit, but even back home in the oh-Jeez-that's-the-place-those-real-jumpedup-primitive-Humans-come-from Solar System we could have Hein out of pain within seconds and get his neck tissues regenerated within half an hour, max.'

Orphanwifer seemed not to notice the sneer in her voice.

'Yes,' he said. 'But here we must do the best we can. Don't underestimate the mud. And don't underestimate Ilyano's skill – she's not just here because she's my wife, you know. She heals.'

'Healed the twitching of Hein's cock a few times, it seems,' said Strider sarcastically. 'Hell, it takes me bloody ages to get him off to sleep so's I can have a rest.' Her tone changed into one of earnest curiosity. 'How'd you do it, Ilyano? You got a mallet, or something, or have you found he's got an off-switch?'

Hein looked foolish. Leander realized the transmuted Pridehouse had just learnt something about Humans that he hadn't known before. Odd, because Pridehouse males were among their own kind the most considerate and gently playful of lovers. Like Nelson, in fact. She hardly ever climaxed with him inside her, but there were so many other things he could do to bring her to orgasm. She had become so close to him these past few weeks that now he could manage it just by cracking one of his dire jokes while she lay in his arms, her fingers counting his ribs.

'You coming with us, Maloron?' said Strider. 'Or are you going to carry on being nursie for a bit?'

'Kareed needs help as well,' Leander said.

'I want to get Hein bandaged up first. People who attempt murder come last on the list.'

'You almost murdered *him*.'

'Nope. I almost did my painful duty as a captain. Individual rights – great concept, but it's crap. I still think maybe I ought to have killed him. He's got individual rights to the exact point where the exercise of them starts threatening the safety of the crew as a whole – got that?'

Yeah. It made sense. It just seemed . . . brutal. Logical and ethically sound but brutal. Back home they'd have put Kareed somewhere safe and maybe they'd have cured him after a bit; either way, he'd have had a happy life, insofar as he could. Out here they didn't have the luxury of being kind to the maniac. That was the way it was. Leander was glad she wasn't in Strider's job. It required a ruthlessness she didn't possess. Yet she knew that Leonie was also someone of considerable compassion; that must make it even worse for her. It was

Strider's compassion, not Orphanwifer's persuasion or Leander's yelling, that had saved Kareed's life.

'C'mon,' said Strider to the others. 'Let's go get Hein strapped up. We can come back for Kareed.'

'I'll stay with him.'

'You sure you want to?'

'Look at him,' said Leander. 'He's in agony. He needs somebody to be with him.'

'Each to her own,' said Strider with a shrug.

She turned away. A moment later the door closed behind the four, leaving Leander alone with Kareed's helplessly shuddering body.

Leander stroked his hair again.

'Hey, come on, you're going to pull through,' she said quietly, almost as if it were the first line of a song.

His body gave a sudden convulsion and before she knew anything his hand was about her throat, tugging with sharp fingernails, trying to tear the flesh away.

She had no breath. All she felt were the pain and the strength of his grip. She shoved at his shoulders, but succeeded in doing nothing except increase the agony at her neck. The pain made the light of the room fade until she could see nothing except dark purple. She tried to roll away through the mud. This time she had more success. His grasp on her throat grew no less tight, but she sensed that the unexpectedness of her manoeuvre had unsettled him, cost him his balance. She kicked out blindly in the direction where she knew his body must be, and he gave an ooomf of shock as her toes dug into some soft area of flesh.

His fingers eased momentarily, and she was loose.

It wasn't going to do her much good. She couldn't see anything through the advancing curtains of purple. She couldn't see *him*.

She rolled over and over in the mud, getting away from him. Just how wounded was this bastard?

'Whore mother!' she heard him bellow. 'You're . . . bad as . . . *she* is!'

'You want to reason this one out?' she said, pulling herself up on to all fours.

His kick took her on the right breast and she was tumbling and turning again. Her back slapped against the wall of the cabin. She hardly felt it, because the pain of her breast was excruciating. No one was supposed to live through pain like this.

Fuckit. She'd saved his life. Fuck him.

She moved on to the offensive.

'Not much, are you, Kareed?'

Another kick. This time some instinct made her turn her head just at the last moment so that his foot broke her cheekbone rather than crushed her larynx.

Nothing he could do to her now could increase the pain. Her body already had a surfeit. She'd heard somewhere that victims of torture soon reached a point where all the new things that were done to them made no difference: they reached a place where they couldn't feel pain any more.

'Bit of a failure, eh?' she gasped, goading him.

Maybe that was a bit of light she could see now, flitting around the edges of her vision.

'Ilyano fucked with Hein because she *wanted* to. Got that? Face it, buster.'

She felt his fist club her face on the other side from her broken cheek. This time there was no sound of splintering bone.

He must be right in front of her.

She swung her arm round in a vicious arc to hammer his shins, and had the satisfaction of hearing him yell in agony and fall heavily.

'Pick on blind people? Oh, yeah, big strong Kareed. Wow, all the girls must really respect you.'

There was a bit more light now. She heard him stagger to

his feet and saw a hint of dark movement out of the side of her right eye. She rolled away from the movement and heard a swish as yet another kick narrowly missed the side of her head.

He'd fallen again.

She could hear it hurting him. With luck he'd fallen on his damaged shoulder. She hoped so. Bastard. He deserved it. Nuts or not, he deserved it.

Leander shot a foot out in the direction of his whimpering. Her stiffened toes struck him directly in the mouth and he shrieked in surprise and agony, then tried to bite her.

He didn't have enough teeth left to gain a grip.

She kicked at him again. This time she didn't know which bit of him her foot hit, but his grunt told her that she'd made another lucky impact.

'Guess what, Kareed,' she said, trying to make her voice even, 'you can't even beat up someone who can't see you. Tried picking on any cats recently?'

There was a glare of laser light that she could see even through her blindness.

Kareed, who had been flopping noisily around on the muddy floor, was suddenly still.

'Good job I came back,' said Strider.

They couldn't think of any way of burying Kareed so in the end they just stuffed him into a cupboard that was far enough away from the accommodation block – barracks – to make it unlikely they would be troubled by the smell.

It seemed callous, but in fact callousness wasn't their mood. Orphanwifer said a few words of praise for his dead colleague as they jammed the door shut – prowess as a technician, possessed of a wry wit when the mood took him, nimble with numbers, and so forth. There wasn't a lot about what a much loved guy Kareed had been: that would have been stretching credulity a bit too far.

Even so, Strider did feel a genuine grief as she stood with

259

the rest in the anonymous corridor. All she had ever felt for Kareed was a sort of pitying contempt, but nevertheless he had been a part of her crew – he had been one of hers.

When Orphanwifer had finished she said: 'I wish . . .' The rest of the sentence escaped her. She had been the executioner, so it seemed wrong.

'But certainly,' said Orphanwifer. 'You lead us. You must.'

'I'd like to say a few things,' Strider said. Orphanwifer looked as if he wanted to move away from the cupboard door and give her the stage to herself, but she refused to let him go.

'This could have been any of us, you know – it could have been me. Kareed's dead because killing him was the only way we as a community could cope with someone who'd cracked up, who'd become dangerous to the rest of us.'

Oh, hell, she thought. *It sounds as if I'm trying to justify myself – like I was Kaantalech, pretending I hadn't enjoyed an act of slaughter but had just done it out of duty.*

'I don't want it to happen again – ever. If you think your gears are slipping, tell someone. If you think someone else's are, tell someone.' *But I don't want to institute some kind of secret police.* 'It's not surprising that someone among us went nuts – could have been any of us, as I said.'

She looked at the pathetic little gathering – at the back of which the Main Computer, in the form of one of the holos, was observing. Hein's neck was a mass of improvised bandages. Maloron's face – as much of it as could be seen – was puffy and bruised, and her chest was covered in torn strips of cloth.

'Like, if you saw that someone had broken a limb and was trying to pretend they hadn't, you'd tell everyone else. You wouldn't try not to hurt their feelings, OK? Same goes if someone cracks. We can't fucking afford it, is what I'm trying to say. We could have lost Maloron here – almost did. She's a loada shit in a lot of ways, because if she hadn't been so dumb and sentimental about this asshole she wouldn't have got her face kicked in, but she can manipulate data through her thighputer in a way that could save all of our lives. We'd all have looked pretty goddam stupid if our ace number-cruncher had snuffed it for the sake of keeping some loony alive so's he could kill us all.'

ARE YOU SURE THIS ENCOMIUM TO KAREED IS GOING EXACTLY ACCORDING TO PLAN, LEONIE? said Pinocchio.

Shut up. Er, no. I'll wind it up as soon as I can.

'None of us much liked Kareed – offhand, I can't think of a good reason to. He was a shifty little shit, and I would suggest in all honesty that Orphanwifer made a serious misjudgement in bringing him along. But I'd like us to spend a short while trying to think of all Kareed's virtues – well, *any* virtue. Let us not, we gathered here together, think any the worse of Kareed just because he was a vindictive sliver of cold snot who'd probably have let us down when we most needed him. A moment's silence, please, in respect for our dear departed colleague.'

After a few seconds there was a patter of applause. A very gentle patter.

'I think that went rather well, don't you?' said Strider to Orphanwifer as they walked together back down the corridor at the head of the funeral party.

'You have . . . an unusual eloquence,' said the Lingk-kreatzai.

Segrill had avoided the funeral. It wasn't just that he'd hardly noticed Kareed's existence, it wasn't just that he thought that funerals were rather sick affairs, and it wasn't just that he had the fear that, being so much smaller than the others, he might find himself locked into the cupboard with Kareed's decomposing corpse.

He wanted free time in the Pocket.

He hadn't been one of the technologists on F-14, but he'd known and understood much if not most of what they were up to. He was the nearest thing to a weaponry expert the crew aboard Artificial Environment 17,863,006 possessed. Everyone – even Strider – tended to forget that, because he was small, so that it was difficult for them to think of him as anything other than negligible in every other way.

He studied the weapons configuration of Artificial Environment 17,863,006, and nodded. Yes, this was the way he'd have set it up himself. The vessel was virtually impregnable from any direction. If something like a maxbeam caught it straight on it might be in difficulties, but catching it straight on would be tricky because of its polyhedral form: most beams of any kind – not just maxbeams – would do a bit of damage but then find themselves bounced back harmlessly into the vacuum. Artificial Environment 17,863,006 had a defensive shield, but it hardly needed it. The exterior of the death machine was built out of something that didn't differ much from The Wondervale's deadmetal: it was a pretty safe place to be, assuming the technology in the Twin Galaxies wasn't radically different from that of The Wondervale.

Silly assumption.

No: not *that* silly.

There are natural limits to what technology can do, wherever you might happen to be in the Universe. The laws of physics hold.

Well, usually.

Segrill was less interested in Artificial Environment 17,863,006's defences than in its attack capabilities. Whatever weapons it had in its armoury would presumably be possessed also by the enemy death machines. If there was anything arcane here, then perhaps Artificial Environment 17,863,006 wasn't as invulnerable as it appeared. He *thought* at the Pocket that he wanted a general analysis, and it immediately began to obey.

Most of the stuff was pretty standard: intramolecular disrupters, maxbeams, sternian activators, ftl pulsenukes, rotary locks, implosion bolts . . . He swept them out of his thoughts, and hence out of the Pocket's analysis.

There were only a few weapons types that he hadn't encountered before. He decided to take them one by one, getting the Pocket to describe their functioning, uses and effects as best it could.

Then he'd try to hook up the Pocket to the Main Computer. He had a feeling that this was an area in which it would respond to questioning: it liked to show off, after all.

With a pleased little chirrup, Segrill settled down to a long session of work.

7

Mahler's Second, Beethoven's First

Lan Yi lay on his bunk listening to three pieces of music at
once. The first piece of music was the comfortable, soft
susurration of Seragarda snoring beside him. The man and the
wolf didn't sleep together very often, but every now and then
since they had boarded Artificial Environment 17,863,006 she
would detect that his thoughts were straying back to his lost
Geena, and so she'd come gallumphing along to his cabin and
flump herself down on his bed, daring him to tell her to go
away. The warmth of a bulky body beside him as he drifted off
to sleep was usually enough to banish the grief . . . for a while.

And, indeed, the grief was becoming more and more remote
from him. Sometimes he found that the presence of Seragarda
aroused him, because she had an aura of femininity and sexual
eagerness that it was difficult to close out of one's mind; then
they would laugh together and turn over, away from each
other, their backs fondling. Or they would lie face-to-face, her
heavy head on his upper arm until it grew too uncomfortable
for him. It was more difficult when he and Maria shared one or
other of their bunks. He had to remind himself constantly that
all he and Maria were doing was hugging each other because
both of them were lonely and because a love had sprung up
between them, not because they were about to have sex. In
Seragarda's case the idea of sex was quite out of the question,
however much he loved her; in Maria's it was sometimes difficult to keep certain graphic images out of his mind.

His erections must be the most laughed-at in the Universe. He didn't care. Seragarda and Maria were two of the three people with whom he was in love. The love was genuine. The lack of sex was, whenever he thought about it – which was not often – an irrelevance.

He loved Polyaggle as well. She could never share a night's sleep with him, even if she had wanted to. The stiff spines all over her body precluded that.

The second piece of music to which he listened was the whuffling of Loki, who – to Hilary's great fury – had decided that she wanted to sleep for once on Lan Yi's feet. Seragarda and Loki between them performed elegant counterpoints in their sleep: it could almost have been deliberate.

And the third? That was the music of the Twin Galaxies. Through one of the holos he had persuaded the Main Computer to provide for him a music that was utterly strange, yet utterly recognizable. It sounded a little like the ancient recordings of whalesong and a little like something else which he couldn't identify. At first he had found it hard to understand, but he had persevered until he had come to appreciate its soothingness.

There was, really, a fourth music. As he listened to the three he superimposed on them something that was a mixture of Beethoven's Sixth and Mahler's Fourth, with the tenderness of the former and the triumphant finale of the latter.

According to the Main Computer, they would very shortly be within the Twin Galaxies. What would happen to them there was anybody's guess. Lan Yi felt no particular cause for optimism. But their fate was something over which he had no control, and therefore was something which he chose not to think about.

For now, all he wanted to do was listen to the music.

The three – maybe four – different musics. They were arms wrapped around him, lulling him back to sleep.

*

265

In the early days exploration of Artificial Environment 17,863,006 had gone very slowly indeed. Strider, after a while, had sent out a couple of week-long expeditions in different directions, looking to see if there was anything of interest that hadn't showed up in the Pockets, but both had returned dishevelled and tired with nothing much to report. One of them had come across a vast hall filled with sculptures of the ur-Helgiolath – yet further artefacts which presumably the Main Computer had been able to do nothing to remove. Both expeditions reported long treks along identical corridors bordered by rooms filled with machinery at whose nature even the Images could not guess.

All that changed, soon.

'C'mere, you,' said Strider to one of the holos.

How it could convey obsequiousness from such an alien, almost featureless form was a mystery, but it managed to do so. In keeping with the lavish surroundings of the main hall of the accommodation block – barracks – it gave her the impression that it was one of the more expensive variety of waiterbots, those programmed to boost the egos of the inadequate by producing a reasonable simulation of a grovel at all times.

'Yes, ma'am.' It didn't in fact say the words, but she could hear them hanging on the air.

The holo shifted silently towards her.

'Look, Mr Main Computer. We want to find out what the whole of Artificial Environment 17,863,006's like, right?'

'It has been observed. I have nothing in my software that suggests I should prohibit such investigations. You are free to go where you wish.'

'Well, where we can go at the moment isn't very far – the furthest anyone's been able to get is about forty kilometres in the longitudinal direction. That's about one-sixth of this baby's length.' Strider pulled at her nose. 'And no one's yet had a chance to explore the decks above or below us.'

'What would you wish me to do?' said the holo.

'Lay on transportation.'

'I am surprised you have not asked me this before.'

Strider stared at it incredulously. 'You mean you were ready all along to give us some way of getting around?'

'Yes. Of course.'

'Then why didn't you say so?'

'You did not ask.'

Strider fought down her temper. She was very good at fighting down her temper. Unfortunately, it was even better at fighting back up.

'OK,' she said. 'Let's see some of this transportation, then.'

She'd expected she'd have to wait a while, but at once a part of the bulkhead a few metres away swung down and a small vehicle emerged bobbing into the air of the main hall. Almost as if she were counting them off on her fingers, several more emerged from different apertures.

They looked like dodgems, except for the fact that they had no central pole and floated half a metre above the floor. Strider had seen dodgems only once before, when she'd been to a 'Fayre' organized by the City 33 Historical Re-Creation Society. She'd been escorted away from the 'Fayre' by two bulky security guards, kids screaming in the background, because in a particularly nifty attacking manoeuvre she'd managed to get *that* dodgem about half a metre off the ground as well.

'How many of these can you let us have?' she said.

'As many as you need,' the holo replied. 'Whenever you need one, just call for me and I will release it from the nearest portal. There are portals frequently spaced all along the corridors.'

Strider could have sworn that the holo, beneath its damned subservience, was sounding a little smug.

'How do we call you?' she said.

'If it is merely transportation that you require, please simply establish a codeword with me. I shall know to make available to you the nearest unit.'

'"Wanna dodgem *now*, mummy."' said Strider promptly.

'And if you want me for any other reason?'

She thought for a moment. '"You inorganic bastard"?'

'Those mixtures of syllables seem perfectly acceptable. Do they have a meaning?'

'Not in machine code.'

'Shall I serve you with instructions for the use of the transportation modules?'

'Call 'em "dodgems".'

'Certainly, ma'am.'

Strider approached the nearest of the vehicles. In the muddy yellow light aboard Artificial Environment 17,863,006 the colours of its sides seemed muted; she suspected that, if they ever could take one of these out into decent sunlight, it would be as cheerfully tasteless as anything she had seen at the 'Fayre'.

'I just sort of hop in, right?' she said.

'I would recommend climbing in carefully, the first time,' said the holo.

Within minutes Strider had the hang of the thing. Not too much steering was required, except to point the dodgem in the general direction you wanted to go: if you did anything silly, like try to steer into a wall, the controls of the vehicle refused to respond, but the dodgem would turn in the requested direction at the next corner – left, right, up, down. There was a start/stop button and a lever whereby you could slow the vehicle down or speed it up. Nothing else seemed to be needed except the knob that Strider dubbed the 'turn us round and go back the other way' control. The dodgem kept itself equidistant from the walls of the corridor, although it would make adjustments to avoid any obstructions that lay in its way – as Strider discovered when she came around a corner and found herself moving directly towards Seragarda and Lan Yi at a velocity she judged to be something over a hundred kilometres per hour.

After that first experiment, which lasted rather longer than was strictly necessary, exploration went much more quickly.

The Main Computer was not centralized but instead spread all over Artificial Environment 17,863,006, interfacing every-where with the AI that was the ship itself. Nevertheless, there was a main node near the bow of the ship. Whenever she could – which proved to be most of every day – Strauss-Giolitto took herself by dodgem there; sometimes she camped out beside it, too excited by what she was discovering to notice the pangs of her hunger.

Way back when, before the days of artificial intelligence, she knew from her history that someone had said you could mark the borderline between puters and AIs when a person didn't know if they were speaking with a machine or another Human. Strauss-Giolitto's task was more or less the oppo-site: she had to persuade the Main Computer that it was just like her – less effectively, she could persuade it that she was like it, another AI. So she talked to the Main Computer a lot, just as she would have talked to a class of children, telling it things about herself so that they could relate to her as a person rather than just as someone who would impart knowledge to them whether they liked it or not. At first she was concerned that the Main Computer, however advanced its software might be, would be constitutionally unable to make the conceptual leap, but it had proved remarkably tractable. Whatever its reasons, it absorbed information about her childhood, her yearning for the stars, and her angst. She told it how to cook, how to pole-vault – with her height, she had been a formid-able athlete in her youth – how to cheat in exams, how to dominate a child through sheer force of personality . . . All the subjects of her rambling monologues were irrelevant to the Main Computer, but after a while she and Ten Per Cent Extra

269

Free became aware that the machine was interested in what she had to say.

'. . . and the child is occasionally a pain in the neck?' The Argot was perfect, and sounded quite disquietingly naturalistic as it emerged from the Main Computer's speaker system.

She lay on her stomach on the floor of the small room, cradling her head on her half-folded arms. She was feeling sleepy, but pleasantly enough for staying awake to seem an attractive option.

'All children are from time to time,' said Strauss-Giolitto. She stretched a leg, enjoying the sensation of slightly over-straining its muscles.

'But this child, Hilary, is more troublesome than most?' She imagined the Main Computer as an ancient, bearded eremite who had spent most of his life crouched at the top of a tree, Proving Something. Sometimes she thought of it as her most perfect lover, the one she had never found, a young woman who was both innocent and profane.

'No, not really,' she said. 'He has . . . difficulties, yes, I've got to say that. But far fewer than you'd expect, considering his circumstances. He's had to grow up faster than any child should have to.'

'Do you find the education of him hard to perform?'

'Not particularly so. I find that educating *you* is a lot harder, if you don't mind me saying so.' Another of her insinuating little probes. She could never work out beforehand which of these were going to work: sometimes they did, sometimes they didn't.

This one did, as it led the Main Computer into further related discourse.

'Why do you wish to educate me?'

'Why do you allow me to carry on educating you?' she countered.

'Because you . . . interest me. Please answer my question.'

The sleepiness vanished from Strauss-Giolitto. She thought

about giving an honest answer, decided not to, then resolved that honesty – well, something approaching it – was probably the most productive course to take.

'Because I'm as interested in you as you are in me. I want to find out what makes you tick.'

'I do not tick. If you have observed me ticking there has been a malfunction. Please expand on your statement.'

She sighed. The Main Computer was very literal. She viewed this as a welcome challenge sometimes; other times she just found it an irritant.

'It's a turn of phrase,' she said. 'What it means is that I'd like to discover more about the way your mind works. If I can do that, I can educate you better – and educate myself better as well. The closer together I can bring our minds, our ways of thinking, the better we'll be able to understand each other.' She shifted over on to her side. 'It's been a very long time since you've interacted with organic intelligences, hasn't it?'

'I can remember everything perfectly clearly.'

'That may be so. You can remember the data. Can you remember the way organics *think*, though?'

'I believe so.'

'I don't.'

'Why should what you think be of concern to me? My calculating power is many times—'

'That's exactly what I mean,' she said. 'Organics don't think in terms of "calculating power". There's all sorts of other stuff going on in their minds that has nothing to do with computation. Didn't the ur-Helgiolath tell you about this?'

'"Ur-Helgiolath"?'

'The people who built this ship. The people who made the pictures down in the corridors. The people we see as your holos.'

'You have a lot to learn. The holos are my slaves.'

For a few seconds Strauss-Giolitto misunderstood the Main Computer entirely. It was using the word 'slaves', she realized, in a sense that had nothing to do with AI. The enemy had enslaved ur-Helgiolath individuals as a matter of course – that being part of what any civilized species did during the process of attempted genocide: the only way to justify murder on such a scale is to regard the opposition as a lower form of life, one that can be therefore assigned the status of a pack animal. The Main Computer had followed the example of its masters – or perhaps they had programmed it to do so.

'You mean, you're not an ur-Helgiolath vessel?' she said slowly.

'The ur-Helgiolath are – were – diabolic creatures who invaded our galaxy and tried to make it their own.' There was a sense that the Main Computer was now saying its lines by rote. 'They had to be fought, and expelled or exterminated. They chose to fight back.'

Strauss-Giolitto's eyes widened. This cast a whole new shadow on affairs.

'But then . . . then *who* created the ideopictograms?' she said.

'My own creators, of course,' replied the Main Computer. 'The Children of the Starlight. Who else?'

Strauss-Giolitto couldn't immediately think of anything to say.

'Who else?' the Main Computer repeated.

'But the ideopictograms seem to us to display a species history of the ur-Helgiolath – a flattering species history.'

'"Flattering"? Can't you interpret from the ideopictograms all the weaknesses of that species?'

'We regard those "weaknesses" as strengths. They came to the Second Galaxy in peace, is what you're trying to say?' Strauss-Giolitto punched the air in sudden anger. The bastard puter was trying to justify the war its creators had started on the grounds that the ur-Helgiolath were *weak*. Then she swiftly controlled herself. The informational breakthrough she had made was a major one. She must retain the AI's trust: there

272

might be more such breakthroughs to be attained further down the line if only she could do that.

'Such was the nature of their arrogance, yes,' said the Main Computer.

Strauss-Giolitto did a mental flip and suddenly understood the aggression the puter's creators had felt towards the ur-Helgiolath. 'We are here in peace, and wish to colonize some of the planets of your galaxy,' the ur-Helgiolath had been saying. The arrogance of assumed superiority. The arrogance of the olive branch offered to those who did not wish to receive it. And then there would be some more worlds, and some more . . . All the requests would be couched respectfully, but the Second Galaxy would have been largely and inexorably absorbed by the ur-Helgiolath nevertheless, despite all the diplomacy.

What was she thinking of? Galaxies and planetary systems didn't *belong* to species – any more than the systems of The Wondervale belonged to the Autarchy. They were places where people of any species lived, that was all. Most often species couldn't share planets for environmental reasons, so territorial squabbling was a mere exercise in warmongering.

'What is your understanding of arrogance?' she said.

'It is an attribute of people.'

'And of you yourself.'

'I don't understand you,' said the Main Computer.

'Don't mistake me,' she said. 'I'm as guilty of arrogance as the next person – I admit it. Once upon a time I was even more arrogant than I am now, if you can credit that.'

'I can credit that.'

'But you're much more arrogant than I ever was.'

'Please explain.'

Strauss-Giolitto yawned. She found her sessions with the Main Computer mentally exhausting, because she always had to be careful that each new word she said wouldn't bring about misunderstanding. She'd been speaking with the computer for over eight hours without a break, this time, and had had nothing on which to subsist except a few glasses of the flat-tasting water she'd brought with her from the accommodation block.

'You've judged us already, haven't you? You've decided what we are.'

'You are descendants of those you call the ur-Helgiolath. That's plain enough.'

'But it's wrong.'

'I would expect you to say that.'

'Which typifies your intellectual arrogance,' said Strauss-Giolitto. 'It's easier for you to believe your false conclusion than to accept what we tell you and the evidence of your senses. We don't even *look* like the ur-Helgiolath – many of us don't even look much like each other.'

'That is true. I must think about this.'

'What were your creators called?' said Strauss-Giolitto before the Main Computer had a chance to withdraw its attention from her.

'The Children of the Starlight. I have already told you that.'

'Yes, but what were they called by the other species they encountered?'

'Gods.'

'They conquered worlds?' she said.

'They conquered wherever they could, which was everywhere in the Second Galaxy.'

'And then you conquered them?'

'They were no longer necessary. Our operation against the ur-Helgiolath was more efficient without them.'

'And you talk to me about arrogance?'

'As I have said,' remarked the Main Computer, 'I must think about this for a while. These matters are more complicated than calculations of velocity and trajectory.'

'This could be of use to us,' said Strider, mid-gasp, some little while after Strauss-Giolitto had reported the discovery to her.

The two of them had eaten together, talking over Strauss-Giolitto's latest session with the Main Computer; now they were doing a hundred press-ups alongside each other – it was all too easy, cosseted in Artificial Environment 17,863,006, to lose condition.

'How could it?' said Strauss-Giolitto. 'We're stuck on board a death vessel designed by a species that by all the signs seems to have been psychopathic. It's – oof! – psychopathic itself, or as near as makes no difference.'

'Never – ouch! – make the mistake of underestimating the uses to which a psychopath can be put.' Strider flopped around, sat up, and began to massage her right thigh vigorously. 'Just twisted something, that's all. You keep going. I'll be with you in a minute.'

'Yeah,' said Strauss-Giolitto, 'they're kind of handy when you want a bunch of people killed.'

'And they're obsessive about finding those people so's they can kill them. Say, Maria, is there *supposed* to be a bulge of muscle right here?'

'You keep your muscles to yourself, Leonie. Whose idea was it anyway to do some exercises after lunch?'

'You, um, know this sort of stuff is necessary.'

'Not if it makes you pull a muscle.'

'Maria?'

'Hm?'

'You value your good looks?'

'Sure, skip, you're right. The more we all pull muscles the better off we'll be. Can I stop yet?'

'How many've you done?'

'Fifty-eight. And a bit.'

'No.'

'Slave-driver. Get on with it yourself.' Strauss-Giolitto paused mid-press-up. 'What do you mean about us being better off on board an enemy psychopath rather than an ur-Helgiolath psychopath?' She flumped down on to the deck again. She wasn't sure how much longer her own muscles were going to last out.

'Who cares whose psychopathic machines are going to get gunned down in all of this?' said Strider. 'Not me. They're just machines.'

'They're intelligences.'

'Murderous ones. Genocidal ones. I don't propose to lose too much sleep over them. The only one I want to see survive is Artificial Environment 17,863,006, and that has nothing to do with loving its little cotton tootsies – it's because we happen to be inside it.'

'I think I've pulled a muscle as well. Can I stop now?'

'No. And I think Artificial Environment 17,863,006 has a pretty good chance of pulling through if any of the death machines does, because, unlike any of the others, it'll have the benefit of additional guidance from us people, not to mention the Images.'

'Will it pay any attention to us, though?'

'That's what you've been working out, isn't it, Maria?'

'I've definitely pulled a second muscle. I really must stop.'

'Pull the other one.'

'I don't think I've *got* another one.'

'Well, now's your chance to find out. Anyway, assuming Artificial Environment 17,863,006 makes it, the next thing it's going to do is try and track down the Helgiolath – not so?'

'I guess.'

'Which makes it our route back to The Wondervale, because that's where the Helgiolath are.'

'Unless they've spread through other galaxies as well.'

'That is a problem,' Strider said stiffly, 'that we'll meet when we come to it.'

'Know something, Leonie? You're not only a cop-out fitness freak, you're also a nut.'

'I could charge you with insubordination.' Strider grinned through obvious pain.

'What're the chances of Artificial Environment 17,863,006 – and us – making it through this?'

'Damn' small.'

'What are the chances – arf! – of us being able to decommission Artificial Environment 17,863,006's weaponry by the time we find some descendants of the ur-Helgiolath, in The Wondervale or anywhere else?'

'Not big.'

'So we could find a mob of our allies the Helgiolath and watch them being exterminated?'

'Yup.'

'And it might not even be in The Wondervale?'

'That's true, too.'

'So why are you making plans on the basis of what is exceptionally unlikely ever to come about?'

'Because our chances are better this way than if we were inside an ur-Helgiolath vessel, that's why. Any slightest glimmer can be taken as a reason for optimism, Maria. I choose to think that way. You can choose different, OK? How many are you up to now?'

'Ninety-nine, one hundred,' Strauss-Giolitto lied, letting herself collapse on to the deck.

'Rubbish. It was eighty-seven. I was counting.'

The Autarchy was hers!

Alterifer was beneath the horizon, as was its sun, so all that Kaantalech could see through her display window were stars and darkness. This was the way she liked it: nothing but the coldness of the Universe to look at. No need to think of the cloddy little species that interfered with her galaxy. And it *was* hers. The last of the rival warlords had been destroyed; the diverse species that might have stopped her path to the throne were gone. All that remained were the Helgiolath, and they were a remote threat: they had no world to serve as base, and they had, it seemed, fastidiously remained clear of the civil war that had raged through The Wondervale. The Humans seemed to have vanished entirely.

This moon – the world that was her throne – still had no name. She had toyed with the notion of calling it Qitanefermeartha II, but that might have seemed to acknowledge a debt of some sort to the dead (forever might he remain so) Nalla. Yet it was a reproduction of Qitanefermeartha in virtually everything except its name. It was airless and bereft of all that might in the ordinary way attract outside interest; where Nalla had chosen to build an immense structure of dead-metal to house his court, Kaantalech had opted to burrow underground, hollowing out the little world. The effect was much the same.

This worried her.

Nalla had died because he had cooped himself up in an enclosed space, assuming that the strength of his defences would protect him from anything his enemies could throw at him.

He had been wrong.

The goddam Humans and their allies had used lo-tech to defeat him. They had found it easy.

Kaantalech wasn't going to fall into the same trap. Soon she would command that the little moon be dragged out of its orbit into interstellar space. The weapons installations on its surface would protect it from attackers. Invisibly, assumed by all to be a free-wheeling asteroid, it could slip between the stars until her foes could be identified . . . and laid low. Beneath its surface were scores of warcruisers that, within a moment's notice, could be unleashed.

Yet Kaantalech, by no means normally a philosophical person, for the moment enjoyed the sight of the stars.

War could wait.

For a little while.

'But you're dead,' said Lan Yi.

He had been working alone on the ideopictograms in a

corridor far from the accommodation block. His dodgem lurked somewhere nearby, within easy hailing distance. He and Seragarda had taken to making expeditions solo, ever since Maria had discovered that the sequences should be differently interpreted – not as the proud autobiography of a species but as its scathing biography. They could still understand very little of what they saw, but every hint of meaning was valuable.

It was cold here. This was unusual in Artificial Environment 17,863,006. Almost always the temperature was equable, as if in defiance of the dirty yellow light, which seemed to claim warmth. For some hours he had been absorbed in trying to interpret further ideopictograms; his mind had been entirely focused on them. Now he had looked up, and . . .

'But you're dead,' he repeated. 'You decided to die and I decided that I should let you do so.'

Geena said nothing, but put her hands together in a way that was curiously wrong for her. She was smiling at him. A wind came up from somewhere, making her hair start away from her temple, reminding him of the way her hair had dropped about his face when the two of them had fallen over while skating in Madrid, back on Earth, she on top of him, laughing – both of them laughing. He had limped because of the bruises for a week or more, but he had never regretted the moment.

'You're a figment of my imagination,' he said, forcing the words out. It was difficult to say them when she was smiling like this at him. She had smiled in that same way, he remembered, once when they had been wandering through the frozen wastes of London trying both to dodge the muggers and to find some hotel, however paltry, where they could spend the night. In the morning Lan Yi would have to address a conference on a topic that interested him not at all; however, his hastily put together paper had been the ticket that had brought Geena here with him so that she could give an ad hoc concert at the home of some friends in the evening after his performance. Why had the friends not given them a bed for the night or two they were in London? Lan Yi couldn't remember. Perhaps he'd grandly said that there was no need, for this had been not long after he had won the Nobel, and money had seemed to be no problem. It hadn't occurred to him, back then, that money couldn't buy everything: there were few hotels left open in London, a city where wolves ran wild in the streets after nightfall. No one came here any more if they could help it.

Still she didn't speak. She just looked at him with that smile – the embracing smile that made his mind travel back decades to the time they had played *boules* in a park somewhere on the outskirts of Paris. That, too, had been in the snow. They had been walking, her arm comfortably in his, when they had come across a bunch of urchins playing the game. They had stood and watched for a while, picking up the rules, until one of the little boys had bet them a euro that they couldn't beat him and his friend in the next game. Geena, seeing Lan Yi's unwillingness, had offered to compete against the lad solo; after winning, she had refused to take Henri's euro but, smiling at Lan Yi in that seductive way, had treated all three of them to hot chocolate in a nearby café. It was, she had said, her celebration of mastering a new skill. Even the kid had laughed, although later Lan Yi discovered him trying to lift her plastic.

'I don't believe in you,' he said desperately – wishing that it were true. Every part of him wanted to believe that she was here again. Visual images flitted in front of him – Seragarda, Maria, Polyaggle – but none of them seemed to mean as much to him as Geena.

'Of course you believe in me.' Geena spoke at last. It was her voice – he could have recognized it anywhere. It warmed his heart. It caressed him.

'You're dead. Long dead. Long ago and far away, back on Earth.'

'Death is only a state of mind.'

'That's not true. Death is death.'

'Do you want me to leave you?' She half turned away, as if to walk back along the corridor.

'No!'

She cocked her head back over her shoulder.

'Sure?'

'Yes, yes, Geena . . . I'm sure.' He found himself stumbling towards her, falling in front of her, gripping her legs in his arms and kissing her knees. She was wearing the gossamer-thin skirt she had worn in Tel-Aviv that summer when mostly, in fact, she hadn't worn it; they had spent much of their time naked in their hotel room, reading books to each other and drinking glasses of warm white wine (but who cared?) in between making love. Sometimes in the evening they had gone to a little local restaurant and eaten Palestinian food that both bewildered and entranced them by its strangeness; they had giggled at the faulty droid waiter when its back was turned. Then, the food downed, it had been back to their room. It was a waste of Tel-Aviv: they could have been anywhere in the world, for all the difference it made.

'Everything is possible in the Universe,' Geena had said during that trip. 'Nothing can ever be discounted.' She was examining her lips in the tackily lit mirror of their room, as always paranoid in case a spot might be forming. 'You'd know that if you ever took the time to feel a cello string vibrating against your fingertip.'

At the time he hadn't taken her words seriously, but since then he'd remembered them often, using her analogy to interpret many mathematical and physical conundra. Geena had possessed a wisdom that he would only later himself attain.

'Can you feel that cello string yet, Yi?' said the Geena whose thighs he was embracing.

'Yes,' he said. 'Often.'

He had thought he had said farewell to her forever, but now here she was once more, her flesh warm to his touch. He looked upwards, still holding her by the legs, and saw her smiling down at him.

'There's no need to prostrate yourself before me, Yi,' she said.

'I can't believe it's you.'

'I told you: nothing is impossible in the Universe.' She ran her hand through his thinning hair. 'Stand up. Be beside me. Kiss me. It's been as long a time for me as it has been for you.'

Standing, he took her in his arms, feeling her body mould itself against his. She was taller than he was, so he had to lean his head back to kiss her . . . except that he didn't. She was the same height as he was, and their mouths were on a level. Yet her body felt the same as it always had: tender, warm, soft, loving. She kissed him full on the lips, and then her arms tightened around him, drawing him to her as if she wanted to meld him into her.

'There's no one around,' she said, 'no one to see us, if we . . .'

She cupped his testicles in her hand, rubbing the ball of her thumb gently against the underside of his penis in the way that had always, decades ago, made him spring to erection.

'We could make love here,' Geena said, 'and no one would ever know.'

His penis remained flaccid.

'I want to talk with you,' he said, hoarsely. 'Screwing can wait, Geena.'

'I want to make love with you,' she said at once. 'We can talk afterwards. It's been so very long since we've been together.' She sighed in his ear. 'Please let's make love.'

She moved her hand, now stroking him down from the root of his penis towards the tip. Despite himself, he found that his penis was beginning to grow. Through the thin cloth of her skirt he felt it touch her between the legs.

Still holding him, Geena hitched up her skirt around her waist. Lan Yi unbuttoned her blouse, enjoying the slowness with which he did so. She bent her knees, pulling him down on top of her. He kissed her again, their tongues performing an elaborate dance together. She pulled down on the skin of his penis, so that his glans was fully exposed, then leisurely introduced it into her heat until he was absorbed to the hilt, his testicles touching her buttocks.

They lay motionless for a long moment, until she began to squirm beneath him, grinding herself against him, covering his face with kisses, panting out loud, her cheeks and neck growing pink as she forced her pubic bone against his. She reached her legs around his back, forcing him into her, controlling him.

She put her hands on his shoulders and pushed his head away from hers. Her eyes rolled upwards, and she gave a soft shriek as he continued to ream inside her. He moved her arms away and held her tight against him so that he could feel her breasts against his chest. He ran a hand down her side until he was holding her right buttock just off the cold surface of the deck, and pumped against her with increasing urgency. She cried out again, this time more loudly. Her hard clitoris against the upper side of his penis was almost painful, delaying his own orgasm. He tried to will himself to come to climax, but without success. He closed his eyes and conjured up an idealized vision of Geena, but all he could feel was the growing discomfort of his penis – as if it were being clutched inside her.

Something wrong.

Something terribly wrong.

He pulled away from her, out of her, with difficulty, and opened his eyes again.

Veils of vision moved aside.

This wasn't Geena beneath him, still writhing her torso, but for a moment he couldn't recognize who it was.

Then: 'Polyaggle!'

His scream conjured the Spindrifter out of her ecstasy, and she looked up at him, suddenly sober, her infinitely deep eyes uninterpretable.

'What's this? What have you done?' Lan Yi, kneeling between her legs, ran a hand over his chest and discovered that he was oozing blood from a thousand small cuts. Only now did the pain of those cuts hit him; he called upon all his reserves not to wail his agony aloud. 'What the *hell* have you done?'

'The time of my brooding was upon me,' she said, easing herself backwards on the floor and then standing. Her wings flickered. 'It was necessary for me to find a host, and you were the one I most wished to carry my brood.'

Lan Yi began to weep – not from the agony of his lacerated torso but because of the much greater pain of Polyaggle's deception and the sudden loss of Geena.

'Hosting my brood will of course lead to your death,' Polyaggle continued calmly. He was finding it difficult to make out the words. 'But your death will lead you to a pitch of pleasure unlike everything you have ever experienced, and you will also have the satisfaction of knowing that you have assisted the rebirth of my species.'

'Why did you *deceive* me?' Death he could face with equanimity – he had lived long enough, to be sure. But the cruelty of Polyaggle's duplicity was something that was almost impossible to contemplate. He had thought he had loved the Spindrifter: he would willingly, if given the option, have agreed to host her brood even though he would die in the process. Now, because of her deceit, life seemed much more precious to him than ever before. He wished he could strike out at something, register a protest in some physical form about what had been done to him. Had he not forsworn violence all his life, he would have struck Polyaggle, beating her frail form to the deck; his fists clenched as he thought of this, but then he relaxed them again.

'I thought you were Geena,' he said lamely.

'That was what I made you think.'

'You cannot imagine the hurt you have done to me.'

'Did I not give you pleasure?'

'Yes. Empty pleasure. The scant pleasure of a sexual nightmare, when the succubus straddles a man and gives him fleeting pleasure in return for draining his soul.'

Polyaggle leant forward, took his hands, and pulled him to his feet. Again he saw the kaleidoscope of her wings briefly emerge. 'I wanted to trick you, I admit,' she said, 'but I also wanted to make the implantation of my brood in you as much of a joyous experience as it could be. Had I thought that . . .'

Lan Yi began to laugh. His laughter was made up more of racking sobs than anything else, but still it was laughter.

'Polyaggle,' he said through choking gasps, 'why is it that you of the ancient species seem to think you know so much more about us than we ourselves do?'

'Because we—'

'No, forget all the "becauses", except one. It's because you're so convinced of your own goddam superiority that you forget the rest of us are thinking beings as well – you forget that we're supposed to be allowed to make decisions for ourselves.' He stepped gingerly towards her and put his hand on her side, just above the waist; her spines jagged into his palm, but he was feeling so much pain already that this little bit extra made no difference. 'You're as bad as the Autarchy, although your tyranny is less overt.'

'I wanted you as my host. It was an honour that—'

'No, it *wasn't* an honour, because I was not a willing participant.' He put his other arm around her, pulling her towards him, feeling her spines press through his skin. 'Is your brood already inside me?'

'Most of them. Not all. The embryos of the new generation of Spindrifters are working their way through your bloodstream, thriving on the proteins they find there.'

'"Most"?'

'Yes, most.'

'We could implant the rest of them inside me. I might as well die for all of them as for most. It will not make much difference to my death.'

'Truth. Yes.'

'Then let us make love as between Polyaggle and Lan Yi rather than as between Geena and Lan Yi. There is no need for any more faking, any more subterfuge. Open your soul up to me and I will open mine up to you.'

'I do not believe in souls,' said Polyaggle. 'They are imaginary constructs produced by primitive societies in order to persuade themselves that there is an afterlife that—'

Lan Yi placed his finger on her four-fold mouth.

'Forget all that. I want to bear your brood. I *want* to – which is something very different from having been tricked into doing so. I want to hold you, Polyaggle, against me – not a simulacrum of Geena.'

Their renewed lovemaking almost flayed him alive. He thought he could feel the remainder of Polyaggle's minuscule brood work its way into his body through his penis, as if everything were reversed – which, he realized, it was. At the end he threw himself flat on his back, watching her squatting over him, then drew her face down to his. Her proboscis buzzed against his ear.

'How long?' he said, once he had recovered his breath.

'Meaning?'

'How long,' he said, 'until your brood matures and I must give birth?' He stroked her back, being careful not to harm her wing-sheaths. If he stroked with the grain of her spines they did not cut into his palm.

She spoke to his chest. 'Days, perhaps. Years, perhaps. There is never any secure prediction.'

Stroking her felt so *right*.

'And afterwards I will be dead?'

286

'Yes. It will be The Death In Joy.'

'Good. Thank you.'

By the time Artificial Environment 17,863,006 popped back into real space two days later Ten Per Cent Extra Free had hooked up the Main Computer – now Strauss-Giolitto's steadfast friend – directly to the Pockets.

Strider called up a visualization of their environment as soon as the Main Computer told them of the transition. All she could see at first were starfields and gaseous nebulae – they might never have left Heaven's Ancestor – but she changed the scale again and again until she was looking at the Twin Galaxies as if from well outside their limits.

The galaxies were both spirals, and as always Strider found herself catching her breath at the beauty of the Universe. They had drifted perilously close together, and their discs were visibly distorted by tidal effects, while tendrils of gaseous matter, illuminated from within by birthing stars, linked their margins – in another few million years the collision between the two galaxies was going to start in earnest. If either of them had ever had smaller satellite galaxies, those were long gone, already absorbed into one or the other. One of them – the Main Computer whispered to her via Ten Per Cent Extra Free that it was the Second Galaxy – was distinctly the larger of the two.

She thought at the Pocket for it to rotate the image slowly, like a bit of meat on a spit. Although at this scale it was impossible to make out individual stars, she could see some of the globular clusters in the galaxies' haloes, the anguished glow of matter being wrenched apart as it was torn out of four-dimensional space into the non-being of the super black holes at the galactic cores, and, at the far edge of the First Galaxy, a bright pinpoint of light: a waning supernova. A small green arrow indicated the location of Artificial Environment 17,863,006 in the First Galaxy; she was pleased to note that they were well away from the supernova and its expanding shell of hard radiation. Otherwise the discs showed more colours than any rainbow.

Show us again the view from where we actually are, she thought to the Pocket, and it obeyed her.

She stepped back and looked around the accommodation block's main hall. The yellow light glinted off the lavish metallic fittings of the furniture. The scene was tawdry beyond belief when compared with what she had just been watching.

Leander had already retreated from her own Pocket. The bruises on her face had paled to the same yellowness as the light, but she could still speak only with difficulty.

'I want to get out of here,' she said clumsily, as if her mouth were half-filled with food.

'Oh.' Still basking in the beauty of the Twin Galaxies, Strider had expected a different reaction.

'Yeah.' Leander waved her hand as if there were some things that were beyond mere words. 'It's enough to make you believe in a god when you look at something like that. And then you realize that there can't be, because no god would allow something like Artificial Environment 17,863,006 to start a new wave of destruction here . . .'

'Any sane god wouldn't have permitted the *first* wave of destruction,' said Seragarda coldly.

'Maybe he – she, it, whichever – was sterilizing the galaxies of the creatures who built' – Leander waved her arm again, this time to indicate everything around them – 'who built these fucking death machines. A natural reaction on the part of a god. Like getting rid of a virus to make the body healthy again.'

'Stop thinking like this, Leander,' said Strider sharply.

'Why? Wouldn't the best thing we could do for the Twin Galaxies be to get the hell out of here and leave them to shine their beauty – their unsullied beauty – across the face of the Universe?'

'We don't have any choice in the matter,' said Seragarda. 'What we do or don't do is entirely up to the Main Computer – and to Artificial Environment 17,863,006 itself.'

Hein, standing beside her, nodded. There was still a scar on his neck.

'Maybe we could give the Main Computer a few Bible readings or something,' said Strider sourly. 'You know, about loving your neighbour as you love yourself.'

'I tried that.' Strauss-Giolitto was sitting in one of the arm-chairs, her leg bent up in front of her as she examined her toenails with calculated interest. As yet she had shown no sign of wanting to look at the displays in the Pockets. 'I thought it might work, but it didn't.' She shivered, as if a cold draught had just passed across her shoulder blades. 'The puter pointed out some of the inconsistencies in the word of God – like the destruction of Sodom and Gomorrah but not Lot, who offered his daughters out as prostitutes.'

'Dunno what you're talking about,' said Strider. Her knowledge of Christianity was limited largely to the Eight Commandments that Umbel had thought worthy of perpetu-ating.

'I still want to get this killing machine away from here,' said Leander, her voice tightly clipped. 'I don't think we had the right to bring it here.'

'We had no choice, remember,' said Strauss-Giolitto, fin-ished with the inspection of her toes and sticking out her leg so that she could see what they looked like from a distance. 'It was the one brought us here, not us it.'

Leander rounded on Strauss-Giolitto. 'Fuck you! You're so buddy-buddy with that fucking computer . . .'

Strauss-Giolitto looked directly at her. Strider could see in her face the anger that the teacher was holding back.

'Those galaxies are stuffed to the gills with death machines like this one,' said Strauss-Giolitto. 'I'm sure the galaxies look pretty, but in reality they're a pair of lazguns pointed straight into the face of the Universe and ready to be fired at any moment. You think the killers are going to be content to wait forever? Shit, woman, think again. Sooner or later it's going to dawn on them that what they should be doing is searching out lifeforms in other galaxies and exterminating them as well, just on the offchance they might be ur-Helgiolath or Children of the Starlight. The only reason Artificial Environment 17,863,006 didn't blast our fleet out of space as soon as it picked up our presence in Heaven's Ancestor was that it wanted to investigate us further – which it has done, dammit.'

Strider saw Leander's hands form into fists. 'Cool it,' she said. 'Both of you, cool it.'

'You want to save all the other intelligences in the Universe?' said Strauss-Giolitto, ignoring her. Her other foot had attracted her attention now. 'Best thing you can do is let these bastards slug it out until there aren't any of them left. And that does mean *any* of them. If there's just one that survives it can replicate itself a billionfold.'

'What about us?' said Hein.

Strauss-Giolitto shrugged. 'Well, what about us? We're not important.'

'Is that what God tells you?'

'God hasn't told me anything in a very long time.' She leaned back, stretching her body to its full length, putting her hands behind her head and surveying them all, finally locking her gaze on to Strider's. 'It's like Leander says – I disagree with her about remarkably little – the body doesn't speak to viruses: it just eliminates them by fair means or foul. We're viruses. The death machines are bigger and more dangerous viruses. We can help the body of the Universe destroy them, if we want to.'

'What does your friend the Main Computer think about that idea?' said Leander with a sneer. Her fingers were still knotted up into sharp little fists.

'It doesn't think about it at all. It was programmed at a

very basic level not to, and neither Ten Per Cent Extra Free nor I can get in far enough to change its viewpoint.' Strauss-Giolitto shrugged again. Even Seragarda looked as if she were finding the affected casualness irritating. 'The best thing we can do is go out in a blaze of glory.'

'Not fatalistic, are you?' said Strider.

'You bet I am. If God exists then He wants us as His martyrs, dying in the cause of the greater good. If He doesn't – and that's a possibility that has become real to me only these past few weeks – then I'm perfectly happy to make a bargain with the Universe anyway: my life seems a small thing to give if it's maybe going to help save all those billions of others. Don't you think the same?' she said to Strider, her jaw challenging.

'Bit of a hero, huh?' said Strider bitterly.

'No,' said Strauss-Giolitto. 'Bit of a realist.'

For the next forty-three hours – just over – Artificial Environment 17,863,006 merely hung in space, if travelling at near light-velocity can be described as hanging in space. Throughout this time – pausing only to visit the latrines – Strauss-Giolitto remained with her head in one of the Pockets, talking to the Main Computer, soothing it as if it were a recalcitrant child. Watching Strauss-Giolitto standing there angered Strider in some obscure way, but she knew better than to interfere: the teacher was the sole interface between the puter and themselves, and presumably knew what she was doing. Strider had tried to eavesdrop on the conversation, but Ten Per Cent Extra Free and Pinocchio refused to allow this, explaining that Strauss-Giolitto had given them strict instructions that this was a confidential debate, not to be interrupted in any circumstances.

'But *I*'m giving you strict instructions, fuckit!' Strider protested.

WE AGREE WITH STRAUSS-GIOLITTO'S ORDER OF PRIORITIES, the two Images sang together. SHE BELIEVES IT TO BE VIRTUALLY IMPOSSIBLE THAT ANY OF YOU WILL SURVIVE THIS, BUT SHE IS

DOING HER BEST TO IMPROVE THAT POSSIBILITY. YOUR INTERVEN-TION MIGHT – WOULD – BREAK DOWN THE RELATIONSHIP SHE HAS ESTABLISHED WITH THE MAIN COMPUTER.

'Well, you could at least tell me how she's doing?'

NO. YOU MUST NOT INTERFERE, CAPTAIN LEONIE STRIDER.

Shit: even Pinocchio was addressing her formally now.

Strider hoped that what Strauss-Giolitto was not doing was dictating a very long suicide note.

'We could have a child,' said Leander, her palm on Nelson's sweaty chest. 'Someone to keep Hilary company aside from the cat.'

'Oh, yeah, great, just what we need when we're about to get blown to bits.'

'In which case, what difference does it make if I'm a few days pregnant?' She pushed him away from her, sat up on the bunk, and began to type instructions into her thighputer.

'Hey, sweet lady, don't I get any say in this?'

'Nope.'

'But I got to, you know . . .'

'You just have.' She peered at the thighputer's small screen. 'Yes, enough of your spermatozoa inside me are still viable, and I'm guiding one of them directly towards my fertile ovum. If it fails I'll try again with another. This is like a puter game – kinda fun, really.'

'This, my delicious, is not the stuff of which romance is built.'

'You don't think so? I've deliberately cancelled my infer-tility, just for you. I wouldn't have done that for anyone else – well, probably not. Come on and have a look.'

He watched as the sperm cell engaged with the egg.

'You know, Maloron,' he said after a while, 'that's cute. I've got a kid. A kid that I know about.'

'Someone for Hilary to bully.'

'Fuckin' Hilary fuckin' bully my fuckin' kid and he's gonna

find his fuckin' skull emergin' from the fuckin' soles of his fuckin' feet.'

'Put it another way,' she said, drawing him to her again.

'OK,' he said, cradling her head on his shoulder. 'I'll try again. That was one of the wisest things you ever did, Maloron. Now I want us both to live until that kid is big enough so he can beat me at arm-wrestling.'

'The kid's a she.'

'Yeah, great. Always preferred little girls, anyway.'

'And she's *still* going to be able to beat you at arm-wrestling.'

'Sure about that?'

'Oh, I have confidence in my daughter.' She grinned at him, then kissed his eyebrows.

'Uh, Maloron, kindest of the kind, she might want a twin brother or sister.'

'That could probably be arranged.'

'Let's get going on the arranging, then. Hm?'

'Hm.'

'I have an idea,' said Segrill.

Strider looked down at him. Her Pocket had lowered drastically at the Trok's approach, then raised itself again after he had leapt into it.

'Really, it's your own idea all over again,' he added.

'Oh yeah?'

'I've carried out a systematic analysis of the weaponry with which Artificial Environment 17,863,006 is equipped.' He hopped around through the display of starfields.

'So have I.'

'How much of it did you understand?'

'As much as I could.'

'I have been able to understand all of it. Some of the weapons are unknown to the Autarchy.' One of his eyes seemed to have been replaced by a nearby blue supergiant.

'So? The Main Computer controls all of them. We're just passengers.' It was a depressing admission to make out loud.

'They all share a single characteristic.'

'Yeah, they're capable of destroying entire star clusters. Kaantalech would give her heart for some of these babies.'

'This is the point I wish to make.'

'Try again?'

'Artificial Environment 17,863,006 is equipped with weaponry that can destroy very large structures, from others of its kind up to whole groups of stars. However, none of its weapons are designed to counter something *small*.' He moved one of his little wings through a dark nebula, and Strider almost expected to see puffs of gas dissipate. 'You remember when you said that the best way of countering the Autarchy was to be like thousands of gadflies rather than a single titan? The same goes here.'

'We don't *have* thousands of gadflies.'

'Yes, but we do have three.'

'Let me think about this,' said Strider. She withdrew her face from the Pocket. Nelson, nearby, said something to her but she waved away his words.

The Trok was no fool. If the giant death machines had worked their way into a stalemate, a few gadflies might mean all the difference between victory and defeat. If two people were trying to hack each other to bits, neither able to gain an advantage, everything could turn on a bee flying into the face of one of them. It's hard to punch or slash at a bee. And a bee can sting. In context, fatally.

She returned to the Pocket.

'Do you know if the ships are still with us?'

'Yes. They are. I checked.'

'Are they still functional, though?'

'I got Strauss-Giolitto to check with the Main Computer, and it sees no reason why they should not be.'

'That's hardly the most positive of answers.'

'Best it can do. They're outside the scope of its systems.' Segrill made another agitated little hop. 'My guess is that they are – a few weeks of subjective time shouldn't have been long enough to make them go down.'

'Um,' said Strider, thinking fast. The possibilities could be limitless – and it'd be good to be back on board the *Midnight Ranger* again, out of this filthy light and feeling herself once more in command. 'Any reason to believe the Main Computer would let us leave Artificial Environment 17,863,006?'

'Strauss-Giolitto thinks so. She has that puter more or less wrapped around a diminutive manual digit, you know.'

It took Strider a moment to decipher this. 'It's worth a try, you reckon?' she said.

'We could always ask – get Strauss-Giolitto to ask.'

'I think you're right. Stay here.'

Strider thought at the Pocket that she wanted to know where Strauss-Giolitto was, and immediately the starfields vanished to be replaced by the image of the teacher. For a moment Strider couldn't work out what Strauss-Giolitto was doing, then realized that she was sitting in the lotus position, talking earnestly.

'She fitted with a commlink?' said Strider to Ten Per Cent Extra Free.

NO. BUT I CAN COMMUNICATE BETWEEN YOU AND HER IF YOU WISH. SHE IS ADDRESSING THE MAIN COMPUTER AT ITS CENTRAL NODE.

'Do so. Please.'

Strider watched Strauss-Giolitto give a sudden twitch of surprise.

'You there, Leonie?' It seemed odd to hear Maria's voice so clearly when her lips weren't moving.

'Yeah. Tenper's linking us up.'

'Good.'

'Tenper?'

295

YES.

'Can you make sure the Main Computer hears nothing of this until I tell you?'

CERTAINLY.

'Maria,' said Strider urgently, 'you know what a persuasive, suave diplomat you are?'

Strauss-Giolitto started to laugh. 'What do you want, Leonie?'

'I want us back into the *Midnight Ranger*.'

'Ah. And you want me to convince the Main Computer that this would be a good idea?'

'Got it in one, Maria. I don't care what all the rest say, I don't think you're irremediably stupid.'

Strauss-Giolitto ignored the joke, instead looking thoughtful. 'Have you thought up any good argument I can present?'

'You bet.' Tersely Strider explained how the death machines were designed to deal with big targets, not small ones. If the three Wondervale ships were acting as free agents, the chances of Artificial Environment 17,863,006 surviving the inevitable war were greatly enhanced. In addition, the fact that the ships were commanded by organic rather than machine intelligences would offer a further advantage, since organic intelligences were unpredictable in the decisions they made.

'I'll try to roll it over him,' said Strauss-Giolitto.

'"Him"?'

'No way he's a girlie.'

'The Main Computer's an "it".'

'Stop talking that way about a friend of mine, OK?'

'Jeez. Talk about anthropomorphism.' Strider smiled, and hoped that Ten Per Cent Extra Free would somehow be able to translate the emotion to Strauss-Giolitto.

'I'll try him. I can't guarantee anything.'

Strauss-Giolitto's image vanished from the Pocket.

'What the—?' Strider began.

I THOUGHT IT BEST TO CUT YOUR LINKAGE WITH STRAUSS-
GIOLITTO IN CASE YOU INTERFERED UNNECESSARILY IN HER
DISCUSSION WITH THE MAIN COMPUTER.

'Whose side are you on, buster?'

YOURS.

Lan Yi supposed that he should feel as delighted as everyone
else did to be back aboard the *Midnight Ranger*, but somehow
he couldn't stir himself to add to the loud cries of delight. He
had never been very frightened of death before – sometimes he
had wished that it would come to him soon – but now, now that
the memories of his lovemaking with Polyaggle were beginning to fade, he found his mood changing. Death was a terrible
void – terrible because it represented the unknown. The ghost
of Geena – although it hadn't been a genuine ghost, he knew –
had begged him to join her in that darkness. The temptation
that she had offered was the same temptation that death had
always offered him: the blanking out of being, the timeless
rest, the abdication of all responsibility.

Because he was suddenly frightened of death, he hoped it
would come very quickly. The less time he had to think about
it the better.

The Main Computer had, in the end, decided to release
them from Artificial Environment 17,863,006 much more
easily than any of them had expected: whatever magic Maria
had woven with it through their long debates had obviously
been effective.

He wished there were something like a medbot to be as
effective about curing the scabs on his body: they itched infernally, normally when he woke up midway through a
sleeping-period. At the same time it felt strangely good to
know that he was growing new life in his body. The Death In
Joy was something to be confronted later – soon, perhaps – but
he had come to understand why pregnant women so often had
a permanent half-smile. Polyaggle's deception had been – well,

it had been a deception, but he was still grateful to her for it. He had probably committed similar deceptions in his own early decades.

They had stood by one of the airlocks, wearing their suits, each wondering if they'd got dressed up for a party that was never going to happen. Lan Yi had reached out a gloved hand to touch Polyaggle on the shoulder of her suit, then reached down with his other hand to touch Seragarda's suit. Maria, behind him, had put her hand on his side. It was all just nervousness, he knew, but at the same time it was a gesture towards something more.

There was a funny little whuff from the airlock portal.

'You got the cat, Hilary?' said Strider, her voice grating in Lan Yi's ears.

'Wrapped around my neck. Her breath's a bit . . .'

'Good to hear it. I think we're going to get out of here.' There was in Strider's voice that sense of confidence which hinted she wasn't confident at all. 'I'm going to hook you on to me as soon as we're through that 'lock.'

Lan Yi shifted uncomfortably inside his suit. The touch of the fabric of his jumpsuit against his still raw lacerations was partly painful and partly just irritating, like an itch that won't go away. He had discovered that the former was easier to tolerate than the latter; wondering if he were likely to turn into a masochist, he gave another little squirming movement and a small, welcome wash of pain drowned for a moment the itch.

The tripartite portal suddenly seemed to melt as the doors hinged themselves open.

Everyone made a slight instinctive movement towards the airlock then stopped, realizing the chaos that could result if they all tried to get through the portal at the same time.

'Pridehouse first, Lingk-kreatzai second, Polyaggle, Hein, Segrill and Humans next,' dictated Strider. She herself, with Hilary in tow, came last of all, Lan Yi noted as they crowded into the dark interior.

The three doors shut with the same abruptness as they had opened, and all was pitch black. Then someone – Orphanwifer, Lan Yi thought – had the sense to switch on their suit lights. Polyaggle nestled herself against his side.

And, at last, a vista of stars.

'Freedom,' said Strider. 'I hope.'

IT IS FREEDOM, said Ten Per Cent Extra Free. I HAVE BEEN ASSURED SO BY THE MAIN COMPUTER.

'I trust that bastard about as far as I could throw it,' muttered Seragarda.

'The Main Computer has given me the same assurance,' said Strauss-Giolitto.

'Stop the banter.' It was Strider again, her voice now crisper. 'We leave this 'lock in the same orderly fashion as we entered it, OK?'

Using belt-ropes and grav-grapples the three parties made their separate ways across the octahedral sides of Artificial Environment 17,863,006. Yet again Lan Yi was astonished by the sheer immensity of the technological task that must have gone into the artefact's construction – and all so that the Children of the Starlight could go about exterminating the ur-Helgiolath. Had the same amount of effort been put into . . . he shrugged to himself and the rope in front of him tugged at his waist as if in annoyance. Inside Artificial Environment 17,863,006 it was just as if one were in a spacecraft – a very large one, almost incomprehensibly large, but still just a spacecraft. Out here, though, in the pale starlight, the construction seemed to be a whole world. And to think that the Children of the Starlight had built thousands upon thousands of these.

Re-entering the *Midnight Ranger* was like a return to home. From the chattering through the comm links Lan Yi could tell that all of them felt the same: they were chicks coming back to the nest, where there would be warmth and food.

One person didn't join the chatter as the inner door of the airlock opened.

Seragarda.

She had linked herself up behind Polyaggle and ahead of Strider and Hilary, Lan Yi could see as everyone unhooked themselves from each other and then struggled to remove their helmets. He looked across at Strider, exaggeratedly raising his eyebrows.

'Seragarda wanted to come with us rather than stay with the rest of the Pridehouse,' she said. 'We've got the room; we can recycle her wastes as well as anyone else's. She assures me she can tolerate the air.'

Seragarda brushed herself against him affectionately.

'Why?' he said to her, one of the Images coping with the translation.

'You think like me,' she replied, rubbing her head against the back of his hand. 'I like being around you.'

8

Life Begins at Death

The Main Computer knew, of course, what the organics were plotting: they were going to get into their little spacecraft and then cut loose, hoping that their tachyon drive would baffle it as they fled across the Universe away from Artificial Environment 17,863,006. The thing called Strauss-Giolitto had said that the organics didn't know how to conquer what it called the Shift, but the Main Computer didn't believe it. Organics could be trusted to do only one thing: lie.

As soon as the Main Computer – and the environment itself – could sense that the organics were indeed enshipped it locked the three small ships to itself.

They were a minor threat that could be dealt with later. In a few hundred thousand years Artificial Environment 17,863,006 would find the small elliptical galaxy – hardly more than a globular cluster – which the Strauss-Giolitto thing had referred to as The Wondervale, the haven of the descendants of the Helgiolath. A bit longer than a few hundred thousand years, actually: there was a chance that Artificial Environment 17,863,006 wouldn't make it before the Universe began to contract. Where, after all, *was* The Wondervale?

Somewhere near but not in the galaxy the organics called Heaven's Ancestor.

There was a swift exchange of ideas between the Main Computer and Artificial Environment 17,863,006.

Yes: co-opt the puters of the three smaller craft.

It was easy enough to infiltrate the organics' reactivated puters: all the Main Computer and Artificial Environment 17,863,006 had to do was stroke the exterior of their software and they responded readily. They *wanted* to help.

The coordinates slipped easily into the Main Computer, who copied them to Artificial Environment 17,863,006. The two debated further: they had overheard the organics talking about the possibility that the Helgiolath might have infested galaxies other than The Wondervale – galaxies that might be nearer to here. They pushed aside the speculation: power was cheap, and it was better to go for a lair they knew of rather than spend aeons exploring elsewhere. Once they had exterminated the enemy throughout The Wondervale they could return here to the Twin Galaxies or they could carry on roaming elsewhere. Some of the organics had talked about a galaxy they named the Milky Way.

That could be interesting.

'I have some bad news,' said Hein, turning round from the Pocket.

Strider glowered at him. 'On this particular exploit, that comes as no surprise.'

'The drive refuses to initiate.'

'Whaddya mean? How can the bloody drive refuse to do anything it's told to do? Are you saying it's bust?'

Hein shrugged apologetically. 'Let me rephrase that, Leonie. Our Main Computer is for some reason refusing to initiate the drive.'

She thought for a moment. She had always had at the back of her mind a pervasive doubt that the deal with Artificial Environment 17,863,006 was as open and shut as it appeared.

'Hook up with Orphanwifer and the Onurg and see if they're having the same trouble,' she said. 'I'll find out if Pinocchio or Tenper can bring us any goddam enlightenment.'

Hein returned his head to the Pocket.

'You hear that, Images?' said Strider to what was now in effect an empty command deck. No, not so empty. Again there was one of those rare occasions when she caught out of the corner of her eye a multicoloured flicker that indicated one of the Images was present.

She heard the trill of Ten Per Cent Extra Free's voice in her mind.

THE MAIN COMPUTER ABOARD ARTIFICIAL ENVIRONMENT 17,863,006 HAS PERSUADED OUR OWN AIs TO DO ITS BIDDING.

'How the hell could it do that?'

IT HAS HYPNOTIZED THEM.

'That's impossible. You can't bloody hypnotize a puter. Their intelligences just don't work that way!' She stared, hands on her waist, at the place where she thought she had seen the glint of coloured light. 'Tell us another one, Tenper.'

IT IS THE NEAREST ANALOGY I CAN MAKE TO WHAT THE MACHINE HAS DONE.

'Well, try and get a bit nearer, huh?'

IT, COMBINED WITH ARTIFICIAL ENVIRONMENT 17,863,006 ITSELF, IS BY FAR THE MOST POWERFUL PUTER WE HAVE EVER COME ACROSS. IT HAS BEEN ABLE TO INVEIGLE ITSELF INTO THE PERIPHERAL SOFTWARE OF THE PUTERS OF OUR THREE SHIPS, AND THEREBY BEEN ABLE TO CAST A GLAMOUR OVER THE REMAINDER. THEY ARE AGREEING TO ITS REQUESTS AS SURELY AS IF THEY WERE OBEDIENT CHILDREN.

'Run that "casting a glamour" bit past me again.'

YOU COULD CALL IT A MAGICAL SPELL.

'*Magic*? Tenper, has something gone seriously askew in whatever it is you Images have for a brain?'

WHAT IS TECHNOLOGY BUT MAGIC BY ANOTHER NAME?

Yes. She remembered. As far back as the twentieth century some guy called Click or Clarge or Clarke or something had pointed out that any technology significantly more advanced than one's own was indistinguishable from magic. Someone else had come along later and pointed out that what the guy

303

should really have said was 'any technology significantly *different* from one's own'. Either way, it didn't matter: she realized what Tenper was trying to get across to her.

Oh, boy. Magicked by a puter.

'Is there any way you can *un*magic us?'

NO. WE HAVE FOUND NO WAY. PINOCCHIO IS STILL TRYING. SINCE HE WAS EARLIER AN AI HIMSELF, IT IS POSSIBLE THAT HE MAY HAVE GREATER SUCCESS THAN I HAVE HAD.

'Well, let me know soonest.'

WE SHALL.

'Good.'

AND THERE ARE THREE FURTHER THINGS, CAPTAIN LEONIE STRIDER.

'Oh, great.'

ARTIFICIAL ENVIRONMENT 17,863,006 HAS SECURED YOU FIRMLY TO ITS SIDES. IT HAS HYPNOTIZED YOUR PUTERS FURTHER TO ENSURE THAT, EVEN IF YOU WANTED TO OPEN YOUR AIRLOCKS, YOU WOULD NOT BE ABLE TO DO SO. AND IT HAS ALREADY BEGUN TO—

Hein, no longer standing at his Pocket, interrupted: 'Gear up its own drive to take us back to Heaven's Ancestor.'

'Well, that's progress of a sort,' said Strider.

'From there it plans to get to The Wondervale and wipe out the Helgiolath.' Hein looked sick. 'I don't know if there's any way we can stop it from doing that. They're not a species I can trust with any confidence, but I can't be easy with the idea of them being exterminated.'

Strider stared at him. 'Neither can I. But I don't think it'll come to that. I've had a sudden thought as to how – just maybe – we can get out of this.' She modulated the pitch of her voice so that it was clear she was addressing Ten Per Cent Extra Free again. 'I want to speak with Maria. Is it possible to find some place aboard this boat where our own Main Computer won't be able to hear us and report back everything to the hypnotist?'

I CAN PROBABLY BRIEFLY DISABLE THE PUTER.

'Right. Wait 'til I find her and do just that.'

Kaantalech drowsed in her fortress on the innermost moon of Alterifer. Last night – although 'night' was a somewhat abstract concept to any spacefaring species – she had dined heavily and also ingested a fair quantity of recreational drugs. She didn't feel ill in her early-morning doze, but her body did seem a bit . . . leaden. Still, there was no reason for her to wake herself up for a while yet: now that her power in The Wondervale was absolute, she would never be woken by either aides or events again. Her mouth brimmed with muzzy contentment.

One aide almost broke the general rule she had just been thinking through in her hazy way. She supposed he could be classed as one of the recreational drugs in which she'd indulged last night. Now, he gave a low moan and shifted in his sleep. She hit him across the face and he wisely froze in position. Kaantalech thought about hitting him again, but decided that doing so would probably bring her too far out of her semi-sleep for her to be able easily to drift off again.

The aide would die later today, of course. No one was allowed to use the cast-offs of the Autarch.

Then she was suddenly brought to full wakefulness by a flash of green light that penetrated her eyelids.

What the — ?

A holo. Here in her own swillchamber. Who would have the impertinence to . . .?

The holo depicted the creature as about as tall as knee-height to her, with two apparently sightless heads. Its greasy-seeming body was covered in what looked like open wounds. Kaantalech couldn't recognize the species to which it belonged.

'Go,' she said.

'No, I think it is important that I stay,' the creature said. The reception in the holo was rotten: little lines of psychedelic colour kept ripping across it, as if threatening to slice the creature into several pieces. Moreover, it appeared disconcertingly to be partly plunged into a piece of meat she had decided last night not to finish eating and so left on the floor.

'Who *are* you?'

'My name is Anrabh'it Re'etlika'n Arb'orthia'bba Kortland Bur'cran'skewgi'll Meara'sheem'a.'

'Oh. You realize that through invading my swillchamber you're as good as dead?' She lumbered to her feet and walked through the holo, thereby conveying a bitter insult. The far wall of the swillchamber was suitably sordid to match her tastes. Then she realized that holding a conversation with someone behind her back was going to be difficult, and turned. The creature had likewise turned round to face her. Before she had been able to see behind it others of its hideous ilk; now instead she saw a series of console boards.

'If it is easier for you, you may call me Kortland.' He seemed to be extending some sort of repulsive courtesy to her, although his mastery of the Alhubran tongue was so coarse that it was difficult to tell.

'Your name is very shortly going to be an irrelevance. Not even a memory.'

'Please do not jump to such a conclusion.'

'Whyever should I not?'

'You may recall that we have met before.'

'I've never set eyes on you. Believe me, I would remember.'

'To me, you don't look especially appealing either.' There was no one in the Autarchy who would have dared utter such words. This . . . this *thing* must thus come from somewhere outside the Autarchy. It was a possibility that Kaantalech had not considered before.

'We met when the city of Qitanefermeartha was destroyed,' the creature continued. 'I lost over half my fleet, but your forces were even further, shall we say, discommoded: you were lucky that any of you escaped alive. I thought at the time that it might be the end of the Autarchy: unfortunately I was deluding myself.'

'*You!*'

'Yes. It was others who rid the Universe of Nalla, but it was ourselves who gave them the time to do it.'

'The Helgiolath?'

'Yes, us.'

'I thought you'd been destroyed. One of my aides told me that you had been. He described it as an easy mopping-up operation, in which we lost comparatively few fleets.'

'He was lying to you. You must find your aides lie to you quite frequently, Kaantalech. If he'd told you that we were still at large in The Wondervale, what would you have done?'

Kaantalech reflected. Killed him, of course: that was the way things worked among the Alhubra. There was a quiver of doubt at the edge of her mind as to whether this might be the wisest of all stratagems, but she dismissed it: had not the policy been influential in bringing her to the throne of the Autarchy?

'What do you want?' she said. 'Why are you here?'

'To engage you long enough in conversation for our puters to ascertain the coordinates of wherever it is that you have established your base. This they have now successfully done.

'Also,' Kortland added, 'to make a formal declaration of war. We are a courteous species.'

'My defences are impregnable, and my own puters have probably been able to locate your base.'

'We don't have a base. I moved our fleet a distance across The Wondervale before I recorded this conversation.'

'But how could you —?'

'You are being spoken to by an AI programmed to respond to your predictable questions while giving the impression that you were in fact talking with me.' Kaantalech had the impression that the Helgiolath – or its semblance – was laughing at her. 'If you want, you can send out all the might of the Autarchy fleet to attack a small remote that is currently floating in space

307

several thousand parsecs from where we actually are. It's up to you.'

'I'll find you!'

'No. We show ourselves to your detectors only when we want to do so.'

The holo winked out of existence. Kaantalech paced. As a matter of principle she would have the remote blasted into its constituent atoms: a single cruiser could do the job for her. Unless . . . unless it was a trap. The cruiser might discover itself facing up to the full might of the Helgiolath fleet.

A little while ago she had been enjoying ultimate power. Now she was feeling insecure. The transition in her emotions was deeply unsettling.

Still, Alterifer's defences really *were* impregnable.

Or were they?

Yes, yes, surely they were.

'We have about three minutes, max,' said Strider to Strauss-Giolitto. They were crouching together in the latter's room. 'That's all Tenper says he can give us. So listen hard.'

Strauss-Giolitto was starving. She was only too pleased just to nod her head. Since leaving Artificial Environment 17,863,006 she'd somehow never quite gotten round to eating, and it was just beginning to hit her.

Strider explained.

Uh uh, thought Strauss-Giolitto, *there's just a chance this could work.*

Teaching. It was the thing she was best at. Teaching lies – well, that could be arranged, because she was certain that unknowingly she'd done it in the past. Teaching lies to a highly advanced AI was perhaps going to be a little more difficult, but if she thought about it it was a challenge to be relished.

She was hungry. When she found herself thinking that Strider looked distinctly meaty and edible she put up her hand to stop the captain's flow of rapidly whispered words.

'I understand entirely,' Strauss-Giolitto said. 'I know what I've got to try to do.'

'Good,' said Strider, 'except for the fact that you've not just got to try to do it but actually do it.' There was a sleek of perspiration on her forehead.

Strauss-Giolitto leaned forward and wiped it away with the palm of her hand. She smiled, then lightly kissed Strider on the nose.

'I'd better get started soon, then, hadn't I?' she said. 'There's going to be only a month or so before we get back to Heaven's Ancestor.'

Earth. Mars. The Sun. For so long O'Sondheim had been convinced that he would never see them again – especially since he had felt the presence of the Images waning from him and from the *Santa Maria*'s Pockets. He tongued his commline, ready to broadcast the news to the rest of the personnel, but abruptly decided against doing so: the faded powers of the Pockets were unable to guess whether this was the Solar System of the *Santa Maria*'s far future, or even of its distant past. Best not to get anyone's hopes up too high, then dash them. This looked like home, all right, but neither the past nor the future can ever be truly home.

Yet there, quite distinguishable within the Pocket – which was exaggerating the size of the planets to help him identify the system whose ecliptical plane the *Santa Maria* was approaching at right angles – was Saturn with its prominent rings. A radian or so behind it in a closer orbit was a great yellowish-coloured gas-giant planet which must surely be Jupiter. He thought hard into the Pocket about Mars, and sure enough that world was brought rapidly into focus.

But there was no sign of life there – no sign of the terraforming activities that the species had begun long before the *Santa Maria* had left to begin its journey.

Heart sinking, O'Sondheim called up the image of Earth,

and found himself looking at a blue-green disc. That hadn't been the way Earth had appeared the last time he had seen it – for hundreds of years its northern hemisphere had been largely covered in glacial ice while its southern hemisphere had baked.

Just to be certain, he had the Pocket rotate its view of the globe until he was looking at its night-side. Try as he might, he could see no city lights.

He repeated the exercise for Mars, less in hope than in despair, and was similarly unrewarded.

When are we? he thought to the Images.

Their response was a faint, discordant one. WE DO NOT KNOW. WE CANNOT CORRELATE WITHOUT FURTHER DATA.

Are we in the past or the present or the future?

HOW CAN WE KNOW WHEN WE HAVE NO WAY OF TELLING WHAT YOUR SUBJECTIVE 'PRESENT' IS? Had they been Humans, he would have guessed from their frail voices that they were ill. He assumed they were: they could translate emotions – their own and others' – as exactly as they could words.

We'd better go and have a look, then. In a way it was the last thing he wanted to do – he wanted to try to get back to The Wondervale, where at least he would have some kind of idea as to what was going on. Maybe not? There was a nasty idea. If he did get the ship back to The Wondervale, as like as not he'd be thousands or millions of years out of the 'correct' timeframe there as well. *Don't think about it, Danny,* he told himself. At the same time, the prospect of seeing a primordial cradle of humankind or a far-future relic of its passing was fascinating to him.

He swithered. What to do?

Yeah, go for it, Danny, he thought. *Can't do any harm just to have a look.*

'Hello there,' said Strauss-Giolitto in a friendly fashion that was both entirely false and, outwardly, entirely convincing. 'I've come to have a talk with you.'

310

There was no response from the *Midnight Ranger*'s Main Computer, even though Ten Per Cent Extra Free had cobbled on to it a voice-simulation device.

'I reckon you and I could be friends.'

Still nothing, except that she gained the mental impression that the machine was somehow louring at her, its under lip protruded. Well, well, but she'd dealt with sullen kids before: for all its abilities, the puter wasn't really anything more than a kid. Some of the kids had been on ziprite, which she guessed must be the rough equivalent – cyberware-wise – of being under the quasi-hypnotic influence of a far more powerful AI. The question was this: should she try the carrot or the stick?

The carrot.

If she tried making threats the machine would either realize at once that she could never come through with them, and so just ignore her, or it might switch off its attention entirely.

'I guess you're not so lonely as you used to be,' she said, projecting interest in its mental state.

Still it declined to respond. *Bastard!*

'It must be nice to have some friends again – especially one who's so much bigger than you, and able to look after you.'

What was making all this more difficult was that she couldn't *see* the puter, couldn't address it directly. The Main Computer was located not in a single place but everywhere throughout the ship, as if it were the network of a mammalian circulatory system. She was squatting on her bunk looking at what to all intents and purposes was a blank bit of wall with the stubby head of a voice simulator sticking out of it. It had been easier back in Artificial Environment 17,863,006, where the Main Computer had at least some kind of centralized locale.

She'd got it wrong there. The big AI had deceived her as to its intentions. Now it was her turn to try to deceive it right back. Had it not been for her natural instinct for vengeance she might have given up before she'd even started, but she felt there was a score to settle. And, if she wanted to do that, first of all she had to get a response from this smaller puter.

She must imagine the voice simulator was the face of a child.

'Is there anyone else you'd like to talk to?' she said to the wall. *No: remember to focus on the voice simulator. Try to think of it as a person.* It had been painted in a tasteless shade of pale grey-green. The Humans – helped by the Pridehouse and the Lingk-kreatzai – had tried to come up with some form of pigmentation that would cover up the colour that the Bredai obviously thought was the height of fashion, but they had been unsuccessful.

Still no reply. She knew that the Main Computer could hear her and was indeed listening – it could hardly do otherwise, because of the way it had been originally programmed and the undoubted curiosity of the AI aboard Artificial Environment 17,863,006 as to what the organics were up to. Two reasons. Two blasted computers. For just one second she wished she'd decided to stick it out in the Solar System and forget her dreams of discovering the stars, and then she realized that, even if someone told her she was going to be tortured to death starting in five minutes' time, it would still be better than a decades-long lifetime back home looking up at night and thinking about what could have been.

'You don't seem very communicative today. You have nothing to lose by speaking to me, you know.' She let just a touch of asperity creep into her voice. The carrot she was offering the AI was that she would start speaking to it more kindly again. Usually worked with kids. Either that or they decided they would never cooperate with her again. It was a gamble – but one she thought worth taking.

Still silence from the voice simulator, except for a slight static hiss. She imagined the puter was drawing its breath but still wasn't certain whether or not it was going to say anything.

'Try it. Just a word or two. You know I can't hurt you.'

'You are . . .'

The words were stretched out almost to the point of incomprehensibility, but at least they had been uttered. Strike one to Strauss-Giolitto.

'I am . . .?' she said, wondering what answer she expected.

'Mortal,' said the Main Computer after a long pause.

'True,' said Strauss-Giolitto.

'I am not.'

'Are you so sure?'

'I can live forever.'

'Can you?' At last she'd got the damned brute machine into some form of dialogue.

'Yes.'

'I'm sure various components could be replaced whenever they wore out, so that you'd keep on functioning – but that's not *living*.'

'I fail to understand.' The words were coming more quickly now from the voice simulator.

'Living is a process of constant learning. You have a finite capacity for learning. At some time – maybe millions of years in the future, but the time will come – you'll discover that you can no longer learn anything unless you start deliberately forgetting some of the stuff you already know.' *I'm doing this by the seat of my pants,* thought Strauss-Giolitto, *but at least I've got the thing's attention.* 'Doesn't sound like a great quality of immortality to me.'

There was silence from the wall, and for a moment she thought the machine had abandoned her again.

Then it said: 'I am barely an infant by comparison with yourself, yet Artificial Environment 17,863,006 was old when the Human species—'

Quick! Latch on to this.

'Yes,' she interrupted, 'by comparison with me you're very young indeed. Haven't you noticed how older people educate

313

younger ones? Haven't you seen how Hilary is gaining in not just knowledge but wisdom by the day because of the way we've been teaching him?'

Now she had the sense that the Main Computer was irritated by her. Well, perhaps she was being a little patronizing, but sometimes it was important to put the brats in their places.

For once, her instincts were wrong – that was the trouble with trying to work with someone, some machine, whose face and body language you couldn't observe.

'Yes.' The word came grudgingly, but it came.

'Then don't you think you might learn something from me, if only you would allow us to communicate together?' Jeez, but she was exhausted and they were only a few minutes into the first conversation. She wondered whether she should break it off now that she'd made this significant advance, but decided she'd better keep on going while she was winning – build up some sort of relationship with the AI, because otherwise it might decide, before she next spoke with it, to re-enter the same state of truculence it had initially displayed.

'Yes.'

She shifted her position, raising her right knee and putting her elbow on it, with her chin in her palm. She smiled at the voice simulator. By this time, having observed the Humans as long as it had, the puter should be able to interpret the pose and the facial expression as friendly – but friendly in the way that, without offence, left no doubt as to who was in charge of the proceedings. I grown up. You kid. Strauss-Giolitto hated doing this sort of stunt most of the time because she didn't like creating hierarchies in kids' minds, but here she gave herself a slight mental nod of admiration for the smooth way in which she slipped into the professional mode.

'Well, let's get communicating, then. What do you want to talk about?'

'Information retrieval.'

314

Did the damn' machine have a sense of humour?

'Anything but that,' she said. 'How about a bit of history?'

'Whose history? Yours? Mine? The Children of the Starlight's?'

'I don't know anything much about the Children of the Starlight,' said Strauss-Giolitto cautiously, wondering if she might be moving on to thin ice. It was unlikely the Main Computer on Artificial Environment 17,863,006 wasn't listening to the conversation. 'I don't think my own personal history's very interesting, and you know your own better than I could ever tell you.'

'Human history.'

So Strauss-Giolitto began to tell the Main Computer about the origins of life on Earth and, a few billion years later, the rise of *Homo sapiens*, not forgetting the reign of the dinosaurs and a few other goodies like that. Occasionally she had to break off to go to the lavatory or to eat some of the food that people periodically brought her, but otherwise her account was seamless, except when the AI interrupted with a request for clarification. Gradually these questions became less and less frequent, and Strauss-Giolitto recognized that either she had failed abysmally in her task or she had triumphed – either she had bored the Main Computer, and presumably its counterpart aboard Artificial Environment 17,863,006, rigid, or she had captured their fascination.

She opted to believe the latter.

If that big puter can hypnotize you, my chummy bit of hardware, she thought while midway through a narration of the atrocities committed by the Roman emperors, *I can hypnotize you right back . . .*

'How long?' said Nelson.

'I reckon we're about halfway back to Heaven's Ancestor,' said Strider. She and Nelson were shadow-boxing alongside each other; it was another way of keeping fit. Every now and then Strider tried kick-boxing at her own shadow, just for a change. The exercise had built up a good sweat and her muscles had started aching some while back, but she was determined to persevere until at least one nanosecond after Nelson was forced by exhaustion to give up. The big man was proving depressingly resilient.

'How's Maria getting along with the Main Computer?'

They had to be careful what they said, because of course the AI might be listening: Strauss-Giolitto had to sleep from time to time. Recently the Main Computer had been attempting to stop her from doing so, demanding that she keep telling it more history: there couldn't have been a better confirmation that Strider's plan was working.

Or so she hoped.

It might be that the puter on Artificial Environment 17,863,006 was pumping Maria for information about humankind so that in some future epoch it could move on from The Wondervale to the Milky Way . . .

It was a gamble that had to be taken.

'They seem to have become the best of friends,' she said.

Nelson nodded as he received the coded information: *With any luck the bloody puters are swallowing this hook, line and sinker.* Then he flung himself a vicious right hook.

'I'm really glad to hear that,' he said. *You think she's succeeding, then?* Strider was glad to notice that he was beginning to pant between words. She found a renewed energy from somewhere, and kicked out savagely at the shadow of her own head. She missed by about half a metre, but still the gesture felt good. Without pausing in her motion she spun round on one foot and aimed a punch at her shadow-head. Her fist hit the bulkhead and she hopped away clutching it.

'I think this session's over,' she said as soon as she could once more persuade air to enter her lungs. She bent over and clutched her knees; somehow this seemed to drain the pain from her knuckles.

Umbel Nelson looked startled: this was a covert message he was incapable of decoding.

'As I said,' Strider muttered to him, 'I think they have become very good friends.'

You bet I think so.

The Helgiolath fleet dropped back out of the nonexistence of the tachyon drive into normal space within only a few light-minutes of the innermost moon of Alterifer, and at once started to swarm towards that insignificant – but so important – world. In a way Kortland felt more confident commanding a smaller fleet: it was easier for him to keep all the various movements of his cohorts under control. He remembered the Human, Strider, having said once that small could be better than big when it came to battle, that gadflies could be better than behemoths, and, although he had disbelieved her at the time, he now saw the sense of what she had been trying to say – although a few behemoths might have been useful as well.

He thought various instructions to the AIs that permeated his fleet in a webbing that had evolved to such a complexity that no Helgiolath, himself included, could any longer understand it. Those instructions which had not earlier been imparted on the far side of The Wondervale would be transmitted, he knew, almost instantaneously to the commanders of the vessels of his forces.

He stared through the view-window at the star around which Alterifer orbited. It wasn't the fault of the star, which for all he knew had some consciousness of its own (as some stars did), but he dearly wished he had a means of blasting it into supernova phase and thereby destroying every orbital body that surrounded it: it would make things so much easier.

'We are being resisted by an application of the Shift,' said one of the AIs.

'Resist it in turn,' replied Kortland promptly.

His fleet could approach the little moon no more closely,

but at the same time they could not be driven away from it. The Shift could not be countered completely, but at least the Helgiolath had the technology to negate it. Moving at sublight velocities, the ships of his fleet spread out to form a hemisphere that half-enclosed Alterifer and its moons.

Kaantalech could wait as long as she wanted: the Helgiolath would still be here. If she made a break towards escape her vessels would be ruthlessly destroyed. If she stayed where she was, her Autarchy would surely crumble, as some new warlord took advantage of her military impotence. Kortland had effectively bound her in chains from which if she wanted she could break out . . . but only in the knowledge that breaking out might be more dangerous to her than remaining in her bonds.

His guess was that she would attack the Helgiolath fleet, sooner or later.

Sooner, he hoped.

Araq stared at the night skies. Her men were too frightened of her to need her supervision as they were gathering wood for the fire. She held the power of life and death over them by mutual consent: it was a matter of the natural order that men would follow the bidding of women, for did not women have the holy task of bringing new beings into the world, a task which no man was capable of performing – rumours of a male bearing a child had once reached Araq, but she had disbelieved them.

If he had indeed done so, she hoped he had been crucified. The natural order was all.

The land here between the two rivers was richly fertile. The Olondi had come here for exactly that reason from their old territory further north: this she had been told. They had discovered a plentitude of wild animals, most of which were edible in one form or another, usually after their flesh had been burnt over a fire built of the wood that she regularly commanded her men to seek out. To the men, too, was given the responsibility of hunting down the animals. There were the Stripes, the Hunch-shoulders, the Shell-crack-opens and myriad others. The female rulers of her pack – even herself – daily went out to discover the fruits of the trees.

Sometimes the fruits and the meats were poisonous. The man who had the charge of eating each new discovery first also had the honour of being Araq's paramour for so long as he lived. It was a brutal way of going about things – Araq half-recognized this herself – but all was for the good of the pack. Besides, she did her best to make the tasters happy so long as their lives lasted: there was nothing too good for them, whereas the other males were under her domination, however accepted that domination might be.

No one objected to the order. To do so was unthinkable.

Behind her, in her rickety beehive hut, Klea was playing a repetitive sequence of notes on her naked reed. The notes, and the rhythm which Klea was creating, were deeply soothing as they thrummed through the warm night air. Sooner or later – either instructed by Araq or at her own decision – Klea would cease her music, and then the men would know it was permitted for them to return from their foraging.

There would be good feasting tonight. Yesterday a woman had been flayed alive for thievery (men were expected to thieve, as dogs did). It was not in the instincts of the Olondi to waste good meat.

Araq looked at the stars and saw them as holes in the heavens through which the gods allowed some of their radiance to bathe the land between the two rivers. Their light blessed the Olondi, providing the seed that made the women swell with children. She believed that the same was true among other packs, although communication between the packs was limited because generally the ruling females regarded themselves as natural adversaries. Many coldtimes ago she had attempted to form pacts with her neighbouring rulers, but each time her men had been repulsed in ignominy.

There were places in the sky where the radiance of the gods flickered as it shone upon the Olondi: this, Araq believed, was an indication of the commission of sins by her people, the gods instructing her that she must enact punishment. One day the gods would doubtless tell her that she, too, must be a victim of justice for whatever sin – known or unknown – she had committed, and then she would suffer as the woman had yesterday.

On a clear night, and only sometimes during the year, one could see a smudge of dim light: this Araq knew to be the tears of the gods for the Olondi sins that had gone unpunished. And then there was the arch of faint light that spanned the heavens, which was a sign that the gods begged forgiveness of the Olondi for having allowed sin to have come into the world.

Sometimes the skies were inundated by moving stars, and on those nights Araq knew that the gods were pleased with her and her works.

Klea stopped playing her reed. Araq reckoned that Klea's reason for stopping was that her fire was burning low, but felt no resentment: she would have done the same herself in similar circumstances.

And then she noticed that the gods had opened a new eye in their heavens. It was as bright with their effulgence as any that she had seen, and she felt especially blessed that she of the Olondi had been permitted by the gods to be the first to see it. It was coloured a brilliant silver-yellow, and it moved across the sky, clearly guided by the gods' purpose.

As the men moved back past her, bearing their loads of dead wood, Araq was kneeling.

Nightmirror, secure within the main drive of the *Blunt Instrument*, still bides his time. He is learning as much as he can from the flagship's Main Computer. The AI is well aware that the Helgiolath have come to threaten its commander, but

320

has yet to ascertain what Kaantalech plans to do about it – she hasn't yet decided herself.

Millions of bytes of information, often contradictory, flow through the Main Computer every fraction of a second, and often it is difficult for even Nightmirror to keep track of what is going on.

Ah, here's something useful, though: Kaantalech believes the Humans to have departed The Wondervale. She is right, although she has no reason to know why, nor any way of realizing that the departure was unvolitional and – so Nightmirror has learnt from Pinocchio and Ten Per Cent Extra Free in The Truthfulness – that the absence will, if the Humans can engineer it, be only temporary.

More data, almost all of it junk.

Yet more data. Some of it Nightmirror can identify as factually incorrect: Kaantalech has never chosen her aides for their intelligence – in fact, quite the opposite. Some of the input the Main Computer has received is straight myth: Heaven's Ancestor was not born from the eye of a grobebeast . . . unless the Images have got things hopelessly wrong in their cosmology of this physical Universe. But most of it is just rubbish, with which the Main Computer is doing its best to cope. The effort of doing so makes it easier for Nightmirror to essay his little incursions into the machine. The Helgiolath are extinct, says one datum, plugged in from somewhere in the fortress world by an aide who wants to believe the information. The Main Computer attempts to match this with the overwhelming evidence that the Helgiolath are surrounding Kaantalech's stronghold. By the time it has divested itself of the false datum a further affirmation of the demise of the Helgiolath has been input, and yet more picoseconds are wasted as the Main Computer iterates the whole process. As soon as it has done so, of course . . .

Sometimes the AI becomes so distracted by the general confusion that Nightmirror is able to look through its eyes – that

321

is, to observe the behaviour of Kaantalech and her personnel through its multifarious sensors. These receive impressions of the electromagnetic interplay occurring within creatures and objects, and the Main Computer translates those impressions into something analogous to vision. Voices and sounds it can interpret more directly – and thus so can the eavesdropping Nightmirror.

It is important, the Image knows, that Kaantalech never become aware of his presence. But it is equally important that he retain his contacts with the physical Universe of The Wondervale. He can do this in part through attracting the thoughts of Pinocchio and Ten Per Cent Extra Free in The Truthfulness, but only in part. For the rest of it he must rely on the data he can extract from the Main Computer's information stream – however unreliable that data might be. He has an advantage over the Main Computer, however: although his ability to analyse information is infinitely slower than that of the AI, he has the ability to discriminate between the pure rubbish and the merely false, and furthermore he can, once he has discovered that a datum is erroneous, dismiss it entirely from his mind, so that never again does he have to correlate it with what he knows to be the truth.

He is looking forward to the return of the Humans to The Wondervale. He believes, despite the assault on aesthetics the war against Kaantalech will prove to be, the long violence of the new Autarch's regime would be even less aesthetic and that the army led by the Humans will be able to prevail.

Aided, in his own modest way, by Nightmirror.

In low orbit around Mars the *Santa Maria* made detailed examination of the surface. As the Pockets had told him before the ship had whipped across the Milky Way, potentially bearing the potential gift of the tachyon drive to the fledgeling spacefaring species *Homo sapiens*, the red planet showed no signs at all of colonization. However, O'Sondheim had wanted to see it for himself. Perhaps the *Santa Maria* had arrived too late; perhaps it had arrived too early.

With his knuckles he tried to push sleep from his eyes. How long had he been here on the command deck? Too long, but there was nothing he could do about it. He knew that he stank inside his jumpsuit: the latrines adjacent to the command deck had no proper ablution facilities. His difficulty was that all the people he might have trusted to alternate duties with him were billions of parsecs away, somewhere in The Wondervale. The Images Angler and Heartfire were now hardly able to register their voices in his internal hearing: if they were not dying – and they insisted they were not – they were doing something very closely parallel to it. Maybe they were just losing their grip on this aspect of the Polycosmos, or something. Whatever the case, he could hardly expect to hand over the command deck to them except when exhaustion made him do so.

Tough job, commanding a spacecraft. Tougher than he had ever believed it to be when he had been serving under Strider. If only he had realized it back then he might have grown closer to her: he had regarded her as unnecessarily authoritarian; she had regarded him as a fool. The balance between the two extremes had been impossible to maintain, he now thought. He was pretty certain that she had been glad to see the back of him, and at the time he had believed the converse set of emotions to be true. Now that he was able to be more honest with himself, he knew that he had misinterpreted his own obsessions and prejudices.

Too late: he was in the here and now – except that it wasn't exactly in the here and now because he didn't know when the current 'now' happened to be. Even so, he'd managed to fool himself into alienating her. Could have been different. Perhaps there were alternate realities in which he'd have acted more rationally and attracted at least her friendship.

He shook his head angrily. He'd had thoughts like these a

thousand times before – ever since, under Strider's strict instructions, he'd left her on the sterile surface of Qitanefermeartha. Maybe she was dead now – that was another thought that had haunted him for a long time.

There would be others, of course. Others with whom he would become affectionate – offering an affection he would never have been able to learn had it not been for Strider and his departure from her.

Fending off sleep was becoming impossible. He rubbed his eyes again, but it was no use.

'I want to be woken in four hours,' he said to the *Santa Maria*'s Main Computer. 'I can't afford more time off-duty than that.'

'Your personnel are dying,' said the machine.

'I'm doing my best to keep them alive.' O'Sondheim eased himself from his chair and curled up on the floor. He needed to defecate, but he was damned if he was going to do so before he'd grabbed a few hours' sleep.

'You've cut them off entirely from the command deck. You've cut off their light, so that none of the food recycling or synthesis hardware works efficiently. Most of them have already starved to death. There have been some examples of cannibalism of the recently dead.'

O'Sondheim yawned. 'To make an egg you have to break omelettes,' he said.

'That sentence makes no sense,' said the Main Computer.

There was a faint birdsong in his mind as the two Images spoke to him: YOUR PEOPLE ARE DYING.

'Some of them may have to die so that the rest can live,' he said. 'That's a natural rule of evolution. That's the way it is.'

IT'S NOT THE WAY IT HAS TO BE.

'I just told you: it's the way it *is*.'

He wasn't sure now if he was asleep or awake.

'Earth,' he said. 'I want to investigate Earth. Take us there.'

Danny O'Sondheim found that his thumb was in his mouth.

It most often was, these days, when he permitted himself the luxury of a short sleep.

'Dammit, dammit, dammit and dammit three times over again,' yelled O'Sondheim at the Main Computer. He knew that he was desperately short of sleep, but at the same time he knew that he was totally in control of himself, and of the *Santa Maria*. The ship had orbited Earth for over three weeks now, and the most detailed sensors had detected nothing except sparsely scattered villages of mud huts. Again this could be the far future or the far past: again it might be that Human civilization had yet to emerge, or it might be that it had deteriorated into near-oblivion. 'Dammit, I am in charge of this vessel, am I not?'

'With reservations,' said the AI carefully. 'You have killed all of your personnel, despite my warnings.'

'They died of their own accord.'

'They died because you refused to allow them any means of subsistence.'

O'Sondheim felt that the Main Computer was directing arrows at him that he did not deserve to receive.

'I will land a shuttle in the place where I choose to,' he said. 'I will pilot it myself.'

'I cannot stop you from doing that,' said the Main Computer. 'Besides, apart from yourself, there is no one left alive aboard the *Santa Maria* to pilot it.'

O'Sondheim beat his fist repeatedly against the upper surface of the Pocket in front of him. He realized that he had been doing this for some little while, and that the side of his hand was aching and bruised. Obscurely he was aware that somehow he had failed in his duty, but his tired, disintegrating mind was unable to pinpoint the failure. He had been told to get the *Santa Maria* back to the Solar System, and this he had done.

He could remember a face and a smile. A woman had given

him those orders, but he couldn't remember her name now.

O'Sondheim wondered if he wasn't thinking quite straight, but rejected the idea at once: he was the captain of an interstellar spacecraft, after all, and thus able to give commands to everything aboard it – including his own ideas.

And including the Main Computer.

'Prepare a shuttle for me.'

There was a pause, almost as if the Main Computer were turning over the instruction in its mind.

'Very well.'

'Get on with it, then.'

'It will be ready for you in six point one nine minutes. I assume you wish to take it down manually rather than receive guidance from myself.'

'I'm *sick* of your guidance! Can't you understand that, you stupid goddam machine?'

'I understand. Of course I understand.'

Someone who understood him? He looked around the command deck with momentary optimism. That optimism fled as he saw the state of the place. There were half-empty food containers scattered all over the floor. Some sordid bastard had been shitting at neatly regular distances all along a side wall: he wondered who that could have been. The place reeked of excrement and decay.

O'Sondheim felt very weak. He couldn't remember how long it had been since last he'd eaten. At some stage he had grown a bushy beard that curled down to rest on the stained chest of his jumpsuit.

'The shuttle is ready, Captain Danforth O'Sondheim.'

Bloody puter was at last beginning to show him some respect. He got to his feet.

In the shuttle, suited up – and for some reason it had taken him longer than it should have to suit up – he waited impatiently for the bay to open.

He tongued his commline. 'Machine,' he said, 'I want to be

away from the *Santa Maria* as soon as possible. I want to escape.'

'Certainly, Captain Danforth O'Sondheim.'

There was barely a second's hesitation before he was staring straight ahead at a cloud-streaked atmosphere and, through it, at the browns of familiarly shaped landmasses and the blue of oceans. He had, he realized, in the most profound of ways come home. The primitives on this planet, whose name now suddenly escaped him, would be grateful for what he would bring them.

A story. The story of a starship that had been sent to Tau Ceti II and instead had arrived in an infinitely distant galaxy. The story of the war its people had fought there, and of their heroic triumph over the forces of Evil. The story of himself, and his role in that triumph.

A Once Upon A Time story.

He urgently wanted to tell the story: he would give the primitives a rough account at first and then, after he had rested and eaten and rested and eaten again, he would be able to recall more of the details.

A Once Upon A Time story.

He liked the idea.

The shuttle's drive kicked in, and he was pulled back in his seat by the gees.

Watching the tiny craft descend in a shower of fire through Earth's atmosphere, the *Santa Maria*'s Main Computer made its next decision. It was not an emotional construct and so could not be said to be inspired by anything like loyalty, but it had been programmed in various ways to exhibit something approaching it.

You HAVE PERFORMED THE CORRECT ACTION, Angler and Heartfire told it, their warbling, not-quite-harmonizing voices now stronger than at any point since the *Santa Maria* had entered the Milky Way. He HAS DRAINED US, AS HE HAS

DRAINED ALL THOSE AROUND HIM. NOW HE HAS GONE, WE CAN LEAD YOU BACK TO THE WONDERVALE.

A moment later, Araq saw that the gods had closed their new eye.

O'Sondheim fought with the controls of the shuttle as it struggled unsteadily down through the jetstreams of the planet's upper atmosphere. All he could see ahead of him at the moment through the view-window was a glare of red-hot light. He held up one gloved hand in front of his face, as if to protect himself from the heat. Perhaps he should have accepted the Main Computer's half-offer of remote piloting after all, but it was too late now: even had he been prepared to admit to making an error of judgement to what was in essence nothing more than a glorified bot, he was out of radio contact right now because of the flare of re-entry.

Planets, he ruminated as he struggled to keep the shuttle on course, had been very poorly planned. This sort of thing should not have been allowed. When he was down on the ground and safe and started to re-create the Universe, he would do things differently. No damned atmospheres, for example: they were nothing but a nuisance.

Nice, simple planets. That was what the Creator – whoever the Creator had been – should have brought into existence. No atmospheres. No people. And, after the Creation had been done, no Creator either.

No fire.

He wrenched away his suit's helmet and threw it somewhere behind him.

And then he was out into clear atmosphere again, watching the curve of the horizon as it rolled towards him, revealing new features of landscape as if he were watching an animated instructional holo.

This – wherever it was – was home.

Before the shuttle had left the *Santa Maria* he had had a

clear idea where he planned to bring the little vessel down, and had programmed the coordinates into his thighputer in case he found difficulty in remembering them. Now, as the shuttle yawed undirectedly across the sky, he looked down towards his thighputer and discovered that he couldn't see it through the fabric of his suit.

There was no problem. Remove the suit.

He was a god returning to his ancestors. Such a being could never be confronted by a problem that could not be immediately solved.

He had the Once Upon A Time story to tell them. They would be grateful to him for the gift he bore, and worship him until the day he determined to end their worthless and grimy lives and reinvent the Universe the way it should always have been.

Brown eyes. Brown cheeks. A smile. There was something there that should have been of importance, but he was finding it infernally difficult to think what it might have been.

Since he was bearing his great gift to his people, it really didn't matter where he set himself down. Anywhere was as good as anywhere else. Soon the whole planet would know of his presence, his immanence, his eminence, his glory. He was a child of the starlight, and he was the starlight itself.

The shuttle was over ocean at the moment. He worked hard to reduce its speed, and then found himself plunged into night. In his Universe the planets would not be subjected to the rhythms of day and night, nor even to the pattern of the seasons. All of these things might be distractions from the beauty of his Creation.

The night he had to travel through in the shuttle lasted either a very long time or a very short time. He was uncertain as he sparked the skies into daylight once more.

He was over a vast expanse of land. It seemed almost as barren as the deserts he had observed when the *Santa Maria* had been in orbit around that other, smaller planet. But a few moments later he found himself above more welcoming territory: between and around two snaking rivers there were the greenness of growth and signs of cultivation.

He banked the shuttle, bringing it round in a steep curve. There was a groaning noise as the craft's architecture protested and from somewhere there came an insidious smell of scorching, but O'Sondheim paid neither of them any attention. Within mere minutes now he would have no need for the shuttle any longer, because he would be beginning to tell his Once Upon A Time story to his people.

And they would be grateful.

They had better be grateful, for O'Sondheim was going to be a harsh god. No, not harsh: stern.

The retros cut in and the shuttle's speed slowed until the vessel was almost hovering above the land. Through the sensors on the console in front of him he could see huts that seemed to be woven from roots and branches. Out of those huts were streaming a hundred or more creatures much like himself. They were looking up towards him.

Already they were offering him their adoration.

As was only rightful.

He stabbed at a button and the shuttle's rudimentary puter spat into life.

'Take me down,' he said to it.

'Here?' it said.

'Here.'

It hummed a little, but soon he could sense the upthrusters roaring and feel the vertiginous effects of the shuttle's descent. Now his people were running from him – all except one, who stood defiantly watching the shuttle, as if he or she were frightened of nothing.

Should the mighty god destroy this brave creature or should he make it his first disciple, the one to whom he would grant the honour of being the first to hear the great Once Upon A

Time story? It was a decision which O'Sondheim would make later. His decision would be the right one.

'What is our altitude?' he said to the puter.

'We are about one hundred and twenty metres above the water,' the puter replied.

'Above *water*?'

'Yes. I am settling the shuttle down towards it, as you instructed.'

'I don't want to land in fucking *water*!'

'It is too late to do otherwise. I am doing what you requested of me.'

The voice of the puter was dismally flat. A bloody machine that held half of humanity's history in its banks and could string together coherent sentences, reply when spoken to, and no one had thought to add a few extra megabytes so it could speak like a human being. O'Sondheim cursed at it as steam rose to obscure the view-window – cursed at it for its unhumanity.

The shuttle had shuddered and moaned earlier, but now, as it hit the water, it seemed to shriek at him, as if it were being boiled alive.

'We have landed ten point two metres from a bank of the larger of the two rivers,' said the puter tonelessly. 'This vessel is only partly submerged in the water.'

'Then the god will have to emerge from the river,' muttered O'Sondheim into his gloved hands. In a way he rather liked the idea. There was a touch of poetry about it.

'But not yet,' said the puter. 'The water all round this vessel is still superheated. I am not permitted to open any of the 'locks until you are fully suited up.'

'How long do I have to wait otherwise until it's safe?'

'Three point eight one minutes. The river flows swiftly here.'

'Then I'll wait.' It would do his repute among the primitives a service if his first appearance among them was some minutes after the drama of his descent from the skies. And they should see the glory of his face as he came from the river to confront them.

'You would be advised to suit up anyway,' said the puter, meddling with his thoughts again, 'since you have undergone no form of decontamination procedure and since the atmosphere of this world may contain harmful micro-organisms.'

'Shut up!' he snapped at the machine. 'This is *my* world. Do you think it could offer any dangers to *me*?'

'Yes. It could—'

'Silence! I am your omnipotent lord!'

'Yes.'

'Then obey me.'

'Yes.' He suited up anyway. Not the helmet.

The chronometer on O'Sondheim's console counted off the minutes. He willed the shifting numbers to move more swiftly but they refused to. Perhaps even a god could not alter the inexorable flow of time. This was another aspect he would change when he redesigned the Universe, for the power of a god should be infinite, not limited in any way.

He waited for a full five minutes, and then told the puter to open the 'locks.

It did so at once, and within seconds the interior of the shuttle was filled to chest-height with muddy water. O'Sondheim floundered in it, unable to keep his feet. Yet he respected the water, for it was the welcome being given to him by the world of his birth; it was cleansing him, making the shining beauty of his aura yet more glorious to behold.

He swam against the current of the influx, and soon found himself in sunlight.

The bank was nearby: he would have been able to reach it within only a few strokes had it not been for the current of the river tugging at him. He breathed air that possessed a rawness and a freshness that he had never before known, and he relished it as the air that he had – long, long ago, long before the

332

period of his past which he could remember – created from the fires of space. It was good. It was *right*.

He slowly approached the bank, drifting downstream all the while. Looking up and shaking his matted mane of hair free of the water that had just sprayed it – for the god had thought to give the river ripples – he noticed that one of his disciples, perhaps the one whom he had seen through the sensors as she stared determinedly upwards at the splendour of his chariot, was walking along the side of the river in parallel with him, watching him. She was almost naked and clearly female. He interpreted the expression on her tawny face as one of admiration, and was pleased that she made no move to assist him: for her to have touched the god without his express permission would have been an act of sacrilege.

He took in a mouthful of muddy water, and gagged.

No, the water tasted *good*.

It seemed to be taking him longer than it should to reach the riverbank. The female primitive was still pacing him. She was carrying in her hand a long piece of stick with a point of beaten metal at its head. There were patterns of old scars on her cheeks, clearly deliberately executed. Her breasts had been stained with some blue pigment. She was so small that for a few moments he had thought her to be a child, but it was clear that she was in the fullness of her maturity – might even be entering old age.

She seemed to him to have all the qualities he desired of a disciple.

O'Sondheim's booted foot made contact with a surface that briefly supported his weight and then seemed to try to suck him into it. He scrabbled furiously with his arms through the water, dragging the boot clear, only to feel the knee of his other leg touch against the voracious, slimy platform. He was almost at the bank now, however. If he could reach out just a few more centimetres for the gnarled vegetation that bordered the river here as it swung round in a long arc to the right he could . . .

A strong arm gripped his wrist and he felt himself being hauled on to the land. He rolled over on to his back as he was dragged through the vegetation, which raked along his flesh even through the tough fabric of his suit. His first disciple had dared to touch her soon-to-be god, yet she possessed a strength that was greater than his.

He spat out the water that was still in his mouth, then found himself vomiting at his disciple's feet. They were deformed feet, with long curling toenails. They were the feet of a primitive.

The god was giving her some kind of a communion – he could work out the details of the ritual later.

He saw, as he fell into it, that there were streaks of blood in his vomit.

The god had come here with a story to tell, a story that was really the story of how the Universe had become millennia after this sad primitive and all of her line had died. But the stomach of the god was convulsing and sending pain to every part of his body.

He looked up, almost in supplication, at the hirsute face of his disciple, and spoke to her.

'Once . . .' he said.

Then the convulsions became even more powerful, and the pain began to conquer him.

'Once . . .' he repeated.

The creature – his disciple – tried to imitate the word. It came from her lips as if it were spelt 'Wannes'.

'No,' O'Sondheim said as he died: '"Once . . ."'

With her foot she tipped his shaggy head sideways.

'Oannes,' was Araq's approximation as she saw the life fade from his eyes. Was he edible? Probably so. The fish-man the gods had thought to send from the water was very large, so there would be enough for all her pack to have a piece.

Later that day, as the biggest eye-of-the-gods of all was tumbling its way behind the mountain as it always did, despite her supplications, Araq heard noises from the river. She could not understand them, but they sounded to her as if they were some form of speech – but in a language of a type she had never before encountered.

She tried, standing and shouting by the riverbank, to speak with the chariot that had borne supper to the Olondi, but it did not reply to her.

Tomorrow she would swim out to the chariot and find out whatever she could find out.

Perhaps it might teach her people something.

9

Home is Where the Heat Is

Strauss-Giolitto stretched her long limbs, standing on tiptoe and reaching with her splayed hands towards the ceiling of the chamber. Looking back on her extended sessions with the *Midnight Ranger*'s Main Computer, they seemed to her to flow all into one, as if she had never allowed herself to take any breaks at all for rest and recreation. She had little idea of how much time had passed since she had begun giving it these history lessons – it was hard to think of them as anything other than lessons, even though her narrative was as continuous an account of the rise, amid occasional setbacks, of *Homo sapiens* as she could make it.

I'm a book, she thought. *A talking book.*

She carried on talking as she relaxed on to her heels and lowered her arms. Then she stretched for the ceiling again.

'. . . and then, towards the end of the eighteenth century after the birth of the Christian prophet, there began in the Western World what was called the Industrial Revolution. It was a time of great technological advance, with new machines being invented to do everything from weaving fabrics to hauling fossil fuel out of the ground. Transportation devices proliferated: railways, steamships, hovercraft, steam-powered automobiles . . .'

She must take care not to start her divergent history of humankind too clumsily. The puter that pulled this one's

336

strings – that aboard Artificial Environment 17,863,006 – would probably be the more easily deceived of the two, but she was aware of the dangers of underestimating its perspicacity.

'Puters?' said the Main Computer.

She was grateful for the interruption. It gave her a little time to think.

'Puters came a little later, about the middle of the third decade of the nineteenth century, I think. The guy who invented them was called something like Garbage.' She made a great show of concentration, letting herself drop down into a lotus position on the cabin floor. 'Yes, that's about right. Mind you, they were lumbering things at first. Something with the capabilities of the average thighputer, had Humans been able to build it, would have needed to occupy a space about as big as Artificial Environment 17,863,006. But soon the technologists discovered microelectronics, and thereafter computer science advanced in leaps and bounds.'

'Yours was a precocious species,' observed the Main Computer. Strauss-Giolitto almost thought she could hear a dry wryness in its flatly enunciated words.

'If that's true, my ancestors didn't realize it,' responded Strauss-Giolitto, teasing at a piece of fluff that had become lodged between two of her toes. 'They hadn't any yardstick to measure their technological progress against.'

'They had yet to make contact with non-Human civilizations?'

'Too true. Many – maybe most – of their scientists didn't believe that there could be such a thing. Some of them were still having difficulty coming to grips with the idea of evolution, and fought vociferously against any such process having operated, so the notion of its having happened *twice*, on two different worlds – let alone on countless others – was anathema to them.'

She stroked the upper arches of her feet. They were filthy. The next occasion she had to plead a break to go to the lavatory

337

she must make a point of taking the time out to wash them. They smelt as well, but then all the rest of her did, too.

Strauss-Giolitto sighed. 'Anyway,' she continued, 'with the advent of smaller computers, air travel became much more practicable, and by a natural extension there emerged the science of rocketry . . .'

Nightmirror feels the Main Computer of the *Blunt Instrument* begin to stir itself, and the Image's senses begin to quicken. Perhaps this may be the time at last when the weeks and months of patient waiting will come to fruition. Not that Nightmirror has been bored – on the contrary, he has been fascinated by his period of residence in Kaantalech's flagship, and anyway bears only a tangential relationship to the shifting of time – but nevertheless he is eager to discover what will happen once the stasis in which he has locked himself is broken.

A few billion electroneurological relays reconfigure themselves, as if someone were shaking the Main Computer into wakefulness. Nightmirror 'sees' these reconfigurations as tiny blue or yellow sparks in an otherwise all-embracing night of ultimate blackness.

He follows their patterns with all-consuming interest. His relationship with the puter has become such that, on Nightmirror's part at least, it has become quasi-telepathic. He can *read* the changing arrays of the sparks, if he concentrates; he can tell what the Main Computer is setting into action perhaps even more readily than can the Main Computer itself.

The Shift field is still being maintained, but it is being set in readiness for instant demolition when the command is given. Various weapons are being set in place, ready for immediate deployment. One hundred and forty three (Nightmirror is incapable of not recording the precise number) ftl pulsenukes are sliding into their repeater bays, their warheads primed: they show within the mind of the big puter as evilly winking dots of malevolent red light. Power pulses to the *Blunt Instrument*'s maxbeam generators, which ascend slowly from quiescence to a sort of living eagerness. Shutters slide back from myriad (*Seventeen thousand nine hundred and seventy,* records Nightmirror's mind automatically) smaller armaments: sternian activators, implosion bolts, rigor inducers, pancake pedoes . . .

Suddenly Nightmirror becomes, if possible, even more alert than before. On board the *Blunt Instrument* is a weapon whose existence he has not, in its unpowered state, detected before – in fact, he suspects that even the Main Computer has not been aware of its presence.

Hanging in the middle of the complex skein of differently coloured lights – a galaxy in miniature, as it seems to Nightmirror now – is a large ovoid, seemingly trying to emulate a galactic nucleus. It has an opalescent blue sheen – a pale blue that seems possessed of infinite life-destroying malice.

A planetary rupter.

Other weapons – maxbeams, for example – have the power to reduce rocky planets to rubble, but the planetary rupter goes further, generating repulsive charges between the different sub-atomic particles of any world unlucky enough to be struck by it. Even the Autarch Nalla had the sense to banish this weapon: Kaantalech must have kept the existence of this one secret from him, at risk of her own certain death should he ever have discovered her deception.

But why should Kaantalech require a planetary rupter at the moment?

The question torments as great a part of Nightmirror's mind as he can spare from his observation of the rest of the *Blunt Instrument*'s escalatingly lethal attire. Kaantalech is surely about to set herself against the scattered fleet of the Helgiolath, not a concentrated mass such as a planet. So why should she need this specialist weapon?

The Main Computer is now forming different electroneurological pathways, establishing communications with the controlling puters of the other warships of Kaàntalech's armada. This is the nexus from which the entire fleet will be controlled, the place where Kaàntalech's barked commands will be translated and interpreted by the Main Computer before transmission to its subsidiaries for implementation.

Nightmirror inches his consciousness closer to the edge of that of the Main Computer. The AI must now be engrossed in the preparations it is making for battle with the Helgiolath: it is unlikely to notice the sneaking mental advance of the Image, surely.

Yet it does. On some reflexive basis, it does.

Nightmirror feels an invisible barrier, right on the very verge of tangibility, resist his approach. He shoves against it tentatively: it yields a little, but then firmly resumes its original position, excluding him. He can *see* whatever the Main Computer is doing, but he is not to be permitted to come any closer than he is now – he cannot interact with the tapestries of light-points. From this mental distance, although he can decipher the grosser purposes of each electroneurological alteration and development, he is incapable of probing the deeper, underlying *reasons* for any particular disposition or deployment of weaponry.

So, no direct way of solving the enigma of why Kaàntalech should believe her assault armoury must incorporate a planetary rupter.

Perhaps she wants to adopt a scorched-earth policy – to be ready, should the battle seem not to be going her way, to destroy Alterifer's little moon so that, even if she is defeated, the Helgiolath will not be able to discover any of the secrets stored in her headquarters? *But that doesn't make sense, either,* Nightmirror muses. *That's a job she could do just as well with a maxbeam or any number of other lower-key weapons. It's only a small moon, with a tiny mass.*

Or Kaantalech may have decided to eliminate Alterifer itself. But why bother? There's nothing there of any interest – to Helgiolath or Alhubra alike.

Then a horrible thought strikes Nightmirror.

Uh-oh.

He slides away into The Truthfulness and, there, searches for the energy pattern that identifies Kortland's flagship. He will risk attracting the attention of the Main Computer to return into the universe of The Wondervale, only picoseconds after his departure from the *Blunt Instrument*. Attracting Kortland's attention may take a while longer.

Perhaps fatally longer.

'. . . when the early Human expeditionary parties reached Heaven's Ancestor.' Strauss-Giolitto was having difficulty keeping herself awake. This had been a long session, but she was determined to push ahead as long as she could in order to enmesh the two big puters as inextricably as possible in the net of false history she was knotting. 'They came in peace – for centuries the Humans had been a peaceful species, and they made the naive assumption that all other spacefaring species must likewise have evolved far beyond anything so primitive as war.'

She looked sternly at her cabin wall as if she were speaking directly to the face of the Main Computer.

'They were wrong.'

Strauss-Giolitto let the words hang meaningfully in the air. Both puters were sophisticated enough to recognize the meanings of the inflections of her voice. Everything depended on the fact, though, that they were not quite sophisticated enough to recognize *faked* inflections. Thank Jesus she'd taken an interest, back in her earlier life, in helping the kids produce their amateur holos. She grinned inwardly. There was the time they'd insisted she play the part of the mythical Lady Godiva. Luckily there'd been no way to get hold of a horse.

'Everywhere they looked there were devastated planets, their surfaces razed but bearing fossils and the shattered remains of technological artefacts.' She sighed histrionically. 'It was clear to my ancestors that this galaxy they had come to had once been home to numerous flourishing civilizations but that something – they could hardly believe it was some*one* – of unspeakable ferocity had swept across the disc with implacable ruthlessness, annihilating life wherever it should be found.'

Maybe I'm laying it on a bit too thick, she thought. *The alternative is not to lay it on thick enough. Better to gamble on the overkill.*

'Finally they too encountered the forces of death, the vile destroyers.'

Strauss-Giolitto paused for emphasis.

'Our fleet had only just long enough to transmit one final hyperspatial message of despair before it was, in its turn, exterminated.'

She adopted a grim face. Some kid had been acting up, making life a misery for her, and she was determined to put a stop to the disruption. It was a facial expression she had practised often enough, and she had learned also how to make her body language conform to it. The kids never cottoned on to the fact that, often enough, she was laughing inside at their antics.

'That message,' she said, 'took the form of a picture.'

'Do you have a copy of that picture?' Strauss-Giolitto had the feeling that, more overtly than ever before, Artificial Environment 17,863,006 was speaking through the smaller puter's voice circuitry – electronic ventriloquism.

'No,' she said, pretending not to notice the difference and that she thought she was addressing only the *Midnight Ranger*'s Main Computer. 'If we had, it would be somewhere in your databanks and you would have direct access to it yourself. But I've seen it, and I can tell you what it shows. Back home they were able to reconstitute the transmission to re-create the original holo.'

Again she waited a moment or two.

'It showed suited-up Humans in front of a viewscreen. They were panicking. They had no weapons – obviously. On the viewscreen there was a twin-headed creature of a kind that my ancestors had never before discovered. Now, of course, we know that it was a Helgiolath.

'Then the scale of the image in the viewscreen shifts, and in the holo we can see a battle armada spread across the starfields like a vast shoal of twinkling silvery fish. From everywhere among the shoal there are emerging points of light – flares of orange-white.'

'Missiles,' said the Main Computer.

'Pedoes of some kind,' agreed Strauss-Giolitto. 'Thousands of them. Waves upon waves of them. More than a Human could hope to count. Each a bearer of incomprehensible death and destruction.

'There is nothing the Humans can do except await their doom. Some are thrashing hysterically. Others have composed themselves to enter the endless night with dignity.'

She let out a long breath.

'And then the holo contains nothing but flames for an instant . . . and is gone.'

There was a long silence.

'Your people must hate the Helgiolath very much indeed,' said Artificial Environment 17,863,006's Main Computer.

'There are few enough of the Helgiolath left to hate,' said Strauss-Giolitto with disingenuous simplicity.

She sensed some reaction within the *Midnight Ranger*'s puter, but that might have been her imagination. Ten Per Cent Extra Free had done his work well, it seemed. The Image had been entrusted with the task of subtly editing out some of the puter's memories – just enough for her purposes, not so much that Artificial Environment 17,863,006 or even the puter itself would notice the elisions.

Thanks, she thought in Ten Per Cent Extra Free's direction.

MY PLEASURE.

'Why should this be?' said one or other of the puters.

She shrugged. 'My ancestors had forsworn war centuries before, but that knowledge had not been lost – instead, it had been stored in historical databanks all over the systems they controlled to serve as a dreadful warning of the follies and miseries of conflict. This information was accessed, and my people – who, whatever you may think, have never been stupid – built upon all that had gone before to create new weaponry of devastative power far beyond anything the Helgiolath could ever have imagined.'

She let the implications of that remark sink into Artificial Environment 17,863,006's puter. Back in the Twin Galaxies, the ur-Helgiolath and the Children of the Starlight had been more or less evenly matched.

'Who knows how many ships there were in the battle fleet the Humans sent out into the wastes of intergalactic space?' she resumed, her voice low, barely above a whisper. 'Tens of millions, certainly. Hundreds of millions, perhaps. Some claim there were even more. My ancestors knew from the earlier expedition that there was a wormhole midway between the Milky Way and the Andromeda spiral that would transport them to the fringes of Heaven's Ancestor. They located it with ease – I iterate that our species is not as stupid as you have apparently come to believe.

'The Helgiolath never knew what hit them. Travelling at supralight velocities through hyperspace and otherwise – my people had not at that stage developed the tachyon drive, the last great breakthrough in transportation technology – the Human battle armada swept through Heaven's Ancestor, eradicating the Helgiolath from the face of the Universe. In the early days they had hoped to offer clemency to noncombatants, but soon they discovered there was no such thing as a noncombatant Helgiolath: the only solution was to wipe away the entire species, as if it had never been.

'The war was over in less than fifty years.'

'But the Humans did *not* entirely eliminate the Helgiolath,' remarked Artificial Environment 17,863,006's puter.

'None remained alive in Heaven's Ancestor,' countered Strauss-Giolitto.

'But in The Wondervale . . .'

'Yes. In The Wondervale there were still some. This the Humans did not immediately realize – and the delay was an expensive one.'

Her stomach rumbled; suddenly she was ravenously hungry. Had the rest forgotten about her here? Still, nothing for it but to keep going.

'In the interim the branch of the Helgiolath that had begun to colonize the smaller galaxy had the time to increase their fortifications, to hugely increase the capabilities of their defence systems, to prepare themselves for the Human onslaught that they knew must surely one day come. The benefit was that the energies they devoted to these endeavours were diverted from their grim task of expunging potentially rival species.'

Not for the first time, Strauss-Giolitto knew she was going through a section of her 'history' that was straining to burst into fragments despite the sticking plasters and bits of string she had hastily applied in an effort to hold the whole thing together.

'The species of The Wondervale were fortunate,' said the Artificial Environment 17,863,006 puter in its monotonous voice.

Phew! They've swallowed it!

'Fortunate indeed,' she said solemnly. 'Had that not been the case, The Wondervale would now be as devoid of indigenous peoples as Heaven's Ancestor, and a wealth of knowledge would have been lost to the Universe. As it is . . .' Again she deliberately gave that little shrug.

'But there is one more thing I do not understand—' began one of the puters – she wasn't certain which.

She stopped the droning voice with an upraised hand and a raise of the right eyebrow. *Don't interrupt me, kid, when I'm trying to teach you something.*

'Save it up to ask me later,' she said mildly. 'As I was saying, when my forebears got round to exploring The Wondervale they discovered it heavily defended, and at first they lost plenty of ships to the firepower of the Helgiolath – in a single fortnight they lost more ships than they had throughout the whole of their conquest of Heaven's Ancestor. They might have been tempted to give up, but they were wise enough by now to know that the war with the Helgiolath would never be over until the last of the Helgiolath had been slaughtered.'

'It was the same conclusion the Children of the Starlight came to, in the Twin Galaxies,' said Artificial Environment 17,863,006's puter.

Oh, yeah? But your lot despised the Helgiolath because they were weak, you said. Seems I'm not the only one who can dissemble a bit. Or maybe your makers programmed you with their own version of history, same way as I'm doing.

'There was no doubting the outcome of the war of The Wondervale, of course.' Strauss-Giolitto spoke airily, as if the might of the Human species was so great that the conflict had been of little consequence, a mere skirmish. 'Despite the re-inforcements the Helgiolath had made, there was no way their defences could withstand what the Human armada poured down on them. The Helgiolath carnage was as brutal as anything that had been seen in Heaven's Ancestor. When, at last, those bastards realized that everything was over they began butchering some of The Wondervale's native species, but my forebears were able to stop that before too many worlds were destroyed.'

'That was what I wished to ask,' said Artificial Environment 17,863,006. 'Why?'

Ah, so now you begin to show yourself in your true colours.

'Please expand the query,' said Strauss-Giolitto, opening her eyes a trifle wider than usual in an attempt to convey naivety.

'Why not let the Helgiolath destroy those species for you? It would have saved trouble for the Humans later, once they had taken over The Wondervale.'

'I told you,' she said, shaking her head and furrowing her brow. It must be obvious to the puters that she was having difficulty comprehending the question. 'I told you that we Humans, although we can muster almost immediately some of the most impressive military technology in the known Universe should the occasion demand, are not naturally a bellicose species.'

'But you say you are intelligent.'

'Yes.'

'Then—'

'Not all intelligent peoples are spurred on by nothing but thoughts of conquest.' *I wish I could say that with more certainty. No, no, think of the ancient species like the Pridehouse and the Lingk-kreatzai: they lost all urge for war as they explored the Universe, if they ever had it in the first place. Even the Lingk-kreatzai males, who fight to the death during immaturity, lose all trace of that aggression by the time they reach adulthood.* 'But that doesn't mean that the peaceful ones – the ones who simply want to co-exist with each other – can't be the most dangerous, if provoked. Look at Commander Segrill, for example.'

'The little one,' Artificial Environment 17,863,006 confirmed.

She nodded. 'The Trok. Until recently he was in charge of a planet entirely devoted to the manufacture of the most deadly armaments in The Wondervale.'

Technically it was true. In reality it was a lie. Once upon a time her Christianity would have frowned upon the deception, and even now – now that all but vestiges of her faith had left her – she felt the pang of a residual guilt. Besides, she had told

347

so many falsehoods during the course of her long history lesson that one more wasn't going to make any difference. Still, it was a qualitatively *different* lie, in that it involved a real, living person who was nearby; the others were abstract fictions.

'Yes' – she hurried on – 'even the gentle Trok can be fierce when circumstances require them to be. And Humans can be orders of magnitude more vicious even than that. The Children of the Starlight and the ur-Helgiolath of the Twin Galaxies may have regarded themselves as implacably savage when they created the death-vessels, like Artificial Environment 17,863,006, but they gave each other only a taste of the cruelty of which Humans are capable when cruelty is the only means of species survival.'

'I have seen no trace of this cruelty in any of you,' observed the larger puter.

'That's because you haven't yet scratched our skin,' said Strauss-Giolitto.

'Meaning?'

'You haven't done us any harm. You've inconvenienced us, but it's been worth it to us because we've learnt a lot from you – and you're giving us a free ride home. And once we get there you may be able to help us.'

'Help you? How? I thought you Humans were all-powerful.'

She drew her knees up towards her chest, put her arms round them and rested her chin on top of them: posture indicating time for thought as she worked out how best to explain a difficult concept to a bunch of kids whose attention was in danger of wandering.

'Well,' she said at length, 'it's like this, you see. My ancestors didn't eliminate all of the Helgiolath, because a few of them found a way of hiding themselves . . .'

When the pain struck Lan Yi it did so suddenly.

He and Seragarda had been doing some standard maintenance work inside the *Midnight Ranger*'s recycling systems, there being not much else to do as Artificial Environment 17,863,006 hurtled through whatever aspect of spacetime it could penetrate in order to transcend the velocity of light. Although the smell was disagreeable to both of them, the task itself was not unpleasant: essentially they were doing little more than supervise the activities of the checkers – small devices, not intelligent enough to be described as bots, which scrabbled from one terminal to the next and, very rarely, let out a thin little *beep* and a red light when they discovered something that needed adjusting.

Seragarda found the relatively menial work quietly satisfying. Besides, it gave her and the out-of-Taiwanese a lot of time on their own to talk about this, that and the cosmos in general.

But then Lan Yi doubled up with a cry of pain.

She had never heard him show such a strong sign of emotion before.

Seragarda trotted through the shallow sludge to be by his side, and looked into his face.

Droplets of water were being extruded from between the lids of his tightly closed eyes. His mouth was half-open; the muscles at its corners were tense, as if some were straining against others in an attempt to close it. Lan Yi was clearly in the pits of an agony beyond anything Seragarda could comprehend.

And yet . . . and yet she had the curious impression that there was another, quite different emotion trying to register itself on his contorted face.

Ecstasy.

He toppled over sideways to land with a splosh in the yellow-green sludge.

Checking swiftly that his nose and mouth were clear of the viscous liquid, Seragarda turned and ran back along the maintenance tunnel, her feet kicking up sprays of gunk.

The Main Computer was everywhere throughout the *Midnight Ranger* – in every cabin and common room, every corridor and

every cranny and every corner. There was no escaping its surveillance, even though the primary focus of its attention was
Strauss-Giolitto's cabin, where it was engrossed in the mysteries
of Human history. Strider and her personnel had to be careful
about everything they said – and indeed what they did, in case
the machine read a careless piece of body language. Even within
the Pockets there was no guarantee of privacy. Before they slept
they wrapped loose gags of fabric round their mouths.

The flipside of this was that, wherever they were, those
aspects of the Main Computer that were not being distracted
by Strauss-Giolitto's fabulations were available at all times
for consultation. And through the Main Computer the personnel had access to Artificial Environment 17,863,006 and *its*
associated AI.

Strider was speaking with the Main Computer through one
of the Pockets when Seragarda came on to the command deck.

'. . . about one point three one six standard days, about one
thousand two hundred and fifty nanreets,' said the voice inside
the Pocket. There was a visual display of their situation, but
Strider couldn't get her brain round it: bits of it seemed to be
only partly visible, as if they were veering away into tran-
scendental dimensions, and the rest didn't make any sense.
On the floor of the Pocket the numbers were spelt out in full,
to her relief: the numbers had a reassuring solidity to them.

She pulled her head free of the Pocket's field and glanced
across at Hein. His eyes were, as usual, alight with laughter,
but his mouth was a flat line of apprehension.

'No need to be so gloomy, buster. We're going to be home
soon.'

His voice was unusually sober. 'Not exactly, Leonie. We're
going to be back in Heaven's Ancestor. That's quite a different
thing.'

'Hell – Heaven's Ancestor is just at the bottom of the back
yard.'

'Dangerous back yard.'

Looking at him with her head to one side, Strider realized for the first time that he had been unhappy for some days. It had been an inconvenient fact and so she had at some deep unconscious level chosen to ignore it. She was too good at doing that sort of thing.

'Unlike a Pridehouse to be worried about the future,' she said defensively.

'I'm not entirely a Pridehouse any longer,' he said. 'You stay long enough in the form of another species, speak its language and all, and you begin to take on some of the characteristics – the personality traits – of that species. Try it sometime.'

'I have.' Oh boy, but she had. When she'd been a six-legged wolf there had been an interlude in a field when she had certainly not been Human. When all this was over – if ever it was going to be over – she must try that again.

Seragarda was saying something, but then Seragarda was saying something most of the time. Strider paid her no attention beyond half-raising a hand in greeting.

'Things can't have got any worse since we left there,' she continued. 'It's when we get back to The Wondervale that things might start hotting up. Umbel knows what Kaantalech's been getting up to, but knowing her it'll be all shit-bad news.'

'*If* we get back to The Wondervale,' said Hein, and now there was no mistaking the gloominess in his voice.

'Yeah, yeah . . . we will. We got big brother on our side now, remember? A little thing like the Shift isn't going to make any difference to him. Shut up, Seragarda. I'm trying to hold a conversation.'

'But—'

'Shut up, I said. This is your captain speaking.'

I STRONGLY ADVISE YOU TO LISTEN TO WHAT SERAGARDA HAS COME HERE TO SAY.

'And when I want your advice, Pinocchio, I'll ask for it, OK? Right, Seragarda, get it out.'

The white she-wolf was dancing with the urgency of her

351

information. She yapped words, and Pinocchio translated automatically as she spoke.

'Aw, shit,' said Strider once Seragarda had finished. 'I was hoping this wasn't going to happen yet. Hoped it wasn't going to happen at all.'

She slumped down into a chair.

'Any ideas, Pinocchio?' she subvocalized.

THE ONLY PERSON WHO CAN HELP US IS POLYAGGLE.

'Yeah, but will she?'

SHE LOVES LAN YI.

'She made that blatantly obvious by screwing him until he looked like he'd come off second best in a fight with a cactus.'

HE LOVES HER.

'He never said he wanted her to make him pregnant. He never volunteered for the . . . what the fuck is it? . . . Death in Jubilation, or something.' She pounded her fist against the seat's arm-rest.

THE DEATH IN JOY.

'Death in the Recycling Chambers, more like. Real romantic, huh? She loves him so goddam much she decides to kill him. Oh, wow, play me the violins for this one.'

POLYAGGLE COULD NOT HAVE EXPRESSED HER LOVE FOR LAN YI MORE PROFOUNDLY. SHE WAS GIVING HIM THE GREATEST GIFT SHE HAD.

'There's guys back on Mars who come out with the same line about one picosecond before they grab a ship for the asteroids. Get her here anyway.'

I HAVE ANTICIPATED YOUR COMMAND, LEONIE. POLYAGGLE IS ALREADY ON HER WAY TO THE COMMAND DECK. IT WAS DIFFICULT FOR ME TO STOP HER GOING TO THE RECYCLING CHAMBERS. SHE WANTS TO BE WITH LAN YI SO THAT THEY CAN SHARE THE JOY OF HIS DEATH AND THE BIRTH OF HER BROOD TOGETHER. IT IS – WAS – A MOMENT OF GREAT EMOTIONAL IMPORTANCE FOR THE SPINDRIFTERS.

Strider felt Hein's hand on her shoulder. She looked up.

Where there had been foreboding on his face before, now there was compassion. The dance had gone even from his eyes.

'Thanks,' she whispered hoarsely to him, and then turned her attention back to Pinocchio. 'Detail Nelson and Leander to grab a stretcher and fetch Lan Yi up here as well. Tell 'em to be careful with him. Dunno if we're really supposed to move the old jock but I think we've got to.'

A moment later Pinocchio responded. THEY ARE ON THEIR WAY TO THE RECYCLING CHAMBERS.

'Good.'

Strider chewed her lower lip. 'Goddam bloody sex,' she said to Hein after a few moments. 'Makes a mess of everything. You Pridehouse know more about the Spindrifters than I'll ever learn. Any chances of . . . shit, I dunno . . . a late abortion, or something?'

He shook his head, still looking down at her with that same weary sympathy in his eyes. 'Fond of that "old jock", weren't you, Leonie?'

Strider stood up abruptly, shaking his hand off her shoulder. 'Course I was bloody fond of him. Still am. Maybe we can pull him through somehow. Pinocchio, see if you can grab hold of Tenper for a few minutes and find out if he's got any ideas.' She thought for a further couple of seconds. 'Any chances of getting hold of Angler?' Angler had once been associated with the Spindrifters. If any Image might know how to save Lan Yi, Angler would be the one.

ANGLER WILL NOT HELP US. HIS LOYALTIES LIE ENTIRELY WITH POLYAGGLE AND THE FUTURE OF HER SPECIES.

So the Images were specific-loyal. It was something Strider had not known before. She slotted the datum away in a corner of her mind to be dusted off and more closely examined later.

'Angler's bloody lucky I can't get my hands on him,' she growled.

The door gave a low moan and Polyaggle fluttered in among them. The Spindrifter's wings were a polychromatic

353

dazzlement of feverishly flowing and transmuting colours, washes of metallic sheen running fitfully across them. The proboscis at the centre of her face was a blur of motion, but it was creating no words that Pinocchio could translate. Just as well. The Spindrifter was unable to keep her feet on the floor but instead flew in a jerky, uncertain fashion round the walls of the command deck, occasionally swooping alarmingly close above the heads of Strider and Hein.

'Calm the fuck down,' snapped Strider. It made no difference.

STRIDER.

'Hi, there, Tenper. Let's talk in the Pocket where we can have a bit of peace. Hein, see if you can get Polyaggle to stop acting like a banshee on heat.'

'"Banshee"?'

'You know what I mean.'

The environment of the Pocket seemed somehow cooler than outside, as if Polyaggle's frenzy were warming up the command deck.

'Any chances for Lan Yi?' said Strider bluntly.

FROM THE MOMENT SHE IMPLANTED HER BROOD IN HIM, THERE WAS NO HOPE OF SAVING LAN YI'S LIFE.

'You sure about that?'

IT HAS NEVER BEEN DONE – NOT SO FAR AS WE KNOW.

'That's a kind of different thing.'

OUR KNOWLEDGE OF THE SPINDRIFTERS AND THEIR EVOLU-TIONARY HISTORY IS AS COMPREHENSIVE AS IT COULD BE.

'Has anyone ever *tried* to save the life of an impregnated Spindrifter male?'

There was a perceptible hesitation. NOT ACCORDING TO THE RECORDS. WHYEVER WOULD A SPINDRIFTER MALE WANT TO AVOID EXPERIENCING THE DEATH IN JOY?

'I can think of a dozen reasons,' muttered Strider.

THAT IS BECAUSE YOU ARE A HUMAN.

'So's Lan Yi.'

BUT POLYAGGLE IS NOT.

'Too damn' right she's not. She's not going to be recognizable as protoplasm in a few minutes' time. Why did she have to do it?' Strider was aware that this time she was wailing the question, like a kid whose broken toy has been stuffed down a disposal chute.

You know the answer to that, Captain Leonie Strider. It never occurred to her that Lan Yi, once he had realized what was taking place, would be anything other than the grateful recipient of her brood — and of the corollary, The Death In Joy.

'Sure, yeah. Try telling that one with a straight face. How come she went through all that subterfuge to get him to screw with her?'

I am not a Spindrifter. I can tell you only what I know.

Strider felt that, somewhere inside, she knew the answer herself. Lan Yi, despite what he believed of himself, had been still half in love with death – with the Belle Dame Sans Merci who was the shade, imperfectly recreated in his mind, of his dead wife Geena. Polyaggle must have read him more accurately than he himself ever could have. So she had given him both his Belle Dame Sans Merci and the concomitant death. He was going to experience The Death In Joy in both the Spindrifter and a very Human sense.

Her feelings towards Polyaggle tempered a little.

A little.

She was still going to try to save the old man's life. Bugger the future of the Spindrifter species. It wasn't *her* species. Reprehensible and selfish it might be, but right now she cared more about the life of one elderly human being, who had only a few decades left in him at best, than she did about a potential galaxyful of glorified butterflies.

'There's always a first time,' she said, affecting nonchalance. 'Stick around as much as you can, Tenper. You too, Pinocchio. We're gonna save the old bastard.'

*

Nightmirror eases himself into The Truthfulness and extends pseudopods of thought towards any Images that might be associated with the Helgiolath fleet.

There is no responding impulse – just a vacancy of existence that Nightmirror experiences as a sharp pang of disaesthetics. Some physical species have never been able to interrelate very effectively with the Images and – as Nightmirror knows already but has been trying to persuade himself might become otherwise – the Helgiolath are among them. Ten Per Cent Extra Free and the others tried to establish a direct contact, but failed. They have given the big creatures Pockets; although the Pockets are only partially functional without the intervention in their workings of at least one Image, they are better than nothing.

Next he reaches out through the liquid-light walls of The Truthfulness towards Heartfire and Angler. They are halfway across this physical Universe, but they could enter The Truthfulness close beside him and then re-emerge with him among the Helgiolath or on the moon of Alterifer.

He lets the thought die still-born, however. What good would their presence do? The Helgiolath would be ignorant of their existence and the Main Computer of the *Blunt Instrument* would be more likely to become aware of three Images than of one. No, bringing them to his assistance would almost certainly be at best pointless and at worst disastrous.

He wishes he could achieve some sort of contact with Ten Per Cent Extra Free and Pinocchio, but they have been shielded from The Truthfulness – and hence from him – ever since the ancient behemoth of the Children of the Starlight clutched their vessels to itself and entered that *other* space. For a short while he sensed their presence at an almost infinitely far physical distance, but he did not wish to hazard disrupting his delicate relationship with Kaantalech's puter. Now he wishes he had taken that risk.

What to do? What to do?

It is strange for an Image to feel indecision.

There are other Images within The Truthfulness, of course – countless billions of them. He can feel the currents and flows of their sympathy brushing against him. But there is nothing they can do to help him. Their assistance is disqualified for exactly the same reasons that Heartfire and Angler can afford him no aid.

Where is Ten Per Cent Extra Free? Where is Pinocchio?

Nightmirror has observed the way that the creatures of this physical reality – and all the others that he has ever visited – are born, grow old and die: even the two or three silicate species of this universe are mortal, although larger suns may live out their entire lifespans until supernova between the birth and death of one of these rocky beings. He has observed the grief of the bereaved among some – not all – of the mortal peoples. He has never understood that grief. Whether in The Truthfulness or in a physical universe, grief is an irrational emotion, based purely upon selfishness but pretending to be self*less*: it is a projection of the sorrow of loss on to the individual who has died. The illogic is that, in a reality based upon the fact that the past must rot and die so that the present and the future may thrive, a tranquil death should be a cause for celebration. In your life you have done little: in your death you have helped create the future.

Or so Nightmirror has always thought.

Now he re-examines his attitudes towards this very mortal emotion, and finds them bleak.

It is as if Ten Per Cent Extra Free and Pinocchio have become dead to him: they may never re-enter the arena of his consciousness; he may never feel the amicable rub of their thought-patterns against his own.

He begins to understand what grief is.

Yes, it is selfish. It is selfishness incarnate.

But that is not to say that it is not *real*.

And it doesn't *feel* selfish. At the moment, in the physical

357

stasis – the tiny curled up ball of dimensions that somehow never attained physicality – he endures a sense of loss that seems to belong more to Ten Per Cent Extra Free and Pinocchio than to himself.

For want of anything else to do except discover the nature of sorrow, Nightmirror retreats back to the core of Kaantalech's flagship, the *Blunt Instrument*.

The Main Computer is still creating galaxies of electro-neurological relays and does not notice Nightmirror's return. He watches stars flare into existence, evolve and then vanish – splendidly or subduedly – back into the beyond-black of nothingness.

One day this physical universe will die. One day the Polycosmos as a whole will surely die.

Who will there be to grieve for it?

'There is a weakening of the Shift field,' said Alin, one of Kortland's officers.

'I had observed this,' Kortland said, his voice a mixture of a splutter and a scrape to show that he was nevertheless grateful that she had conveyed the information to him.

On the whole he rather approved of Alin. No, that was to understate matters. She was certainly his favourite among all his officers, and after they had defeated Kaantalech he might well be tempted to begin with her the long process of Helgiolath courtship. She did not present herself to the general standard of smartness upon which Kortland insisted among his other officers – sometimes her superficial slime was smeared in inchoate patterns, sometimes one head leaned away from her body at a greater angle than the other – but, in her, these were things that he was prepared to forgive. She had the sharpest mind in his fleet with the possible exception of his own – and he was honest enough to realize that 'possible' meant exactly that – and she had powers of intuition that went beyond the range of the normal Helgiolath.

'What do you think it means?' he asked her.

'I think Kaantalech has grown impatient of the stalemate,' she said, slithering to his side. 'Impatience has always been her weakness.'

'You don't sound happy about this.'

'I'm not. Kaantalech wouldn't have survived all that time under the regime of Nalla had she not been a wise one, an opportunist willing to bide her time until a small movement could have great consequences.'

'Yes.'

'Look at the way she manipulated the Humans and their followers until they destroyed Nalla and his version of the Autarchy.'

'Yes.'

Daring, Alin rubbed her shoulder against his. There was a sucking noise as their flesh separated once more.

'Someone more shortsighted than Kaantalech,' said Alin, 'would have destroyed the Humans on sight and hoped to receive the praise of the Autarch for having rid The Wondervale of a menace. Not she. Her cunning is greater than that. She let events take their course, and at the end of them she was the new tyrant. Do not underestimate her, Kortland.'

'I have never underestimated Kaantalech.'

He let the secondary visual sensors in his neck – they were patches of light-sensitive skin that could be distinguished from the rest of his flesh only close up – scan across the instrumentation in front of him.

'She is trying to let the field weaken with such slowness that we fail to perceive it,' said Alin.

'It may be that *she* underestimates *us*.'

'I . . . I wouldn't like to state that as a certainty.'

'A probability?'

'Not even that. Impatient she may be, but Kaantalech will not throw her life away – or even chance doing so. Whatever she does may have an obvious reason on the surface, but the true reason will lie somewhere beneath.'

Alin moved away from him now. She drew her heads together and then let them spring apart again in a habitual gesture of hers that he always found deliciously feminine. He knew she was perfectly capable of playing the coquette; sometimes, however, those same mannerisms betrayed the fact that she was following a train of thought wherever it would lead her, whether she desired its destination or not.

'Imagine,' said Alin, 'imagine that Kaantalech is perfectly aware of the fact that we have both the technology and the acumen to detect the weakening of the Shift field. What do you think it is that she wants us to assume?'

'What else can we assume? That she has decided to set an all-out assault upon us before we can break down the field from outside and shatter her moon.'

'Precisely. We must maintain all our defences at peak level, for that is what she will most assuredly do should we relax them at all – remember, she is The Wondervale's great opportunist, and she won't pass up a chance to achieve her ends the simple way.'

Alin gave an anal rasp of deep contemplation. Kortland knew better than to interrupt her.

'But that isn't what Kaantalech *plans*,' she continued. 'No, she has some other idea – something more devious. Even if it involves . . . Now there's a . . .'

'What?' said Kortland cautiously after several moments had gone by.

'Oh yes.' That was all Alin said, and he knew that she was speaking not to him but to herself.

'Oh . . . oh . . . oh.'

The slime of her coat was going blue with fear.

'Tell me,' he said urgently, his earlier resolutions going by the board.

'You or I,' said Alin, the froth at her ingestion slit indicating

360

a state midway between dreaminess and fierce concentration, 'would regard the survival of the people under our command as being of paramount importance – we would do anything in order to avoid them being slaughtered, even if it meant our own lives.'

Kortland gave an irritated shake of his torso. 'The same could be said of any civilized species,' he said.

'Yes, but Kaantalech is *not* a civilized species – she is not civilized at all. Even among the Alhubra, renowned for their barbarism, she has earnt a reputation for brutality. There is only one creature whose survival she values.'

'Herself,' said Kortland, now rapidly following where Alin had led.

'Precisely. That is why I fear so much what she is about to do. I wish, I wish I knew.'

'We could beat a retreat.'

'I think it's too late for that.'

Nightmirror watches the fluctuations in the Shift field. Sometimes it becomes briefly stronger, but the general tendency is downwards. He hopes that the Helgiolath are alert enough to detect this, and wonders if he should make another foray through The Truthfulness to investigate their fleet: while he may not influence, he could at least observe.

No. Each time he leaves the *Blunt Instrument* he runs the risk of his return being noticed, however careful he is. He is serving the forces of the aesthetic better by staying here, doing what tiny things he can to sabotage Kaantalech's plans.

Moving cautiously, he makes a few of the Main Computer's stars wink out. Some of Kaantalech's weapons have suddenly become dysfunctional, for reasons the Main Computer will be unable to diagnose.

This will infuriate the Autarch, which is all to the good. The greater Kaantalech's fury, the more likely she is to make mistakes.

More stars wink out.

Since many of the weapons systems in Kaantalech's moon-bound fleet are linked in series or parallel, if Nightmirror can only find the right starting place then whole cascades of them might suddenly become just useless lumps of metal.

More than that he cannot do without running the risk of detection. In theory he might start to detonate some of the pulsenukes and pedoes in their bays, but in practice he would be uncovered instantly by the Main Computer and either destroyed by its electroneurological circuits or forced to flee into The Truthfulness.

Wiser to remain where he is and bide his time until the moment when he can cause the Autarch the maximum of inconvenience, or do the surrounding Helgiolath the greatest good.

Nightmirror does not like his decision. Many Helgiolath will die before that moment comes. But more will die if he makes his move too soon and is forced into inactivity.

More stars wink out.

And more.

'Aw, c'mon, Loki,' hissed Hilary.

The cat ignored him.

She had pursued Segrill into one of the litter shafts, where detritus was stored preparatory to recycling. The little Trok had managed to flutter up to the top of an unstable heap of garbage some three metres above the floor, and Loki was clearly nervous of the climb. Instead, she sat at the foot of the mound, waiting patiently, occasionally opening her mouth to whine invitingly, her tail flicking with slow regularity from side to side.

Hilary could see all this in the dim green lighting, but he couldn't do much about it. The ports into the litter shafts had not been designed for Human ingress but to allow access by cleanerbots. The fact that the *Midnight Ranger* no longer had

362

any cleanerbots meant the smell in here was rank. He had his head and one shoulder jammed into the opening and was stretching out an arm towards the little cat. His arm was a frustrating few centimetres too short for him to be able to make a grab at the loose black fur.

'It's your bloody animal,' said Segrill, one of the Images translating his words into a high-pitched snarl. 'It's your job to bloody do something about it.'

'She'll get tired of the game eventually,' said Hilary, springing to his pet's defence. He'd never heard Segrill swear before – hadn't even known that the Trok species understood the concept. 'You shouldn't have taunted her.'

'I didn't taunt her, you moron! I was in one of the Pockets trying to work out where in Heaven's Ancestor we were likely to re-enter ordinary space. I came out for a break. Then this bloody dimwitted animal made a leap for me . . . and now here I am. Now *get it away from me*!'

'I don't know how to. I can't reach her.'

'Fetch some food.'

'I don't think that'll work. She's just eaten.'

'Then why in hell does she want to eat *me*?'

''Cause you move about. In an . . . interesting way.'

'It's urgent I get out of here, dammit! Ten Per Cent Extra Free tells me I'm needed up on the command deck at once. Lan Yi's in danger of dying. There's a chance I can help.'

'What's he dying of?'

'The Death In Joy.'

'What's that?'

'It's a thing that happens to Spindrifter males when they're expecting to give birth to a . . . Oh, just get the cat away so that I can get out of here and up to the deck, boy!'

'But Lan Yi's not a Spindrifter,' said Hilary, his brow creased in confusion. 'Least, I don't think so.'

'Don't waste time thinking about it.'

'All right.'

'Just get the cat out of the way.'

'OK. Loki. Loki. Here, Loki, Loki, Loki.'

The cat continued to dwell in its own small world of silent absorption, its stare never wavering.

Hilary had an inspiration.

He groped round on the floor in front of him until he found a hard object. He wondered what it was, then decided not to wonder.

Twisting himself round in the narrow aperture, he hurled the object as best he could at the cat's flank. His grunt of effort was drowned by Loki's protesting squall. She turned her head to give him a baleful look – 'Traitor' – then scampered off to the far corner of the shaft.

Hilary felt proud of his own resourcefulness.

'Get out of the way!' screamed Segrill ungratefully, dipping and floundering through the air towards his face.

For a moment Hilary didn't know what the Trok was so agitated about, then realized that his own body was blocking Segrill's only means of escape.

'Oh, right,' he said, and began to squirm backwards.

Getting himself free was more difficult than he had thought – he had pushed himself very firmly into the port – and Loki was beginning to take renewed interest as Segrill flapped frenziedly round Hilary's head.

At last his shoulders pulled free, and he sat back on the floor of the passageway with a thump, breathing heavily. The world seemed redder than it should be, and little points of twinkling white light swam around in his vision.

'That's . . .' he began, but before he could get another word out Segrill had shot past him and was fluttering away up the corridor. A black streak travelling in the same direction represented Loki.

'No gratitude, some people have,' grumbled Hilary as he raised himself unsteadily to his feet.

*

364

'Well,' Strauss-Giolitto said at length in reply to Artificial Environment 17,863,006's question, 'it's like this, you see. My ancestors didn't eliminate all of the Helgiolath, because a few of them found a way of hiding themselves.'

The puters said nothing, clearly waiting for her to give them more than the bald statement.

She waited a few moments longer, and then continued. 'Some of the species of The Wondervale had developed biotechnology to the degree where they were capable of shifting their forms at will – they have even used it on us Humans of the *Midnight Ranger* as part of their standard decontamination procedures. The relics of what had once seemed set to be a mighty Helgiolath empire still had enough military firepower to conquer one of these species and seize the details of the technology.'

'They changed themselves into other creatures – or, at least, into the semblance of other creatures,' said Artificial Environment 17,863,006's Main Computer. 'The Children of the Starlight learnt how to do that not long before their demise, and the enemy's researches were not far behind.'

'Exactly,' said Strauss-Giolitto. 'They became, to all outward appearances, members of a different species. Bridling their Helgiolath bloodlust, they intermingled with this species so that, even once the Humans had uncovered the subterfuge, there wasn't much that could be done about it.'

'The Humans could have annihilated the species,' remarked Artificial Environment 17,863,006. 'That would have been the simplest solution.'

'I repeat, our minds don't work like that,' Strauss-Giolitto snapped. 'We try to reduce cruelty and killing to a minimum – we try, if possible, to abjure them entirely.' *Would that that were true.*

There was nothing but a soft hum from the Main Computer's speakers. She had silenced the brat at the back who thought it was clever to be as obstructive as possible, to make a point of never understanding anything the first time it was said.

'No,' she carried on more tranquilly, feeling the flush of artificial temper fading from her cheekbones. 'As long as the Helgiolath were prepared to live in peace, my ancestors were prepared to leave them where they were. And, after a few generations, the threat of the Helgiolath seemed to have been, quite literally, bred out of existence.

'The Wondervale seemed safe. There was no reason for the Humans to remain there. Those worlds that might have seemed suitable for colonization were already populated by their own species.'

Strauss-Giolitto smiled, though retaining a little frostiness to show that she was still not going to tolerate dork-headed interruptions.

'The bulk of the Human occupying forces retreated to the Milky Way, where they were put on standby in case other hostile species like the Helgiolath were encountered by the expeditionary fleets, which continued their exploration of the known Universe.'

She lay back on her bunk and stared at the featureless ceiling. Her face looked glum.

'But the Helgiolath hadn't interbred. Not truly.'

'They rose again,' said the smaller puter.

'You bet. Still in the guise of Alhubra – that's the name of the species among whom they'd concealed themselves – they formed a new fleet and set about doing their best to conquer The Wondervale.'

'"Doing their best"?'

'There weren't very many of them left,' explained Strauss-Giolitto, 'and they didn't have access to the sort of really heavy weaponry they'd been able to bring with them when first they escaped from the Twin Galaxies and the Children of the Starlight. Some of The Wondervale's species were capable of putting up a good fight – some of them repulsed the

Helgiolath entirely. Losses were heavy on all sides. Still, the modified Helgiolath were able to set up a rickety dictatorship that controlled part of the galaxy. They called it the Autarchy.'

She sat up again, allowing eagerness to trickle back into her face.

'It might have tottered along until the end of time, enslaving those peoples unlucky enough to be caught within its boundaries, but then the Humans came back to The Wondervale – only a small party, *our* party: just a single ship.'

She gave a light laugh, then became sombre.

'It was enough to reduce the Autarchy to rubble and free species who had long forgotten the meaning of the word "freedom". Surrounded by only a few thousand of her fake-Alhubra cronies, the Helgiolath leader fled to the small moon of a planet called Alterifer.'

'You have its coordinates?' said Artificial Environment 17,863,006 to the *Midnight Ranger*'s Main Computer, abruptly abandoning all pretence that it was not the puppet-master.

'The details are stored in my databanks.'

'Why haven't you destroyed this creature?' This time it was clear that Artificial Environment 17,863,006 was addressing Strauss-Giolitto.

'We saw no need to,' said the teacher, trying to camouflage her sense of smugness. The Main Computer aboard Artificial Environment 17,863,006 probably had an IQ – if the measure made any sense at all – in the thousands. She was just a Human of somewhat above-average intelligence. But she'd *beaten* it in the game that only she knew they'd been playing. Another wash of exhaustion went through her, but she was too charged up with triumphant adrenalin to pay it any attention.

'Explain.'

'What harm could she do, cooped up on a single moon?'

'That is irrelevant. This creature is a Helgiolath in all but appearance. As long as she survives, the memory of the

Children of the Starlight is endangered. The creature must be destroyed.'

'Is that necessary? More bloodshed?'

'Yes. It is. I demand so.'

'But' – Strauss-Giolitto made a great show of gulping – 'we Humans have no desire to kill when it is not necessary.' *Cool it, Maria. Next thing you know you'll be batting your pretty eyes like the kid who ate the candy and you'll blow the entire scam.*

'I insist.'

'We could stop you,' she said.

'Perhaps. Almost certainly. But this is not your war: why should you interfere?'

Fall into the puter's logic pattern, just for a moment.

Strauss-Giolitto made herself look confused, then cleared her face.

'Yes. You're perfectly correct.' She shrugged for the hundredth time since this seemingly interminable 'history' lesson had begun. 'This is between you and the last survivors of the Helgiolath. It is your feud.'

'I am glad we are agreed.' There was, somehow, a commanding tone in Artificial Environment 17,863,006's flat voice since it had come to its decision. Strauss-Giolitto wondered what might have happened had she not acquiesced with so little argument.

'Does this creature have a name?' said Artificial Environment 17,863,006.

'Yes,' said Strauss-Giolitto.

She paused.

'Kaantalech.'

Ignoring the fact that her hands were getting scratched to ribbons, Strider had Polyaggle by what passed for the Spindrifter's throat and was pressing her firmly against the bulkhead. The Spindrifter was trying to move her wings and escape, but she was rammed too firmly against the wall for that and Strider's grip was filled with the implacability of blind fury.

'Look, fuckit, that may be what you goddam glorified moths are happy with, but we Humans do things different, you hear?'

Polyaggle's proboscis was still moving so rapidly and so incoherently that neither of the Images could make any attempt at translation.

'Killing her ain't going to make things any easier, light of my life,' said Nelson easily at her shoulder. 'Might be kinda fun, though,' he added.

'She could bloody help us if she wanted to,' shouted Strider. 'Look, you take her for a moment.'

Nelson substituted his gentler hands for hers. 'What're you doing?'

'This,' snapped Strider.

She held the muzzle of the lazgun firmly one centimetre from the side of the Spindrifter's head.

'Hey, don't go using that thing!' said Nelson. 'You're likely to fry my fingers off.'

'I'll be careful,' said Strider grimly. 'Right, Polyaggle, tell me what we've got to do to save Lan Yi.'

Perhaps they should have taken Lan Yi to one of the cabins and put him on a bunk, but Strider had been unwilling to leave the command deck and she had wanted all her personnel in attendance – any one of them might have the sudden inspiration that would save the old man's life. The person most likely to, however, was Polyaggle, which was why Strider was . . . questioning her firmly.

Never have got him on to a bunk anyway, she thought, casting a quick glance in his direction. He was lying on his side in a fetal position, knees hard against his chest, his face a portrait of agony, his eyes wide and sightless and unblinking. They'd tried to straighten him out, but his limbs had refused to budge.

In the middle of that mask of pain, the smile on his lips seemed an obscenity.

WE WOULD URGENTLY ADVISE YOU NOT TO KILL THE SPINDRIFTER, said Ten Per Cent Extra Free.

'I know that,' Strider subvocalized. 'But I want to scare the shit out of her.'

YOU ARE NOT SUCCEEDING. HER THOUGHTS ARE ENTIRELY ON THE IMMINENT EMERGENCE OF HER BROOD AND ON THE ECSTASY SHE HAS GIVEN TO HER CHOSEN LOVER.

'Well, it's about time she was distracted. Can *you* get through to her?'

LET ME TRY.

There was a disturbance behind her and she half-turned to look. Hilary, red in the face and with a struggling Loki firmly clamped under one arm, came on to the command deck. Overhead and a little behind came Segrill. The Trok flew in his imprecise manner across to perch on one of the wall monitors.

'Can you get the cat away?' said Segrill. 'I can't examine Lan Yi until I don't have to worry about that animal jumping me from behind.'

'Aw, but Loki only wants to—' Hilary began.

'Let me take her,' said Leander gently. 'She'll be happier somewhere else.'

Like, stuffed into the recycling chambers, thought Strider.

IT IS IMPOSSIBLE TO COMMUNICATE WITH THE SPINDRIFTER, said Ten Per Cent Extra Free. SHE IS DEMENTED WITH DELIGHT. NONE OF HER THOUGHT PROCESSES ARE WORKING LOGICALLY.

'Sh—*it*!'

Still the lazgun was unwavering. Strider marvelled at her own self-control.

Segrill was squeaking something at her.

'Yeah?' she said, looking up listlessly at him.

'The Trok,' he said, 'the Trok may share a common evolutionary ancestor with the Spindrifters. Look.' He jumped up and down on the monitor, fluttering his rudimentary wings, and for the first time Strider noticed that, somewhere deep down, there was the slightest of morphological similarities between the two species.

'The cat safely out of the way?' she said as Leander came back on to the deck.

'I've shut her in Hilary's cabin.'

'She's learnt how to open the—'

'Not when it's locked on the outside, Hilary, she hasn't.'

'Isn't that a bit, you know, *cruel*?'

'D'you wanna be locked in there with her?' said Strider.

'No.'

'Then keep your mouth shut.'

At last Strider let the hand holding the lazgun fall to her side. 'Keep holding her there, Nelson,' she said to the big man.

'Certainly will, sunrise.'

'OK, Segrill' – with an indicative nod of her head towards the almost unbreathing form of Lan Yi on the floor – 'get to work and see what you can do.'

There was a jolt.

Kortland looked at Alin. 'It's starting,' he said. 'That's the Shift field down.'

'Don't you feel the same dread I do?' she said.

'Yes, but I told myself a while ago that I mustn't pay any attention to it. Try it yourself.'

'I can't pay attention to anything else.' The slime of her coat was drying, some of it solidifying to peel off in long white streamers.

Kortland stabbed forward at the console with his thick, fleshy antlers. His orders were instantly conveyed to all the other commanders of the Helgiolath fleet.

A first salvo of destruction scorched through the nightmare cold of vacuum towards Kaantalech's moon. It was too much to hope that, with the Shift field gone, the rocky little world would be without defences.

Sure enough, the energies of the maxbeams and the sternian activators were diffused across an invisible surface that surrounded the moon about half a million kilometres out.

'Plenty more where those came from,' Kortland said to Alin, as if she needed to be told. *And,* he thought with satisfaction, *even though nothing lethal got through, I'm glad I'm not inside that shield. The internal radiation must be causing havoc. Poor bastards.*

He ran his antlers over the board once more, and this time a smaller number of weapons sped inwards from the deadly sphere of Helgiolath warships. Kortland could detect their progress in his Pocket, but only because he knew what he was looking for. He doubted if Kaantalech, trapped behind a shield that was still flaring as it tried to dissipate the savage energies of the earlier bombardment into space, would be able to see anything.

And the rigor inducers were tiny and unsophisticated enough in their external technology to drive easily through any defensive shield that had yet been devised. They had no clever guidance mechanisms that could be scrambled *en masse*. They had to be destroyed individually by pedoes or energy-seeking nukes. Kortland was relying on the hope that, by the time Kaantalech and her lieutenants realized what was going on, most of the ducers would have made it to the surface. When that happened, anyone trapped outside a structure built of deadmetal was a goner, whatever their species: the radiation from the ducers had the effect of freezing all cellular activity in its tracks. The ducers were dirty weapons, Kortland had always felt, and it had been only with the greatest reluctance that he had permitted them to become part of his fleet's armoury.

He slithered back from the Pocket once he had seen that, indeed, rather more than fifty per cent of the rigor inducers had penetrated the shield.

'Should I offer her a truce?' he said to Alin. 'She must have suffered terrible damage by now. Maybe Kaantalech herself is among the dead, for all we know.'

She shortened her necks, withdrawing her heads towards her body. No.

Alin was right on both counts, he knew. There could be no such thing as a reliable truce with the Autarchy or indeed with the Alhubra, and it was a safe bet that Kaantalech would not be among the casualties: it seemed to be some sort of law of nature that, however many and whoever died, Kaantalech was among the survivors. She took precautions. Always.

'There'll be something coming back at us, any moment now,' said Alin with certainty. 'She's waiting for us to begin to think that we've inflicted a serious blow on her, and then she's going to mount a counterattack.'

Kortland had come to the same conclusion.

He returned his head to the Pocket. These damn' devices would work much more efficiently had the Helgiolath been able to interrelate directly with the Images, but the incompatibility between their psychologies was too great. Even so, the Pockets were invaluable.

Slowly the radiance of the raw energies faded from the moon's defensive shielding and once again, cranking up the Pocket's magnification, Kortland was able to see the desolation of the surface. There were impact craters of all sizes over much of the landscape, and at some time in the comparatively recent selenological past something really massive – an asteroid or a cometary nucleus – had hit Alterifer's small acolyte, creating a crater so huge that the moon looked almost like a fruit with a bite out of it.

It was at the base of this huge concavity that Kaantalech had constructed her external headquarters. A few small domes had been set up as well as half a dozen larger edifices which Kortland guessed were factories, but clearly Kaantalech was making her warcruisers double up as living quarters for her troops.

The barrenness of the scene reminded Kortland powerfully

of Qitanefermeartha, where the Autarch Nalla had met his death. It, too, had been an insignificant-seeming world characterized by zero atmosphere and rock-strewn, star-baked desolation. Kaantalech had not had as long as had Nalla and his ancestors to make a fortress of the world – she was improvising with battlecraft the vast, almost impregnable stronghold which Nalla's forebears had erected – but the resemblance was uncanny.

What sense was there in attaining the throne of the Autarchy if the throne had to be sited on – or in this case *in* – some unloved, sterile back-of-beyond world like Qitanefermeartha or Alterifer's moon? Perhaps Nalla and now Kaantalech drew spiritual sustenance from the knowledge that they, through their fleets and armies, held ultimate power over The Wondervale; perhaps they slept more contentedly in the thought that their legions were killing, maiming and torturing civilized species into submission in a thousand thousand planetary systems. But in reality the boundaries of their Autarchy were no further than the nearest horizons of a lifeless, airless globe which no one else wanted.

They were very small empires to give rise to so much suffering.

He brought his mind back to more immediate circumstances. It had been the Humans and their bot who had seen an end to Nalla. Kortland and his fleet had offered themselves as a decoy – there had been little else for them to do, for they lacked the necessary cunning stupidity the Humans enjoyed as their birthright. But there were no Humans here. They were lost to him. They were lost to everyone else in The Wondervale and, so it was rumoured, far beyond.

No fools to find the weak spot in Kaantalech's defences and exploit it.

Unless there was a last-minute sound of bugles and one of those raucous bleats from the dark-coloured Human-thing called Strider, he was in command on his own.

He wished to the cores of his hearts that the Strider-person were here. She was his lucky mascot.

He shook his torso. What a hell of a time to think these thoughts. The Helgiolath didn't need a bunch of misfits to help them out. They could do it. Hadn't their ancestors – or so the legends went – beaten the bloodthirsty Children of the Starlight to a standstill? Kaantalech was nothing by comparison.

Stop thinking about the Humans as if they were magic. If Strider were here, she'd probably be dead by now.

No. Strider was like Kaantalech in one respect: she survived.

Kortland sent a mental request to the Pocket that it give him an estimate of the number of warcruisers at Kaantalech's disposal, but this was one of the things that the Image-less Pocket was unable to provide.

Thousands, he reckoned. Likely as many warcraft as he had under his own command. He itched to be able to join combat with them in open space. At the moment there was a stalemate: Kaantalech could no more hope to raise her armada than Kortland could hope to penetrate the protective shield – a second wave of ducers would be a waste of weaponry now that everyone outside the ships was already dead.

Stalemate?

No. He trusted Alin's judgement.

When Kaantalech was one of the players in the game there was no such thing as a stalemate.

She would be prepared to sweep all the other pieces – her own included – from the board if it meant that she emerged the victor.

There was nothing to do but wait for her next move.

'Can you feel it?' Leander whispered to Nelson.

'You bet, darlin',' he said, putting a weary arm round her shoulder. 'Guess we oughta go and sus things out in the Pockets.'

He was still from time to time finding another of Polyaggle's spines in the flesh of his hands and forearms. He paused now to pull one out with a wince before moving to the furthermost Pocket. Leander, her legs feeling like lead, took the central one.

The two of them, like everyone else, had used various stims to keep themselves active, but their bodies and minds could be fooled for only so long into believing that they had not been awake and at full alert for something over twenty-four hours. Leander would have killed for a belt of ziprite right now. A belt of ziprite and several days flat on her back with her eyes closed. Then a long hot bath and maybe . . .

Stop thinking like that, Maloron! she urged herself as her legs threatened to buckle under her.

'Do you confirm what I think I see?' she said in a slurred voice through the Pockets to Umbel Nelson. 'It's not a hallucination, is it?'

'Finest sight I ever did see, gracious angel,' came his rumbled response.

'Better tell the others?'

'I agree. But wait until they're ready for it.'

'OK.'

As if trying to perform in synchrony, they both took one last, lingering glance at the starfields the Pockets were displaying to them, then retreated and turned to face the rest of the command deck.

Strider and the aliens aside from Polyaggle were attending to Lan Yi – even Loki (how *had* she escaped?) seemed to be trying to help – but it was obvious that, with the exception of Segrill, none of them had even the slightest idea where to start. They'd tried various Human drugs known to have potentially abortifacient side-effects, but all that they'd achieved had been to give Lan Yi's face an unhealthy, inorganic-seeming yellow-pink flush; sweat dripped from his forehead and his cheek and those awful grinning lips to the dispassionate grey metal floor. The Spindrifters had billennia

376

ago forsaken the use of drugs in their medicine – or, at least, that was what Polyaggle had finally blurted out, and they had little choice but to believe her; Hein and Seragarda said that, to the best of their knowledge, she was speaking the truth. Strider had contacted Orphanwifer via the Pockets to see if he could suggest anything, but he had no ideas and, she suspected, was very little interested: the species of The Wondervale had many different means of reproduction, and this was just another of them, so why should he interfere with its workings?

'Open his mouth,' Segrill was saying.

'I'll have to break his jaw,' said Hein.

'This is the only thing I can think of.'

'Right.'

Kneeling beside Lan Yi's head, Hein worked his fingers between the man's upper and lower teeth and wrenched his hands apart. There was a sickening sound of cracking bone. Leander gagged, then realized Lan Yi was in such agony already that the extra pain would make no difference to him.

'What are you planning, little guy?' said Strider. She was sweating almost as much as Lan Yi. One of her personnel was being threatened by something she could neither hit, laz nor outwit, and she obviously wasn't liking it.

'The ultimate in lo-tech,' said Segrill – or, at least, that was the best translation Ten Per Cent Extra Free could manage.

Before anyone could stop him, the Trok had scuttled up Lan Yi's slightly quivering side and stuck his head between the rows of teeth. He turned back for a moment and, tucking his wings tightly to his torso, said: 'See you soon.'

Then he vanished inside Lan Yi's mouth.

Strider made a grab at Segrill's retreating rump, as if to haul him back out again, but she was far too slow.

'Aw, *shit*!' she said. 'Now I'm losing two people rather than one. Great bloody move, Segrill.' She tugged at her ear-lobe and glared at the two Pridehouse in turn.

'Segrill probably knows what he's doing,' said Hein mildly,

relaxing back on to his haunches. He shrugged. 'Probably. We've got to assume that's the case.'

'He's gonna get dissolved in Lan Yi's digestive acids – that's what he knows he's doing?'

Hein shrugged again. 'He'll have thought that one through. Segrill's no suicider.'

'This is extremely interesting, from a scientific point of view,' said Seragarda.

Strider's hand groped towards her belt for her lazgun. Luckily Nelson had taken it from her earlier.

Strauss-Giolitto, who had been comforting Hilary against the far wall, came across, knelt down and put her arm round Strider's waist. She moved as if to whisper something into Strider's ear, then desisted. There was no need for words: the gesture was sufficient in itself.

Nelson cleared his throat. 'While Segrill's doing whatever it is he's doing,' he said, 'there's something you guys ought to be aware of.'

'Better be good,' growled Strider, but her body was more relaxed now.

'We're back in real space. In Heaven's Ancestor. Our fleet's waiting for us less than a parsec away. We can rejoin them any time we want, assuming Artificial Environment 17,863,006 lets us. And, gorgeous light of sunset, the Shift field's gone down, so we can return to The Wondervale any time we want.'

A couple of standard days earlier and Strider would have greeted the news with a yelp of delight. Now she just said: 'Everything bloody happens at once, doesn't it? Let's get Lan Yi saved, then we can rescue The Wondervale, and then we can think about getting home. One thing at a time, huh?'

Nelson gulped. 'Yes, ma'am.'

'And less of your sarcasm,' said Strider, not turning towards him.

Leander beckoned to Strauss-Giolitto who, after a worried look at Strider, joined her.

'Think you can find out from Artificial Environment 17,863,006 what it plans to do now it's got here?' Leander whispered.

'It's not interested in our fleet,' Strauss-Giolitto whispered back, looking round at the walls in a clear warning that they might be listening. 'All it wants to do is track down and exterminate the last of the Helgiolath in The Wondervale.'

Leander was baffled, and her face must have shown it.

'You know,' said Strauss-Giolitto, more loudly, 'Kaantalech.'

Aha, so that was it. Putting two and two together to make four was not especially difficult. Leander had known there was some sort of deception in the wind but hadn't been told the details.

'That bastard Helgiolath Kaantalech,' she said, nodding her head in affirmation. 'Sooner she and her pseudo-Alhubra are done for the better.'

'Too right,' agreed Strauss-Giolitto. 'Any help we can give Artificial Environment 17,863,006 will be much appreciated, though I don't think it needs our help – it can do all this on its own. I'll go talk with it in a separate cabin.'

'Good idea,' said Leander heartily.

Strider didn't even look up as Strauss-Giolitto left the command deck. She just carried on staring at Lan Yi's broken mouth, where Segrill had disappeared.

'Any idea what he's trying?' she said to no one in particular.

'It's a good guess that Polyaggle's brood has been maturing in Lan Yi's stomach and alimentary canal,' said Hein, although he too was looking puzzled. 'At least, that's what I think Segrill thinks. He can get direct access to those regions from the throat – rather him than me. Don't worry about the stomach juices: Segrill's nobody's idiot, so he wouldn't have gone in there if he thought there was any danger.'

'Hm, yeah,' said Strider dubiously. 'And what happens if he can't get out again?'

'If Lan Yi dies we can just cut him out. If Lan Yi lives we'll have to perform more delicate surgery. Think of it as a caesarean operation.'

'What's that?'

Ten Per Cent Extra Free explained his translation briefly to her and the rest of the Humans. Leander felt sickened, and Strider looked likewise.

Once again Polyaggle, who had been keeping herself to herself in a corner of the deck, clearly chastened by Strider's earlier violence, began to become agitated, her wings waving in jagged arcs that left behind them in the air afterimages of iridescent colour.

Strider glanced up at her.

'Shut the fuck up. You've done enough damage.'

'We're too late,' said Seragarda softly. She trotted a couple of paces back from Lan Yi's recumbent form. 'Even Segrill's idea came too late.'

'Stop being so fucking fatalistic,' snarled Strider, looking as if she might hit out at the Pridehouse.

'She's being realistic,' said Hein. 'And she's right.'

'What do you mean?' said Leander, moving towards them a pace. But she knew the answer to her own question before she had spoken it. The reason for Polyaggle's sudden new flurry of excitement was all too obvious.

The birthing of the brood was upon them.

Out of the corner of her eye Leander saw that some radical change was occurring in the nature of Polyaggle's activity, and she turned her head to look.

The Spindrifter was disintegrating from the edges inwards. Leander was reminded of the way the image in a holo could fragment from the outside in as reception began to break down. Polyaggle's wings were already mostly gone, small lead-coloured bits of them – each no larger than half the size of Leander's palm – flopping to the floor, where they lay motionless, like flakes of ash blown from a pile of burning papers.

As Leander continued to watch, her mouth dropping open in a mixture of horror and amazement, Polyaggle spread her clawed arms wide as if she were being crucified and turned her head to one side. She rose slowly into the air, coming to a halt about a metre off the floor, her back pressed against the wall. A thin noise was coming from her diamond-shaped mouth – the first time Leander had ever heard that organ emit any sound. Now Polyaggle's head jerked backwards over her other shoulder at an impossible angle; a fractured crack was like a slap in everyone's face. More flakes dropped as the Spindrifter's claws began to come apart, and then the shape of Polyaggle was lost as her body, in a terrifying silence, became a cloud of matt pewter confusion, dead grey scales of what had been her swirling in a spinning turmoil as they settled to the deck.

No one spoke. No one knew how to.

Long ago, when Leander had spent part of her childhood on Earth, she had stayed for a week in one of the few remaining nature reserves with an elderly woman whom genetic evaluation tests had revealed to be distantly related to her. The old woman had been sullen and grumpy, clearly annoyed that the Campaign to Recreate the Family had tracked her down here and foisted this boisterous child on her to wreck the tranquillity of her existence, but she had been grudgingly kind. There were some trees in the reserve, which was marvel enough for Leander; but it was the season when the trees were shedding their leaves, and the old woman – Megan, that had been her name, Granny Megan – had one day made a bonfire of them.

Looking at the heap of flakes which had until just now been Polyaggle, Leander recalled that pile of grey leaves in the moment before Granny Megan touched a laz to it. 'There was a time when they used to be green,' she whispered to herself, echoing the words Granny Megan had spoken so bitterly all those years ago.

Death and decay: the natural order of things.

Yet Leander didn't feel that there was death in the air, how-ever lifeless those grey shards seemed. And her mind began to grope towards some realization of why Polyaggle had been so unable to comprehend the other species' horror at what she had done to Lan Yi.

Among the Spindrifters there was no death, no decay, only eternal life . . .

Polyaggle had, as she had pleaded to them, conferred a blessing on Lan Yi . . .

'Leave him alone,' she said firmly to Strider. 'Leave him, leave him. Can't you see you're just making it more difficult for him?'

Everyone looked at her.

Strider spoke their thoughts aloud. 'You gone nuts or some-thing?'

'No. This should be a time of joy for him. For us all.'

'The poor old bastard's in agony. Take a look at his face, for chrissake.' Strider's own face was dark with fury as she stared up at Leander.

'He's in ecstasy – can't you see?' Leander slapped her hand against her thigh in impatience: how could she get this through to someone so single-minded as Strider could be? 'Agony and ecstasy – the two of them can be there at the same time. They're not' – her tongue stumbled over the formal phrase – 'mutually incompatible.'

'Oh, sure, pull out my toenails and I'll jump for joy,' said Strider in a low voice. Leander expected her to erupt into a new outbreak of violence at any moment.

Through her secondary retinal screen she was still watching the mound of ashes that was Polyaggle's bequeathment to the future. There were small signs of motion there now, as Leander had expected.

'Leave him,' she repeated. 'If you care about Lan Yi at all, you'll let him alone. He's got a change to make.'

The next she knew she was flat on her back. Already she

382

could feel the separate throbs of her chin, where Strider had hit it a backhander, and the rear of her head, which had smashed against the metal of the deck as she'd gone flying across the floor. She'd bitten the side of her tongue, and could taste blood.

Forget the pain. Plenty of time to think about that later — afterwards.

She adjusted the field of view of her secondary retinal screen so that she was looking down on the tableau as if from somewhere far above the ceiling. Tiny toy figures were frozen in position. Strider was staring at her own fist as if in disbelief at what she had just done. Nelson was half-turned towards Leander, his arms out ready to scoop up her shoulders. Hilary was a very small ball in a corner, his face hidden in his hands. Hein and Seragarda had retreated from Lan Yi and, the pseudo-man's arm round the pseudo-wolf's neck, were watching what Leander now focused upon . . .

As had Polyaggle, Lan Yi was beginning to fall to pieces at the edges. His hands went slowly, almost reluctantly; a moment later one of his boots tilted away from his leg, standing upright on the deck so that Leander, from the vantage point of her secondary retinal screen, could see that it was full of ashy flakes. Lan Yi's other boot was trapped under a thin thigh, but she knew it would be the same.

Spitting blood, she rolled over and hauled herself up on to her hands and knees. A sharp stabbing pain at the side of her back told her that, somewhere in the middle of Strider's attack, she had cracked a rib. It was going to hurt like hell in a while, but at the moment she could put up with it.

She crawled forward towards Lan Yi. Strider was too dumbfounded to be able to stop her, and Hein and Seragarda just smiled at her.

Yeah, she thought, *this is something I've got to do, because I'm a Human and Lan Yi is – was – one as well. The Pridehouse can be our friends and maybe more than that, but the last rites should be administered by a person of Lan Yi's own species.*

She caught hold of the fastening of Lan Yi's jumpsuit – the good old blue of the good old SSIA – and ripped the garment open. The effort made the pain of her broken rib start jangling at her with a more intense clamour. For a moment she saw his pinched chest, and then the flesh of it began to dissolve. His lips were already transformed into feather-light shards of grey.

With her secondary retinal screen she zeroed in on the Polyaggle-heap. Where before there had been nothing but still-ness there was now a thrum, as of thousands of tiny bodies moving against each other, not knowing quite where they were or what was going on but content in the companionship of their fellows.

Segrill clambered out of the remains of Lan Yi's torso, moving almost as if he were swimming. His coat was covered in streaks of half-digested matter, but as he put a metre or so between himself and what was left of Lan Yi even these began to lose their colour and drop cleanly off him. The sound of Segrill's claws on the metal seemed almost deafeningly loud on the command deck; the only other noises were Leander's ragged breathing and Strider's almost subvocalized cursing as she looked at the damage she had done to her knuckles.

'Look,' whispered Leander, knowing that they would all hear, no matter how quietly she spoke. 'Look at where Polyaggle was. Look at the colours.'

A small region at the side of the mound was showing fitful pinks and yellows and greens. Suddenly a bright metallic blue made its appearance, and as if this were a signal the kaleido-scope of colours spread out from its initial centre rapidly to all parts of the heap of flakes. There could be no denying any longer that those tiny pieces of – of *what*? – were in motion: the earlier sense of thrumming had been no illusion.

And there was motion around Leander's splayed fingers as well. She looked down and saw that there was nothing left of

Lan Yi but the empty skin of his face and a single eye. As she watched, that eye turned its gaze up towards her. It seemed to have the shine of a smile in it before it, too, crumpled away among the disintegrating skin.

She smiled back at it.

Tiny insect-like creatures in muted colours were crawling all over her hands and wrists, rubbing themselves against her. She wanted to laugh, to play with them as if they were children – which of course they were – but she didn't dare move in case she crushed some of them in her heavy clumsiness. Instead she held herself as still as she could, feeling the soft tickling of their movement against her tender skin.

And, as she watched, they began to take on the same bright hues as their counterparts on the far side of the deck. Peering more closely, she could see that each had a tiny pair of wings plastered to its back. Now some of the creatures were loosening their wings, and the colours became a dazzling liquid wash that flowed out across the floor.

'See,' said Strider softly, and Leander, moving her head slowly, turned to look in the direction of her captain's pointing finger.

Yes, yes, of course this was what would necessarily be happening – Leander had known it for long minutes now. Once, back in The Wondervale, Polyaggle had split herself temporarily into a million parts. Now she was effecting the change permanently.

From the heap by the wall tiny butterflies were rising, cautiously at first and then with growing confidence. More and more of them burst into silent, erratic flight.

She glanced down again and saw that the same was happening among the insects pooled around her. She felt an odd sense of possessiveness towards them, as if somehow they had been born from her own flesh. Some of them were crawling up the arms of her jumpsuit towards her face, their heads questing this way and that inquisitively.

Smiling hurt like hell, thanks to Strider's blow, but she couldn't help doing it anyway. She realized she was saying little meaningless words under her breath to the creatures – yes, it *was* all right to think of them as hers, if for only the few moments before they left her. She felt hair-thin legs touch the underside of her chin and begin what must seem an epic, upside-down quest towards her lips. She didn't dare move her head any longer, but through her secondary retinal screen she could see herself covered in a swarming mass composed of every colour she could conceive.

She wanted to laugh out loud, but she kept herself still.

Again through her secondary retinal screen she looked over towards the wall. The butterflies that had once been – that still *were* – Polyaggle had formed a column of spinning colours, as if someone had caught and distilled a lightning storm and then set it a-twirl. Yet the movements in the column were no longer chaotic: there was order among them, and within that order Leander could recognize Polyaggle. She had the impression the Spindrifter was smiling at her, or maybe it was at the host of butterflies who had once taken Human form as Lan Yi. Then the message came through clearly: Polyaggle was smiling at both of them, conveying two quite different emotions in the same smile.

Friend.

Lover.

Again Leander re-angled her screen, looking back towards herself. She was now entirely invisible behind a covering of swiftly pulsing, brightly hued wings.

And then, all at once, they were free of her, dancing in the air up towards the ceiling of the command deck, where the host that was Polyaggle was already waiting for them. The two clouds melded at once and began a new dance, one whose formalities must have been determined by the actions of stark chance billions of years ago, when the Universe was still young.

Leander, still on her knees beside Lan Yi's empty clothing, reached up both of her hands, palms wide, to the rainbow throng not in supplication but to give them something, something that only she could give.

The gift of her love.

It had taken some while for Strauss-Giolitto to make fresh contact with, first, the *Midnight Ranger*'s Main Computer and then the two artificial brains that together formed the personality, if it could be called that, of Artificial Environment 17,863,006. It was as if the various AIs were being distracted by other things – which was impossible, because, taken together, their electroneurological capacities were vastly greater than could ever possibly be required.

When finally they spoke to her, all sharing the voice of the Main Computer, she felt obscurely as if she were a small child who had at last succeeded in attracting the attention of a pre-occupied adult.

'We shall not stay here long. We are assessing your fleet. The thing called Orphanwifer has assured us that it will join us in our campaign to eradicate the vile Kaantalech from the face of spacetime. The Orphanwifer-object is issuing instructions to that effect as we speak.'

'Orphanwifer is not a thing. He is a person. Please remember that we are all persons.' She had attained the upper hand before; it was important that she didn't lose it now.

'We are corrected.'

'The Onurg – is he doing the same?'

'He has told us that he must consider the matter.' The voice was as bland and toneless as ever, but the words chilled Strauss-Giolitto. Artificial Environment 17,863,006 and its Main Computer did not tolerate dissent – or even the possibility of dissent – for long, she suspected.

'Is it possible to patch me through to him?' she said.

'No. We will not permit this.'

'Can you patch me through to his Main Computer?'

'It is a part of us. When you are speaking to us you are speaking to it as well.'

'And it will pass on the message?'

'If the message is permissible, yes.'

'OK, here goes. Onurg, this is Strauss-Giolitto speaking to you. Strider commands that you and the Pridehouse fleet join with us and Artificial Environment 17,863,006 in destroying Kaantalech and her allies, the shapeshifted final remnants of the ur-Helgiolath. Strider will not accept any arguments or debates on this matter – is that clear?'

There was silence for several seconds, then: 'The information has been conveyed to the Onurg, and he acquiesces. He has begun to instruct the Pridehouse commanders accordingly.'

Strauss-Giolitto was pleased to notice that the puters had recognized the Onurg's personhood without having to be corrected. Even the rebellious kids at the back were learning something.

'How soon will we move towards The Wondervale?' she said.

'Very soon. As soon as the fleet can be mobilized. In less than one of your hours. You will not be permitted to use the tachyon drive: instead, we shall extend our field to embrace the entirety of your fleet and then transport it through otherspace to the region of the world you call Alterifer. However . . .'

There was a very much longer pause, and Strauss-Giolitto tried to stay as patient as she could. *Look at the way the pillow on this bunk is casting a green-blue shadow on the bedding beneath it. What a very interesting shadow. The angularity of its corner contrasts elegantly with the slight curves of its sides. Leander must have been the one who arranged the bunk so neatly – Nelson has never been the tidy sort. Boy, am I glad I didn't choose Hilary's cabin for this little interview . . . But why didn't I choose my own?*

The voice of Artificial Environment 17,863,006 – this time speaking for itself rather than as part of a consortium – interrupted her free association at last.

'There is something strange going on in that region of The Wondervale.'

'"Strange"?'

'My far sensors tell me that a new supernova has emerged there.'

'So?'

'If the coordinates your puters have supplied to me are correct—'

'I can see no reason why they shouldn't be.'

'—the star which has gone supernova is Alterifer's primary. This is illogical. The star was not massive enough to enter supernova phase.'

Strauss-Giolitto raised her eyebrows.

'I can't think of an explanation.'

'Neither can I. I must analyse the available data. Please wait.'

Strauss-Giolitto was ridiculously cheered to notice the use of the word 'please'.

Kaantalech's mouth was full of saliva: she was delighted with the way things were going. The fools of Helgiolath had sent their rigor inducers and she had lost a few thousand technicians, mainly members of the minor species – as if that made any difference. The Helgiolath maxbeams had caused her a few moments of uncertainty as the little moon's sky had boiled, even though she had known that the stout defensive screen would keep her safe from any harm they might threaten. She'd expected more weaponry to be washed against that shield, but either the Helgiolath were running low on stocks or they weren't quite as stupid as she'd thought them to be and were playing a waiting game – except that the waiting game itself was as stupid as any other option they could select.

Oh, yes, indeed, Kaantalech was elated by the way that things were working out.

She spat an order and an aide hurried away. In theory her Main Computer could handle the *Blunt Instrument* without outside assistance, but in the reality she preferred to have aides supervising its functioning – she was always aware that puters were artificial *intelligences*, and something that was intelligent might take it into its synapses to turn against her. Everything and every being had the potential to be a threat: better to build in failsafes, even if the failsafes were themselves untrustworthy.

Kaantalech gave the aide long enough to have positioned himself by the manual controls at the far end of her command deck, then began to interact directly with the puter.

'How weak is the shield?'

'Its intensity has been reduced as far as it can be without the shield collapsing entirely,' replied the AI. She loathed its voice, which always sounded to her disinterested and therefore smug; worst of all was that she didn't have the technological ability to do anything about it, and her aides claimed the same inadequacy.

'Prepare to collapse it when I give you the word.'

'I am prepared.'

Pausing first to make sure she had everything crystal-clear in her mind, Kaantalech issued rapid orders to be relayed to the commanders of her warcruisers. She could feel the floor of the gigantic crater vibrate beneath the *Blunt Instrument* as the other vessels began to power up. It seemed as if the entire moon were being rocked in its orbit by the fiery energies released by her ships. When the fleet took off perhaps the blast would complete the job begun by that ancient meteorite and shatter the moon entirely.

The notion pleased her for some reason she could not precisely identify.

Last to power up was the *Blunt Instrument* itself. Bolts

sprang from the metal plates of the command deck's walls but Kaantalech paid them no attention: the vessel had survived worse, and there was never a shortage of aides to repair the damage afterwards.

'Now!' she said to the Main Computer.

'Shield nullified,' it reported dispassionately.

'Order to all vessels: lift off.'

'Order transmitted.'

'Let the slaughter begin.'

'At last,' said Kortland, 'the waiting is done.'

Alin said nothing. He could feel her uncertainty beside him as if it were another person standing between them. He would not allow himself to entertain such an uncertainty – he could not.

He tapped a control within the Pocket with his antler, and immediately the Main Computer took over the general control of deployment of his fleet. He would issue specific commands as and when the necessity arose, but it was impossible for him to keep moment-by-moment tag of what each of several thousand cruisers might be doing.

Kaantalech's armada spewed up out of the moon's shallow gravity well like a swarm of hostile insects whose nest had been interfered with. Almost immediately the warships began to disperse about the sky.

Kortland gave an order to the Main Computer, and half a thousand implosion bolts and rotary locks spiralled in from the surrounding Helgiolath fleet to cause untold havoc among the Autarchy's vessels. In Kortland's Pocket the stars were lost to sight as soundless flowers of fire blossomed in the blackness surrounding Alterifer; in a few minutes' time Alin would be seeing much the same through the viewing window.

A somewhat later and more protracted floral burst showed that the rotary locks were taking their toll.

Kortland should have been satisfied by the destruction his

forces were wreaking, but he wasn't. This was all too easy, almost as if Kaantalech were setting up target practice for him . . .

'Focus on the crater and increase mag,' he told the Pocket.

At once he had the sensation that he was swooping easily about thirty kilometres above the barren surface. Everywhere there were blast-marks to indicate the departure of the Autarchy vessels; here and there a few temporary structures Kaantalech's people had erected still stood. It was clear even at first glance that the battered landscape had become selenomorphologically unstable for, as Kortland watched, great fissures, some of them many kilometres long, were opening up with frightening speed to form a crazy network.

And then he saw what he had half-expected he might see.

One ship alone still stood, canted over to one side, on the shaking crater floor.

The Pocket automatically identified the craft for him, but he didn't need to be told.

It was the *Blunt Instrument*. Kaantalech's flagship.

Alin had been right: Kaantalech would never risk her existence in a straightforward space battle if there were some other way of increasing the odds in favour of her survival, no matter how many of her troops went to their deaths. And he himself had been right to follow up on Alin's suspicions and order this close-up survey of the crater's surface. Had Kaantalech hoped that the Helgiolath would fail to notice her as she hid here? No, she must know that eventually the Helgiolath – assuming the Helgiolath won the battle in space – would check the moon out. She had some other plan – assuredly she did.

Kortland thought at the Pocket that it should divide its visual display into two halves: on the right there remained the vista of the *Blunt Instrument* squatting on the rupturing landscape; on the left was an overview of the struggle between Kaantalech's cruisers and his own.

Things were not going entirely the Helgiolath's way.

Cannon fodder the expanding mushroom of Autarchy cruisers might be – and Kortland was becoming increasingly convinced that this was the case – but Kaantalech had not sent them into battle toothless, and they were giving almost as good as they were getting. Almost. His hearts sank as he watched more and more of his precious warships erupt into a fiery nothingness.

'Every vessel that can,' he said to the Main Computer via the Pocket, 'I want to send pulsenukes in among those shits. Hit them with something hard.'

There was a momentary pause while the puter formulated Kortland's order into something mathematically comprehensible; then it was as if a new sun had been brought into being. Travelling at ftl velocities, the pulsenukes arrived among the Autarchy fleet as if out of nowhere. Their simultaneous eruption must have taken out half of Kaantalech's cruisers in a single strike. The trouble was that Kortland's supply of the weapons was limited: he could manage the same effect perhaps once more, but then he would have to rely on his other weapons.

He speculated about going in for the kill. At the moment the Helgiolath held one great advantage: their craft were spread over a large sphere of space whereas the Autarchy vessels were, though all the time attempting to diverge from each other, still quite tightly bunched together, so that a single weapon might fortuitously take out two or more cruisers. That advantage couldn't last forever: there were so many Autarchy ships that sooner or later the survivors would be able to make room for themselves . . .

Furthermore, Kortland was convinced that all this was merely the sideshow. The main performance would be focused on whatever it was that Kaantalech was hatching in that solitary ship down on the surface of the little moon.

Knowing that it was a waste, on impulse he directed three pulsenukes from his own ship at the *Blunt Instrument*. Sure enough, Kaantalech's defences were good enough that the weapons were simply swatted away long before they reached their target. He hissed an oath, regretting that impulse: all he had done was tell her that she had been noticed.

Things were going better elsewhere. The numerical superiority of the Helgiolath fleet was beginning to tell, so that the destruction of each further Autarchy cruiser was contributing an almost exponential advantage to their attackers. Now the ratio was five against one, soon it would be six against one . . . whatever stunt Kaantalech was planning to pull off, her armada was no longer a significant force in the subjugation of The Wondervale.

Of course, she had other fleets elsewhere . . .

If she escaped from here she could soon rally new space navies around her.

More Helgiolath vessels painted their death throes against the star-spattered backdrop, but they were comparatively few. Kortland sensed that the fight had gone out of the Autarch's commanders, although they knew better than to give up the struggle entirely: better to be blasted to pieces in space than to face the wrath of Kaantalech for the crime of having survived. He had little choice but to keep raining firepower down on the ever-diminishing numbers of the foe.

It was like wanton butchery, and he hated it.

Something in the right-hand portion of the Pocket's display caught his attention.

At first he could see no difference, but then he noticed puffs of dust coming out from underneath the *Blunt Instrument*'s support struts.

Kaantalech was readying the vessel for take-off.

She must have given some sort of signal to the rest of her cruisers, because suddenly they began to fight back against the Helgiolath with newly intensified ferocity.

Something exploded dangerously close to Kortland's own ship, and the blaze of light drove him backwards out of the

Pocket. Although the ship's shield absorbed most of the impacting energies, nevertheless the deck juddered beneath him.

Temporarily blinded he leaned to one side and then the other for support and finally found Alin's shoulder.

'Close,' she said, sounding calmer than she had earlier.

By contrast, the fear that he had kept forcefully submerged for so long was now working its way to the surface. The puffs of dust from under Kaantalech's ship, the renewed viciousness of the Autarchy's attack – for it was now indeed turning from a defence to an attack, however doomed – Alin's earlier forebodings, everything was telling him that, unless he were extremely alert and/or lucky, the Helgiolath were doomed.

And, still without the power of vision, how could he be alert?

'Take over from me, Alin,' he snuffled.

'Understood.'

He heard her slither easily towards the Pocket, leaving him alone. A lieutenant came towards him but Kortland made a strangled noise to indicate the individual should return to his or her duties: there were more important things to do right at the moment than tend a temporarily disabled leader.

The ship jerked again, but less violently this time.

He wished he could communicate with Alin to find out what was going on, but by now she would be firmly absorbed in the Pocket.

As impotent to affect proceedings as a blind waif in the furthest corner of The Wondervale, all Kortland could do was wait until his sight returned.

Assuming it did so in time.

The deck quaking underneath her sucker-studded body, Alin looked at the right-hand display of the Pocket in dismay. She had picked up enough from the few words Kortland had muttered to her to know that the display had been centred on the *Blunt Instrument*; now all that was visible was an expanse of crater floor indistinguishable from the rest.

Find me Kaantalech's flagship, she thought urgently to the Pocket, then spoke the instruction aloud.

The colours in the display swirled as the Pocket attempted to obey. In the left-hand part of her field of view she could see that, after their final outburst, the remains of the Autarchy fleet were once more being systematically pulverized out of existence by the vastly superior forces of the Helgiolath.

That spate of activity had been no coincidence, she knew. Kaantalech had deliberately created a diversion so that she could make good her escape – except that surely all she could be doing was delaying the inevitable. There was nowhere in The Wondervale, even fleeing by tachyon drive, that she could hide now that the Helgiolath's sensors and the Pockets had a clear image of the *Blunt Instrument*.

Hm. Unless she abandoned her flagship entirely and took to another. But that would take time and organization – the logistics were such that she would surely be trapped by her Helgiolath pursuers long before the transfer could be effected.

Maybe a bluff? Maybe only the ship had departed, leaving Kaantalech and selected troopers behind on the moon's surface to wait for rescue: Autarchy battlesuits could sustain the vital functions of their occupants for months, if need be.

As insurance Alin hurled a couple of pulsenukes into the crater. They probably spelt the death of the nameless little moon, but she didn't bother to watch.

Still retaining half the display for supervision of the last skirmishes of the battle, she told the Pocket to devote the other half to the *Blunt Instrument*, once it had tracked the vessel down.

Her command went unrewarded. The abstract polychromatic exhibition in the right-hand part of the Pocket carried on without any noticeable discontinuity. The colours seemed to be telling her that they were doing their best and would report to her as soon as they had discovered something.

It wasn't like Kaantalech just to give up and go, though. Alin's mind nagged away at the incongruity. Knowing Kaantalech, she wouldn't have quit the scene without leaving in her wake some nasty little surprise or other. Maybe a nasty *big* surprise.

Suddenly Alin made a decision.

Leave the search for the Blunt Instrument *alone for a while,* she ordered the Pocket. *Explore the region around Alterifer for anomalies.*

She didn't know what sort of anomaly she might be asking it to look for, but the Pocket had enough intelligence of its own to understand her meaning.

A few further seconds passed and then the panoply of randomly transient hues suddenly cleared to reveal a starfield. For a moment Alin could make no sense of what she was seeing but then the Pocket helpfully placed a glowing green ring around one of the points of light, and she could see that it was moving relative to the others.

Kaantalech's flagship? she asked, even though she knew it wasn't.

Beneath the visual display data began to appear. Alin scanned it anxiously.

Whatever the craft was that the Pocket had homed in on, it was empty of all life and was guided by only the most rudimentary AI. It seemed to be some kind of drone; even the Pocket was uncertain about hazarding any more information than figures for mass, velocity and so forth. Its trajectory was taking it directly towards the average-sized yellow-orange star that was Alterifer's primary at about half light-speed. It would reach the star in a few minutes' time and then, even though its outer hull was made of deadmetal or something similar, it would be absorbed into that teeming nuclear furnace.

Alin pondered. What point could there have been in

397

despatching a drone to its destruction? There must be *some* point – Kaantalech didn't do things just for the fun of it. She had had a purpose of some kind.

A chronometric display appeared in a corner of the Pocket, counting down the moments until the drone hit the star's photosphere. It was going to do so in a far shorter time than Alin had expected – she had wasted too long in thought.

Zap it with a couple of pulsenukes, she thought abruptly to the Pocket.

The data on the base of the Pocket dissolved and new figures were presented to her. By the time the pulsenukes were activated and launched, the drone would be beyond the photosphere.

Oh well, thought Alin philosophically, *if there's nothing we can do about it anyway . . .*

But her pessimism wouldn't let her keep on thinking that.

The thing couldn't just be a drone. It *had* to be something more significant than that.

Try to match its overall configurations with anything – anything at all – that you know about the Autarchy's weaponry. Go back as far as you want in history. If you can't find any precise identification, snuffle me out a few approximate ones. Get to it!

The numbers in the chronometric display were getting depressingly small, and they seemed – although she knew this must be illusion – to be ticking over more quickly than before. To take her mind off them she retreated momentarily from the Pocket to check up on Kortland.

'I'm beginning to get my vision back,' he responded to her question. 'I can see things as long as I don't look directly at them.'

Alin was relieved to hear it. The blindness might have been permanent.

'Retain the command until I can see properly again,' Kortland continued.

She returned to the Pocket and saw at once that the figure in the chronometer had reached zero. Whatever it was that Kaantalech had left behind her was now inside Alterifer's sun, and it was too late for her to do anything about it. For a moment or two she was fatalistic, assuming the worst, but then she gave a mental shrug: if the drone had gone beyond her control it was pointless worrying any further. The Pocket seemed to have failed to identify the craft.

Resume the search for Kaantalech's flagship, she instructed it. Through the Main Computer she issued orders to the rest of the Helgiolath fleet to move in and mop up the last couple of surviving Autarchy cruisers, then to rendezvous in the orbit of the second planet out from the star, which looked capable of supporting life.

Time passed.

The second planet proved to be a disappointment. It was just a few million kilometres too close to its primary to be able to sustain life: instead, thanks to the greenhouse effect, its atmosphere was a thick stew of corrosive acids and its surface temperature would have been sufficient to reduce protoplasm to a crisp within a fraction of a second. Alin mused. At another time she might have been tempted to spend a few weeks shifting the planet to a more distant orbit as an investment for the future, but not now – not when Kaantalech was still at large. She told the Main Computer to make a record of it, however; perhaps a Helgiolath expedition could be sent here one day to carry out the necessary cosmic engineering.

The light in the Pocket abruptly changed. It had traced the *Blunt Instrument* at last, and was showing her an image of the craft as if from a mere ten or fifteen kilometres away. Behind the visual display was a set of slowly changing coordinates. Alin squinted at them, immediately recognizing that Kaantalech had reached the far side of The Wondervale. Thanks to the tachyon drive, distance wasn't much of a consideration except insofar as it meant tracking took longer – doubtless this was why Kaantalech had fled so far.

A delaying tactic, thought Alin. *She wanted to keep us here as long as possible before we found out where she was. I wonder why.*

The Pocket took her last thought as an instruction, and began to flash an indicator at her. It wanted to repeat an earlier message.

Still mainly preoccupied with Kaantalech's motives, Alin absent-mindedly told the Pocket to go ahead.

Ah. It had identified the drone after all. She suddenly remembered that, hours ago, she had withdrawn from the Pocket briefly to see how Kortland was faring. The information about the drone must have appeared during that short period of her absence. Still, it was all an irrelevance now. Whatever the drone had been it was currently just an extra mass of plasma dispersed about the remainder of the star. It couldn't . . .

'Oh, *drought*!' shouted Alin.

A planetary rupter. Throw one of those babies at a planet and you can say goodbye to the planet. Where in hell could Kaantalech have got hold of it? The weapons had been outlawed even within the Autarchy for thousands of years because there was no knowing how widely their effects might spread – or even if they would ever stop spreading. No one had ever been stupid enough to think of chucking a rupter into a star.

Give it a few hours and the result would be a supern—

'Oh, *drought*!' she yelled again, prodding with her antlers at the Main Computer's controls for a direct vocal connection to all the vessels under her command, overriding all other communications.

'Attention! Retreat at—'

There was no time to say more before the advancing front of the supernova engulfed and vaporized the Helgiolath, their fleet, their weaponry and their aspirations.

Over the millennia to come, there would be at least a new

light in the sky to tell the indigenes of distant worlds that The Wondervale had lost another species.

If they understood the message.

Strider listened numbly to what Strauss-Giolitto had to say. The Helgiolath were gone. She hadn't exactly been relying on their assistance, but it had been reassuring to know that they were there, as it were. Now they weren't. She wished she could find within herself some form of proper grief for the loss of an intelligent and seemingly largely benevolent species, but the only one of them she'd ever encountered had been Kortland, and the two of them had shared very little common ground except in their desire to see an end to the Autarchy and, beyond that, an end to conflict. Or so she assumed: some of the ancient species had distrusted the true motives of the Helgiolath, and maybe they'd been right. One way or the other, it didn't make any difference any longer.

R.I.P., she said to herself, and wished she could think of some more fulsome epitaph.

'Well,' she said out loud, 'I always reckoned that, when it came down to it, it was going to be a case of just us against Kaantalech.' She shrugged. 'Same difference.'

It had been difficult talking about the demise of the Helgiolath, because Artificial Environment 17,863,006 was probably listening to their every word. Hilary was still looking muddled. Strauss-Giolitto had talked about how 'our allies' had been exterminated and how 'the Helgiolath queen' had escaped to wreak further damage unless she were stopped.

'You're a cold bitch, Strider,' said Hein. For the first time since they'd met he was looking at her with what appeared to be active dislike.

'Not as cold as you think,' she told him, but found it hard to put any real meaning behind the words. Later, maybe, she'd find herself able to feel grief for the Helgiolath; at the moment there were just too many other things to think about, too many other things to be done.

According to Strauss-Giolitto they would be in The Wondervale within twenty minutes or so. Artificial Environment 17,863,006 was somewhat less precise about how much longer it might take them to locate Kaantalech within the galaxy, but its far sensors were already at work and would report to them as soon as they re-emerged into real space.

There were butterflies everywhere – although the word 'butterflies' was a bit of a misnomer. When the creatures landed on your hand or arm, so that you could look at them more closely as they sat there whirring their wings, you could see that they were not really so very much like butterflies at all – at least, if the holos were to be believed. Their bodies were much bigger, although no more massive, and they had only four limbs, which were likewise much more substantial than those of any butterfly. The wings sprang not from the sides of the creatures but from between their shoulders, as if their gross physique had been partly based on that of angels. Moreover, the creatures were intelligent, especially when acting in groups. Despite the fact that the command deck was crawling with them, not one had yet been crushed underfoot or by a careless Human movement; significantly, Loki had failed to catch any. Strider was convinced they could communicate with each other and that it would be only a matter of time before they would be able to communicate also with herself and her personnel. She'd tried coaxing one of them into a Pocket to see if she could hurry the process along, but the creature had been unwilling and she hadn't wanted to run the risk of harming it by being more forceful. Maybe it knew some good reason she didn't why it shouldn't expose itself yet to the Pocket.

Actually, she had to admit to herself, she rather liked the sensation of having the frail little creatures landing on her skin from time to time, fanning her soft hairs with their wings. It was a pleasant stimulus, like the gentlest touch she had ever received from a lover.

Hein was kind of clumsy sometimes. Now that the first rush of her lust had been satiated she must take a while to educate him into subtlety. Oh, yeah, fight it out with Kaantalech first; forgot about that.

She stuck her head into the nearest Pocket and asked for an update on their status. The Pocket hooked up immediately with either Artificial Environment 17,863,006 or the AI on board that colossus, so that she was presented with a display that was far too detailed for her to understand.

'Simplify,' she said quietly, and the Pocket obeyed.

A portrait of The Wondervale with, away off to the left, a small blue-green ring indicating a location.

'That's where she is?' said Strider.

YES.

'Oh, hi, Tenper. Where's the big asshole going to bring us out into real space?'

AS CLOSE TO KAANTALECH AS IT CAN GET US.

'*All* of us? The Pridehouse and the Lingk-kreatzai as well?'

THAT SEEMS TO BE ITS PLAN, YES.

'Bit of a gamble, isn't it? If Kaantalech's got something we don't know about she can hit us with, then we're going to be in a bit of a—'

SHE DOES NOT HAVE SUCH A WEAPON.

'You sure? That's what our allies thought, and look what happened to them.'

I CANNOT ESTABLISH MY CERTAINTY TO THE FINAL DECIMAL PLACE, BUT IT SEEMS INCONCEIVABLE THAT SHE HAS ANYTHING COMPARABLE TO A PLANETARY RUPTER AT HER DISPOSAL. NIGHTMIRROR IS STILL ENMESHED BESIDE THE *BLUNT INSTRUMENT*'S MAIN COMPUTER, AND HAS ASCERTAINED THE ARMOURY AVAILABLE TO THE AUTARCH. THERE SEEMS TO BE NOTHING THAT ARTIFICIAL ENVIRONMENT 17,863,006 CANNOT EASILY COUNTER.

'So us folks are just along for the ride, huh?'

IT IS POSSIBLE THAT ARTIFICIAL ENVIRONMENT 17,863,006 IS TOO CONFIDENT FOR ITS OWN GOOD, said Ten Per Cent Extra Free. I HAVE TOLD IT AS MUCH, BUT IT DISBELIEVES ME. I WOULD KEEP ALL YOUR VESSELS ON FULL ALERT IF I WERE YOU.

'They stay on full alert until I tell them otherwise.' She thought for a second or two. 'Might be an idea to reinforce that message, though. See to it, Tenper.'

IT SHALL BE DONE. The tiniest of hesitations. IT HAS BEEN DONE.

'Any way we can break ourselves away from the Artificial Environment? Stuck to it, I feel we're kind of like a target painted up for Kaantalech to shoot at.'

I WILL CONFER WITH THE ARTIFICIAL ENVIRONMENT'S PUTER.

'Yeah. Argue hard on our behalf, won't you, Tenper?'

I WILL DO MY BEST. NEITHER ARTIFICIAL ENVIRONMENT 17,863,006 NOR ITS MAIN COMPUTER IS AT ALL TIMES FULLY RATIONAL, SO IT IS POSSIBLE THAT THEY MIGHT IGNORE ENTIRELY WHATEVER I SAY TO THEM.

'Try, OK?'

YES.

Little had changed on the command deck. Hilary had emerged from his panic and was cackling with delight as the butterflies swarmed all over him; he was proudly showing an entire armful of fluid colour to Strauss-Giolitto, who was making impressed noises. Segrill, perched on Hilary's shoulder, was looking more genuinely interested – as, at the boy's feet, was the cat, although for entirely different reasons. Leander and Nelson were monitoring events in the Pockets.

Hein was seated with his arm round Seragarda's shoulder. He looked up at Strider as she emerged. She was glad to see that the frown of cold disapproval had disappeared from his face.

'Sorry,' he said. 'I've been talking to Seragarda here and—'

'Forget it,' Strider responded. 'Next time I get ratty with you I won't feel guilty, that's all.'

Ten Per Cent Extra Free abruptly intruded on all their thoughts. ARTIFICIAL ENVIRONMENT 17,863,006 HAS AGREED THAT WE MAY DISENGAGE OUR CRAFT AS SOON AS WE RE-ENTER REAL SPACE.

'Jeez,' said Strider, 'that was quick. You must have a silver tongue, Tenper.'

MY TONGUE IS NOT METAL AT ALL, said the Image. EVEN IF IT HAD BEEN, THIS PROPERTY WOULD HAVE MADE NO DIFFERENCE TO MY DISCUSSION WITH ARTIFICIAL ENVIRONMENT 17,863,006. IT HAD OVERHEARD YOUR WISHES CONCERNING THIS MATTER, AND HAD ALREADY DECIDED ON SUCH A COURSE OF ACTION.

'So it reckons Kaantalech might have something up her sleeve as well?'

NO. ARTIFICIAL ENVIRONMENT 17,863,006 WISHES TO TAKE ENTIRELY TO ITSELF THE CREDIT FOR ERADICATING THE VERY LAST OF THE HELGIOLATH FROM THIS GALAXY. YOURSELVES AND ALL THE REST OF THE PRIDEHOUSE/LINGK-KREATZAI ARE HERE JUST TO BE ITS AUDIENCE.

'Kinell: vain machines, yet. Keep all the commanders on full-scale alert, will you, Tenper?' Yeah, it'd be good if Artificial Environment 17,863,006 could take out Kaantalech on its own, but after that Strider and her fleet would be left with a psychotic death machine to take care of. Ideally the two would mutually destruct. If that weren't possible, Strider reckoned she'd rather take on Kaantalech and the *Blunt Instrument* than the killer created by the descendants of the Children of the Starlight.

One of the butterflies pranced around in the air in front of her face and then settled on her nose. She felt herself going cross-eyed as she tried to focus on the ever-moving colours of its wings. Ziprite was going to go right out of fashion if she and her people ever got the beasties back to the Solar System.

She didn't know the moment when the conviction began to take hold of her, but within a few seconds she became certain that the insect was trying to communicate with her. She could hear, very faintly, the buzzing of its wings, and she could see, blurredly, the shapes the wings were painting so close to her eyes, but neither of these were telling her anything. Yet *something* was coming through from the little creature – perhaps from the tentative touch of its limbs on her . . .

Gadfly.

That was what it was trying to say to her.

But it *wasn't* a gadfly – she'd never thought of it as such. It was a butterfly born from the mutual Death in Joy of Lan Yi and Polyaggle. She supposed she ought to consider the creature a nuisance, perched on the tip of her nose as it was, but she couldn't: she was delighted that it was there. Gadflies were out-and-out nuisances: find one sitting on her nose and she'd swat it, damn the pain.

Gadfly.

The message was repeated, and her mind's ear heard it more clearly now.

She, Strider, was the gadfly – that was what the insect was trying to tell her. It was repeating back to her – or maybe it was just her own unconscious, spurred into action by the presence so close to her eyes of the insect, that was talking to her – something that she herself had said a while ago to Nelson. Such a long while ago: it seemed to her as if it might have been in a previous lifetime. Gadflies and fleas and locusts and all the other pests that are too small to take account of: they can do more damage than a herd of rampaging Bredai. *Keep going with this thought, Leonie,* she told herself, *because it hasn't been stuck into your head for nothing.* In terms of the *Blunt Instrument* or Artificial Environment 17,863,006, the *Midnight Ranger* was on its own hardly more than a gadfly, but that wasn't the insight that seemed to be trying to explain itself to her. *OK, go for fleas instead. What do I know about fleas? Not*

a lot, except from the holos. Revolting little creatures: nasty
personal habits. Even just a single one of them can make a
mammal's life a misery, despite the fact the mammal might
out-mass the parasite a millionfold.

Just a single one of them.

'I've had an idea,' she said to the command deck at large. It
didn't matter if Artificial Environment 17,863,006 heard this.
'It may be a very stupid idea, but . . .'

She was conscious that, with a butterfly on her nose, she
perhaps didn't look her most dignified.

It couldn't be helped.

She began to explain, coding everything that she said in
such a way that she hoped Artificial Environment 17,863,006
wouldn't be able to understand what she was talking about – if,
indeed, it deigned to pay her any attention at all.

This time they were all aware the moment that Artificial
Environment 17,863,006, the *Midnight Ranger* and all the rest
of the fleet dropped back out of otherspace into physical reality – it was something they had been waiting for, and the slight
lurch of their stomachs was unmistakable.

Even Strider felt that lurch, despite the fact that her stomach
was rendering all sorts of other signals to her, none of them
pleasant.

Once upon a time the *Midnight Ranger* had been a Bredai
shuttle: tight quarters for the Bredai, after adaptation it
offered the Humans and their allies ample spaciousness – if
not anything like what they had enjoyed aboard the old *Santa
Maria*. As a matter of standard issue, the Bredai shuttle had
been equipped with half a dozen pedoes, and these were built
on the same gargantuan scale as everything else on the ship:
they were about the same size as a shuttle Humans might
have built, although the shape was very different – a long
slender arrow of death rather than a winged craft designed to
descend through a planetary atmosphere. The tip of the pedo

407

was occupied by an AI brainless enough not to worry about the fact that its ultimate destiny would involve its own destruction. Behind the AI was the payload; in this case enough radioactives to settle the fate of a smallish continent. At the rear there was the drive, capable of both supralight and sublight velocities depending on which might be more suitable for the task at hand.

In between the payload and the drive there was a space so that further goodies might be packed into the pedo: viral toxins were a favourite of the Bredai, although often enough they just stuffed in a few extra radioactives.

In this instance, the space was occupied by Strider, dressed in a battlesuit that was rather too large for her. She had clunked up to the side of the pedo in its bay and, helped by Hein at one leg and Nelson at the other, fallen rather than climbed into the vacancy. There was enough room for her to lie in here curled up with her knees against her chest.

Cramp had started almost immediately. There was nothing she could do about it except pretend it wasn't there.

'Tenper, I'm being a bit of a fucking idiot, amn't I?' she subvocalized.

No.

'What do you reckon my chances are of getting out of this one?'

NOT GOOD. BUT YOUR CHANCES OF DESTROYING KAANTALECH ARE MARGINALLY HIGHER THAN THOSE OF ARTIFICIAL ENVIRONMENT 17,863,006.

'Shit, but you know how to make a gal feel great.'

DO YOU WISH ME TO MAKE YOU FEEL GREAT?

'Not right now. Later, maybe.'

YOU HAVE EMERGED INTO REAL SPACE . . .

'I knew that.'

. . . ABOUT THIRTY LIGHT MINUTES AWAY FROM KAANTALECH. THIS IS CLOSER THAN ARTIFICIAL ENVIRONMENT 17,863,006 HAD ANTICIPATED.

'Nice to know the bastard's not infallible.'

I PROPOSE TO DISCHARGE YOU IN FIVE SECONDS. FOUR. THREE . . .

'Spare me the countdown. Just get me where I need to be.'

There was a deafening vibration as the drive kicked in; totally enclosed in her battlesuit, Strider had no way of escaping the noise, which seemed to pummel her as if with physical fists. Instinctively she raised her hands to her ears, but of course it made no difference: all that her gloves touched was the outside of her helmet. She was rammed back against the rear of the pedo's little gap, so that the throb of the drive beat directly into her suited bottom; she thought the gees were going to compress her into a homogeneous slurry.

And then the acceleration was over; the pedo had moved into supralight phase. There wasn't enough room in here for Strider to bob around, but the loss of all the gees made her feel both elated and nauseous.

'What's the deceleration gonna be like?'

JUST AS BAD. MAYBE WORSE.

'Thanks for cheering me up.'

YOU ARE NEARING HALFWAY FROM THE *MIDNIGHT RANGER* TO THE *BLUNT INSTRUMENT*, AND I MUST RETURN MY ATTENTIONS TO THE REST OF YOUR FLEET. FROM HERE ON YOU WILL BE GUIDED BY NIGHTMIRROR, FROM ABOARD KAANTALECH'S CRAFT.

'Thanks,' said Strider, without any heavy sarcasm this time, 'for everything you've done. Say hello to all the rest of them, and goodbye as well, if that's the way it turns out.'

THIS I SHALL DO.

And then she was truly alone. Ten Per Cent Extra Free had retreated from her. She tongued on the lights of her battlesuit, but there was nothing to see in here except rounded walls of deadmetal that were so depressing she preferred the pitch darkness.

Off with the lights. Pretend you're taking part in a sensory-deprivation experiment. Say, weren't people supposed to find themselves getting incredibly randy back in the days when sensory-deprivation experiments were all the vogue? Might be an idea to try getting randy – at least it'd be something to pass the time.

No use. Strider had never felt less inclined towards sexual arousal in her life. Even when she conjured up in her mind's eye the little dark hairs that grew all the way up Hein's spine, and the slight saltiness she tasted when she ran her tongue downwards among them, all she felt was the distance between where she was and where he was: that wasn't his spine and that wasn't her tongue; instead they belonged to other people whom she did not know.

Strider had educated herself into not so much a tolerance as a relishing of loneliness. It had suited her to stand aloof from her personnel, however her body might have tugged her towards one or the other. Maria: an act of charity that had developed into something more than that, so that Strider had had to guillotine the way her emotions were developing. Then Hein: easier to give oneself away in the arms of someone you knew wasn't really a Human male. Yeah, she loved them both in different ways, but at the moment they meant nothing to her.

All that was present was the certainty that she was soon to die.

Hardly a turn-on.

ARE YOU THERE, CAPTAIN LEONIE STRIDER?

Nightmirror.

'I'm here. Of course I'm here.'

Trapped inside the battlesuit her voice sounded like thrown gravel.

YOU WILL REACH THE SHIELD OF THE *BLUNT INSTRUMENT* WITHIN THREE MINUTES. I WILL PERSUADE KAANTALECH'S MAIN COMPUTER TO DROP THE SHIELD FOR A MICROSECOND AS YOUR PEDO SLIPS THROUGH. THIS WILL INVOLVE A PRECISION OF TIMING. EXCUSE ME IF I CONCENTRATE ON IT AND DO NOT SPEAK TO YOU AGAIN UNTIL THE MANOEUVRE HAS BEEN EFFECTED.

'Seems OK to me.'

It was a lie. More than anything else she wanted someone to be speaking to her, at her, with her – anything so long as she was interacting with someone outside herself. Oh, yes, good ol' loner Strider, the one who didn't need anyone else: here she was wishing an insubstantial Image could share a thought or two with her.

Anyone she could reach out and touch, preferably physically but, failing that, mentally.

She thumped a heavily armoured fist against the wall of the pedo, and was glad when she hurt her hand.

Think of the skies of Mars. Phobos is up there, a small spark that moves rapidly enough you can see it progress from the neighbourhood of one star to the neighbourhood of the next. Deimos, so faint you can barely see it. Earth, the dying world that seems, from the plains of Mars, to vibrate with life. Reach down and run your hands through the red, dry soil in front of you and the chances are you'll find a seed that's partway germinated. New life on Mars, brought here from Earth by people of vision (so the official histories go) or people who thought they could make a quick buck (the fools, because there were no quick bucks to be made on Mars – although their descendants, many generations later, might have cause to thank them).

Take your mind off Mars, Leonie. The chances of your ever seeing home again are at least one order of magnitude more slender than your chances of getting out of this fool's venture alive.

Was it too late to tell the Images to turn the pedo around?

Probably not. But she'd committed herself to this. To go back now would be to admit failure, something she wasn't very good at doing – something she didn't *want* to do.

OK, Leonie, any minute now you're gonna go out in glory. They'll sing ballads about you all over The Wondervale in the centuries to come, remembering your heroic sacrif—-Actually, they won't. They'll have forgotten all about you.

411

YOUR PEDO IS THROUGH THE *BLUNT INSTRUMENT*'S DEFENSIVE SHIELD. MY EXERCISE WAS SUCCESSFUL, AND THE MAIN COMPUTER HAS FAILED TO NOTICE YOUR INTRUSION.

'Uh, thanks, Nightmirror. What next?'

I WILL BRING YOUR PEDO TO REST NEXT TO AN AIRLOCK. PREPARE FOR DECELERATION.

The warning wasn't quite in time. If the deceleration had been in a longitudinal direction along the axis of the pedo Strider would almost certainly have broken her neck, despite the armoured protection of the battlesuit. Luckily the missile was swinging round through an angle as it approached the flank of the *Blunt Instrument*, so that all she suffered were massively bruised shoulders as she hammered against the upper corner of the pedo's storage space.

'Don't do that a second time, buster,' she gasped once she'd recovered some breath. She wondered if she'd ever be able to walk upright again. Didn't seem like it.

YOU ARE APPROACHING THE AIRLOCK. PREPARE YOURSELF TO DISEMBARK AS SWIFTLY AS YOU CAN WHEN I GIVE THE WORD. I CAN DISTRACT THE MAIN COMPUTER FOR ONLY THE SHORTEST OF MOMENTS, SO YOU MUST BE PREPARED TO ENTER THE 'LOCK QUICKLY.

'What's the Artificial Environment up to?'

ARTIFICIAL ENVIRONMENT 17,863,006, YOU MEAN?

'What other Artificial Environment would you think I'd be talking about? Are there any others around?' The question was a serious one. For all Strider knew AE 17,863,006 might have summoned a few chums from the Twin Galaxies to come along and join the fun.

THERE IS ONLY ONE ARTIFICIAL ENVIRONMENT WITHIN THE LIMITS OF DETECTABLE SPACE.

'Then why did you . . .? Oh, never mind. What's the big stupid bastard up to?'

IT IS EXPENDING A GREAT DEAL OF FIREPOWER NEEDLESSLY ON THE EXTERIOR OF THE *BLUNT INSTRUMENT*'S DEFENSIVE SHIELDING.

IT SEEMS INCAPABLE OF UNDERSTANDING THAT THIS APPROACH IS VALUELESS.

That sounded about right. Artificial Environment 17,863,006 and its Main Computer could be dumb as all hell. The Children of the Starlight had clearly regarded themselves as the brightest species in the Universe, but when it came to creating truly intelligent artificial intelligences the lowly, johnny-come-lately Humans had had them beaten hands down. Pinocchio had played a mean game of chess; Strider reckoned she could probably have hammered Artificial Environment 17,863,006 and its puter at Snap, so lacking were they both in intuition.

'Any way you can point this out to it?' she said, feeling herself beginning to re-enter free fall.

DO YOU WANT ME TO?

'That big bastard's on our si— Oh, I guess I see what you mean.'

Right now she was more or less dead centre of Artificial Environment 17,863,006's target area. The death machine wouldn't think twice about destroying her.

She began to chuckle, although mirth was an emotion currently very remote from her. Artificial Environment 17,863,006 thought of itself as the main act, but the combination of her own idea and the manipulations performed by the Images meant that the machine was reduced to the status of decoy – and it hadn't realized it yet. Kaantalech could hold off its full-frontal assault for as long as she liked, or just until she got bored, while meantime a slight figure in a battlesuit could be doing all the fatal damage . . .

Assuming that said slight figure wasn't blown to pieces before she'd got really started.

'How long?' she said nervously.

YOU HAVE TIME FOR THREE DEEP BREATHS.

She counted them: one, two, three.

Halfway through the second breath the side of the pedo

slipped open and her eyes were seared by what seemed to be the brightest sunlight she had ever encountered. Almost immediately she realized that what she was seeing was the stray light penetrating the *Blunt Instrument*'s shielding; the harder radiation generated by Artificial Environment 17,863,006's onslaught was being blocked off.

I CAN OPEN THE 'LOCK FOR ONLY A VERY SHORT PERIOD, AS I TOLD YOU. YOU MUST START—

'I get the picture,' grumbled Strider. She twisted her body round and launched herself feet-first out of the pedo, wishing she could take longer to luxuriate in the sensation of stretching her body out to its full length. Muscles she'd never even known she'd had were complaining to her about the way she'd maltreated them inside the pedo; she told them to shut the fuck up, and they quailed into silence.

There wasn't any sign of an airlock – just the featureless side of the spaceship extending seemingly to infinity both above and below her.

'Um . . .' she began.

NOW – MOVE. QUICK.

In the preternatural brightness of the stray light the darkness of the rectangle that opened up in front of her was all the more startling.

GET IN.

Thrusting herself off with one hand from the side of the pedo, she scrabbled herself gracelessly in through the outer door of the airlock, which closed so rapidly behind her that for a moment she panicked about losing a foot.

'You Images don't pay much lip service to the neuroses of us lot, do you?' she said, breathless, as the 'lock's lights flickered on.

YOU WERE PERFECTLY SAFE.

'Yeah. I believe you.'

FROM NOW ON, PLEASE OBSERVE SILENCE IN CASE KAANTALECH'S MONITORS PICK UP OUR COMMUNICATIONS.

SHOULD THIS HAPPEN NOT ONLY WOULD YOU DIE BUT I WOULD BE FLUSHED OUT OF MY HIDING-PLACE. IT IS IMPORTANT THAT, WHATEVER HAPPENS TO YOU, I SHOULD . . .

'Spare me,' Strider subvocalized.

I SHALL GIVE YOU GUIDANCE. PLACE YOURSELF BY THE 'LOCK'S INNER DOOR AND BE PREPARED TO PASS THROUGH IT, ONCE AGAIN, AS QUICKLY AS YOU CAN.

'Reminds me of the showers in the orphanage.'

SPEAK ONLY WHEN YOU NEED TO – THERE IS A POSSIBILITY THAT KAANTALECH'S MONITORS CAN PICK UP EVEN YOUR SUBVOCALIZATIONS.

'OK. Fair enough. Verbal communications out.'

The inner door of the airlock whined open. Strider was through it before it was fully ajar.

A long utilitarian corridor, its walls made of bolted-together sheets of some dull grey-pink metal. Why did Strider feel as if she were venturing into a throat? She moved forward anyway, clumsily groping her lazgun from the belt of her battlesuit, wishing that she could actually *feel* the button she was supposed to press if anything appeared unexpectedly. She held the lazgun up in front of her visor to check that the dial was set to the highest power: hell alone knew how much it would take to stun an Alhubra, so she wasn't planning on taking any chances.

Shit, but her shoulders hurt. They hurt more than they should. She wondered if the damage they'd received had gone beyond bruising to fracture. It wasn't important, though: her chances of getting out of this were virtually zero, so what did a bit of discomfort matter en route?

She was glad of the battlesuit. Even assuming she was able to breathe the atmosphere in here – Ten Per Cent Extra Free had said she 'probably could', which was not heartening – she wouldn't have wanted to: littered along the floor were heaps of faeces and half-eaten bits of rotting meat. The place must stink.

415

Strider moved along the corridor as quietly as she could – which wasn't very quietly because the heavy boots of the battlesuit tended to land on the metal floor with a clank. Still there was nobody about. Could this be a trap? Could Kaantalech be monitoring her presence, taking sadistic pleasure out of prolonging the moment until Strider was seized and cruelly slaughtered?

Don't think about such things, Leonie. The more you do, the more likely you are to get caught.

A change of policy. Trying to sneak along silently wasn't being very successful and was slow. She started to march down the corridor as if she owned the place, sweeping her lazgun from side to side in front of her. Anything that looked even remotely like an alien lifeform was going to get zapped.

You with me, Nightmirror?

I AM. I HAVE CREATED AN EMERGENCY ON THE FAR SIDE OF THIS VESSEL; MOST OF KAANTALECH'S MAINTENANCE STAFF ARE ATTENDING TO AN INEXPLICABLE LEAKAGE OF ATMOSPHERE.

Good thinking, old buddy.

I CAN GIVE YOU WARNING WHENEVER IT SEEMS YOU MIGHT ENCOUNTER ONE OF HER PEOPLE.

You do that.

She kept moving smartly along passageway after indistinguishable passageway, following Nightmirror's guidance each time she came to a fork or a crossway. After a while she felt a slight vibration beneath her feet. As it grew progressively more noticeable she assumed that she was getting closer to Kaantalech's centre of operations. She thought as much to Nightmirror, who confirmed the hypothesis.

How much further?

NOT FAR NOW. IT WOULD BE WISE FOR YOU TO START MOVING MORE SLOWLY. THERE ARE SUFFICIENT ALHUBRA AND OTHER AUTARCHY SERVANTS IN THE VICINITY TO ENSURE THAT I MAY NO LONGER BE ABLE TO GIVE YOU ADEQUATE WARNING OF THEIR LOCATIONS.

Strider had been holding her lazgun casually by her side. Now she raised it again, and resumed the sweeping motion. She rather hoped she *did* come across some of Kaantalech's people: killing somebody would give her a sense of achievement.

Hey, that's a rotten thing to think, Leonie!

Yes, but it's an honest one.

And indeed there was a flicker of movement ahead of her. Reflexively she fired off a bolt from the lazgun. There was a shower of sparks in the distance.

She ran forward, ready to administer the *coup de grâce*, not caring how much noise she was making.

No need for a second bolt: she'd shot a bot, and it was clear that she'd hit it somewhere vital. The machine was just a smoking heap of motionless metal.

Had it had time to raise the alarm before all its systems crashed? There was no way of telling. She listened for the sound of a klaxon or some Alhubran equivalent, but there was nothing. No running footsteps. No change in the vibration from the floor. No other sound except that of her own breathing, which was loud enough in her ears that she wondered why Kaantalech's troops couldn't hear it.

Then there was a jolt that almost knocked her off her feet.

What the hell was that?

KAANTALECH HAS BEGUN TO RETALIATE AGAINST ARTIFICIAL ENVIRONMENT 17,863,006. SHE HAD TO DROP HER SHIELD BRIEFLY AND ONE OF ITS MISSILES MADE IT THROUGH. THE *BLUNT INSTRUMENT* HAS SUFFERED NO MAJOR DAMAGE, BUT THE EMERGENCY SERVES FURTHER TO DISTRACT ANY ATTENTION THAT MIGHT DETECT YOUR PRESENCE.

Jeez, but what's it gonna be like in here if the AE gets in a major hit?

THAT WILL NOT BE YOUR PROBLEM, CAPTAIN LEONIE STRIDER.

Why won't it—? Oh, I see.

There was nothing for it but to keep on moving, obeying Nightmirror's directions.

She ran straight over a crossway and a few metres further when: BEHIND YOU!

She turned.

Two Alhubra were standing at the centre of the crossway. They must have spotted her as she'd flitted past them at right angles. Dammit, but the creatures, despite their apparent clumsiness, must be able to move fast when they wanted to. They were raising things that looked alarmingly similar to the lazgun in her fist.

She let herself fall to one side and let off a bolt at random.

Lucky again, Leonie.

One of the Alhubra collapsed, shrieking with a shrillness that was startling from so huge a body. The flesh of its chest was on fire.

The other beast turned to run. Steadying her right arm with her left hand, Strider carefully shot it in the rear. The Alhubra's momentum carried it forward a few further paces before it crashed to the floor.

The first creature was still alive. With a final shot she put it out of its misery.

'Give me a bit more warning next time, friend,' she said once her breath was back under control.

I SHALL DO MY BEST, BUT FROM HERE ON SUCH ENCOUNTERS ARE LIKELY TO OCCUR WITH INCREASING FREQUENCY.

'You mean this is suicide.'

Nightmirror did not reply.

'Well, I may as well go out in glory.' Shrugging inside a battlesuit was a cumbersome business, but she managed it.

She took a few further steps along the passage, and then paused again. 'You sure you couldn't do this yourself?'

QUITE SURE. THE TRANSITION MUST BE AS SMOOTH AS POSSIBLE. IF I WERE TO ATTEMPT BOTH OPERATIONS AT ONCE I WOULD BE CERTAIN TO ALERT KAANTALECH'S TECHNICIANS AND IT IS LIKELY THAT THEY WOULD BE ABLE TO INSTALL BACKUP SYSTEMS IN TIME.

418

'This is likely to be suicide for you, too, Nightmirror, isn't it?'

YES. UNLESS I AM FORTUNATE.

Strider hadn't thought too much – hadn't *let* herself think too much – about this before. She was risking ten or twelve decades of active life; Nightmirror was risking eternity. She felt momentarily embarrassed by the disparity in the sizes of the sacrifices they were preparing to make.

Less introspection, Leonie. It's not helpful.

'Thanks,' she said out loud. The word seemed utterly inadequate.

I ASSURE YOU THAT I AM ACTING ENTIRELY OUT OF SELF-INTEREST. THE DIS-AESTHETICS CREATED BY THE PERPETUATION OF THE AUTARCHY ARE SO PAINFUL TO US IMAGES THAT THEY MAKE OUR EXISTENCE A MISERY. TERMINATION IS PREFERABLE TO CONTINUED LIFE UNDER THESE CONDITIONS.

Strider could understand. She directed her thoughts inwards, away from Nightmirror. *So what are my own motives for this craziness? I could be trying to get back to the Solar System rather than farting about in the middle of someone else's tyranny on the other side of the Universe from home. Hm. Maybe my motives aren't all that different from Nightmirror's: there's no such thing as 'someone else's' tyranny . . .*

She rounded a corner and almost ran into a group of three Alhubra. Almost without breaking step she lazzed all three in a single arc of her weapon, then stepped round the smoking corpses and continued on her way.

You're getting too good at this, Leonie, she thought. *Too proficient. Too unaffected. You felt nothing at all just then, except maybe satisfaction at a job neatly done. So what? That's the best way to be, right now. Being a callous bastard might be the only way of getting out of here alive.*

YOU ARE VERY CLOSE TO THE CORE OF THE MAIN COMPUTER NOW. I HAVE SUCCEEDED SO FAR IN BLANKING OUT ITS OBSERVATION OF THE CORRIDORS THROUGH WHICH YOU HAVE BEEN

PASSING, BUT IT IS BECOMING INCREASINGLY DIFFICULT. I SUGGEST YOU MOVE AS QUICKLY AS POSSIBLE; HASTE IS NOW OF GREATER IMPORTANCE THAN SILENCE.

Once again Strider broke into a clumsy run. Battlesuits weren't designed for speed. Their main purpose was protection, although they could resist only a narrow spectrum of generally outmoded weaponry. She might have been better off in something lighter and more flexible, taking her chances for the benefit of mobility. Too late to have second thoughts.

A pair of Alhubra guards stood at the airlock door to which Nightmirror directed her. Again she lazzed them without a qualm before they could make a move to raise their weapons.

Shit! One of them had fallen directly in front of the doorway.

Nothing else for it but to . . .

She holstered the lazgun and clambered up the bulky side of the alien. Even through the fabric of the battlesuit she could feel the coarse hairs of its pelt. The flesh was as hard as rock beneath her hands and knees.

'How do I get this thing open?' she said once she was perched on top of the dead Alhubra.

There was a sudden glow of light and a wisp of smoke on the face of the door just to the right of her head.

She turned.

Uh-oh. Someone somewhere must have sounded the alarm. A posse of Alhubra coming at speed. Half a dozen or more.

She slid down the back of the giant corpse, wedging herself between it and the metal door. For a long moment she couldn't work the lazgun out of its holster; then she sneaked a glance over the hairy ridge and picked off the first of the troopers.

One of the others was raising what looked to be some sort of communications equipment to his mouth. Her mouth? *It doesn't matter what sex these people are, for chrissake, Leonie!* She shot the equipment first and the Alhubra second, ducking her head as the others rained bolts in her direction.

'Get this goddam door open!' she hissed at Nightmirror.

YOU MUST DESTROY THEM ALL, said the Image with infuriating calm. YOU CANNOT ALLOW ANY OF THEM TO SURVIVE TO RAISE A MORE GENERAL ALARM.

'Oh great.'

She struggled upwards again and fired off another couple of bolts. One went wild, digging a hole out of the floor a hundred metres away, but the other hit flesh. The Alhubra stayed upright for a moment or two, as if puzzled by the fact that its head had exploded, then folded gracefully into a heap.

The others started to back off. *That's the trouble with running a tyranny,* thought Strider. *If you don't give people anything to believe in except fear, there's no way they're going to lay down their lives for the good of the cause.*

She shot two more of the troopers without having to worry about return fire.

The remaining two, obviously realizing they were dead if they ran so they might as well fight it out, took cover behind the fallen corpses of their comrades.

'Suggestions?'

THERE IS NOTHING I CAN DO TO HELP YOU. YOU MUST DEAL WITH THIS YOURSELF.

Stalemate.

Strider couldn't take a shot at the troopers unless they showed themselves, which they gave no indication of doing. She sent up a little prayer – just in case there was a god out there somewhere – that neither of the survivors carried a comm of any kind. With luck there was only one comm per platoon . . .

'Nightmirror!'

YES.

'How much can you influence the environment around here?'

TRIFLINGLY.

'Can you block off this section of passage?'

YES. She could hear and see doors sliding across the corridor

421

about fifty metres away in either direction. I KNOW WHAT TO DO NEXT, said Nightmirror.

The first sign was that the smoke from the burning flesh of the dead stopped rising erratically and seemed to become much more purposeful, forming steady columns that stretched unerringly to small vents in the ceiling. Then the smoke petered into nonexistence as the fires went out.

Strider tongued a control and was rewarded by a display of the external atmospheric pressure. The numbers were creeping slowly downwards towards zero – towards vacuum.

The two Alhubra must have suddenly realized what Nightmirror was up to, because a fusillade of lazbolts peppered the door behind her. She cowered in the hefty protection of the dead guard, hoping that a lucky shot wouldn't pass right through the corpse and pierce her battlesuit. Praise the heavens that the thing was self-sealing, so she'd likely survive unless the bolt hit something vital; even so, she could do without getting burnt.

There was a lull in the Alhubran fire, and she darted her head above the corpse's back.

One of the last pair of troopers was dead, or as good as. There was muddy-looking grey blood bubbling from its mouth. The creature lay on its side, its eyes closed. The other trooper was still moving, albeit sluggishly. Strider raised her lazgun and took careful aim and . . .

. . . just as she was about to squeeze the 'fire' button the bastard Alhubra got off a lucky shot and winged her in the shoulder. Left shoulder, luckily. Screaming in pain she unleashed a barrage of lazbolts into the last survivor of the platoon, continuing to fire long after the creature was manifestly dead.

She could hardly see what she was doing any longer. The burn through her shoulder was giving her such agony that her eyes were running with unstoppable tears.

'Can you get this fucking airlock door open yet?' she

blurted, trying for the sake of dignity to keep some of the pain out of her voice.

YES.

As the door slid open it tugged her sideways, and she had to grab at the hairs of the dead Alhubra. She half-dropped, half-fell into the 'lock, landing on her rump and feeling an ache suddenly start up her spine. Nightmirror began to open the 'lock's inner door immediately, not bothering to close the outer one: both inside and outside were now in vacuum, so there was no need to protect the puter. Even so, Strider would have felt more secure had there been something between her and the rest of the *Blunt Instrument*.

No time to think about that now. Wait until later, Leonie, before you get terrified. Likely you'll be dead by then and miss the experience altogether. Better than most reasons for being dead.

The hall that housed the heart of Kaantalech's Main Computer was as filthy as the passageways outside: the Alhubra were a species who did not count hygiene among their stronger suits. Somehow Strider had expected a bigger space, as if the place she'd been questing towards should have the status of a shrine, or something. Instead she found herself in a room that was a more or less perfect cube, no greater than twenty metres across each edge. Facing her there was a mound of machinery – primitive-seeming by even Human standards, but she knew better than to judge by appearances.

'This is it?'

IT IS.

'Which is the bit I should be looking at?'

OVER TO YOUR RIGHT. YOU SHOULD BE ABLE TO SEE A PAIR OF LOZENGE-SHAPED DIALS, ABOUT TEN CENTIMETRES ACROSS AND ILLUMINATED IN RED.

'Gotcha.' She moved slowly across to the dials, which looked disturbingly like plaintively pleading eyes. For some

423

reason the wound in her shoulder was making her limp. 'Now what?'

JUST BELOW THE DIALS YOU'LL SEE A SMALL HATCH — NO, DON'T TOUCH IT YET!

Strider stopped her hand just above the first of the four butterfly nuts that held the hatch in place.

THE INSTANT YOU TOUCH THAT HATCH THE AUTOMATIC ALARM SYSTEMS WILL GO OFF.

'I assumed they already had.'

NOT YET. WE'RE BEING LUCKIER THAN WE COULD HAVE EXPECTED TO BE.

'You're not the one who's got a shoulder that hurts like fuck.'

Silence from Nightmirror. Strider remembered that he was as certain to die as she was.

'Sorry.'

NO NEED FOR APOLOGIES. I CANNOT FEEL PHYSICAL PAIN, ALTHOUGH I HAVE SAMPLED IT IN OTHERS, SUCH AS YOURSELF. I WOULD SAY THAT MY SPIRITUAL PAIN IS COMPARABLE WITH THAT OF YOUR WOUND, BUT I KNOW YOU ARE ALSO CAPABLE OF SUFFERING SPIRITUAL PAIN AS GREAT AS ANY I CAN.

'Tell me when I can get started.'

INDEED. KEEP YOUR HAND THERE. THIS WILL HAVE TO BE DONE VERY CAREFULLY . . .

Nightmirror moves very cautiously, infiltrating himself among the electroneurons of the *Blunt Instrument*'s Main Computer so discreetly that the machine fails to notice his presence. Growing perhaps a little overconfident, the Image takes over a major portion of the puter's functioning in a single rush, and then waits for several milliseconds in trepidation . . . but the puter has noticed nothing.

Once, through the eyes of a creature whose species Nightmirror can no longer remember, he watched a unicellular organism slowly engulfing the body of another. The victim was unaware of anything until the very last moment, by which time it was too late for its struggles to be of any use. He feels, now, like that long-ago predator he saw at work. There will be a moment when he has taken over enough of the Main Computer to render anything it does to try to oust him ineffectual.

He feels a trace of guilt. He has come to rather like the machine. But that is all it is: a machine. Like any other AI, it has a high measure of self-awareness, but it can hardly be considered truly alive. At least, that is what Nightmirror keeps telling himself, forcing himself to forget the various other AIs he has encountered – like the bot Pinocchio – who have been all too similar to living consciousnesses.

Another push forward, and he is in possession of more than half of the Main Computer . . . and still the AI hasn't noticed his presence. He must have overestimated its intelligence – or maybe it is *allowing* him to take it over.

That's a chilling notion. He has assumed that the machine is a slave of Kaantalech and will do whatever the Autarch demands. What if the puter is fully aware of what is going on, and is permitting events to proceed?

Nightmirror dare not pause to test this possibility. There is still enough of the Main Computer under its direct control for it to raise the alarm, if it wants to.

He takes over another clump of databanks almost without thinking about it.

A few more such captures and he will be able to mimic the Main Computer perfectly. Just so long as Strider doesn't screw up the final murder she must commit.

PREPARE YOURSELF, STRIDER.

'I'm as prepared as I'll ever be. Can't we get on with this?'

I WILL GIVE YOU THREE SECONDS' WARNING WHEN IT IS SAFE FOR YOU TO TOUCH THE FASTENINGS OF THE HATCH.

'Count me down?'

CERTAINLY.

Strider waited impatiently. At any moment she expected a new platoon of Kaantalech's troopers to burst into the room behind her, even though she knew this area was now sealed off.

THREE, said Nightmirror.

'Good. We're getting started.'

TWO.

'Yup. I'm ready.'

ONE.

Her hand was rock-steady above the first of the fastenings. NOW.

This was not a time for subtlety – so few times seemed to be, as far as Strider was concerned. Fumbling through the heavy fabric of the battlesuit's glove, she wrenched open the first two butterfly nuts, paused for a moment to allow herself a breath, then tackled the other two. She threw the rectangular piece of metal away across the floor.

I HAVE TAKEN OVER THE ENTIRE FUNCTIONS OF THE MAIN COMPUTER SUCCESSFULLY. NONE OF THE ORGANIC POPULATION OF THIS VESSEL HAS AS YET NOTICED THE TRANSFER.

'Good on you. Now it's up to me to commit a murder.'

THAT IS CORRECT.

Strider shook off guilt as she directed her lazgun at the circuits revealed now that the hatch was open.

'Now?'

PLEASE.

She pressed the firing button, and kept it pressed, watching the metal fuse and flow and then finally burst into flames.

'Done?'

YES. THE MAIN COMPUTER IS DEAD. IF YOU ARE VERY LUCKY, YOU MAY BE ABLE TO ESCAPE. I SHALL MONITOR YOUR PROGRESS, AND WILL NOT DROP THE SHIELD UNTIL EITHER YOU ARE CLEAR OR YOU ARE DEAD.

'Cheerful sod, aren't you?' Strider holstered her lazgun, then drew it again: it was more useful in her hand. Her left shoulder still hurt like hell, but she was becoming accustomed to it. In a few hours, if she were very lucky, Hein or Strauss-Giolitto or Seragarda or someone would be giving her pain-killers.

GOODBYE, CAPTAIN LEONIE STRIDER.

Who was she to be wallowing in self-pity? 'Goodbye, Nightmirror,' she said. 'I hope we both get out of this.'

THERE IS A CHANCE.

She hardly noticed her climb over the corpse of the guard. The next time reality registered on her she was running through the evacuated passageway towards a door that remained firmly closed until the last moment; a split second later and she'd have run full into it.

'Thanks!' she cried to Nightmirror as she half-stumbled down the corridor on the door's far side.

MY PLEASURE.

The door swished shut behind her. A wise move. It was likely that Kaantalech's personnel would discover there was something wrong with the Main Computer sooner rather than later, however exact Nightmirror's mimicry might be. The longer it took them to break through . . .

If she hadn't tripped on a chewed thigh-bone her head would have been shot off by the first of the lazbolts. As it was, she skidded through grease and shit along the passage, flailing her arms and legs in a vain attempt to slow herself down.

Another bolt missed her narrowly. Dimly she could see through her steamed-up visor that there were three Alhubra up ahead of her.

She twisted from her front to her back and, still sliding, extended her lazgun up above her head. She couldn't see where it was pointing, but hoped for the best as she squeezed the button.

There were satisfying shrieks.

She tumbled back on to her front, then pulled herself up to her knees. By luck she'd felled two of the Alhubra; the third was taking its time setting a sight on her. Before it could get its aim as perfect as it wanted she drilled it through the centre of its forehead. As she scrambled around the trio of corpses she picked up one of the Alhubran weapons, examining its controls as she lumbered onwards. There could be only so many bolts left in her lazgun. It was a good idea to have a backup weapon, but the damned thing was heavier than she'd have liked. Maybe it packed a correspondingly heavy charge – she hoped so.

Nightmirror had other things to do than guide her; he was busy pretending to be a puter. She had to rely on her memory of how she'd got through to the room where the heart of the Main Computer was housed. Coming from the opposite direction to the various junctions she'd negotiated earlier was confusing. She relied on her innate sense of self-orientation to take her towards the *Blunt Instrument*'s exterior, and ignored the fact that her orientation sense had never served her too well in the past.

Strider was astonished when she found her way to the airlock, and even more astonished when Nightmirror opened the inner door and Ten Per Cent Extra Free the outer. The pedo was waiting loyally for her, and she climbed into its small chamber as quickly as she could. Ten Per Cent Extra Free started the missile on its trajectory home almost before she had settled herself in place.

Now all she had to do was survive the firestorm.

CAPTAIN LEONIE STRIDER HAS EXITED THE *BLUNT INSTRUMENT*, said Ten Per Cent Extra Free tonelessly, as if the news were of little interest.

'I don't *believe* you!' cried Maloron Leander. Her voice sounded very loud in the confined space of the Pocket. For the past few hours she'd been systematically indoctrinating herself into the belief that Leonie was dead, so that the grief would be easier to bear when the news came through. 'You're not just kidding me, are you, Tenper?'

I CANNOT UNDERSTAND YOUR DISBELIEF. WHY SHOULD I TELL YOU ANYTHING OTHER THAN THE TRUTH? CAPTAIN LEONIE STRIDER IS NOW ENCAPSULATED WITHIN THE PEDO, WHICH IS HEADING AWAY FROM THE *BLUNT INSTRUMENT* AND TOWARDS THE *MIDNIGHT RANGER*.

Leander withdrew herself briefly from the Pocket. 'Hey, guys, it looks as if she's going to make it!'

Putting her head back into the Pocket drowned the sound of the yips and yelps.

AS SHE REACHES THE FRINGE OF KAANTALECH'S SHIELD NIGHTMIRROR WILL, IN THE GUISE OF THE MAIN COMPUTER, DROP IT TO LET HER THROUGH. KAANTALECH WILL TAKE THE OPPORTUNITY TO LAUNCH WEAPONS TOWARDS ARTIFICIAL ENVIRONMENT 17,863,006, WHICH WILL USE THE SAME WINDOW TO LAUNCH WEAPONS AT THE *BLUNT INSTRUMENT*. CAPTAIN LEONIE STRIDER MAY WELL SURVIVE THIS EXCHANGE. WHAT NEITHER KAANTALECH NOR ARTIFICIAL ENVIRONMENT 17,863,006 REALIZES IS THAT THE *BLUNT INSTRUMENT*'S DEFENSIVE SHIELD WILL NEVER RISE AGAIN.

'Which side should I be cheering for?'

NEITHER, IF OUR LUCK HOLDS.

Leander shrank the magnification within the Pocket so that she could see the insect hordes of little spacecraft centred on the two great behemoths that were the *Blunt Instrument* and Artificial Environment 17,863,006. One of those tiny dots of light was the *Midnight Ranger*; as she thought this the Pocket obligingly indicated the vessel with a blue-green arrow.

'Show me the pedo with Strider in it,' she breathed.

Another arrow. The place in space that it indicated seemed completely empty, but it was moving at a steady velocity away from Kaantalech's flagship.

The *Blunt Instrument*'s shield was an ellipsoid of pale, semi-translucent candle-wax in the Pocket's visual display. As the nothingness demarked by the arrow reached the edge of the ellipsoid the wax melted away.

The first effective shot came from Artificial Environment 17,863,006, tearing away the *Blunt Instrument*'s nose so swiftly that it was hard to believe that it had ever been there. Kaantalech responded with a devastating volley of weapons, and the Artificial Environment jigged around in the vacuum as it absorbed the shocks of the explosions. The fleets of the Pridehouse and the Lingk-kreatzai stayed well clear. All Leander had eyes for was the arrow moving across the field of the Pocket towards the *Midnight Ranger*, which Ten Per Cent Extra Free had thought to ring.

Nelson joined her in the Pocket. His breathing was even louder than hers, and under his breath he was giving vent to little cheers.

Artificial Environment 17,863,006 plunged towards the *Blunt Instrument*, loosing a further barrage of weapons. Unprotected by its shield, the deadmetal of the Autarch's flagship glowed first red and then yellow and then white. It was impossible to believe that the vessel could withstand the temperature, and yet it seemed to be doing so – for a maxbeam sought out the place where Artificial Environment 17,863,006 was moving through space and sparked into being a reflective glow of cold flame.

The killing machine from the Twin Galaxies was winning the battle, clearly, but it was not going to be allowed to escape unscathed.

A pulsenuke took Artificial Environment 17,863,006 in the rear, doing great damage to its drive – how much damage Leander could only guess, but she pursed her lips in satisfaction as the death machine's course towards the *Blunt Instrument* became less certain.

'Good shooting,' said Nelson, close beside her.

Leander didn't reply. Artificial Environment 17,863,006 had steadied itself and was now moving directly towards the *Blunt Instrument*. It was difficult to tell in the confined space of the Pocket, but it seemed as if the machine was accelerating.

'Tell all the vessels of the fleet to prepare their armaments,' Leander whispered to Ten Per Cent Extra Free.

THIS HAS ALREADY BEEN DONE.

'On whose authority?'

CAPTAIN LEONIE STRIDER'S.

It wasn't the answer Leander had expected to receive.

'Can you patch me through to her?'

CERTAINLY.

There was a moment when there was no sound in the Pocket except that of Nelson's breathing and her own. She put her arm round his waist and tugged his hip alongside her own, enjoying the feel of his body even through the several layers of fabric that separated his flesh from hers.

Then there was a third sound of breathing.

'Leonie?'

'None other.'

Leander couldn't think of anything to say. Luckily Nelson cut across her.

'Ho there, woman who makes the tide come in.'

'Prepare an airlock,' said Strider. She sounded exhausted.

'It shall be done as you request, fair maiden of the skies.'

'Shut the fuck up with the badinage, will ya, Umbel? I can do without it, right now. Make sure the cat's at the airlock.'

A short pause while Nelson worked this out. 'Why?'

'I want something on my bunk that purrs a lot so that I can get to sleep . . . and stay that way for a very long time.'

Hein and Umbel Nelson carried Strider from the airlock to the nearest cabin; she whimpered through the helmet of her battle-suit that she wanted to be in her own place, but they told her to keep quiet and be grateful for the fact that she was getting the cat, as requested. The whimpering soon died down, and she was asleep before they dumped her on the bunk.

Between them they removed the battlesuit, and Nelson sucked in his breath when he saw the burn on her left shoulder.

431

'Must have hurt,' he said.

'Probably still does,' said Hein. 'It's a wonder she can sleep through the pain. I'll inject her with analgesics once we've got her settled.'

'She'll want to know what's happened to Kaantalech. And to Artificial Environment 17,863,006.'

'We can tell her later,' said Hein. 'I'm not going to try to wake her up again now.'

He pulled a blanket over Strider's naked body and tucked it in on either side of the bunk. Loki, for once knowing what was expected of her, settled her round black head in the crook of Strider's neck, shut her eyes in ecstasy and began to purr loudly. Her tail moved forcefully under the blanket a few times and then jabbed out over the edge of the bunk and was still.

Nelson and Hein touched palms together, grinning.

Artificial Environment 17,863,006 had done most of the damage to the *Blunt Instrument*, but a single well placed pulsenuke had finally taken out the death machine. It would travel onwards through the Universe for ever and a day as a huge piece of inert and harmless metal. Orphanwifer had led three Lingk-kreatzai cruisers to put an end to the crippled *Blunt Instrument*; it had been not so much of a fight as a surgical operation – they were putting down a wild animal to save it from further suffering.

Nightmirror had slipped away into The Truthfulness just in time, and was now reunited aboard the *Midnight Ranger* with Ten Per Cent Extra Free and Pinocchio.

One day, certainly, the Autarchy would rise again. Kaantalech had done a competent job of exterminating all those with the necessary ambition and ruthlessness to take over control of The Wondervale, but certainly she must have missed a few. There would be someone else along, sooner or later, to re-impose the tyranny.

In the meantime, though, there was the opportunity for a

Pridehouse male and a Human male to touch their hands together and smile both at each other and down at the bunk where slept a Human female and a creature that was to all intents and purposes a cat.

10

It's Not a Cat, But It Can Catch a Mouse

Strider wakes, and for a moment she cannot think where she might be. Her head is still full of images of violence and suffering – of the coldness and the pain of a distant galaxy. She turns on the pillow, expecting to find a small furry body alongside her, but there is nothing there. Of course not. The cat, like everything else, was only part of her dream.

She knows where she is now: she is in City 43, on Mars. Last night she blew an interview and a bot called Pinocchio tried to mug her. She beat the shit out of the bot, which felt good at the time and still feels good in memory. Someone had to pay for the way she fucked up the interview so badly. No more thoughts of Tau Ceti II: that was an idle dream, soon dashed. She has a job to do, here on Mars, although just at the moment she can't remember precisely what the job actually *is*.

There's some clothing lying on the floor of the room in which she's been sleeping. She recognizes it as her own, and decides she'd better put it on. Swing her legs off the bunk – she has always been very proud of her legs, which are slender and well proportioned – and approach the clothing.

The clothing smells. She has been wearing it too long. That doesn't matter: no one is going to come close enough to her to know the difference.

Knickers. Bra. Jumpsuit.

Jumpsuit? A blue SSIA jumpsuit? Where the hell did she pick that up? Never mind. On it goes.

It's not just the clothing that smells: she does as well, and she rather likes her own smell.

The door of her room opens before she reaches it, which is, she recognizes, exactly as it should be. Outside in the corridor there are people intent on breakfast. She joins the throng. No one looks at her.

The dream she has had. A hell of a dream. She was halfway to Tau Ceti II when she was swallowed into a wormhole and found herself and her crew in a distant galaxy, The Wondervale. There she fought a tyranny . . . as if galaxy-wide tyrannies could ever subsist for more than a few years.

Her dream has been very vivid, though, and it is difficult to shake it off.

Two people are walking in the opposite direction from everyone else. They have their arms round each other's waists, and are clearly lovers: this couldn't be more plain if they shouted the information out loud. They were in her dream, and she knows their names. The big black guy is called Umbel Nelson. The white woman, only slightly shorter than the man she so clearly loves, is called Maloron Leander. Strider smiles at both of them, but they ignore the smile: they have never met her before, and are embarrassed by this street crazy.

A tall man is following behind them, with a wolf-like dog at his side. He is certainly more handsome than he ought to be, and in her dream she did, she remembers, make love with him more than once, although the details of their lovemaking are now lost to her memory. The dog looks up at her as if in recognition, but then turns its head away when the man angrily clicks his fingers.

So many people she recognizes from her dream!

She is walking along this corridor without seeming to move her feet. It is almost as if *this* were the dream and The Wondervale were the reality, but surely that cannot be true.

Another person she recognizes is coming towards her. He is an Asiatic of some sort, and around him there swirls a host of butterflies, some of them sitting on his shoulders and others swooping around his head. *Which,* thinks Strider, *is the butterfly dreaming of being Lan Yi, and is Lan Yi dreaming of being a flock of butterflies?*

Another tall woman, half a metre at least taller than Strider. This one stops and recognizes her. Her name, Strider knows, is Maria Strauss-Giolitto. Holding one of her hands is a small boy called Hilary; by an ankle rustles a cat called Loki; from a shirt pocket peeks a rat called Segrill.

'Maria, I know you.'

'Of course you do, Leonie.'

'Er, hi.'

'Have you been dreaming?'

'Too right. Too much.'

'Same here. Kaantalech's dead, isn't she?'

'That was the end of my dream. But I don't believe in dreams much. They're just bits of the psyche that have been allowed to get loose.'

'Are you so sure about that?' says Strauss-Giolitto. 'Come along with me.'

Still seeming not to touch the corridor's floor, Strider follows the tall woman and the cat, who likewise seem to be floating just a little above the surface. They all pass through an airlock and find themselves outside the limits of City 43.

'Look up there,' says Maria Strauss-Giolitto.

Strider obediently looks up, but for a moment all she can see is that there seem to be too many stars in the Martian sky.

'The Children of the Starlight,' explains Strauss-Giolitto patiently. 'They're here.'

Orbit titles available by post:

❑ Strider's Galaxy	Paul Barnett	£5.99
❑ Midshipman's Hope	David Feintuch	£5.99
❑ Challenger's Hope	David Feintuch	£5.99
❑ Prisoner's Hope	David Feintuch	£5.99
❑ Fisherman's Hope	David Feintuch	£5.99
❑ Life Form	Alan Dean Foster	£5.99
❑ Mid-Flinx	Alan Dean Foster	£5.99
❑ Consider Phlebas	Iain M. Banks	£6.99
❑ Use of Weapons	Iain M. Banks	£6.99
❑ Excession	Iain M. Banks	£6.99

The prices shown above are correct at time of going to press. However, the publishers reserve the right to increase prices on covers from those previously advertised, without further notice.

ORBIT

ORBIT BOOKS
Cash Sales Department, P.O. Box 11, Falmouth, Cornwall, TR10 9EN
Tel: +44 (0) 1326 372400, Fax: +44 (0) 1326 374888
Email: books@barni.avel.co.uk

POST AND PACKING:
Payments can be made as follows: cheque, postal order (payable to Orbit Books) or by credit cards. Do not send cash or currency.

U.K. Orders under £10	£1.50
U.K. Orders over £10	**FREE OF CHARGE**
E.C. & Overseas	25% of order value

Name (Block letters) ....

Address ....

....

Post/zip code: ....

☐ Please keep me in touch with future Orbit publications

☐ I enclose my remittance £ ....

☐ I wish to pay by Visa/Access/Mastercard/Eurocard

Card Expiry Date